**Praise for #1 *New York Times* bestselling author Nora Roberts:**

"The publishing world might be hard-pressed to find an author with a more diverse style or fertile imagination than Roberts."
*–Publishers Weekly*

"You can't bottle wish fulfillment, but Nora Roberts certainly knows how to put it on the page."
*–New York Times*

"[Nora] Roberts... is at the top of her game."
*–People*

"Roberts' bestselling novels are some of the best in the romance genre. They are thoughtfully plotted, well-written stories featuring fascinating characters."
*–USA TODAY*

"Her stories have fueled the dreams of twenty-five million readers."
*–Entertainment Weekly*

"Roberts is indeed a word artist, painting her story and her characters with vitality and verve."
*–Los Angeles Daily News*

"Roberts has a warm feel for her characters and an eye for the evocative detail."
*–Chicago Tribune*

"Compelling and dimensional characters, intriguing plots, passionate love stories—Nora Roberts... romance at its finest."
*–Rendezvous*

# NORA ROBERTS

## Finding Home

lesley shepparcard
416 568- 27[illegible]8
lesley_world_traveller@yahoo.ca

facbook
lesley sharp Sheppard .

Mills & Boon™

First Published 1985
Fourth Australian Paperback Edition 2009
ISBN 978 0 733 59672 8

First Published 1986
Fifth Australian Paperback Edition 2009
ISBN 978 0 733 59672 8



Published by
Harlequin Mills & Boon®
Level 5
15 Help Street
CHATSWOOD NSW 2067
AUSTRALIA



Printed and bound in Australia by
McPherson's Printing Group

# CONTENTS

**Also available from Mills & Boon by Nora Roberts**

A WILL AND A WAY
ALL I WANT FOR CHRISTMAS
BEST LAID PLANS
BLITHE IMAGES
CAPTIVATED
CHARMED
COURTING CATHERINE
DANCE OF DREAMS
DANCE TO THE PIPER
ENCHANTED
ENTRANCED
FIRST IMPRESSIONS
FOR NOW, FOREVER
GABRIEL'S ANGEL
HER MOTHER'S KEEPER
HOME FOR CHRISTMAS
IN FROM THE COLD
ISLAND OF FLOWERS
LAWLESS
LESS OF A STRANGER
LOCAL HERO
LOVING JACK
MIND OVER MATTER
NIGHT SHADOW
NIGHT SHIFT
NIGHT SMOKE
NIGHTSHADE
PARTNERS
RULES OF THE GAME
SEARCH FOR LOVE
SKIN DEEP
SONG OF THE WEST
STORM WARNING
TEMPTATION
TEMPTING FATE
THE HEART'S VICTORY
THE LAST HONEST WOMAN
THE NAME OF THE GAME
THE RIGHT PATH
THE WELCOMING
TIME WAS
TIME CHANGE
UNFINISHED BUSINESS
UNTAMED
WITHOUT A TRACE

# Night Moves

To the mountains I live in,
and the people who love them.

# *Chapter 1*

"What the hell are you doing in a place like this?"

Maggie, on her hands and knees, didn't look up. "C.J., you're playing the same old song."

C.J. pulled down the hem of his cashmere sweater. He was a man who made worry an art, and he worried about Maggie. Someone had to. Frustrated, he looked down at the sable-brown hair twisted untidily into a knot on top of her head. Her neck was slender, pale, her shoulders curved slightly forward as she rested her weight on her forearms. She had a delicate build, with the kind of fragility C.J. had always associated with nineteenth-century English aristocratic ladies. Though perhaps they, too, had possessed endless stores of strength and endurance under frail bones and porcelain skin.

She wore a T-shirt and jeans that were both faded and slightly damp from perspiration. When he looked at her hands, fine-boned, elegant hands, and saw they were grimy, he shuddered. He knew the magic they were capable of.

A phase, he thought. She was just going through a phase. After two marriages and a few affairs, C.J. understood that women went through odd moods from time to time. He brushed at his trim, sandy mustache with one finger. It was up to him to guide her back, gently, to the real world.

As he glanced around at nothing but trees and rocks and isolation, he wondered, fleetingly, if there were bears in the woods. In the real world, such things were kept in zoos. Keeping a nervous lookout for suspicious movements, he tried again.

"Maggie, just how long are you going to go on this way?"

"What way is that, C.J.?" Her voice was low, husky, as if she'd just been awakened. It was a voice that made most men wish they'd awakened her.

The woman was infuriating. C.J. tugged a hand through his carefully styled, blow-dried hair. What was she doing three thousand miles from L.A., wasting herself on this dirty work? He had a responsibility to her and, damn it, to himself. C.J. blew out a long breath, an old habit he had whenever he met with opposition. Negotiations were, after all, his business. It was up to him to talk some sense into her. He shifted his feet, careful to keep his polished loafers out of the dirt. "Babe, I love you. You know I do. Come home."

This time Maggie turned her head, looking up with a flash of a smile that involved every inch of her face—the mouth that stopped just short of being too wide, the chin a bit pointed, the sweep of cheekbones that gave her face a diamond shape. Her eyes, big, round and shades darker than her hair, added that final spark of animation.

It wasn't a stunning face. You'd tell yourself that while you tried to focus in on the reason you were stunned. Even now, without makeup, with a long streak of topsoil across one cheek, the face involved you. Maggie Fitzgerald involved you because she was exactly what she seemed. Interesting. Interested.

Now she sat back on her haunches, blowing a wisp of hair out of her eyes as she looked up at the man who was frowning at her. She felt a tug of affection, a tug of amusement. Both had always come easily to her. "C.J., I love you, too. Now stop acting like an old woman."

"You don't belong here," he began, more exasperated than insulted. "You shouldn't be grubbing around on your hands and knees—"

"I like it," she said simply.

It was the very simplicity of the tone that told him he had a real problem. If she'd shouted, argued, his chances of turning her around would've been all but secured. But when she was like this, calmly stubborn, changing her mind would be like climbing Mount Everest. Treacherous and exhausting. Because he was a clever man, C.J. changed tactics.

"Maggie, I can certainly understand why you might like to get away for a while, rest a bit. No one deserves it more." That was a nice touch, he thought, because it was true. "Why don't you take a couple weeks in Cancún, or go on a shopping spree in Paris?"

"Mmm." Maggie shifted on her knees and fluffed up the petals of the pansies she was planting. They looked, she decided, a bit sick. "Hand me that watering can, will you?"

"You're not listening."

"Yes, I am." Stretching over, she retrieved the can herself. "I've been to Cancún, and I have so many clothes now I left half of them in storage in L.A."

Without breaking stride, C.J. tried a different turn. "It's not just me," he began again, watching as she drenched the pansies. "Everyone who knows you, who knows about this, thinks you've—"

"Slipped a gear?" Maggie supplied. Overdid the water, she decided as the saturated blossoms drooped. She had a lot to learn about the basics of country life. "C.J., instead of nagging me and trying to talk me into doing something I've no intention of doing, why don't you come down here and give me a hand?"

"A hand?" His voice held the slightly appalled note it might have if she'd suggested he dilute prime scotch with tap water. Maggie chuckled.

"Pass me that flat of petunias." She stuck the small spade in the ground again, fighting the rocky soil. "Gardening's good for you. It gets you back in touch with nature."

"I've no desire to touch nature."

This time she laughed and lifted her face to the sky. No, the closest C.J. would come to nature would be a chlorinated pool—solar-heated. Up to a few months ago she'd barely gotten much closer herself. She'd certainly never attempted to. But now she'd found something—something she hadn't even been looking for. If she hadn't come to the East Coast to collaborate on the score for a new musical, if she hadn't taken an impulsive drive south after the long, grueling sessions had ended, she never would've happened on the sleepy little town tucked into the Blue Ridge.

Do we ever know where we belong, Maggie wondered, unless we're lucky enough to stumble onto our own personal space? She only knew that she'd been heading nowhere in particular and she'd come home.

Maybe it had been fate that had led her into Morganville, a cluster of houses cupped in the foothills that boasted a population of 142. From the town proper, it spread out into farms and isolated mountain homes. If fate had taken her to Morganville, it had again taken her past the sign that listed the sale of a house and twelve acres. There'd been no moment of indecision, no quibbling over the price, no last-minute doubts. Maggie had met the terms and had had the deed in her hand within thirty days.

Looking up at the three-story frame house, with shutters still hanging crooked, Maggie could well imagine her friends and colleagues wondering about her mental state. She'd left her Italian-marble entrance hall and mosaic-tiled pool for rusty hinges and rocks. She'd done it without a backward glance.

Maggie patted the dirt around the petunias, then sat back. They looked a bit more spritely than her pansies. Maybe she was beginning to get the hang of it. "What do you think?"

"I think you should come back to L.A. and finish the score."

"I meant the flowers." She brushed off her jeans as she rose. "In any case, I am finishing the score—right here."

"Maggie, how can you work here?" C.J. exploded. He tossed out both arms in a gesture she'd always admired for its unapologetic theatrics. "How can you live here? This place isn't even civilized."

"Why? Because there's no health club and boutique on every other corner?" Wanting to temper the words, she tucked a hand through C.J.'s arm. "Go ahead, take a deep breath. The clean air won't hurt you."

"Smog's underrated," he mumbled as he shifted his feet again. Professionally he was her agent, but personally C.J. considered himself her friend, perhaps her best friend since Jerry had died. Thinking of that, he changed his tone again. This time it was gentle. "Look, Maggie, I know you've been through some rough times. Maybe L.A. has too many memories for you to deal with right now. But you can't bury yourself."

"I'm not burying myself." She put her hands on his forearms, squeezing for both emphasis and support. "And I buried Jerry nearly two years ago. That was another part of my life, C.J., and has nothing to do with this. This is home. I don't know how else to explain it." She slid her hands down to his, forgetting hers were smeared with earth. "This is my mountain now, and I'm happier here, more settled, than I ever was in Los Angeles."

He knew he was beating his head against a wall, but opted to give it one more shot. "Maggie." He slipped an arm around her shoulder, as if, she thought ruefully, she was a small child needing guidance. "Look at that place." He let the silence hang a moment while they both studied the house on the rise above. He noticed that the porch was missing several boards and that the paint on the trim was peeling badly. Maggie saw the sun reflecting off the window glass in rainbows. "You can't possibly be serious about living there."

"A little paint, a few nails." She shrugged it away. Long ago she'd learned that surface problems were best ignored. It was the problem simmering under the surface, not quite visible, that had to be dealt with. "It has such possibilities, C.J."

"The biggest one is that it'll fall down on your head."

"I had the roof fixed last week—a local man."

"Maggie, I'm not at all convinced there are any local men, or women, within ten miles. This place doesn't look fit for anything but elves and gnomes."

"Well, he might've been a gnome." Her sense of fun spurred her on as she stretched her back muscles. "He was about five foot five, stocky as a bull and somewhere around a hundred and two. His name was Bog."

"Maggie—"

"He was very helpful," she went on. "He and his boy are coming back to deal with the porch and some of the other major repairs."

"All right, so you've got a gnome to do some hammering and sawing. What about this?" He swept his hand around to take in the surrounding land. It was rocky, uneven and overgrown with weeds and thickets. Not even a dedicated optimist could've considered any part of it a lawn. A burly tree slanted dangerously toward the house itself, while thorny vines and wildflowers scrambled for space. There was a pervading smell of earth and green.

"Like Sleeping Beauty's castle," Maggie murmured. "I'll be sorry in a way to hack it down, but Mr. Bog has that under control, too."

"He does excavation work, too?"

Maggie tilted her head and arched her brows. It was a look that made anyone over forty remember her mother. "He recommended a landscaper. Mr. Bog assures me that Cliff Delaney is the best man in the county. He's coming by this afternoon to take a look at the place."

"If he's a smart man, he'll take one look at that gully you call a road leading up here and keep on going."

"But you brought your rented Mercedes all the way up." Turning, she threw her arms around his neck and kissed him. "Don't think I don't appreciate that or the fact that you flew in from the Coast or that you care enough to be concerned. I appreciate all of it. I appreciate you." She ruffled his hair, something no one else would've gotten away with. "Trust my judgment on this, C.J. I really do know what I'm doing. Professionally, my work can't do anything but improve here."

"That's yet to be seen," he muttered, but lifted a hand to touch her cheek. She was still young enough to have foolish dreams, he thought. Still sweet enough to believe in them. "You know it's not your work I'm worried about."

"I know." Her voice softened, and with it her eyes, her mouth. She was not a woman who guided her emotions, but one who was guided by them. "I need the peace here. Do you know, this is the first time in my life I've gotten off the merry-go-round? I'm enjoying the solid ground, C.J."

He knew her well and understood that there was no moving her, for the moment, from the position she'd taken. He understood, too, that from birth her life had been ribboned with the stuff of fantasies—and of nightmares. Perhaps she did need to compensate, for a time.

"I've got a plane to catch," he grumbled. "As long as you insist on staying here, I want you to call me every day."

Maggie kissed him again. "Once a week," she countered. "You'll have the completed score for *Heat Dance* in ten days." With her arm around his waist, she led him to the end of the uneven, overgrown path where his Mercedes sat in incongruous splendor. "I love the film, C.J. It's even better than I thought it would be when I first read the script. The music's all but writing itself."

He only grunted and cast one look behind him at the house. "If you get lonely—"

"I won't." With a quick laugh, Maggie nudged him into the car. "It's been enlightening discovering how self-sufficient I can be. Now, have a nice trip back and stop worrying about me."

Fat chance, he thought, automatically reaching in his briefcase to make certain his Dramamine was there. "Send me the score, and if it's sensational, I might stop worrying…a little."

"It is sensational." She backed off from the car to give him room to turn around. "*I'm* sensational!" she shouted as the Mercedes began to inch around. "Tell everyone back on the Coast that I've decided to buy some goats and chickens."

The Mercedes stopped dead. "Maggie…"

Laughing, she waved at him and backed down the path. "Not yet…but maybe in the fall." She decided it was best to reassure him, or else he might get out and start again. "Oh, and send me some Godiva chocolates."

That was more like it, C.J. thought, and put the car in gear again. She'd be back in L.A. in six weeks. He glanced in his rearview mirror as he started to drive away. He could see her, small and slender, still laughing, against the backdrop of the overgrown land, greening trees and dilapidated house. Once again he shuddered, but this time it wasn't from an offense of his sensibilities. This time it was from something like fear. He had a sudden flash of certainty that she wasn't safe there.

Shaking his head, C.J. reached in his pocket for his antacids as the car bumped noisily over a rock. Everyone told him he worried too much.

Lonely, Maggie thought as she watched the Mercedes bump and wind its way down her excuse for a lane. No, she wasn't lonely. She was as certain as she'd ever been about anything that she'd never be lonely here. She felt an unexpected sense of foreboding that she shrugged off as ridiculous.

Wrapping her arms around herself, she turned in two slow circles. Trees rose up out of the rocky hillside. The leaves were hardly more than buds now, but in a few weeks they would grow and spread, turning the woods into a lush cover of green. She liked to imagine it that way and to try to picture it in the dead of winter—white, all white and black with ice clinging to the branches and shimmering on the rocks. In the fall there'd be a tapestry outside every window. She was far from lonely.

For the first time in her life, she had a chance to put her own stamp on a place. It wouldn't be a copy of anything she'd had before or anything that'd been given to her. It was hers, absolutely, and so were any mistakes she made here, any triumphs. There'd be no press to compare this isolated spot in western Maryland with her mother's mansion in Beverly Hills or her father's villa in the south of France. If she was lucky, very, very lucky, Maggie thought with a satisfied sigh, there'd be no press at all. She could make her music and live her life in peace and solitude.

If she stood very still, if she closed her eyes and didn't move, she could hear the music all around her. Not birdsong but the ruffle of air through branches and tiny leaves. If she concentrated, she could hear the faint trickle of the narrow creek that ran along the other side of the lane. The quality of silence was rich, flowing over her like a symphony.

There was a place for glitz, she mused, and for glamour. She simply didn't want that place any longer. The truth was she hadn't wanted that place for a very long time but hadn't known the way out. When your birth had been celebrated by the international press, your first step, your first words, cataloged for the public, it was natural to forget there was another way of life.

Her mother had been one of the greatest blues and ballad singers in America, her father a child actor turned successful film director. Their courtship and marriage had been followed religiously by fans around the world. The birth of their daughter had been an event treated like the birth of royalty. And Maggie had lived the life of a pampered princess. Gold carousels and white fur coats. She'd been lucky because her parents had adored her, and each other. That had compensated for the make-believe, often hard-edged world of show business, with all its demands and inconstancy. Her world had been cushioned by wealth and love, rippled continually with publicity.

The paparazzi haunted her on dates through her teenage years—to her amusement but often to the boys' frustration. Maggie had accepted the fact that her life was public domain. It had never been otherwise.

And when her parents' private plane had crashed into the Swiss Alps, the press had frozen her grief in glossies and newsprint. She hadn't tried to stop it; she'd realized that the world had mourned with her. She'd been eighteen when the fabric of her world had torn.

Then there had been Jerry. First friend, then lover, then husband. With him, her life had drifted into more fantasy, and more tragedy.

She wouldn't think of any of that now, Maggie told herself as she picked up her spade and began to fight the tough soil again. All that was really left of that portion of her life was her music. That she would never give up. She couldn't have if she'd tried. It was part of her the way her eyes and ears were part of her. She composed words and music and twined them together, not effortlessly, as it sometimes seemed from the fluid finished result, but obsessively, wonderingly, constantly. Unlike her mother, she didn't perform but fed other performers with her gift.

At twenty-eight, she had two Oscars, five Grammies and a Tony. She could sit at the piano and play any song she'd ever written from memory. The awards were still in the packing boxes that had been shipped from L.A.

The little flower plot she was planting in a spot perhaps no one would see but herself was a labor of love with no guarantee of success. It was enough that it gave her pleasure to add her own peculiar spot of color to the land she'd claimed as hers. Maggie began to sing as she worked. She'd completely forgotten her former feeling of apprehension.

Normally he didn't do the estimating and initial planning on a job himself. Not anymore. For the past six years Cliff Delaney had been in the position of being able to send one or two of his best men out on the first stage of a project; then he would fine-tune. If the job was interesting enough, he would visit the site while work was in progress, perhaps handle some of the grading and planting himself. He was making an exception.

He knew the old Morgan place. It had been built by a Morgan, even as the tiny community a few miles away had been named after one. For ten years, since William Morgan's car had crashed into the Potomac, the house had stood empty. The house had always been stern, the land formidable. But with the right touch, the right insight,

Cliff knew, it could be magnificent. He had his doubts that the lady from L.A. had the right insight.

He knew of her. Naturally he knew of her. Anyone who hadn't spent the last twenty-eight years in a cave knew Maggie Fitzgerald. At the moment, she was the biggest news in Morganville—all but eclipsing the hot gossip of Lloyd Messner's wife running off with the bank manager.

It was a simple town, the kind that moved slowly. The kind of town where everyone took pride in the acquisition of a new fire engine and the yearly Founder's Day parade. That's why Cliff chose to live there after he'd reached a point where he could live anywhere he chose. He'd grown up there and understood the people, their unity and their possessiveness. He understood their failings. More, perhaps much more, than that, he understood the land. He had serious doubts that the glamorous song writer from California would understand either.

C.J. had estimated six weeks before she flew back. Cliff, without ever setting eyes on her, cut that in half. But perhaps before Maggie Fitzgerald grew bored with her shot at rural living, he could put his own mark on the land.

He turned off the paved road onto the quarter-mile lane that cut through the Morgan property. It had been years since he'd been on it, and it was worse than he remembered. Rain and neglect had worn ruts in the dirt. From both sides of the lane, branches reached out to whip at the truck. The first order of business would be the lane itself, Cliff thought as his small pickup bounced over ruts. It would be graded, leveled, filled. Drainage ditches would have to be dug, gravel spread.

He went slowly, not for the truck's sake but because the land on either side of the lane appealed to him. It was wild and primitive, timeless. He'd want to work with that, incorporate his own talents with the genius of nature. If Maggie Fitzgerald wanted blacktop and hothouse plants, she'd come to the wrong place. He'd be the first one to let her know.

If he had a distrust of outsiders, Cliff considered he'd come by it honestly. They came, often from the rich suburbs of D.C., and wanted their lawns flat and free of the poplar and oak that had first claim. They wanted neat little flowers in orderly rows. Lawns should be even, so that their mowers could handle the weekly cutting effortlessly. What they wanted, Cliff thought derisively, was to say they lived *in the country* while they brought city attitudes and city tastes with them. By the time he rounded the last bend, he was already out of patience with Maggie Fitzgerald.

Maggie heard the truck coming before it was in sight. That was something else she liked about her new home. It was quiet—so quiet that the sound of a truck, which would have been ignored in the city, brought her to attention. Halfheartedly brushing her hands on the seat of her pants, she rose from her planting, then shielded her eyes against the sun.

While she watched, the truck rounded the curve and parked where the Mercedes had been only an hour before. A bit dusty from the road, with its chrome dull rather than gleaming, the truck looked much more comfortable than the luxury car had. Though she couldn't yet see the driver through the glare of sun on windshield, Maggie smiled and lifted a hand in greeting.

The first thing Cliff thought was that she was smaller than he'd expected, more delicate in build. The Fitzgeralds had always been larger than life. He wondered, with a quick grunt, if she'd want to raise orchids to match her style. He got out of the truck, convinced she was going to annoy him.

Perhaps it was because she'd been expecting another Mr. Bog that Maggie felt a flutter of surprise when Cliff stepped out of the truck. Or perhaps, she thought with her usual penchant for honesty, it was because he was quite simply a magnificent example of manhood. Six-two, Maggie decided, with an impressive breadth of shoulders. Black hair that had been ruffled by the wind through the open truck windows fell over his forehead and ears in loose waves. He didn't smile, but his mouth was sculpted, sensual. She had a fleeting regret that he wore dark glasses so that his eyes were hidden. She judged people from their eyes.

Instead, Maggie summed him up from the way he moved—loosely, confidently. Athletic, she concluded, as he strode over the uneven ground. Definitely self-assured. He was still a yard away when she got the unmistakable impression that he wasn't particularly friendly.

"Miss Fitzgerald?"

"Yes." Giving him a neutral smile, Maggie held out a hand. "You're from Delaney's?"

"That's right." Their hands met, briefly, hers soft, his hard, both of them capable. Without bothering to identify himself, Cliff scanned the grounds. "You wanted an estimate on some landscaping."

Maggie followed his gaze, and this time her smile held amusement. "Obviously I need something. Does your company perform miracles?"

"We do the job." He glanced down at the splash of color behind her, wilted pansies and soggy petunias. Her effort touched something in him that he ignored, telling himself she'd be bored long before it was time to pull the first weeds. "Why don't you tell me what you have in mind?"

"A glass of iced tea at the moment. Look around while I get some; then we'll talk about it." She'd been giving orders without a second thought all her life. After giving this one, Maggie turned and climbed the rickety steps to the porch. Behind the tinted glasses, Cliff's eyes narrowed.

Designer jeans, he thought with a smirk as he watched the graceful sway of hips before the screen door banged shut at her back. And the solitaire on the thin chain around her neck had been no less than a carat. Just what game was little Miss Hollywood playing? She'd left a trace of her scent behind, something soft and subtle that would nag at a man's senses. Shrugging, he turned his back on the house and looked at the land.

It could be shaped and structured without being tamed. It should never lose its basic unruly sense by being manicured, though he admitted the years of neglect had given the rougher side of nature too much of an advantage. Still, he wouldn't level it for her. Cliff had turned down more than one job because the client had insisted on altering the land's personality. Even with that, he wouldn't have called himself an artist. He was a businessman. His business was the land.

He walked farther away from the house, toward a grove of trees overrun with tangling vines, greedy saplings and thistles. Without effort he could see it cleared of undergrowth, richly mulched, naturalized perhaps with jonquils. That one section would personify peace, as he saw it. Hitching his thumbs in his back pockets, Cliff reflected that from the reams that had been written about Maggie Fitzgerald over the years, she didn't go in much for peace.

Jet-setting, the fast lane, glitter and glitz. What the hell had she moved out here for?

Before he heard her, Cliff caught a fresh whiff of her perfume. When he turned, she was a few paces behind him, two glasses in her hand. She watched him steadily with a curiosity she didn't bother to hide. He learned something more about her then as she stood with her eyes on his face and the sun at her back. She was the most alluring woman he'd ever met, though he'd be damned if he knew why.

Maggie approached him and offered a glass of frosty tea. "Want to hear my ideas?"

The voice had something to do with it, Cliff decided. An innocent question, phrased in that sultry voice, conjured up a dozen dark pleasures. He took a slow sip. "That's what I'm here for," he told her with a curtness he'd never shown any potential client.

Her brow lifted at the tone, the only sign that she'd noticed his rudeness. With that attitude, she thought, he wouldn't have the job for long. Then again, he didn't strike her as a man who'd work for someone else. "Indeed you are, Mr....?"

"Delaney."

"Ah, the man himself." That made more sense, she decided, if his attitude didn't. "Well, Mr. Delaney, I'm told you're the best. I believe in having the best, so..." Thoughtfully, she ran a fingertip down the length of her glass, streaking the film of moisture. "I'll tell you what I want, and you tell me if you can deliver."

"Fair enough." He didn't know why her simple statement should annoy him any more than he could understand why he was just noticing how smooth her skin was and how compelling were those large velvet eyes. Like a doe's, Cliff realized. He wasn't a man who hunted but a man who watched. "I'll tell you up front that my company has a policy against destroying the natural terrain in order to make the land into something it's not. This is rough country, Miss Fitzgerald. It's supposed to be. If you want an acre or two of manicured lawn, you've bought the wrong land and called the wrong landscaper."

It took a great deal to fire up her temper. Maggie had worked long and hard to control a natural tendency toward quick fury in order to block the label of temperamental daughter of temperamental artists. "Decent of you to point it out," she managed after three long, quiet breaths.

"I don't know why you bought the place," he began.

"I don't believe I've offered that information."

"And it's none of my business," Cliff finished with an acknowledging nod. "But this—" he indicated the property with a gesture of his hand "—is my business."

"You're a bit premature in condemning me, aren't you, Mr. Delaney?" To keep herself in check, Maggie took a sip of tea. It was cold, with a faint bite of lemon. "I've yet to ask you to bring on the bulldozers and chain saws." She ought to tell him to haul his buns into his truck and take off. Almost before she could wonder why she didn't, the answer came. Instinct. Instinct had brought her to Morganville and to the property she now stood on. It was instinct that told her he was indeed the best. Nothing else would do for her land. To give herself a moment to be sure she didn't do anything rash, Maggie took another sip from her glass.

"That grove there," she began briskly. "I want it cleared of undergrowth. It can't be enjoyed if you have to fight your way through thorns and thickets to walk in it." She shot him a look. "Don't you want to take notes?"

He watched her, consideringly. "No. Go on."

"All right. This stretch right here, in front of the porch—I imagine that was a lawn of sorts at one time." She turned, looking at the knee-high weeds. "It should be again, but I want enough room to plant, I don't know, some pines, maybe, to keep the line between lawn and woods from being too marked. Then there's the way the whole thing just sort of falls away until it reaches the lane below."

Forgetting her annoyance for the moment, Maggie made her way across the relatively flat land to where it sloped steeply down. Weeds, some of them as tall as she, grew in abundance wherever the rocks would permit. "It's certainly too steep for grass to be practical," she said half to herself. "But I can't just let all these weeds have their way. I'd like some color, but I don't want uniformity."

"You'll want some evergreens," he said from behind her. "Some spreading junipers along the bottom edge of the whole slope, a few coming farther up over there, with some forsythia mixed in. Here, where the grade's not so dramatic, you'd want some low ground cover." He could see phlox spilling and bumping over the rocks. "That tree's got to come down," he went on, frowning at the one that leaned precariously toward her roof. "And there's two, maybe three, on the rise behind the house that've got to be taken down before they fall down."

She was frowning now, but she'd always believed in letting an expert set the plan. "Okay, but I don't want you to cut down anything that doesn't have to be cleared."

Maggie could only see her own reflection in his glasses when he faced her. "I never do." He turned and began to walk around the side of the house. "That's another problem," Cliff continued without checking to see if she was following. "The way that dirt wall's eroding down from the cliff here. You're going to end up with a tree or a boulder in your kitchen when you least expect it."

"So?" Maggie tilted her head so she could scan the ridge behind her house. "You're the expert."

"It'll need to be recut, tapered back some. Then I'd put up a retaining wall, three, maybe four, foot high. Crown vetch'd hold the dirt above that. Plant it along the entire slope. It's hardy and fast."

"All right." It sounded reasonable. He sounded more reasonable, Maggie decided, when he was talking about his business. A man of the land, she mused, and wished again she could see beyond the tinted glass to his eyes. "This part behind the house has to be cleared." She began to fight her way through the weeds and briars as she talked. "I think if I had a walkway of some kind from here to the lane, I could have a rockery…here." A vague gesture of her hands indicated the spot she had in mind. "There're plenty of rocks," she muttered, nearly stumbling over one. "Then down here—"

Cliff took her arm before she could start down the slope on the far side of the house. The contact jolted both of them. More surprised than alarmed, Maggie turned her head.

"I wouldn't," Cliff said softly, and she felt a tiny trickle, an odd excitement, sprint up her spine.

"Wouldn't what?" Her chin automatically tilted, her eyes challenged.

"Walk down there." Her skin was soft, Cliff discovered. With his hand wrapped around her arm, he could touch his fingertips to his thumb. Small and soft, he mused, enjoying the feel of his flesh against hers. Too small and soft for land that would fight back at you.

Maggie glanced down to where he held her. She noticed the tan on the back of his hand; she noticed the size and the strength of it. When she noticed her pulse wasn't quite steady, she lifted her gaze again. "Mr. Delaney—"

"Snakes," he said simply, and had the satisfaction of seeing her take two quick steps back. "You're almost sure to have some down in a spot like that. In fact, with the way this place is overgrown, you're likely to have them everywhere."

"Well, then—" Maggie swallowed and made a herculean effort not to shudder "—maybe you can start the job right away."

For the first time, he smiled, a very slight, very cautious, curving of lips. They'd both forgotten he still held her, but they were standing much closer now, within a hand span of touching. She certainly hadn't reacted the way he'd expected. He wouldn't have been surprised if she'd screeched at the mention of snakes, then had dashed into the house, slamming and locking the door. Her skin was soft, Cliff mused, unconsciously moving his thumb over it. But apparently she wasn't.

"I might be able to send a crew out next week, but the first thing that has to be dealt with is your road."

Maggie dismissed this with a shrug. "Do whatever you think best there, excluding asphalt. It's only a means of getting in and out to me. I want to concentrate on the house and grounds."

"The road's going to run you twelve, maybe fifteen, hundred," he began, but she cut him off again.

"Do what you have to," she told him with the unconscious arrogance of someone who'd never worried about money. "This section here—" She pointed to the steep drop in front of them, making no move this time to go down it. At the base it spread twenty feet wide, perhaps thirty in length, in a wicked maze of thorny vines and weeds as thick at the stem as her thumb. "I want a pond."

Cliff brought his attention back to her. "A pond?"

She gave him a level look and stood her ground. "Allow me one eccentricity, Mr. Delaney. A small one," she continued before he could comment. "There's certainly enough room, and it seems to me that this section here's the worst. It's hardly more than a hole in the ground in a very awkward place. Do you have an objection to water?"

Instead of answering, he studied the ground below them, running through the possibilities. The truth was, she couldn't have picked a better spot as far as the lay of the land and the angle to the house. It could be done, he mused. It wouldn't be an easy job, but it could be done. And it would be very effective.

"It's going to cost you," he said at length. "You're going to be sinking a lot of cash into this place. If you're weighing that against resale value, I can tell you, this property won't be easy to sell."

It snapped her patience. She was tired, very tired, of having people suggest she didn't know what she was doing. "Mr. Delaney, I'm hiring you to do a job, not to advise me on real estate or my finances. If you can't handle it, just say so and I'll get someone else."

His eyes narrowed. The fingers on her arm tightened fractionally. "I can handle it, Miss Fitzgerald. I'll draw up an estimate and a contract. They'll be in the mail tomorrow. If you still want the job done after you've looked them over, call my office." Slowly, he released her arm, then handed her back the glass of tea. He left her there, near the edge where the slope gave way to gully as he headed back toward his truck. "By the way," he said without turning around, "you overwatered your pansies."

Maggie let out one long, simmering breath and dumped the tepid tea on the ground at her feet.

## *Chapter 2*

When she was alone, Maggie went back inside, through the back door, which creaked ominously on its hinges. She wasn't going to think about Cliff Delaney. In fact, she doubted if she'd see him again. He'd send crews out to deal with the actual work, and whatever they had to discuss would be done via phone or letter. Better that way, Maggie decided. He'd been unfriendly, abrupt and annoying, though his mouth had been attractive, she reflected, even kind.

She was halfway through the kitchen when she remembered the glasses in her hand. Turning back, she crossed the scarred linoleum to set them both in the sink, then leaned on the windowsill to look out at the rise behind her house. Even as she watched, a few loose stones and dirt slid down the wall. A couple of hard rains, she mused, and half that bank would be at her back door. A retaining wall. Maggie nodded. Cliff Delaney obviously knew his business.

There was just enough breeze to carry a hint of spring to her. Far back in the woods a bird she couldn't see sang out as though it would never stop. Listening, she forgot the eroding wall and the exposed roots of trees that were much too close to its edge. She forgot the rudeness, and the attraction, of a stranger. If she looked up, far up, she could see where the tops of the trees met the sky.

She wondered how this view would change with the seasons and found herself impatient to experience them all. Perhaps she'd never realized how badly she'd needed a place to herself, time to herself, until she'd found it.

With a sigh, Maggie moved away from the window. It was time to get down to work if she was to deliver the finished score as promised. She walked down the hall where the wallpaper was peeling and curled and turned into what had once been the back parlor. It was now her music room.

Boxes she hadn't even thought of unpacking stood in a pile against one wall. A few odd pieces of furniture that had come with the house sat hidden under dustcovers. The windows were uncurtained, the floor was uncarpeted. There were pale squares intermittently on the walls where pictures had once hung. In the center of the room, glossy and elegant, stood her baby grand. A single box lay open beside it, and from this Maggie took a sheet of staff paper. Tucking a pencil behind her ear, she sat.

For a moment she did nothing else, just sat in the silence while she let the music come and play in her head. She knew what she wanted for this segment—something dramatic, something strong and full of power. Behind her closed eyelids she could see the scene from the film sweep by. It was up to her to underscore, to accentuate, to take the mood and make it music.

Reaching out, she switched on the cassette tape and began.

She let the notes build in strength as she continued to visualize the scene her music would amplify. She only worked on films she had a feeling for. Though the Oscars told her she excelled in this area of work, Maggie's true affection was for the single song—words and music.

Maggie had always compared the composing of a score to the building of a bridge. First came the blueprint, the overall plan. Then the construction had to be done, slowly, meticulously, until each end fit snugly on solid ground, a flawless arch in between. It was a labor of precision.

The single song was a painting, to be created as the mood dictated. The single song could be written from nothing more than a phrasing of words or notes. It could encapsulate mood, emotion or a story in a matter of minutes. It was a labor of love.

When she worked, she forgot the time, forgot everything but the careful structuring of notes to mood. Her fingers moved over the piano keys as she repeated the same segment again and again, changing perhaps no more than one note until her instincts told her it was right. An hour passed, then two. She didn't grow weary or bored or impatient with the constant repetition. Music was her business, but it was also her lover.

She might not have heard the knock if she hadn't paused to rewind the tape. Disoriented, she ignored it, waiting for the maid to answer before she recalled where she was.

*No maids, Maggie,* she reminded herself. *No gardener, no cook. It's all up to you now.* The thought pleased her. If there was no one to answer to her, she had no one to answer to.

Rising, she went back into the hall and down to the big front door.

She didn't have to develop the country habit of leaving the doors unlocked. In L.A., there'd been servants to deal with bolts and chains and security systems. Maggie never gave them a thought. Taking the knob in both hands, she twisted and tugged. She reminded herself to tell Mr. Bog about the sticking problem as the door swung open.

On the porch stood a tall, prim-looking woman in her early fifties. Her hair was a soft, uniform gray worn with more tidiness than style. Faded blue eyes studied Maggie from behind rose-framed glasses. If this was the welcome wagon lady, Maggie thought after a glance at the unhappy line of the woman's mouth, she didn't seem thrilled with the job. Much too used to strangers' approaches to be reserved, Maggie tilted her head and smiled.

"Hello, can I help you?"

"You are Miss Fitzgerald?" The voice was low and even, as subdued and inoffensive as her plain, pale coatdress.

"Yes, I am."

"I'm Louella Morgan."

It took Maggie a moment; then the name clicked. Louella Morgan, widow of William Morgan, former owner of the house that was now hers. For an instant Maggie felt like an intruder; then she shook the feeling away and extended her hand. "Hello, Mrs. Morgan. Won't you come in?"

"I don't want to disturb you."

"No, please." As she spoke, she opened the door a bit wider. "I met your daughter when we settled on the house."

"Yes, Joyce told me." Louella's gaze darted around and behind Maggie as she stepped over the threshold. "She never expected to sell so quickly. The property had only been on the market a week."

"I like to think it was fate." Maggie put her weight against the door and pushed until she managed to close it. Definitely a job for Bog, she decided.

"Fate?" Louella turned back from her study of the long, empty hall.

"It just seemed to be waiting for me." Though she found the woman's direct, unsmiling stare odd, Maggie gestured toward the living room. "Come in and sit down," she invited. "Would you like some coffee? Something cold?"

"No, thank you. I'll stay only a minute." Louella did wander into the living room, and though there was a single sofa piled with soft, inviting pillows, she didn't accept Maggie's invitation to sit. She looked at the crumbling wallpaper, the cracked paint and the windows that glistened from Maggie's diligence with ammonia. "I suppose I wanted to see the house again with someone living in it."

Maggie took a look at the almost-empty room. Maybe she'd start stripping off the wallpaper next week. "I guess it'll be a few weeks more before it looks as though someone is."

Louella didn't seem to hear. "I came here as a newlywed." She smiled then, but Maggie didn't see anything happy in it. The eyes, she thought, looked lost, as if the woman had been lost for years. "But then, my husband wanted something more modern, more convenient to town and his business. So we moved, and he rented it out."

Louella focused on Maggie again. "Such a lovely, quiet spot," she murmured. "A pity it's been so neglected over the years."

"It is a lovely spot," Maggie agreed, struggling not to sound as uncomfortable as she felt. "I'm having some work done on both the house and the land..." Her voice trailed off when Louella wandered to the front window and stared out. *Heavens,* Maggie thought, searching for something more to say, *what have I got here?* "Ah, of course I plan to do a lot of the painting and papering and such myself."

"The weeds have taken over," Louella said with her back to the room.

Maggie's brows lifted and fell as she wondered what to do next. "Yes, well, Cliff Delaney was out this afternoon to take a look around."

"Cliff." Louella's attention seemed to focus again as she turned back. The light coming through the uncurtained windows made her seem more pale, more insubstantial. "An interesting young man, rather rough-and-ready, but very clever. He'll do well for you here, for the land. He's a cousin of the Morgans, you know." She paused and seemed to laugh, but very softly. "Then, you'll find many Morgans and their kin scattered throughout the county."

A cousin, Maggie mused. Perhaps he'd been unfriendly because he didn't think the property should've been sold to an outsider. Resolutely, she tried to push Cliff Delaney aside. He didn't have to approve. The land was hers.

"The front lawn was lovely once," Louella murmured.

Maggie felt a stirring of pity. "It will be again. The front's going to be cleared and planted. The back, too." Wanting to reassure her, Maggie stepped closer. Both women stood by the window now. "I'm going to have a rock garden, and there'll be a pond where the gully is on the side."

"A pond?" Louella turned and fixed her with another long stare. "You're going to clear out the gully?"

"Yes." Uncomfortable again, Maggie shifted. "It's the perfect place."

Louella ran a hand over the front of her purse as if she were wiping something away. "I used to have a rock garden. Sweet william and azure Adams. There was wisteria beneath my bedroom window, and roses, red roses, climbing on a trellis."

"I'd like to have seen it," Maggie said gently. "It must've been beautiful."

"I have pictures."

"Do you?" Struck with an idea, Maggie forgot her discomfort. "Perhaps I could see them. They'd help me decide just what to plant."

"I'll see that you get them. You're very kind to let me come in this way." Louella took one last scan of the room. "The house holds memories." When she walked out into the hall, Maggie went with her to tug open the front door again. "Goodbye, Miss Fitzgerald."

"Goodbye, Mrs. Morgan." Her pity stirred again, and Maggie reached out to touch the woman's shoulder. "Please, come again."

Louella looked back, her smile very slight, her eyes very tired. "Thank you."

While Maggie watched, she walked to an old, well-preserved Lincoln, then drove slowly down the hill. Vaguely disturbed, Maggie went back into the music room. She hadn't met many residents of Morganville yet, she mused, but they were certainly an interesting bunch.

The noise brought Maggie out of a sound sleep into a drowsy, cranky state. For a moment, as she tried to bury her head under the pillow, she thought she was in New York. The groan and roar sounded like a big, nasty garbage truck. But she wasn't in New York, she thought as she surfaced, rubbing her hands over her eyes. She was in Morganville, and there weren't any garbage trucks. Here you piled your trash into the back of your car or pickup and hauled it to the county dump. Maggie had considered this the height of self-sufficiency.

Still, something was out there.

She lay on her back for a full minute, staring up at the ceiling. The sunlight slanted, low and thin, across her newly purchased quilt. She'd never been a morning person, nor did she intend to have country life change that intimate part of her nature. Warily, she turned her head to look at the clock: 7:05. Good heavens.

It was a struggle, but she pushed herself into a sitting position and stared blankly around the room. Here, too, boxes were piled, unopened. There was a precariously stacked pile of books and magazines on decorating and landscaping beside the bed. On the wall were three fresh strips of wallpaper, an ivory background with tiny violets, that she'd hung herself. More rolls and paste were pushed into a corner. The noise outside was a constant, irritating roar.

Resigned, Maggie got out of bed. She stumbled over a pair of shoes, swore, then went to the window. She'd chosen that room as her own because she could see out over the rolling pitch of what would be her front yard, over the tops of the trees on her own property to the valley beyond.

There was a farmhouse in the distance with a red roof and a smoking chimney. Beside it was a long, wide field that had just been plowed and planted. If she looked farther still, she could see the peaks of mountains faintly blue and indistinct in the morning mist. The window on the connecting wall would give her a view of the intended pond and the line of pines that would eventually be planted.

Maggie pushed the window up the rest of the way, struggling as it stuck a bit. The early-spring air had a pleasant chill. She could still hear the constant low sound of a running engine. Curious, she pressed her face against the screen, only to have it topple out of the window frame and fall to the porch below. One more thing for Mr. Bog to see to, Maggie thought with a sigh as she leaned through the opening. Just then the yellow bulk of a bulldozer rounded the bend in her lane and broke into view.

So, she thought, watching it inch its way along, leveling and pushing at rock and dirt, Cliff Delaney was a man of his word. She'd received the promised estimate and contract two days after his visit. When she'd called his office, Maggie had spoken to an efficient-sounding woman who'd told her the work would begin the first of the week.

And it's Monday, she reflected, leaning her elbows on the sill. Very prompt. Narrowing her eyes, she looked more closely at the man on top of the bulldozer. His build was too slight, she decided, his hair not quite dark enough. She didn't have to see his face to know it wasn't Cliff. Shrugging, she turned away from the window. Why should she have thought Cliff Delaney would work his own machines? And why should she have wanted it to be him? Hadn't she already decided she wouldn't see him again? She'd hired his company to do a job; the job would be done, and she'd write out a check. That was all there was to it.

Maggie attributed her crankiness to the early awakening as she snatched up her robe and headed for the shower.

Two hours later, fortified with the coffee she'd made for herself and the bulldozer operator, Maggie was on her knees on the kitchen floor. Since she was up at a barbaric hour, she thought it best to do something physical. On the counter above her sat her cassette tape player. The sound of her score, nearly completed, all but drowned out the whine of machinery. She let herself flow with it while words to the title song she'd yet to compose flitted in and out of her mind.

While she let her thoughts flow with the music she'd created, Maggie chipped away at the worn tile on the kitchen floor. True, her bedroom had only one wall partially papered, and only the ceiling in the upstairs bath was painted, *and* there were two more steps to be stripped and lacquered before the main stairway was finished, but she worked in her own way, at her own speed. She found herself jumping from project to project, leaving one partially done and leaping headlong into the next. This way, she reasoned, she could watch the house come together piece by piece rather than have one completed, out-of-place room.

Besides, she'd gotten a peek at the flooring beneath the tile when she'd inadvertently knocked an edge off a corner. Curiosity had done the rest.

When Cliff walked to the back door, he was already annoyed. It was ridiculous for him to be wasting time here, with all the other jobs his firm had in progress. Yet he was here. He'd knocked at the front door for almost five minutes. He knew Maggie was inside, her car was in the driveway, and the bulldozer operator had told him she'd brought out coffee an hour or so before. Didn't it occur to her that someone usually knocked when they wanted something?

The music coming through the open windows caught his attention, and his imagination. He'd never heard the melody before. It was compelling, sexy, moody. A lone piano, no backdrop of strings or brass, but it had the power of making the listener want to stop and hear every note. For a moment he did stop, both disturbed and moved.

Shifting the screen he'd found into his other hand, Cliff started to knock. Then he saw her.

She was on her hands and knees, prying up pieces of linoleum with what looked like a putty knife. Her hair was loose, falling over one shoulder so that her face was hidden behind it. The deep, rich sable brown picked up hints of gold from the sunlight that streamed through the open door and window.

Gray corduroys fit snugly over her hips, tapering down to bare ankles and feet. A vivid red suede shirt was tucked into the waist. He recognized the shirt as one sold in exclusive shops for very exclusive prices. Her wrists and hands looked impossibly delicate against it. Cliff was scowling at them when Maggie got too enthusiastic with the putty knife and scraped her knuckle against a corner of the tile.

"What the hell are you doing?" he demanded, swinging the door open and striding in before Maggie had a chance to react. She'd barely put the knuckle to her mouth in an instinctive move when he was crouched beside her and grabbing her hand.

"It's nothing," she said automatically. "Just a scratch."

"You're lucky you didn't slice it, the way you're hacking at that tile." Though his voice was rough and impatient, his hand was gentle. She left hers in it.

Yes, his hand was gentle, though rough-edged, like his voice, but this time she could see his eyes. They were gray; smoky, secret. Evening mists came to her mind. Mists that were sometimes dangerous but always compelling. That was the sort of mist she'd always believed had cloaked Brigadoon for a hundred years at a time. Maggie decided she could like him, in a cautious sort of way.

"Who'd be stupid enough to put linoleum over this?" With the fingers of her free hand, she skimmed over the hardwood she'd exposed. "Lovely, isn't it? Or it will be when it's sanded and sealed."

"Get Bog to deal with it," Cliff ordered. "You don't know what you're doing."

So everyone said. Maggie withdrew a bit, annoyed by the phrase. "Why should he have all the fun? Besides, I'm being careful."

"I can see that." He turned her hand over so that she saw the scrape over her thumb. It infuriated him to see the delicacy marred. "Doesn't someone in your profession have to be careful with their hands?"

"They're insured," she tossed back. "I think I can probably hit a few chords, even with a wound as serious as this." She pulled her hand out of his. "Did you come here to criticize me, Mr. Delaney, or did you have something else in mind?"

"I came to check on the job." Which wasn't necessary, he admitted. In any case, why should it matter to him if she was careless enough to hurt her hand? She was just a woman who had touched down in his territory and would be gone again before the leaves were full-blown with summer. He was going to have to remember that, and the fact that she didn't interest him personally. Shifting, he picked up the screen he'd dropped when he'd taken her hand. "I found this outside."

It wasn't often her voice took on that regal tone. He seemed to nudge it out of her. "Thank you." She took the screen and leaned it against the stove.

"Your road'll be blocked most of the day. I hope you weren't planning on going anywhere."

Maggie gave him a level look that held a hint of challenge. "I'm not going anywhere, Mr. Delaney."

He inclined his head. "Fine." The music on the tape player changed tempo. It was more hard-driving, more primitive. It seemed something to be played on hot, moonless nights. It drew him, pulled at him. "What is that?" Cliff demanded. "I've never heard it before."

Maggie glanced up at the recorder. "It's a movie score I'm composing. That's the melody for the title song." Because it had given her a great deal of trouble, she frowned at the revolving tape. "Do you like it?"

"Yes."

It was the most simple and most direct answer he'd given her thus far. It wasn't enough for Maggie.

"Why?"

He paused a moment, still listening, hardly aware that they were both still on the floor, close enough to touch. "It goes straight to the blood, straight to the imagination. Isn't that what a song's supposed to do?"

He could have said nothing more perfect. Her smile flashed, a quick, stunning smile that left him staring at her as though he'd been struck by lightning. "Yes. Yes, that's exactly what it's supposed to do." In her enthusiasm she shifted. Their knees brushed. "I'm trying for something very basic with this. It has to set the mood for a film about a passionate relationship—an intensely passionate relationship between two people who seem to have nothing in common but an uncontrollable desire for each other. One of them will kill because of it."

She trailed off, lost in the music and the mood. She could see it in vivid colors—scarlets, purples. She could feel it, like the close, sultry air on a hot summer night. Then she frowned, and as if on cue, the music stopped. From the tape came a sharp, pungent curse, then silence.

"I lost something in those last two bars," she muttered. "It was like—" she gestured with both hands, bringing them up, turning them over, then dropping them again "—something came unmeshed. It has to build to desperation, but it has to be more subtle than that. Passion at the very edge of control."

"Do you always write like that?" Cliff was studying her when she focused on him again, studying her as he had her land—thoroughly, with an eye both for detail and an overview.

She sat back on her haunches, comfortable now with a conversation on her own turf. He could hardly frustrate her in a discussion of music. She'd lived with it, in it, all her life. "Like what?" she countered.

"With the emphasis on mood and emotions rather than notes and timing."

Her brows lifted. With one hand, she pushed back the hair that swept across her cheek. She wore an amethyst on her finger, wine-colored, square. It caught the light, holding it until she dropped her hand again. As she thought it over, it occurred to her that no one, not even her closest associates, had ever defined her style so cleanly. It pleased her, though she didn't know why, that he had done so. "Yes," she said simply.

He didn't like what those big, soft eyes could do to him. Cliff rose. "That's why your music is good."

Maggie gave a quick laugh, not at the compliment, but at the grudging tone with which he delivered it. "So, you can say something nice, after all."

"When it's appropriate." He watched her stand, noting that she moved with the sort of fluidity he'd always associated with tall, willowy women. "I admire your music."

Again, it was the tone, rather than the words, that spoke to her. This time it touched off annoyance, rather than humor. "And little else that has to do with me."

"I don't know you," Cliff countered.

"You didn't like me when you drove up that hill the other day." With her temper rising, Maggie put her hands on her hips and faced him squarely. "I get the impression you didn't like me years before we met."

That was direct, Cliff decided. Maggie Fitzgerald, glamour girl from the Coast, didn't believe in evasions. Neither did he. "I have a problem with people who live their lives on silver platters. I've too much respect for reality."

"Silver platters," Maggie repeated in a voice that was much, much too quiet. "In other words, I was born into affluence, therefore, I can't understand the real world."

He didn't know why he wanted to smile. Perhaps it was the way color flooded her face. Perhaps it was because she stood nearly a foot beneath him but gave every appearance of being ready to Indian-wrestle and win. Yet he didn't smile. Cliff had the impression that if you gave an inch to this lady, you'd soon be begging to give a mile. "That about sums it up. The gravel for the lane'll be delivered and spread by five."

"Sums it up?" Accustomed to ending a conversation when she chose, Maggie grabbed his arm as he started to turn for the door. "You're a narrow-minded snob, and you know nothing about my life."

Cliff looked down at the delicate hand against his tanned muscled arm. The amethyst glowed up at him. "Miss Fitzgerald, everyone in the country knows about your life."

"That is one of the most unintelligent statements I've ever heard." She made one final attempt to control her temper, then forgot it. "Let me tell you something, Mr. Delaney—" The phone interrupted what would have been a stream of impassioned abuse. Maggie ended up swearing. "You stay there," she ordered as she turned to the wall phone.

Cliff's brows lifted at the command. Slowly, he leaned against the kitchen counter. He'd stay, he decided. Not because she'd told him to, but because he'd discovered he wanted to hear what she had to say.

Maggie yanked the receiver from the wall and barked into it. "Hello."

"Well, it's nice to hear that country life's agreeing with you."

"C.J." She struggled to hold down her temper. She wanted neither questions nor I-told-you-sos. "Sorry, you caught me in the middle of a philosophical discussion." Though she heard Cliff's quick snort of laughter, she ignored it. "Something up, C.J.?"

"Well, I hadn't heard from you in a couple of days—"

"I told you I'd call once a week. Will you stop worrying?"

"You know I can't."

She had to laugh. "No, I know you can't. If it relieves your mind, I'm having the lane fixed even as we speak. The next time you visit, you won't have to worry about your muffler falling off."

"It doesn't relieve my mind," C.J. grumbled. "I have nightmares about that roof caving in on your head. The damn place is falling apart."

"The place is not falling apart." She turned, inadvertently kicking the screen and sending it clattering across the floor. At that moment, her eyes met Cliff's. He was still leaning against the counter, still close enough to the back door to be gone in two strides. But now he was grinning. Maggie looked at the screen, then back at Cliff, and covered her mouth to smother a giggle.

"What was that noise?" C.J. demanded.

"Noise?" Maggie swallowed. "I didn't hear any noise." She covered the mouth of the receiver with her hand when Cliff laughed again. "Shh," she whispered, smiling. "C.J.," she said back into the phone, knowing she needed to distract him, "the score's nearly finished."

"When?" The response was immediate and predictable. She sent Cliff a knowing nod.

"For the most part, it's polished. I'm a little hung up on the title song. If you let me get back to work, the tape'll be in your office next week."

"Why don't you deliver it yourself? We'll have lunch."

"Forget it."

He sighed. "Just thought I'd try. To show you my heart's in the right place, I sent you a present."

"A present? The Godiva?"

"You'll have to wait and see," he said evasively. "It'll be there by tomorrow morning. I expect you to be so touched you'll catch the next plane to L.A. to thank me in person."

"C.J.—"

"Get back to work. And call me," he added, clever enough to know when to retreat and when to advance. "I keep having visions of you falling off that mountain."

He hung up, leaving her, as he often did, torn between amusement and annoyance. "My agent," Maggie said as she replaced the receiver. "He likes to worry."

"I see."

Cliff remained where he was; so did she. That one silly shared moment seemed to have broken down a barrier between them. Now, in its place, was an awkwardness neither of them fully understood. He was suddenly aware of the allure of her scent, of the slender line of her throat. She was suddenly disturbed by his basic masculinity, by the memory of the firm, rough feel of his palm. Maggie cleared her throat.

"Mr. Delaney—"

"Cliff," he corrected.

She smiled, telling herself to relax. "Cliff. We seem to've gotten off on the wrong foot for some reason. Maybe if we concentrate on something that interests us both—my land—we won't keep rubbing each other the wrong way."

He found it an interesting phrase, particularly since he was imagining what it would feel like to run his hands over her skin. "All right," he agreed as he straightened from the counter. He crossed to her, wondering who he was testing, himself or her. When he stopped, she was trapped between him and the stove.

He didn't touch her, but both of them could sense what it would be like. Hard hands, soft skin. Warmth turning quickly to heat. Mouth meeting mouth with confidence, with knowledge, with passion.

"I consider your land a challenge." He said it quietly, his eyes on hers. She didn't think of mists now but of smoke—of smoke and fire. "Which is why I've decided to give this project quite a bit of my personal attention."

Her nerves were suddenly strung tight. Maggie didn't back away, because she was almost certain that was what he wanted. Instead, she met his gaze. If her eyes weren't calm, if they'd darkened with the first traces of desire, she couldn't prevent it. "I can't argue with that."

"No." He smiled a little. If he stayed, even moments longer, he knew he'd find out how her lips tasted. That might be the biggest mistake he'd ever make. Turning, he went to the back door. "Call Bog." He tossed this over his shoulder as he pushed the screen door open. "Your fingers belong on piano keys, not on putty knives."

Maggie let out a long, tense breath when the screen door slammed. Did he do that on purpose, she wondered as she pressed a hand to her speeding heart. Or was it a natural talent of his to turn women into limp rags? Shaking her head, she told herself to forget it. If there was one thing she had experience in, it was in avoiding and evading the professional lothario. She was definitely uninterested in going a few rounds with Morganville's leading contender.

With a scowl, she dropped back to her knees and picked up the putty knife. She began to hack at the tile with a vengeance. Maggie Fitzgerald could take care of herself.

# *Chapter 3*

For the third morning in a row, Maggie was awakened by the sound of men and machinery outside her windows. It occurred to her that she'd hardly had the chance to become used to the quiet when the chaos had started.

The bulldozer had been replaced by chain saws, industrial weed eaters and trucks. While she was far from getting used to the early risings, she was resigned. By seven-fifteen she had dragged herself out of the shower and was staring at her face in the bathroom mirror.

Not so good, she decided, studying her own sleepy eyes. But then she'd been up until two working on the score. Displeased, she ran a hand over her face. She'd never considered pampering her skin a luxury or a waste of time. It was simply something she did routinely, the same way she'd swim twenty laps every morning in California.

She'd been neglecting the basics lately, Maggie decided, squinting at her reflection. Had it been over two months since she'd been in a salon? Ruefully, she tugged at the bangs that swept over her forehead. It was showing, and it was time to do something about it.

After wrapping her still-damp hair in a towel, she pulled open the mirrored medicine-cabinet door. The nearest Elizabeth Arden's was seventy miles away. There were times, Maggie told herself as she smeared on a clay mask, that you had to fend for yourself.

She was just rinsing her hands when the sound of quick, high-pitched barking reached her. C.J.'s present, Maggie thought wryly, wanted his breakfast. In her short terry-cloth robe, which was raveled at the hem, her hair wrapped in a checked towel and the clay mask hardening on her face, she started downstairs to tend to the demanding gift her agent had flown out to her. She had just reached the bottom landing when a knock on the door sent the homely bulldog puppy into a frenzy.

"Calm down," she ordered, scooping him up under one arm. "All this excitement and I haven't had my coffee yet. Give me a break." The pup lowered his head and growled when she pulled on the front door. Definitely city-oriented, she thought, trying to calm the pup. She wondered if C.J. had planned it that way. The door resisted, sticking. Swearing, Maggie set down the dog and yanked with both hands.

The door swung open, carrying her a few steps back with the momentum. The pup dashed through the closest doorway, poking his head around the frame and snarling as if he meant business. Cliff stared at Maggie as she stood, panting, in the hall. She blew out a breath, wondering what could happen next. "I thought country life was supposed to be peaceful."

Cliff grinned, tucking his thumbs in the front pockets of his jeans. "Not necessarily. Get you up?"

"I've been up for quite some time," she said loftily.

"Mmm-hmm." His gaze skimmed over her legs, nicely exposed by the brief robe, before it lingered on the puppy crouched in the doorway. Her legs were longer, he mused, than one would think, considering the overall size of her. "Friend of yours?"

Maggie looked at the bulldog, which was making fierce sounds in his throat while keeping a careful distance. "A present from my agent."

"What's his name?"

Maggie sent the cowering puppy a wry look. "Killer."

Cliff watched the pup disappear behind the wall again. "Very apt. You figure to train him as a guard dog?"

"I'm going to teach him to attack music critics." She lifted a hand to push it through her hair—an old habit—and discovered the towel. Just as abruptly, she remembered the rest of her appearance. One hand flew to her face and found the thin layer of hardened clay. "Oh, my God," Maggie murmured as Cliff's grin widened. "Oh, damn." Turning, she raced for the stairs. "Just a minute." He was treated to an intriguing glimpse of bare thighs as she dashed upstairs.

Ten minutes later, she walked back down, perfectly composed. Her hair was swept back at the side with mother-of-pearl combs; her face was lightly touched with makeup. She'd pulled on the first thing she'd come to in her still-unpacked trunk. The tight black jeans proved an interesting contrast to the bulky white sweatshirt. Cliff sat on the bottom landing, sending the cowardly puppy into ecstasy by rubbing his belly. Maggie frowned down at the crown of Cliff's head.

"You weren't going to say a word, were you?"

He continued to rub the puppy, not bothering to look up. "About what?"

Maggie narrowed her eyes and folded her arms under her breasts. "Nothing. Was there something you wanted to discuss this morning?"

He wasn't precisely sure why that frosty, regal tone appealed to him. Perhaps he just liked knowing he had the ability to make her use it. "Still want that pond?"

"Yes, I still want the pond," she snapped, then gritted her teeth to prevent herself from doing so again. "I don't make a habit of changing my mind."

"Fine. We'll be clearing out the gully this afternoon." Rising, he faced her while the puppy sat expectantly at his feet. "You didn't call Bog about the kitchen floor."

Confusion came and went in her eyes. "How do you—"

"It's easy to find things out in Morganville."

"Well, it's none of your—"

"Hard to keep your business to yourself in small towns," Cliff interrupted again. It amused him to hear her breath huff out in frustration. "Fact is, you're about the top news item in town these days. Everybody wonders what the lady from California's doing up on this mountain. The more you keep to yourself," he added, "the more they wonder."

"Is that so?" Maggie tilted her head and stepped closer. "And you?" she countered. "Do you wonder?"

Cliff knew a challenge when he heard one, and knew he'd answer it in his own time. Impulsively, he cupped her chin in his hand and ran his thumb over her jawline. She didn't flinch or draw back, but became very still. "Nice skin," he murmured, sweeping his gaze along the path his thumb took. "Very nice. You take good care of it, Maggie. I'll take care of your land."

With this, he left her precisely as she was—arms folded, head tilted back, eyes astonished.

By ten, Maggie decided it wasn't going to be the quiet, solitary sort of day she'd moved to the country for. The men outside shouted above the machinery to make themselves heard. Trucks came and went down her newly graveled lane. She could comfort herself that in a few weeks that part of the disruption would be over.

She took three calls from the Coast from friends who wondered how and what she was doing. By the third call, she was a bit testy from explaining she was scraping linoleum, papering walls, painting woodwork and enjoying it. She left the phone off the hook and went back to her putty knife and kitchen floor.

More than half of the wood was exposed now. The progress excited her enough that she decided to stick with this one job until it was completed. The floor would be beautiful, and, she added, thinking of Cliff's comments, she'd have done it herself.

Maggie had barely scraped off two more inches when there was a knock behind her. She turned her head, ready to flare if it was Cliff Delaney returned to taunt her. Instead, she saw a tall, slender woman of her own age with soft brown hair and pale blue eyes. As Maggie studied Joyce Morgan Agee, she wondered why she hadn't seen the resemblance to Louella before.

"Mrs. Agee." Maggie rose, brushing at the knees of her jeans. "Please, come in. I'm sorry." Her sneakers squeaked as she stepped on a thin layer of old glue. "The floor's a bit sticky."

"I don't mean to disturb your work." Joyce stood uncertainly in the doorway, eyeing the floor. "I would've called, but I was on my way home from Mother's."

Joyce's pumps were trim and stylish. Maggie felt the glue pull at the bottom of her old sneakers. "We can talk outside, if you don't mind." Taking the initiative, Maggie walked out into the sunshine. "Things are a little confused around here right now."

"Yes." They heard one of the workers call to a companion, punctuating his suggestion with good-natured swearing. Joyce glanced over in their direction before she turned back to Maggie. "You're not wasting any time, I see."

"No." Maggie laughed and eyed the crumbling dirt wall beside them. "I've never been very patient. For some reason, I'm more anxious to have the outside the way I want it than the inside."

"You couldn't have picked a better company," Joyce murmured, glancing over at one of the trucks with *Delaney's* on the side.

Maggie followed her gaze but kept her tone neutral. "So I'm told."

"I want you to know I'm really glad you're doing so much to the place." Joyce began to fiddle with the strap of her shoulder bag. "I can hardly remember living here. I was a child when we moved, but I hate waste." With a little smile, she looked around again and shook her head. "I don't think I could live out here. I like being in town, with neighbors close by and other children for my children to play with. Of course, Stan, my husband, likes being available all the time."

It took Maggie a moment; then she remembered. "Oh, your husband's the sheriff, isn't he?"

"That's right. Morganville's a quiet town, nothing like Los Angeles, but it keeps him busy." She smiled, but Maggie wondered why she sensed strain. "We're just not city people."

"No." Maggie smiled, too. "I guess I've discovered I'm not, either."

"I don't understand how you could give up—" Joyce seemed to catch herself. "I guess what I meant was, this must be such a change for you after living in a place like Beverly Hills."

"A change," Maggie agreed. Was she sensing undercurrents here, too, as she had with Louella's dreaminess? "It was one I wanted."

"Yes, well, you know I'm glad you bought the place, and so quickly. Stan was a little upset with my putting it on the market when he was out of town, but I couldn't see it just sitting here. Who knows, if you hadn't come along so fast, he might've talked me out of selling it."

"Then we can both be grateful I saw the sign when I did." Mentally, Maggie was trying to figure out the logistics of the situation. It seemed the house had belonged exclusively to Joyce, without her husband or her mother having any claim. Fleetingly, she wondered why Joyce hadn't rented or sold the property before.

"The real reason I came by, Miss Fitzgerald, is my mother. She told me she was here a few days ago."

"Yes, she's a lovely woman."

"Yes." Joyce looked back toward the men working, then took a deep breath. Maggie no longer had to wonder if she was sensing undercurrents. She was sure of it. "It's more than possible she'll drop in on you again. I'd like to ask you a favor, that is, if she begins to bother you, if you'd tell me instead of her."

"Why should she bother me?"

Joyce let out a sound that was somewhere between fatigue and frustration. "Mother often dwells on the past. She's never completely gotten over my father's death. She makes some people uncomfortable."

Maggie remembered the discomfort she'd felt on and off during Louella's brief visit. Still, she shook her head. "Your mother's welcome to visit me from time to time, Mrs. Agee."

"Thank you, but you will promise to tell me if—well, if you'd like her to stay away. You see, she'd often come here, even when the place was deserted. I don't want her to get in your way. She doesn't know who you are. That is—" Obviously embarrassed, Joyce broke off. "I mean, Mother doesn't understand that someone like you would be busy."

Maggie remembered the lost eyes, the unhappy mouth. Pity stirred again. "All right, if she bothers me, I'll tell you."

The relief in Joyce's face was quick and very plain. "I appreciate it, Miss Fitzgerald."

"Maggie."

"Yes, well..." As if only more uncertain of her ground, Joyce managed a smile. "I understand that someone like you wouldn't want to have people dropping by and getting in the way."

Maggie laughed, thinking how many times the phone calls from California had interrupted her that morning. "I'm not a recluse," she told Joyce, though she was no longer completely sure. "And I'm not really very temperamental. Some people even consider me normal."

"Oh, I didn't mean—"

"I know you didn't. Come back when I've done something with that floor, and we'll have some coffee."

"I'd like to, really. Oh, I nearly forgot." She reached into the big canvas bag on her shoulder and pulled out a manila envelope. "Mother said you wanted to see these. Some pictures of the property."

"Yes." Pleased, Maggie took the envelope. She hadn't thought Louella would remember or bother to put them together for her. "I hoped they might give me some ideas."

"Mother said you could keep them as long as you liked." Joyce hesitated, fiddling again with the strap of her bag. "I have to get back. My youngest gets home from kindergarten at noon, and Stan sometimes comes home for lunch. I haven't done a thing to the house. I hope I see you sometime in town."

"I'm sure you will." Maggie tucked the envelope under her arm. "Give my best to your mother."

Maggie started back into the house, but as she put her hand on the doorknob, she noticed Cliff crossing to Joyce. Curiosity had her stopping to watch as Cliff took both the brunette's hands in his own. Though she couldn't hear the conversation over the din of motors, it was obvious that they knew each other well. There was a gentleness on Cliff's face Maggie hadn't seen before, and something she interpreted as concern. He bent down close, as if Joyce were speaking very softly, then touched her hair. The touch of a brother? Maggie wondered. Or a lover?

As she watched, Joyce shook her head, apparently fumbling with the door handle before she got into the car. Cliff leaned into the window for a moment. Were they arguing? Maggie wondered. Was the tension she sensed real or imaginary? Fascinated with the silent scene being played out in her driveway, Maggie watched as Cliff withdrew from the window and Joyce backed out to drive away. Before she could retreat inside, Cliff turned, and their gazes locked.

There were a hundred feet separating them, and the air was full of the sounds of men and machines. The sun was strong enough to make her almost too warm in the sweatshirt, yet she felt one quick, unexpected chill race up her spine. Perhaps it was hostility she felt. Maggie tried to tell herself it was hostility and not the first dangerous flutters of passion.

There was a temptation to cross those hundred feet and test both of them. Even the thought of it stirred her blood. He didn't move. He didn't take his eyes from her. With fingers gone suddenly numb, Maggie twisted the handle and went inside.

Two hours later, Maggie went out again. She'd never been one to retreat from a challenge, from her emotions or from trouble. Cliff Delaney seemed connected with all three. While she'd scraped linoleum, Maggie had lectured herself on letting Cliff intimidate her for no reason other than his being powerfully male and sexy.

And different, she'd admitted. Different from most of the men she'd encountered in her profession. He didn't fawn—far from it. He didn't pour on the charm. He wasn't impressed with his own physique, looks or sophistication. It must have been that difference that had made her not quite certain how to handle him.

A very direct, very frank business approach, she decided as she circled around the back of the house. Maggie paused to look at the bank fronting her house.

The vines, briars and thick sumac were gone. Piles of rich, dark topsoil were being spread over what had been a tangled jungle of neglect. The tree that had leaned toward her house was gone, stump and all. Two men, backs glistening with sweat, were setting stone in a low-spreading wall where the edge of the slope met the edge of the lawn.

Cliff Delaney ran a tight ship, Maggie concluded, and made her way through the new dirt toward the side yard. Here, too, the worst had been cleared out. An enormous bearded man in bib overalls sat atop a big yellow backhoe as easily as another might sit in an armchair. At the push of a lever, the digger went down into the gully, bit into earth and rock and came up full.

Maggie shaded her eyes and watched the procedure while the puppy circled her legs and snarled at everything in sight. Each time the digger would open its claws to drop its load, the dog would send up a ruckus of barks. Laughing, Maggie crouched down to scratch his ears and soothe him.

"Don't be a coward, Killer. I won't let it get you."

"I wouldn't get any closer," Cliff said from behind her.

She turned her head, squinting against the sun. "This is close enough." Disliking the disadvantage of looking up and into the sun, Maggie stood. "You seem to be making progress."

"We need to get the plants in and the wall of this thing solid—" he gestured toward the gully "—before the rain hits. Otherwise, you'll have a real mess on your hands."

"I see." Because he wore the frustrating tinted glasses again, she turned from him to watch the backhoe work. "You certainly have a large staff."

Cliff's thumbs went into his pockets. "Large enough." He'd told himself he'd imagined that powerful sexual pull hours before. Now, feeling it again, he couldn't deny it.

She wasn't what he wanted, yet he wanted her. She wasn't what he would have chosen, yet he was choosing her. He could turn away logic until he'd learned what it was like to touch her.

Maggie was very aware of how close they stood. The stirring she'd felt hours before began to build again, slowly, seductively, until she felt her whole body tense with it. She understood that you could want someone you didn't know, someone you passed on the street. It all had to do with chemistry, but her chemistry had never reacted this way before. She had a wild urge to turn into his arms, to demand or offer the fulfillment, or whatever it was, that simmered between them. It was something that offered excitement, and pleasure she had only glimpsed before. So she did turn, completely uncertain as to what she would say.

"I don't think I like what's happening here."

Cliff didn't pretend to misunderstand her. Neither of their minds was on the pond or the machine. "Do you have a choice?"

Maggie frowned, wishing she was more certain of her moves. He wasn't like the men she'd known before; therefore, the standard rules didn't apply. "I think so. I moved here because it was where I wanted to live, where I wanted to work. But I also moved here because I wanted to be on my own. I intend to do all those things."

Cliff studied her a moment, then gave the backhoe driver an absent wave as he shut off the machine to take his lunch break. "I took this job because I wanted to work this land. I intend to do it."

Though she didn't feel the slightest lessening of tension, Maggie nodded. "Then we understand each other."

As she started to turn away, Cliff put a hand on her shoulder, holding her still. "I think we both understand quite a bit."

The muscles in her stomach tightened and loosened like a nervous fist. With his fingers so light on the bulky sweatshirt, she shouldn't have felt anything. But hundreds of pulses sprang to life in her body. The air seemed to grow closer, hotter, the sounds of men more distant. "I don't know what you mean."

"Yes, you do."

Yes, she did. "I don't know anything about you," Maggie managed.

Cliff caught the tips of her hair in his fingers. "I can't say the same."

Maggie's temper flared, though she knew when she was being baited. "So, you believe everything you read in the tabloids and glossies." She tossed her head to free her hair from his fingers. "I'm surprised that a man who's obviously so successful and talented could be so ignorant."

Cliff acknowledged the hit with a nod. "I'm surprised a woman who's obviously so successful and talented could be so foolish."

"Foolish? What the hell's that supposed to mean?"

"It seems foolish to me to encourage the press to report every area of your life."

She clenched her teeth and tried deep breathing. Neither worked. "I don't encourage the press to do anything."

"You don't discourage them," Cliff countered.

"Discouragement *is* encouragement," she tossed back. Folding her arms under her breasts as she'd done earlier, she stared out over the open gully. "Why am I defending myself?" she muttered. "You don't know anything about it. I don't need you to know anything about it."

"I know you gave an interview about yourself and your husband weeks after his death." He heard her quick intake of breath even as he cursed himself for saying something so personal, and so uncalled-for.

"Do you have any idea how the press hammered at me during

those weeks?" Her voice was low and strained, and she no longer looked at him. "Do you know all the garbage they were printing?" Her fingers tightened on her own arms. "I chose a reporter I could trust, and I gave the most honest, most straightforward interview I could manage, knowing it was my only chance to keep things from sinking lower. That interview was for Jerry. It was the only thing I had left to give him."

He'd wanted to prod, perhaps even to prick, but he hadn't wanted to hurt. "I'm sorry." Cliff put his hand on her shoulder again, but she jerked away.

"Forget it."

This time he took both of her shoulders, turning her firmly to face him. "I don't forget blows below the belt, especially when I'm the one doing the punching."

She waited to speak until she was certain she had some control again. "I've survived hits before. My advice to you is not to criticize something you have no capacity for understanding."

"I apologized." He didn't release her shoulders when she tried to draw away. "But I'm not very good at following advice."

Maggie became still again. Somehow they had gotten closer, so that now their thighs brushed. The combination of anger and desire was becoming too strong to ignore. "Then you and I don't have any more to say to each other."

"You're wrong." His voice was very quiet, very compelling. "We haven't begun to say all there is to say."

"You work for me—"

"I work for myself," Cliff corrected.

She understood that kind of pride, admired it. But admiration wouldn't remove his hands from her shoulders. "I'm paying you to do a job."

"You're paying my company. That's business."

"It's going to be our only business."

"Wrong again," he murmured, but released her.

Maggie opened her mouth to hurl something back at him, but the dog began to bark in quick, excited yelps. She decided turning her back on him to investigate her pet was a much grander insult than the verbal one she'd planned. Without a word, she began to make her way around the slope of the gully to the pile of earth and rock and debris the backhoe had dumped.

"All right, Killer." The going was so rough that she swore under her breath as she stumbled over stones. "You'll never find anything worthwhile in that pile, anyway."

Ignoring her, the puppy continued to dig, his barking muffled as his nose went farther in, his backside wriggling with either effort or delight in the new game.

"Cut it out." She bent to pull him out of the heap and ended up sitting down hard. "Damn it, Killer." Staying as she was, she grabbed the dog with one hand, dragging him back and unearthing a small avalanche of rock.

"Will you be careful?" Cliff shouted from above her, knowing she'd been lucky not to have one of the rocks bounce off her shin.

"It's the stupid dog!" Maggie shouted back as she lost her grip on him again. "God knows what he thinks is so fascinating about this mess. Nothing but dirt and rocks," she muttered, pushing at the pile that had landed near her hip.

"Well, grab him and get back up here before you're both hurt."

"Yeah," she muttered under her breath. "You're a big help." Disgusted, she started to struggle up when her fingers slid into the worn, rounded rock her hand had rested on. Hollow, she thought curiously. Her attention torn between the gully and the dog's unrelenting barks, Maggie glanced down.

Then she began to scream, loud and long enough to send the puppy racing for cover.

Cliff's first thought as he raced down the slope to her was snakes. When he reached her, he dragged her up and into his arms in an instinctive move of protection. She'd stopped screaming, and though her breathing was shallow, Maggie grabbed his shirt before he could carry her back up the slope. "Bones," she whispered. Closing her eyes, she dropped her head on his shoulder. "Oh, my God."

Cliff looked down and saw what the machine and dog had unearthed. Mixed with the rock and debris was a pile of what might have been mistaken for long white sticks layered with dirt.

But lying on the bones, inches from where Maggie had sat, was a human skull.

# *Chapter 4*

"I'm all right." Maggie sat at the kitchen table and gripped the glass of water Cliff had handed her. When the pain in her fingers finally registered, she relaxed them a bit. "I feel like an idiot, screaming that way."

She was still pale, he noted. Though the hands on the glass were steady now, they were still white at the knuckles. Her eyes were wide and shocked, suddenly too big for the rest of her face. He started to stroke her hair, then stuck his own hands in his pockets. "A natural enough reaction."

"I guess." She looked up and managed a shaky smile. She was cold, but prayed she wouldn't begin to shiver in front of him. "I've never found myself in that sort of…situation before."

Cliff lifted a brow. "Neither have I."

"No?" Somehow she'd wanted to think it had happened before. If it had, it might make it less horrible—and less personal. She looked down at the floor, not realizing until that moment that the dog lay across her feet, whimpering. "But don't you dig up a lot of—" She hesitated, not sure just how she wanted to phrase it. "Things," Maggie decided weakly, "in your line of work?"

She was reaching, Cliff thought, and whether she knew it or not, those big brown eyes were pleading with him for some sort of easy explanation. He didn't have one to give her. "Not that kind of thing."

Their gazes held for one long, silent moment before Maggie nodded. If there was one thing she'd learned in the hard, competitive business she'd chosen, it was to handle things as they came. "So, neither of us has a tidy explanation." The little expulsion of breath was the last sign of weakness she intended to show him. "I guess the next step is the police."

"Yeah." The more determined she became to be calm, the more difficult it became for him. She was weakening something in him that he was determined to keep objective. His hands were balled into fists inside his pockets in his struggle not to touch her. Distance was the quickest defense. "You'd better call," Cliff said briskly. "I'll go out and make sure the crew keeps clear of the gully."

Again, her answer was a nod. Maggie watched as he crossed to the screen door and pushed it open. There he hesitated. He'd have cursed if he'd understood what it was he wanted to swear at. When he looked back, she saw the concern on his face she'd seen when he'd spoken to Joyce. "Maggie, are you all right?"

The question, and the tone, helped her to settle. Perhaps it had something to do with her knowing just what it was like to be pressured by another's weakness. "I will be. Thanks." She waited until the screen door banged shut behind him before she dropped her head on the table.

Good heavens, what had she walked into here? People didn't find bodies in their front yard. C.J. would've said it was totally uncivilized. Maggie choked back a hysterical giggle and straightened. The one unarguable fact she had to face was that she had found one. Now she had to deal with it. Taking deep breaths, she went to the phone and dialed the operator.

"Get me the police," she said quickly.

A few minutes later, Maggie went outside. Though she'd hoped the practical routine of reporting what she'd found would calm her, it hadn't worked. She didn't go near the gully, but she found she couldn't sit inside, waiting alone. Circling around the front of the house, she found a convenient rock and sat. The puppy stretched out in the patch of sunlight at her feet and went to sleep.

She could almost believe she'd imagined what she'd seen in that pile of dirt and rock. It was too peaceful here for anything so stark. The air was too soft, the sun too warm. Her land might be unruly, but it held a serenity that blocked out the harsher aspects of life.

Was that why she'd chosen it, Maggie wondered. Because she wanted to pretend there wasn't any real madness in the world? Here she could cocoon herself from so many of the pressures and demands that had threaded through her life for so long. Was this spot the home she'd always wanted, or was it in reality just an escape for her? She squeezed her eyes shut. If that were true, it made her weak and dishonest, two things she couldn't tolerate. Why had it taken this incident to make her question what she hadn't questioned before? As she tried to find her tranquillity again, a shadow fell over her. Opening her eyes, Maggie looked up at Cliff.

For some reason it toughened her. She wouldn't admit to him that she'd begun to doubt herself or her motives. No, not to him.

"Someone should be here soon." She linked her folded hands over one knee and looked back into the woods.

"Good." Several minutes passed while they both remained silent, looking into the trees.

Eventually, Cliff crouched down beside her. Funny, but he thought that she looked more apt to fall apart now than she had when he'd carried her into her kitchen. Reaction, he decided, had different speeds for different people. He wanted to hold her again, hard and close, as he'd done all too briefly before. The contact had made something strong and sultry move through him. Like her music—something like her music.

He wished like hell he'd turned down the job and had walked away the first time he'd seen her. Cliff looked past her to the slope that led to the gully.

"You talked to Stan?"

"Stan?" Blankly, Maggie stared at Cliff's set profile. At that moment, he was close enough to reach but seemed miles away. "Oh, the sheriff." She wished he'd touch her, just for a moment. Just a hand on her. "No, I didn't call him. I called the operator and asked for the police. She connected me with the state police in Hagerstown." She lapsed into silence, waiting for him to make some comment on her typical city response.

"Probably for the best," Cliff murmured. "I let the crew go. It'll be less confusing."

"Oh." She must've been in a daze not to notice that the trucks and men were gone. When she forced herself to look, she saw that the backhoe remained, sitting on the rise above the gully, big and yellow and silent. The sun was warm on her back. Her skin was like ice. Time to snap out of it, Maggie told herself, and straightened her shoulders. "Yes, I'm sure you're right. Should I call your office when the police say it's all right to start work again?" Her voice was businesslike. Her throat was dry with the thought of being left alone, completely alone, with what was down by the gully.

Cliff turned his head. Without speaking, he took off his sunglasses so that their eyes met. "Thought I'd hang around."

Relief washed over her. Maggie knew it must've shown in her face, but she didn't have the will to put pride first. "I'd like you to. It's stupid, but—" She glanced over in the direction of the gully.

"Not stupid."

"Maybe weak's a better word," she mumbled, trying to smile.

"Human." Despite his determination not to, Cliff reached out and took her hand. The touch, one designed to comfort, to reassure her, set off a chain reaction of emotion too swift to stop.

It ran through her head that she should rise swiftly and go inside. He might stop her, or he might let her go. Maggie didn't ask herself which she wanted, nor did she move. Instead, she sat where she was, meeting his gaze and letting the sensation of torrid, liquid heat flow through her. Nothing else existed. Nothing else mattered.

She felt each of his fingers tense individually on her hand. There was a sense of power there; whether it was his or hers, she wasn't sure. Perhaps it was the melding of both. She saw his eyes darken until the irises were only shades lighter than the pupils. It was as if he were looking through her, into her chaotic thoughts. In the quiet of midafternoon, she heard each breath he drew in and expelled. The sound stirred the excitement that vibrated in the air between them.

Together they moved toward each other until mouth molded itself to mouth.

Intensity. She hadn't known anything between two people could be so concentrated, such pure sensation. She understood that if years passed, if she was blind and deaf, she would know this man just by the touch of his lips. In one instant she became intimate with the shape of his mouth, the taste and texture of his tongue. Her mouth was on his, his hand on hers, and they touched nowhere else. In that moment there was no need to.

There was an aggressiveness, even a harshness, to the kiss that Maggie hadn't expected. It held none of the sweetness, the hesitation, that first kisses often do, yet she didn't back away from it. Perhaps it was all part of the attraction that had begun the moment he'd stepped from the truck. Different, yes, he was different from the other men who'd touched her life—different still from the man she'd shared her body with. She'd known that from the first encounter. Now, with his mouth stirring her senses, she found herself grateful for it. She wanted nothing to be the same as it had been, no reminders of what she'd had once and lost. This man wouldn't pamper or worship. He was strong enough to want strength in return. She felt his tongue tangle with hers, probing deeper. Maggie reveled in the demands.

It was easy, almost too easy, to forget her delicate build, her fragile looks, when her mouth was so ardent on his. He should've known there'd be deep, restless passion in a woman who created music with such sexuality. But how could he have known that passion would call to him as though he'd been waiting for years?

It was much too easy to forget she wasn't the kind of woman he wanted in his life when her taste was filling him. Again, he should have known she'd have the power to make a man toss aside all logic, all intellect. Her lips were warm, moist, the taste as pungent as the scent of newly turned earth around them. The urge rose to take her in his arms and fulfill, there under the clear afternoon sun, all the needs that welled inside him. Cliff drew back, resisting that final painful twist of desire.

Breathless, throbbing, Maggie stared at him. Could that one searing meeting of lips have moved him as it had moved her? Were his thoughts swimming as hers were? Was his body pulsing with wild, urgent needs? She could tell nothing from his face. Though his eyes were fixed on hers, their expression was unreadable. If she asked, would he tell her that he, too, had never known a wave of passion so overwhelming or so mesmerizing? She would ask, and would know, as soon as she had the voice to question. As she sat, struggling to catch her breath, the events of the day came flashing back into her mind. Abruptly, Maggie sprang to her feet.

"God, what are we doing?" she demanded. With a hand that shook, she pushed the hair away from her face. "How can we sit here like this when that—that thing's only a few yards away?"

Cliff took her arm, turning her back to face him. "What does one have to do with the other?"

"Nothing. I don't know." With her insides churning, she looked up at him. Her emotions had always been too dominant. Though she knew it, Maggie had never been able to change it. It had been years since she'd really tried. Confusion, distress, passion, radiated from her as tangible things. "What we found, it's dreadful, unbelievably dreadful, and a few moments ago I was sitting there wondering what it would be like to make love with you."

Something flashed in his eyes, quickly controlled. Unlike Maggie, Cliff had learned long ago to channel his emotions and keep them to himself. “You obviously don’t believe in evading the issue.”

“Evasions take too much time and effort.” After letting out a long breath, Maggie managed to match his even, casual tone. “Listen, I didn’t expect that sort of—eruption,” she decided. “I suppose I’m wound up over all of this, and a bit too susceptible.”

“Susceptible.” Her choice of words made him smile. Somehow, when she became cool and calm, he became tempted to prod. Deliberately, he lifted a hand and ran his fingertips down her cheek. Her skin was still warm with desire. “I wouldn’t have described you that way. You seem to be a woman who knows what she wants and how to get it.”

If he’d wanted to fire her up, he’d found the perfect key. “Stop it.” In one sharp move, she pushed his hand from her face. “I’ve said it before—you don’t know me. Every time we’re together, I become more certain that I don’t want you to. You’re a very attractive man, Cliff. And very unlikable. I stay away from people I don’t like.”

It occurred to him that he’d never gone out of his way to argue with anyone before. A lot of things were changing. “In a small community like this, it’s hard to stay away from anyone.”

“I’ll put more effort into it.”

“Nearly impossible.”

She narrowed her eyes and fought to keep her lips from curving. “I’m very good when I put my mind to something.”

“Yeah.” He put his sunglasses back on. When he grinned, the deliberate cockiness was almost too appealing to resist. “I bet you are.”

“Are you trying to be smart, or are you trying to be charming?”

"I never had to try to be either one."

"Think again." Because she was having trouble controlling the grin, Maggie turned away. As luck would have it, she found herself staring out over the gully. A chill raced up her spine. Swearing, she folded her arms under her breasts. "I can't believe it," she muttered. "I can't believe I'm standing here having a ridiculous conversation when there's a—" She found she couldn't say it and detested herself. "I think the whole world must be going mad."

He wasn't going to let her get shaky on him again. When she was vulnerable, she was much more dangerous. "What's down there's been there for a long time." His voice was brisk, almost hard. "It doesn't have anything to do with you."

"It's my land," Maggie tossed back. She whirled around, eyes glowing, chin angled. "So it has everything to do with me."

"Then you better stop shaking every time you think about it."

"I'm not shaking."

Without a word, he drew her hand away from her elbow so they could both see the tremor. Furious, Maggie snatched it away again. "When I want you to touch me, I'll let you know," she said between her teeth.

"You already have."

Before she could think of an appropriate response, the dog scrambled up and began to bark furiously. Seconds later, they both heard the sound of an approaching car.

"He might make you a decent watchdog, after all," Cliff said mildly. The pup bounded around in circles like a mad thing, then hid behind the rock. "Then again…"

As the official car came into sight, he bent down to pat the dog on the head before he walked toward the end of the drive. Maggie hurried to keep pace. Her land, her problem, her responsibility, she told herself. *She'd* do the talking.

A trooper climbed out of the car, adjusted his hat, then broke into a grin. "Cliff, didn't expect to see you out here."

"Bob." Because the greeting didn't include a handshake, Maggie assumed the men knew each other well and saw each other often. "My company's handling the landscaping."

"The old Morgan place." The trooper looked around with interest. "Been a while since I was back here. You dig up something we should know about?"

"So it seems."

"It's the Fitzgerald place now," Maggie cut in briskly.

The trooper touched the brim of his hat and started to make a polite comment. His eyes widened when he took his first good look at her. "Fitzgerald," he repeated. "Hey, aren't you Maggie Fitzgerald?"

She smiled, though the recognition, with Cliff beside her, made her uncomfortable. "Yes, I am."

"I'll be damned. You look just like your pictures in all the magazines. I guess there isn't a song you've written I can't hum. You bought the Morgan place."

"That's right."

He pushed the hat back on his head in a gesture that made her think of cowboys. "Wait till I tell my wife. We had 'Forever' played at our wedding. You remember, Cliff. Cliff was best man."

Maggie tilted her head to look at the man beside her. "Really?"

"If you've finished being impressed," Cliff said mildly, "you might want to take a look at what's down by the gully."

Bob grinned again, all amiability. "That's why I'm here." They began to walk toward the gully together. "You know, it isn't easy to tell what's from a human and what's from an animal just by looking. Could be, ma'am, that you uncovered a deer."

Maggie glanced over at Cliff. She could still feel the way her hand had slid into the hollow opening of what she'd taken for a rock. "I wish I could think so."

"Down here," Cliff said without acknowledging the look. "The going's rough." In a smooth, calculated move, he blocked Maggie's way before she could start down. It forced her to pull up short and grab his arm for support. "Why don't you wait here?"

It would've been easy to do so. Much too easy. "It's my land," Maggie said, and, brushing by him, led the way down herself. "The dog started digging in this pile." She heard the nerves in her own voice and fought against them. "I came down to pull him away, and that's when I saw..." Trailing off, she pointed.

The trooper crouched down, letting out a low whistle. "Holy hell," he murmured. He turned his head, but it was Cliff he looked at, not Maggie. "It doesn't look like you dug up any deer."

"No." In a casual move, Cliff shifted so that he blocked Maggie's view. "What now?"

Bob rose. He wasn't smiling now, but Maggie thought she detected a gleam of excitement. "I'll have to call the investigation section. Those boys are going to want to take a look at this."

Maggie didn't speak when they climbed up the slope again. She waited in silence while the trooper went to his car to radio in his report. When she did speak, she deliberately avoided the reason they were all standing outside in the middle of the afternoon.

"So you two know each other," she commented as though it were any normal remark made on any normal day.

"Bob and I went to school together." Cliff watched a big black crow swoop over the trees. He was remembering the look on Maggie's face the moment before she'd begun to scream. "He ended up marrying one of my cousins a couple of years ago."

Bending over, she plucked a wildflower and began to shred it. "You have a lot of cousins."

He shrugged. The crow landed and was still. "Enough."

"A few Morgans."

That caught his attention. "A few," he said slowly. "Why?"

"I wondered if it was your connection with them that made you resent my having this land."

Cliff wondered why, when he normally respected candor, it annoyed him from her. "No."

"But you did resent it," Maggie insisted. "You resented me before you even saw me."

He had, and perhaps the resentment had grown since he'd had a taste of her. "Joyce had the right to sell this property whenever, and to whomever, she wanted."

Maggie nodded, looking down to where the puppy scrambled in the new dirt. "Is Joyce a cousin, too?"

"What are you getting at?"

Lifting her head, Maggie met his impatient look. "I'm just trying to understand small towns. After all, I'm going to be living here."

"Then the first thing you should learn is that people don't like questions. They might volunteer more information than you want to hear, but they don't like to be asked."

Maggie acknowledged this with a lift of a brow. "I'll keep that in mind." Rather pleased that she'd annoyed him, Maggie turned to the trooper as he approached.

"They're sending out a team." He glanced from her to Cliff, then over his friend's shoulder toward the gully. "Probably be here for a while, then take what they find with them."

"What then?"

Bob brought his attention back to Maggie. "Good question." He shifted his feet as he considered it. "To tell you the truth, I've never been in on anything like this before, but my guess would be they'd ship everything off to the medical examiner in Baltimore. He'd have to check the, ah, everything out before they could start an investigation."

"Investigation?" she repeated, and felt something tighten in her throat. "What kind of investigation?"

The trooper ran his thumb and forefinger down his nose. "Well, ma'am, as far as I can see, there's no reason for anything like that to be buried down in that gully unless—"

"Unless someone buried it there," Cliff finished.

Maggie stared out into the peaceful spread of greening wood across the lane. "I think we could all use some coffee," she murmured. Without waiting for an acknowledgment, she went back toward the house.

Bob took off his hat and wiped at the sweat on his forehead. "This is one for the books."

Cliff followed his friend's long look at the woman climbing the rickety front steps. "Which? Her or that?" With one hand he gestured toward the gully.

"Both." Bob took out a pack of gum and carefully unwrapped a piece. "First place, what's a woman like her, a celebrity, doing holed up here in the woods?"

"Maybe she decided she likes trees."

Bob slipped the gum into his mouth. "Must be ten, twelve acres of them here."

"Twelve."

"Looks to me like she bought more than she bargained for. Holy hell, Cliff, we haven't had anything like this down in this end of the county since crazy Mel Stickler set those barn fires. Now, in the city—"

"Taken to the fast pace, have you?"

Bob knew Cliff well enough to catch both the dig and the humor. "I like some action," he said easily. "Speaking of which, the lady songwriter smells like heaven."

"How's Carol Ann?"

Bob grinned at the mention of his wife. "Just fine. Look, Cliff, if a man doesn't look, and appreciate, he'd better see a doctor. You're not going to tell me you haven't noticed just how nice that lady's put together."

"I've noticed." He glanced down at the rock beside him. She'd sat there when he'd kissed her. It wouldn't take any effort to remember each separate sensation that had run through him in that one moment. "I'm more interested in her land."

Bob let out a quick laugh. "If you are, you've done a lot of changing since high school. Remember when we used to come up here—those blond twins, the cheerleaders whose parents rented the place for a while? That old Chevy of yours lost its muffler right there on that turn."

"I remember."

"We had some interesting walks up there in the woods," Bob reminisced. "They were the prettiest girls in school till their daddy got transferred and they moved away."

"Who moved in after that?" Cliff wondered, half to himself. "That old couple from Harrisburg—the Faradays. They were here a long time, until the old man died and she went to live with her kids." Cliff narrowed his eyes as he tried to remember. "That was a couple months before Morgan ran off the bridge. Nobody's lived here since."

Bob shrugged; then both of them looked toward the gully. "Guess it's been ten years since anybody lived here."

"Ten years," Cliff repeated. "A long time."

They both looked over at the sound of a car. "The investigators," Bob said, adjusting his hat again. "They'll take over now."

From the corner of the porch, Maggie watched the proceedings. She'd decided that if the police crew needed her, they'd let her know. It appeared to her that they knew their business. She would just be in the way down there, Maggie reasoned as she drank another cup of black coffee.

She watched them shovel, sift and systematically bag what they'd come for. Maggie told herself that once it was off her property, she'd forget it. It would no longer concern her. She wished she could believe it. What was now being transferred into plastic bags had once been a living being. A man or a woman who'd had thoughts and feelings had lain, alone, only yards from what was now her home. No, she didn't believe she'd be able to forget that.

Before it was over, she'd have to know who that person had been, why they had died and why their grave had been on her land. She'd have to have the answers if she were to live in the home she'd chosen. She finished the last swallow of coffee as one of the police crew broke away from the group and came toward the porch. Maggie went to the steps to meet him.

"Ma'am." He nodded to her but, to her relief, didn't offer his hand. Instead, he took out a badge, flashing the cover up briefly. "I'm Lieutenant Reiker."

She thought he looked like a middle-aged accountant and wondered if he carried a gun under his jacket. "Yes, Lieutenant."

"We're just about finished up. Sorry for the inconvenience."

"That's all right." She gripped her hands together over the cup and wished she could go inside, to her music.

"I've got the trooper's report, but I wonder if you could tell me how you happened to find the remains."

Remains, Maggie thought with a shudder. It seemed a very cold word. For the second time, she related her story of the puppy's digging. She did so calmly now, without a tremor.

"You just bought the place?"

"Yes, I only moved in a few weeks ago."

"And you hired Delaney to do some landscaping."

"Yes." She looked down to where Cliff stood talking to another of the team. "The handyman I hired recommended him."

"Mmm-hmm." In a very casual way, the investigator took notes. "Delaney tells me you wanted the gully there dug out for a pond."

Maggie moistened her lips. "That's right."

"Nice place for one," he said conversationally. "I'd like to ask you to hold off on that for a while, though. We might need to come back and take another look around."

Maggie's hands twisted on the empty cup. "All right."

"What we'd like to do is block off that area." He hitched at his belt, then settled one foot on the step above the other. "Some chicken wire," he said easily, "to keep your dog and any other stray animal from digging around in there."

And people, Maggie thought, deciding it didn't take a genius to read between the lines. Before the day was over, this would be the biggest news flash in the county. She was learning fast. "Do whatever you need to do."

"We appreciate the cooperation, Miss Fitzgerald." He twirled the pen in his fingers, hesitating.

"Is there something else?"

"I know it's a bad time," he said with a sheepish smile, "but I can't pass it up. Would you mind signing my pad? I was a big fan of your mother's, and I guess I know most all of your songs, too."

Maggie laughed. It was far better to laugh. The day had been a series of one ludicrous event after another. "Of course." She took the offered pad and pen. "Would you like me to say anything special?"

"Maybe you could just write—to my good friend Harvey."

Before she could oblige, she glanced up and caught Cliff's eyes on her. She saw his lips twist into something between a sneer and a smile. With a silent oath, she signed the pad and handed it back.

"I don't know much about this kind of thing," she began briskly, "but I'd appreciate it if you kept me informed on whatever's being done."

"We'll have the medical examiner's report in a few days." Pocketing his pad, the investigator became solidly professional again. "We'll all know more then. Thanks for your time, Miss Fitzgerald. We'll be out of your way as soon as we can."

Though she felt Cliff's gaze still on her, Maggie didn't look over. Instead, she turned and walked back into the house. Moments later, music could be heard through the open windows.

Cliff remained where he was, though he'd answered all the questions that he could answer. His thoughts were focused on the sounds coming from the music room. It wasn't one of her songs, he concluded, but something from the classics, something that required speed, concentration and passion. Therapy, he wondered, frowning up at the window. With a shrug, he started toward his car. It wasn't his concern if the lady was upset. Hadn't she told him she'd moved back here to be on her own?

Turning his head, he saw the investigators preparing to leave. Within moments, he reflected, she'd be alone. The music pouring out of the windows was tense, almost desperate. Swearing, Cliff stuffed his keys back in his pocket and strode toward the steps.

She didn't answer his knock. The music played on. Without giving it a second thought, he pushed open the front door. The house vibrated with the storm coming from the piano. Following it into the music room, he watched her from the doorway.

Her eyes were dark, her head was bent, though he didn't think she even saw the keys. Talent? There was no denying it, any more than there could be any denying her tension or her vulnerability. Later, he might ask himself why all three made him uncomfortable.

Perhaps he did want to comfort her, he told himself. He'd do the same for anyone, under the circumstances. She didn't have to mean anything to him for him to want to offer a diversion. Strays and wounded birds had always been weaknesses of his. Dissatisfied with his own logic, Cliff waited until she'd finished.

Maggie looked up, startled to see him in the doorway. Damn her nerves, she thought, carefully folding her hands in her lap. "I thought you'd gone."

"No. They have."

She tossed the hair out of her eyes and hoped she looked composed. "Was there something else?"

"Yeah." He walked over to run a finger over the piano keys. No dust, he noted, in a house nearly choked with it. Her work was obviously of first importance.

When he didn't elaborate, Maggie frowned. Cliff preferred the impatience he saw in her eyes now. "What?"

"I had a steak in mind."

"I beg your pardon?"

The cool response made his lips curve. Yes, he definitely preferred her this way. "I haven't eaten."

"Sorry." Maggie began to straighten her sheet music. "I don't happen to have one handy."

"There's a place about ten miles out of town." He took her arm to draw her to her feet. "I have a feeling they'd treat a steak better than you would, anyway."

She pulled away, stood her ground and studied him. "We're going out to dinner?"

"That's right."

"Why?"

He took her arm again, so that he wouldn't ask himself the same question. "Because I'm hungry," Cliff said simply.

Maggie started to resist, though he didn't appear to notice. Then it struck her how much she wanted to get out, to get away, just for a little while. Sooner or later, she'd have to be alone in the house, but right then— No, right then, she didn't want to be alone anywhere.

He knew, understood, and whatever his approach, Cliff was offering her exactly what she needed.

Though their thoughts weren't particularly calm, neither of them spoke as they walked through the door together.

## *Chapter 5*

Maggie set aside the next day to complete the title song for the movie score. She made a conscious effort to forget everything that had happened the day before. Everything. She wouldn't think of what had been buried and unearthed so close to her house, nor would she think of police or investigators or medical examiners.

In exactly the same way, she refused to think of Cliff, of the one wildly exciting kiss or of the oddly civilized dinner they'd shared. It was difficult to believe that she'd experienced both with the same man.

Today, she was Maggie Fitzgerald, writer of songs, creator of music. If she thought of only that, *was* only that, perhaps she could convince herself that everything that had happened yesterday had happened to someone else.

She knew there were men outside spreading seed, planting. There were shrubs going in, mulch being laid, more brush being cleared. If the landscape timbers she'd seen brought in that morning meant what she thought, construction was about to begin on her retaining wall.

None of that concerned her. The score demanded to be completed, and she'd complete it. The one form of discipline she understood perfectly was that a job had to be done no matter what went on around you. She'd seen her father direct a movie when his equipment had broken down and his actors had thrown tantrums. She'd known her mother to perform while running a fever. Much of her life might have been lived in a plush, make-believe world, but she'd learned responsibility.

The score came first today, and the title song would be written. Perhaps she'd even add some clever little aside to C.J. at the end of the tape before she mailed it off.

It certainly wouldn't do to mention what was going on in her side yard, Maggie thought as she meticulously copied notes onto staff paper. C.J. wouldn't be able to find enough antacids in L.A. to handle it for him. Poor man, she mused, he'd been worried about the roof caving in on her. In a totally unexpected way, it certainly had. If he knew there'd been policemen swarming over her land with plastic bags, he'd catch the next plane and drag her back to L.A.

She wondered if Cliff would've dragged her from the house the night before if she hadn't gone voluntarily. Fortunately, it hadn't been an issue, because Maggie thought him perfectly capable of it. Yet he'd been the ideal dinner companion. While she hadn't expected consideration from him, he'd been considerate. She hadn't expected subtle kindness, but it had been there. Finding both had made it difficult to remember she considered him an unlikable man.

They hadn't spoken of what had been found on her property that day, nor had there been any speculation on the whys and hows. They hadn't discussed his work or hers, but had simply talked.

Looking back, Maggie couldn't say precisely what they'd talked about, only that the mood had been easy. So easy, she had almost forgotten the passion they'd pulled from each other in the quiet afternoon sunlight. Almost forgotten. The memory had been there, quietly nagging at her throughout the evening. It had made her blood move a little faster. It had made her wonder if he'd felt it, too.

Maggie swore and erased the last five notes she'd copied down. C.J. wouldn't appreciate the fact that she was mixing her bass and tenor. She was doing exactly what she'd promised herself she wouldn't do, and as she'd known it would, the upheaval of yesterday was affecting her work. Calmly, she took deep breaths until her mind was clear again. The wisest course was to switch the recorder back on to play and start from the beginning. Then the knock on the front door disrupted her thoughts. Quiet country life. She asked herself where she'd ever heard that expression as she went to answer.

The gun on the man's hip made her stomach twist. The little badge pinned to the khaki shirt told her he was the sheriff. When she took her gaze up to his face, she was surprised by his looks. Blond, tanned, with blue eyes fanned by lines that spoke of humor or sun. For a moment, she had the insane notion that C.J. had sent him out from central casting.

"Miss Fitzgerald?"

She moistened her lips as she tried to be rational. C.J. worried too much for practical jokes. Besides, the gun looked very, very real. "Yes."

"I'm Sheriff Agee. Hope you don't mind me dropping by."

"No." She tried a polite smile, but found it strained. Guns and badges and official vehicles. Too many police in too short a time, Maggie told herself.

"If it wouldn't put you out too much, I'd like to come in and talk to you for a few minutes."

It did put her out. She wanted to say it did, then close the door on him and everything he wanted to talk about. *Coward,* she told herself, and stepped back to let him in. "I suppose you're here about what we found yesterday." Maggie put her shoulder to the door to shut it. "I don't know what I can tell you."

"I'm sure it was a nasty experience, Miss Fitzgerald, and one you'd just as soon forget." His voice held just the right trace of sympathy mixed with professionalism. She decided he knew his business. "I wouldn't feel I was doing my duty as sheriff or as a neighbor if I didn't give you whatever help I can."

Maggie looked at him again. This time her smile came a bit more easily. "I appreciate that. I can offer you coffee, if you don't mind the mess in the kitchen."

He smiled and looked so solid, so pleasant, Maggie almost forgot the gun at his hip. "I never turn down coffee."

"The kitchen's down here," she began, then laughed. "I don't have to tell you, do I? You'd know this house as well as I do."

He fell into step beside her. "Tell you the truth, I've been around the outside, hacking at the weeds now and again or hunting, but I've only been inside a handful of times. The Morgans moved out when Joyce was still a kid."

"Yes, she told me."

"Nobody's lived here for more'n ten years. Louella just let it go after the old man died." He glanced up at the cracked ceiling paint.

"She held it in trust till Joyce inherited it at twenty-five. You probably heard I held Joyce off from selling."

"Well..." Uncertain how to respond, Maggie busied herself at the stove.

"Guess I thought we'd fix it up eventually, rent it out again." To her, he sounded like a man who knew about dreams but never found the time for them. "But a big old place like this needs a lot of time and money to put right. Joyce probably did the right thing, selling out."

"I'm glad she did." After switching on the coffeemaker, Maggie indicated a chair.

"With Bog handling repairs and Delaney working on the grounds, you picked the right men." When Maggie just looked at him, the sheriff grinned again. "Nothing travels fast in small towns but news."

"No, I suppose not."

"Look, what happened yesterday..." He paused, clearing his throat. "I know it must be rough on you. I gotta tell you, Joyce was worked up about it. A lot of people who'd find something like that a stone's throw from their house would just pull up stakes and take off."

Maggie reached in the cabinets for cups. "I'm not going anywhere."

"Glad to hear it." He was silent a moment, watching her pour the coffee. Her hands looked steady enough. "I understand Cliff was here yesterday, too."

"That's right. He was overseeing some of the work."

"And your dog dug up—"

"Yes." Maggie set both cups on the table before she sat down. "He's just a puppy. Right now he's asleep upstairs. Too much excitement."

The sheriff waved away her offer of cream, sipping the coffee black. "I didn't come to press you for details. The state police filled me in. I just wanted to let you know I was as close as the phone if you needed anything."

"I appreciate that. I'm not really familiar with the procedure, but I suppose I should've called you yesterday."

"I like to take care of my own territory," he said slowly, "but with something like this—" He shrugged. "Hell, I'd've had to call in the state, anyway." She watched his wedding ring gleam dully in the sunlight. Joyce had had a matching one, Maggie recalled. Plain and gold and solid. "Looks like you're redoing this floor."

Maggie looked down blankly. "Oh, yes, I took up the old linoleum. I've got to get to the sanding."

"You call George Cooper," the sheriff told her. "He's in the book. He'll get you an electric sander that'll take care of this in no time. Just tell him Stan Agee gave you his name."

"All right." She knew the conversation should've eased her mind, but her nerves were jumping again. "Thank you."

"Anything else you need, you just give us a call. Joyce'll want to have you over for dinner. She bakes the best ham in the county."

"That'd be nice."

"She can't get over someone like you moving here to Morganville." He sipped at his coffee while Maggie's grew cold. While he leaned back in the chair, relaxed, she sat very straight with tension. "I don't keep up with music much, but Joyce knows all of your songs. She reads all those magazines, too, and now somebody's who's in them's living in her old house." He glanced idly at the back door. "You ought to speak to Bog about putting some dead bolts on."

She looked over at the screen, remembering the hinges needed oiling. "Dead bolts?"

With a laugh, he finished off his coffee. "That's what happens when you're sheriff. You're always thinking of security. We've got a nice, quiet community, Miss Fitzgerald. Wouldn't want you to think otherwise. But I'd feel better knowing you had some good solid locks on the doors, since you're back here alone." Rising, he tugged absently at his holster. "Thanks for the coffee. You just remember to call if you need anything."

"Yes, I'll remember."

"I'll go on out this way and let you get back to work. You call George Cooper, now."

"All right." Maggie walked to the back door with him. "Thank you, Sheriff."

For a moment she just stood there by the door, her head resting against the jamb. She hated knowing she could be so easily worked up. The sheriff had come to reassure her, to show her that the community she'd chosen to live in had a concerned, capable law enforcer. Now her nerves were raw from talking to so many police. So many police, Maggie mused, just as it had been when Jerry died. All the police, all the questions. She thought she'd been over it, but now everything was coming back again, much too clearly.

"Your husband drove off the road, Mrs. Browning. We haven't located his body yet, but we're doing everything we can. I'm sorry."

Yes, there'd been sympathy at first, Maggie remembered. She'd had sympathy from the police, from her friends, Jerry's friends. Then questions: "Had your husband been drinking when he left the house?" "Was he upset, angry?" "Were you fighting?"

God, hadn't it been enough that he'd been dead? Why had they picked and pulled at all the reasons? How many reasons could there be for a twenty-eight-year-old man to turn his car toward a cliff and drive over it?

Yes, he'd been drinking. He'd done a lot of drinking since his career had started to skid and hers had kept climbing. Yes, they'd been fighting, because neither of them had understood what had happened to the dreams they'd once had. She'd answered their questions; she'd suffered the press until she had thought she'd go mad.

Maggie squeezed her eyes tight. That was over, she told herself. She couldn't bring Jerry back and solve his problems now. He'd found his own solution. Turning from the door, she went back to the music room.

In her work she found the serenity and the discipline she needed. It had always been that way for her. She could escape into the music so that her emotions found their outlet. She could train her mind on timing and structure. Her drive had always been to release the emotions, hers by the creation of a song and the listener's by hearing it. If she was successful in that, she needed no other ambition.

Talent wasn't enough in itself, she knew. It hadn't been enough for Jerry. Talent had to be harnessed by discipline; discipline, guided by creativity. Maggie used all three now.

As time passed, she became absorbed in the music and in the goal she'd set. The title song had to be passionate, full of movement and sexuality, as the title itself suggested. When it was played, she wanted it to stir the senses, touch off needs, build longings.

No one had been signed to perform it yet, so she was free to use whatever style she chose. She wanted something bluesy, and in her mind she could hear the moan of a sax. Sexy, sultry. She wanted the quiet wail of brass and the smoky throb of bass. Late the night before, when she'd been restless, she'd written down a few phrases. Now she experimented with them, twining words to music.

Almost at once she knew she'd found the key. The key was unexplained passion, barely controlled. It was desire that promised to rip aside anything civilized. It was the fury and heat that a man and woman could bring to each other until both were senseless from it. She had the key now, Maggie thought as her pulse began to pound with the music, because she'd experienced it herself. Yesterday, on the rise, in the sun, with Cliff.

Madness. That was the word that streamed through her mind. Desire was madness. She closed her eyes as words and melody flowed through her. Hadn't she felt that madness, the sweetness and the ache of it, when his mouth had moved on hers? Hadn't she wanted to feel him against her, flesh to flesh? He'd made her think of dark nights, steamy, moonless nights when the air was so thick you'd feel it pulse on your skin. Then she hadn't thought at all, because desire was madness.

She let the words come, passionate, wanton promises that simmered over the heat of the music. Seductive, suggestive, they poured out of her own needs. Lovers' words, desperate words, were whispered out in her low, husky voice until the room was charged with them. No one who heard would be unmoved. That was her ambition.

When she was finished, Maggie was breathless and moved and exhilarated. She reached up to rewind the recorder for playback when, for the second time, she saw Cliff standing in the doorway.

Her hand froze, and her pulse, already fast, went racing. Had she called him with the song, she wondered frantically. Was the magic that strong? When he said nothing, she switched off the recorder and spoke with studied calm. "Is it an accepted habit in the country for people to walk into homes uninvited?"

"You don't seem to hear the door when you're working."

She acknowledged this with an inclination of her head. "That might mean I don't like to be disturbed when I'm working."

"It might." Disturbed. The word almost made him laugh. Perhaps he had disturbed her work, but that was nothing compared to what the song had done to him—to what watching her sing had done to him. It had taken every ounce of his control not to yank her from the piano stool and take her on the littered, dusty floor. He came closer, knowing before it reached him that her scent would be there to add to her allure.

"I lost quite a bit of time yesterday." Maggie swallowed whatever was trying to block her voice. Her body was still throbbing, still much too vulnerable from the passion she'd released. "I have a deadline on this score."

He glanced down at her hands. He wanted to feel them stroke over him with the same skill she'd used on the piano keys. Slowly, he took his gaze up her arms, over the curve of her shoulder to her face. For both of them, it was as if he'd touched her.

Her breath wasn't steady; her eyes weren't calm. That was as he wanted it now. No matter how often or how firmly he told himself to back off from her, Cliff knew he was reaching a point when it would be impossible. She wasn't for him—he could convince himself of that. But they had something that had to be freed and had to be tasted.

"From what I heard," he murmured, "you seem to be finished."

"That's for me to decide."

"Play it back." It was a challenge. He saw from her eyes that she knew it. A challenge could backfire on either of them. "The last song—I want to hear it again."

Dangerous. Maggie understood the danger. As she hesitated, his lips curved. It was enough. Without a word, she punched the rewind button. The song was a fantasy, she told herself as the tape hurried backward. It was a fantasy, just as the film was a fantasy. The song was for the characters in a story and had nothing, absolutely nothing, to do with her. Or with him. She flicked the recorder to play.

She'd listen objectively, Maggie decided as the music began to spill into the room. She'd listen as a musician, as a technician. That was what her job demanded. But she found, as her own voice began to tempt her, that she was listening as a woman. Rising, she walked to the window and faced out. When a hunger was this strong, she thought, distance could mean everything.

Wait for night when the air's hot and there's madness
I'll make your blood swim
Wait for night when passion rises like a flood in the heat dance
Desire pours over the rim

He listened, as he had before, and felt his system respond to the music and the promises that low voice made. He wanted all that the song hinted at. All that, and more.

When Cliff crossed the room, he saw her tense. He thought he could feel the air snap, hissing with the heat the song had fanned.

Before he reached her, Maggie turned. The sun at her back shot a nimbus around her. In contrast, her eyes were dark. Like night, he thought. Like her night music. The words she'd written filled the room around them. It seemed those words were enough.

He didn't speak, but circled the back of her neck with his hand. She didn't speak, but resisted, forcing her body to stiffen. There was anger in her eyes now, as much for herself as for him. She'd taken herself to this point by allowing her own needs and fantasies to clear the path. It wasn't madness she wanted, Maggie told herself as she drew back. It was stability. It wasn't the wild she sought, but serenity. He wouldn't offer those things.

His fingers only tightened as she pulled back. That surprised them both. He'd forgotten the rules of a civilized seduction, just as he'd forgotten he'd only come there to see how she was. The music, the words, made the vulnerability that had concerned him a thing of the past. Now he felt strength as his fingers pressed into her skin. He saw challenge in her stance, and a dare, mixed with the fury in her eyes. Cliff wanted nothing less from her.

He stepped closer. When she lifted a hand in protest, he took her wrist. The pulse throbbed under his hand as intensely as the music throbbed on the air. Their eyes met, clashed, passion against passion. In one move, he pulled her against him and took her mouth.

She saw the vivid colors and lights she'd once imagined. She tasted the flavor of urgent desire. As her arms pulled him yet closer to her, Maggie heard her own moan of shuddering pleasure. The world was suddenly honed down to an instant, and the instant went on and on.

Had she been waiting for this? This mindless, melting pleasure?

Were these sensations, these emotions, what she'd poured out into music for so long? She could find no answers, only more needs.

He'd stopped thinking. In some small portion of his brain, Cliff knew he'd lost the capacity to reason. She made him feel, outrageously, so that there was no room for intellect. His hands sought her, skimming under her shirt to find the soft, heated skin he knew he'd dreamed about. She strained against him, offering more. Against his mouth, he felt her lips form his name. Something wild burst inside him.

He wasn't gentle, though as a lover he'd never been rough before. He was too desperate to touch to realize that he might bruise something more fragile than he. The kiss grew savage. He knew he'd never be able to draw enough from her to satisfy him. More, and still more, he wanted, though her mouth was as crazed and demanding as his.

He was driving her mad. No one had ever shown her a need so great. Hunger fueled hunger until she ached with it. She knew it could consume her, perhaps both of them. With a fire so hot, they could burn each other out and be left with nothing. The thought made her moan again, and cling. She wanted more. Yet she feared to take more and find herself empty.

"No." His lips at her throat were turning her knees to water. "No, this is crazy," she managed.

He lifted his head. His eyes were nearly black now, and his breathing was unsteady. For the first time, Maggie felt a twinge of fear. What did she know of this man? "You called it madness," he murmured. "You were right."

Yes, she'd been right, and it had been him she'd thought of when she'd written the words. Yet she told herself it was sanity she needed. "It's not what either of us should want."

"No." His control was threatening to snap completely. Deliberately, he ran a hand down her hair. "But it's already too far along to stop. I want you, Maggie, whether I should or not."

If he hadn't used her name— Until then she hadn't realized that he could say her name and make her weak. As needs welled up again, she dropped her head on his chest. It was that artless, unplanned gesture that cleared his frenzied thoughts and tugged at something other than desire.

This was the kind of woman who could get inside a man. Once she did, he'd never be free of her. Knowing that, he fought back the overwhelming need to hold her close again. He wanted her, and he intended to have her. That didn't mean he'd get involved. They both knew that what had ignited between them would have to be consummated sooner or later. It was basic; it was simple. And they'd both walk away undamaged.

Whereas the arousal he'd felt hadn't worried him, the tenderness he was feeling now did. They'd better get things back on the right road. He took her by the shoulders and drew her back.

"We want each other." It sounded simple when he said it. Cliff was determined to believe it could be.

"Yes." She nodded, almost composed again. "I'm sure you've learned, as I have, that you can't have everything you want."

"True enough. But there's no reason for either of us not to have what we want this time."

"I can think of a few. The first is that I barely know you."

He frowned as he studied her face. "Does that matter to you?"

Maggie jerked away so quickly his hands fell to his sides. "So, you do believe everything you read." Her voice was brittle now, and her eyes were cold. "Los Angeles, land of sinning and sinners. I'm sorry to disappoint you, Cliff, but I haven't filled my life with nameless, faceless lovers. This fills my life." She slapped her hand down on the piano so that papers slid off onto the floor. "And since you read so much, since you know so much about me, you'll know that up to two years ago I was married. I had a husband, and as ridiculous as it sounds, was faithful for six years."

"My question didn't have anything to do with that." His voice was so mild in contrast to hers that she stiffened. Maggie had learned to trust him the least when he used that tone. "It was more personal, as in you and me."

"Then let's just say I have a rule of thumb not to hop into bed with men I don't know. You included."

He crossed the room, then laid his hand over hers on the piano. "Just how well do you have to know me?"

"Better, I think, than I ever will." She had to fight the urge to snatch her hand away. She'd made a fool of herself enough for one day. "I have another rule about steering clear of people who don't like who and what I am."

He looked down at the hand beneath his. It was pale, slender and strong. "Maybe I don't know who and what you are." His gaze lifted to lock on hers. "Maybe I intend to find out for myself."

"You'll have to have my cooperation for that, won't you?"

He lifted a brow, as if amused. "We'll see."

Her voice became only more icy. "I'd like you to leave. I've a lot of work to do."

"Tell me what you were thinking about when you wrote that song."

Something fluttered over her face so quickly he couldn't be certain if it was panic or passion. Either would have suited him.

"I said I want you to leave."

"I will—after you tell me what you were thinking of."

She kept her chin angled and her eyes level. "I was thinking of you."

He smiled. Taking her hand, he brought her palm to his lips. The unexpected gesture had thunderbolts echoing in her head. "Good," he murmured. "Think some more. I'll be back."

She closed her fingers over her palm as he walked away. He'd given her no choice but to do as he'd asked.

It was late, late into the night, when she woke. Groggy, Maggie thought it had been the dream that had disturbed her. She cursed Cliff and rolled onto her back. She didn't want to dream of him. She certainly didn't want to lie awake in the middle of the night, thinking of him.

Staring up at the ceiling, she listened to the quiet. At times like this, it struck her how alone she was. There were no servants sleeping downstairs, as there had been all her life. Her closest neighbor was perhaps a quarter of a mile away through the woods. No all-night clubs or drugstores, she mused. So far, she'd yet to even deal with getting an outside antenna for television. She was on her own, as she'd chosen.

Then why, Maggie wondered, did her bed suddenly seem so empty and the night so long? Rolling to her side, she struggled to shake off the mood and her thoughts of Cliff.

Overhead, a board creaked, but she paid no attention. Old houses made noises at night. Maggie had learned that quickly. Restless, she shifted in bed and lay watching the light of the waning moon.

She didn't want Cliff there, with her. Even allowing herself to think that she did was coming too close to dangerous ground. It was true her body had reacted to him, strongly. A woman couldn't always control the needs of her body, but she could control the direction of her thoughts. Firmly, she set her mind on the list of chores for the next day.

When the sound came again, she frowned, glancing automatically at the ceiling. The creaks and groans rarely disturbed her, but then, she'd always slept soundly in this house. Until Cliff Delaney, she thought, and determinedly shut her eyes. The sound of a door shutting quietly had them flying open again.

Before panic could register or reason overtake it, her heart was lodged in her throat, pounding. She was alone, and someone was in the house. All the nightmares that had ever plagued a woman alone in the dark loomed in her mind. Her fingers curled into the sheets as she lay stiffly, straining to hear.

Was that a footstep on the stairs, or was it all in her imagination? As terror flowed into her, she thought of the gully outside. She bit down on her lip to keep herself from making a sound. Very slowly, Maggie turned her head and made out the puppy sleeping at the foot of the bed. He didn't hear anything. She closed her eyes again and tried to even her breathing.

If the dog heard nothing that disturbed him, she reasoned, there was nothing to worry about. Just boards settling. Even as she tried to convince herself, Maggie heard a movement downstairs. A soft squeak, a gentle scrape. The kitchen door? she asked herself as the panic buzzed in her head. Fighting to move slowly and quietly, she reached for the phone beside the bed. As she held it to her ear, she heard the buzz that reminded her she'd left the kitchen extension off the hook earlier so as not to be disturbed. Her phone was as good as dead. Hysteria bubbled and was swallowed.

*Think,* she ordered herself. *Stay calm and think.* If she was alone, with no way to reach help, she had to rely on herself. How many times in the past few weeks had she stated that she could do just that?

She pressed a hand against her mouth so that the sound of her own breathing wouldn't disturb her concentrated listening. There was nothing now, no creaks, no soft steps on wood.

Careful to make no sound, she climbed out of bed and found the fireplace poker. Muscles tense, Maggie propped herself in the chair, facing the door. Gripping the poker in both hands, she prayed for morning.

# Chapter 6

After a few days, Maggie had all but forgotten about the noises in her house. As early as the morning after the incident, she'd felt like a fool. She'd been awakened by the puppy licking her bare feet while she sat, stiff and sore from the night in the chair. The fireplace poker had lain across her lap like a medieval sword. The bright sunlight and birdsong had convinced her she'd imagined everything, then had magnified every small noise the way a child magnifies shadows in the dark. Perhaps she wasn't quite as acclimated to living alone as she'd thought. At least she could be grateful she'd left the downstairs extension off the hook. If she hadn't, everyone in town would know she was a nervous idiot.

If she had nerves, Maggie told herself, it was certainly understandable under the circumstances. People digging up skeletons beside her house, the local sheriff suggesting she lock her doors, and Cliff Delaney, Maggie added, keeping her up at night. The only good thing to come out of the entire week was the completed score. She imagined that C.J. would be pleased enough with the finished product not to nag her about coming back to L.A., at least for a little while.

Maggie decided the next constructive thing to do was to take the tape and sheet music she'd packaged to the post office and mail it off. Perhaps later she'd celebrate her first songs written in her new home.

She enjoyed the trip to town and took it leisurely. The narrow little roads were flanked by trees that would offer a blanket of shade in a few short weeks. Now the sun streamed through the tiny leaves to pour white onto the road. Here and there the woods were interrupted by fields, brown earth turned up. She could see farmers working with their tractors and wondered what was being planted. Corn, hay, wheat? She knew virtually nothing of that aspect of the home she'd chosen. Maggie thought it would be interesting to watch things grow until the summer or autumn harvest.

She saw cows with small calves nursing frantically. There was a woman carrying a steel bucket to what must have been a chicken coop. A dog raced along a fenced yard, barking furiously at Maggie's car.

Her panic of a few nights before seemed so ridiculous she refused to think of it.

She passed a few houses, some of them hardly more than cabins, others so obviously new and modern they offended the eyes. She found herself resenting the pristine homes on lots where trees had been cleared. Why hadn't they worked with what was there, instead of spoiling it? Then she laughed at herself. She was sounding too much like Cliff Delaney. People had a right to live where and how they chose, didn't they? But she couldn't deny that she preferred the old weathered brick or wood homes surrounded by trees.

As she drove into Morganville, she noted the homes were closer together. That was town life, she decided. There were sidewalks here, and a few cars parked along the curb. People kept their lawns trimmed. Maggie decided that from the look of it, there was quite a bit of pride and competition among the flower gardens. It reminded her to check her own petunias.

The post office was on the corner, a small redbrick building with a two-car parking lot. Beside it, separated by no more than a two-foot strip of grass, was the Morganville bank. Two men stood beside the outside mailbox, smoking and talking. They watched as Maggie pulled into the lot, as she stepped out of the car and as she walked toward the post office. Deciding to try her luck, she turned her head and flashed them a smile.

"Good morning."

"Morning," they said in unison. One of them pushed back his fishing cap. "Nice car."

"Thank you."

She walked inside, pleased that she had had what could pass for a conversation.

There was one woman behind the counter already engaged in what appeared to be casual gossip with a younger woman who toted a baby on her hip. "No telling how long they've been there," the postmistress stated, counting out stamps. "Nobody's lived out there since the Faradays, and that's been ten years last month. Old lady Faraday used to come in for a dollar's worth of stamps once a week, like clockwork. 'Course, they were cheaper then." She pushed the stamps across the counter. "That's five dollars' worth, Amy."

"Well, I think it's spooky." The young mother jiggled the baby on her hip while he busied himself gurgling at Maggie. Gathering up the stamps, she stuffed them into a bag on her other shoulder. "If I found a bunch of old bones in my yard, I'd have a for-sale sign up the next day." Hearing the words, Maggie felt some of her pleasure in the day fade. "Billy said some drifter probably fell in that gully and nobody ever knew about it."

"Could be. Guess the state police'll figure it out before long." The postmistress closed the conversation by turning to Maggie. "Help you?"

"Yes." Maggie stepped up to the counter. The young woman gave her one long, curious look before she took her baby outside. "I'd like to send this registered mail."

"Well, let's see what it weighs." The postmistress took the package and put it on the scale. "You want a return receipt?"

"Yes, please."

"Okay." She took the pencil from behind her ear to run the tip along a chart taped to the scale. "Cost you a bit more, but you'll know it got there. Let's see, it's going to zone—" She broke off as she caught the return address on the corner of the package. Her gaze lifted, focusing sharply on Maggie, before she began to fill out the form. "You're the songwriter from California. Bought the Morgan place."

"That's right." Because she wasn't sure what to say after the conversation she'd overheard, Maggie left it at that.

"Nice music." The postmistress wrote in meticulously rounded letters. "Lot of that stuff they play I can't even understand. I got some of your mama's records. She was the best. Nobody else comes close."

Maggie's heart warmed, as it always did when someone spoke of her mother. "Yes, I think so, too."

"You sign this here." As she obeyed, Maggie felt the postmistress's eyes on her. It occurred to her that this woman saw every piece of correspondence that came to or from her. Though it was an odd feeling, she found it wasn't unpleasant. "Big old house, the Morgan place." The woman figured the total on a little white pad. "You settling in all right out there?"

"Bit by bit. There's a lot to be done."

"That's the way it is when you move into a place, 'specially one's been empty so long. Must be a lot different for you."

Maggie lifted her head. "Yes. I like it."

Perhaps it was the direct eyes or perhaps it was the simple phrasing, but the postmistress seemed to nod to herself. Maggie felt as though she'd found her first full acceptance. "Bog'll do well by you. So will young Delaney."

Maggie smiled to herself as she reached for her wallet. Small towns, she thought. No secrets.

"You had a shock the other day."

Because she'd been expecting some kind of comment, Maggie took it easily. "I wouldn't care to have another like it."

"Nope, guess nobody would. You just relax and enjoy that old house," the postmistress advised. "It was a showcase in its day. Louella always kept it fine. Let the police worry about the rest of it."

"That's what I'm trying to do." Maggie pocketed her change. "Thank you."

"We'll get this off for you right away. You have a nice day."

Maggie was definitely feeling pleased with herself when she walked back outside. She took a deep breath of soft spring air, smiled again at the two men still talking beside the mailbox, then turned toward her car. The smile faded when she saw Cliff leaning against the hood.

"Out early," he said easily.

He'd told her it was difficult to avoid anyone in a town that size. Maggie decided it was his accuracy that annoyed her. "Shouldn't you be working somewhere?"

He grinned and offered her the bottle of soda he held. "Actually, I just came off a job site and was on my way to another." When she made no move to take the soda, he lifted the bottle to his lips again and drank deeply. "You don't see too many of these in Morganville." He tapped a finger against the side of her Aston Martin.

She started to move around him to the driver's door. "If you'll excuse me," she said coolly, "I'm busy."

He stopped her effortlessly with a hand on her arm. Ignoring her glare, as well as the interested speculation of the two men a few yards away, Cliff studied her face. "You've shadows under your eyes. Haven't you been sleeping?"

"I've been sleeping just fine."

"No." He stopped her again, but this time he lifted a hand to her face, as well. Though she didn't seem to know it, every time her fragile side showed, he lost ground. "I thought you didn't believe in evasions."

"Look, I'm busy."

"You've let that business in the gully get to you."

"Well, what if I have?" Maggie exploded. "I'm human. It's a normal reaction."

"I didn't say it wasn't." The hand on her face tilted her chin back a bit farther. "You fire up easily these days. Is it just that business that has you tense, or is there something else?"

Maggie stopped trying to pull away and stood very still. Maybe he hadn't noticed the men watching them, or the postmistress in the window, but she had. "It's none of your business whether I'm tense or not. Now, if you'll stop making a scene, I have to go home and work."

"Do scenes bother you?" Amused now, he drew her closer. "I wouldn't have thought so, from the number of times you've had your picture snapped."

"Cliff, cut it out." She put both hands on his chest. "For heaven's sake, we're standing on Main Street."

"Yeah. And we've just become the ten-o'clock bulletin."

A laugh escaped before she even knew it was going to happen. "You get a real kick out of that, don't you?"

"Well..." He took advantage of her slight relaxing and wrapped his arms around her. "Maybe. I've been meaning to talk to you."

A woman walked by with a letter in her hand. Maggie noticed that she took her time putting it into the box. "I think we could find a better place." At his snort of laughter, she narrowed her eyes. "I didn't mean that. Now, will you let go?"

"In a minute. Remember when we went out to dinner the other night?"

"Yes, I remember. Cliff—" She turned her head and saw that the two men were still there, still watching. Now the woman had joined them. "This really isn't funny."

"Thing is," he continued easily, "we have this custom around here. I take you out to dinner, then you reciprocate."

Out of patience, she wriggled against him and found that only made her blood pressure rise. "I haven't the time to go out to dinner right now. I'll get back to you in a few weeks."

"I'll take potluck."

"Potluck?" she repeated. "At *my* house?"

"Good idea."

"Wait a minute. I didn't say—"

"Unless you can't cook."

"Of course I can cook," she tossed back.

"Fine. Seven o'clock?"

She aimed her most deadly, most regal stare. "I'm hanging wallpaper tonight."

"You have to eat sometime." Before she could comment, he kissed her, briefly but firmly enough to make a point. "See you at seven," he said, then strolled over to his truck. "And Maggie," he added through the open window, "nothing fancy. I'm not fussy."

"You—" she began, but the roar of the truck's engine drowned her out. She was left standing alone, fuming, in the center of the parking lot. Knowing there were at least a dozen pair of eyes on her, Maggie kept her head high as she climbed into her own car.

She cursed Cliff repeatedly, and expertly, on the three-mile drive back to her house.

Maggie expected the men from Cliff's crew to be there when she returned. The discreet black car at the end of her driveway, however, was unexpected. She discovered as she pulled alongside it that she wasn't in the mood for visitors, not for neighbors calling to pay their respects or for curiosity-seekers. She wanted to be alone with the sander she'd rented from George Cooper.

As she stepped from the car, she spotted the rangy man with the salt-and-pepper hair crossing her front yard from the direction of the gully. And she recognized him.

"Miss Fitzgerald."

"Good morning. Lieutenant Reiker, isn't it?"

"Yes, ma'am."

What was the accepted etiquette, Maggie wondered, when you came home and found a homicide detective on your doorstep? Maggie decided on the practical, marginally friendly approach. "Is there something I can do for you?"

"I'm going to have to ask for your cooperation, Miss Fitzgerald." The lieutenant kept his weight on one foot, as if his hips were troubling him. "I'm sure you'd like to get on with all your landscaping plans, but we want you to hold off on the pond a while longer."

"I see." She was afraid she did. "Can you tell me why?"

"We've received the medical examiner's preliminary report. We'll be investigating."

It might've been easier not to ask, not to know. Maggie wasn't certain she could live with herself if she took the coward's way out that she was obviously being offered. "Lieutenant, I'm not sure how much you're at liberty to tell me, but I do think I have a right to know certain things. This is my property."

"You won't be involved to any real extent, Miss Fitzgerald. This business goes back a long way."

"As long as my land's part of it, I'm involved." She caught herself worrying the strap of her bag, much as Joyce had done on her visit. She forced her hands to be still. "It'd be easier for me, Lieutenant, if I knew what was going on."

Reiker rubbed his hand over his face. The investigation was barely under way, and he already had a bad taste in his mouth. Maybe things that'd been dead and buried for ten years should just stay buried. Some things, he decided grimly. Yes, some things.

"The medical examiner determined that the remains belonged to a Caucasian male in his early fifties."

Maggie swallowed. That made it too real. Much too real. "How long—" she began, but had to swallow again. "How long had he been there?"

"The examiner puts it at about ten years."

"As long as the house has been empty," she murmured. She brought herself back, telling herself that it wasn't personal. Logically, practically, it had nothing to do with her. "I don't suppose they could determine how he died?"

"Shot," Reiker said flatly, and watched the horror fill her eyes. "Appears to've been a thirty-gauge shotgun, probably at close range."

"Good God." Murder. Yet hadn't she known it, sensed it almost from the first instant? Maggie stared out into the woods and watched two squirrels race up the trunk of a tree. How could it have happened here? "After so many years—" she began, but had to swallow yet again. "After so many years, wouldn't it be virtually impossible to identify the—him?"

"He was identified this morning." Reiker watched as she turned to him, pale, her eyes almost opaque. It gave him a bad feeling. He told himself it was because, like every other man in the country, he'd had a fantasy love affair with her mother twenty years before. He told himself it was because she was young enough to be his daughter. At times like this, he wished he'd chosen any other line of work.

"We found a ring, too, an old ring with a lot of fancy carving and three small diamond chips. An hour ago, Joyce Agee identified it as her father's. William Morgan was murdered and buried in that gully."

But that was wrong. Maggie dragged a hand through her hair and tried to think. No matter how bluntly, how practically, Reiker put it, it was wrong. "That can't be. I was told that William Morgan had an accident—something about a car accident."

"Ten years ago, his car went through the guardrail of the bridge crossing into West Virginia. His car was dragged out of the Potomac, but not his body. His body was never found...until a few days ago."

Through the rail, into the water, Maggie thought numbly. Like Jerry. They hadn't found Jerry's body, either, not for nearly a week. She'd lived through every kind of hell during that week. As she stood, staring straight ahead, she felt as though she were two people in two separate times. "What will you do now?"

"There'll be an official investigation. It has nothing to do with you, Miss Fitzgerald, other than we need for you to keep that section of your property clear. There'll be a team here this afternoon to start going over it again, just in case we missed something."

"All right. If you don't need anything else—"

"No, ma'am."

"I'll be inside."

As she walked across the lawn toward the house, she told herself that something that had happened ten years before had nothing to do with her. Ten years before, she'd been dealing with her own tragedy, the loss of her parents. Unable to resist, she looked back over her shoulder at the gully as she climbed the steps to the porch.

Joyce Agee's father, Maggie thought with a shudder. Joyce had sold her the house without knowing what would be discovered. She thought of the pretty, tense young woman who had been grateful for a simple kindness to her mother. Compelled, Maggie went to the pad scrawled with names and numbers beside the phone. Without hesitating, she called the number for Joyce Agee. The voice that answered was soft, hardly more than a whisper. Maggie felt a stab of sympathy.

"Mrs. Agee—Joyce, this is Maggie Fitzgerald."

"Oh… Yes, hello."

"I don't want to intrude." Now what? Maggie asked herself. She had no part of this, no link other than a plot of land that had lain neglected for a decade. "I just wanted you to know that I'm terribly sorry, and if there's anything I can do…I'd like to help."

"Thank you, there's nothing." Her voice hitched, then faltered. "It's been such a shock. We always thought—"

"Yes, I know. Please, don't think you have to talk to me or be polite. I only called because somehow—" She broke off, passing a hand over her hair. "I don't know. I feel as though I've set it all off."

"It's better to know the truth." Joyce's voice became suddenly calm. "It's always better to know. I worry about Mother."

"Is she all right?"

"I'm not— I'm not sure." Maggie sensed fatigue now, rather than tears. She understood that form of grief, as well. "She's here now. The doctor's with her."

"I won't keep you, then. Joyce, I understand we hardly know each other, but I would like to help. Please let me know if I can."

"I will. Thank you for calling."

Maggie replaced the receiver. That accomplished nothing, she reflected. It accomplished nothing, because she didn't know Joyce Agee. When you grieved, you needed someone you knew, the way she'd needed Jerry when her parents had been killed. Though she knew Joyce had a husband, Maggie thought of Cliff and the way he'd taken the woman's hands, the look of concern on his face, when he'd spoken to her. He'd be there for her, Maggie mused, and wished she knew what they meant to each other.

To give her excess energy an outlet, she switched on the rented sander.

The sun was low, the sky rosy with it, when Cliff drove toward the old Morgan property. His mind was full of questions. William Morgan murdered. He'd been shot, buried on his own property; then someone had covered the trail by sending his car into the river.

Cliff was close enough to the Morgans and to the people of Morganville to know that every other person in town might've wished William Morgan dead. He'd been a hard man, a cold man, with a genius for making money and enemies. But could someone who Cliff knew, someone he'd talk to on the street any day of the week, have actually murdered him?

In truth, he didn't give a damn about the old man, but he worried about Louella and Joyce—especially Joyce. He didn't like to see her the way she'd been that afternoon, so calm, so detached, with nerves snagged at the edge. She meant more to him than any other woman he'd known, yet there seemed to be no way to help her now. That was for Stan, Cliff thought, downshifting as he came to a corner.

God knew if the police would ever come up with anything viable. He didn't have much faith in that after ten years. That meant Joyce would have to live with knowing that her father had been murdered and that his murderer still walked free. Would she, Cliff mused, look at her neighbors and wonder?

Swearing, Cliff turned onto the lane that led to the Morgan place. There was someone else he worried about, he thought grimly, though he didn't have the excuse of a long, close friendship with this woman.

Damned if he wanted to worry about Maggie Fitzgerald. She was a woman from another place, who liked glittery parties and opening nights. Where he'd choose solitude, she'd choose crowds. She'd want champagne; he, cold beer. She'd prefer trips to Europe; he, a quiet ride down the river. She was the last person he needed to worry about.

She'd been married to a performer who'd flamed like a comet and who'd burned out just as quickly. Her escorts had been among the princes of the celebrity world. Tuxedos, silk scarves and diamond cufflinks, he thought derisively. What the hell was she doing in the middle of a mess like this? And what the hell, he asked himself, was she doing in his life?

He pulled up behind her car and stared broodingly at her house. Maybe with all that was going on she'd decide to go back west. He'd prefer it that way. Damned if he didn't want to believe he would. She had no business crashing into his thoughts the way she had lately. That music. He let out a long stream of curses as he remembered it. That night music. Cliff knew he wanted her the way he'd wanted no woman before. It was something he couldn't overcome. Something he could barely control.

So why was he here? Why had he pushed his way into a meeting she hadn't wanted? Because, he admitted, when he thought of the way it had been between them, he didn't want to overcome it. Tonight he didn't want control.

As he walked toward the front door, he reminded himself that he was dealing with a woman who was different from any he'd known. Approach with caution, he told himself, then knocked at the front door.

From the other side, Maggie gripped the knob with both hands and tugged. It took two tries before she opened the door, and by that time Killer was barking nonstop.

"You should have Bog take care of that," Cliff suggested. He bent down to ruffle the dog's fur. Killer flopped on his back, offering his belly.

"Yeah." She was glad to see him. Maggie told herself she would've been glad to see anyone, but when she looked at him, she knew it was a lie. All through the afternoon she'd waited. "I keep meaning to."

He saw tension in the way she stood, in the way one hand still gripped the doorknob. Deliberately, he gave her a cocky smile. "So, what's for dinner?"

She let out a quick laugh as some of the nerves escaped. "Hamburgers."

"Hamburgers?"

"You did invite yourself," she reminded him. "And you did say not to fuss."

"So I did." He gave Killer a last scratch behind the ears, then rose.

"Well, since it's my first dinner party, I thought I'd stick with my speciality. It was either that or canned soup and cold sandwiches."

"If that's been your staple since you moved in, it's no wonder you're thin."

Frowning, Maggie glanced down at herself. "Do you realize you make a habit of criticizing?"

"I didn't say I didn't like thin women."

"That's not the point. You can come back and complain while I cook the hamburgers."

As they walked down the hall, Cliff noticed a few bare spots where she'd removed strips of wallpaper. Apparently she was serious about taking on the overwhelming job of redoing the house. When they passed the music room, he glanced in at her piano and wondered why. She was in the position of being able to hire a fleet of decorators and craftsmen. The job could be done in weeks, rather than the months, even years, it promised to take this way. The freshly sanded floor in the kitchen caught his eye.

"Nice job." Automatically, he crouched down to run his fingers over the floor's surface. The dog took this as an invitation to lick his face.

Maggie lifted a brow. "Well, thank you."

Catching the tone, he looked up at her. He couldn't deny that he'd been giving her a hard time from the outset. He had his reasons. The primary one as Cliff saw it now was her effect on him. "The question is," he said, rising again, "why you're doing it."

"The floor needed it." She turned to the counter to begin making patties.

"I meant why *you're* doing it."

"It's my house."

He wandered over to stand beside her. Again, he found himself watching her hands. "Did you sand your own floors in California?"

"No." Annoyed, she set the patties under the broiler. "How many can you eat?"

"One'll do. Why are you sanding floors and hanging wallpaper?"

"Because it's my house." Maggie grabbed a head of lettuce from the refrigerator and began to shred it for salad.

"It was your house in California, too."

"Not the way this is." She dropped the lettuce and faced him. Impatience, annoyance, frustration—the emotions were plainly on the surface for him to see. "Look, I don't expect you to understand. I don't *care* if you understand. This house is special. Even after everything that's happened, it's special."

No, he didn't understand, but he discovered he wanted to. "The police have contacted you, then."

"Yes." She began to shred lettuce with a vengeance. "That investigator, Lieutenant Reiker, was here this morning." Her fingers dug into the cold, wet leaves. "Damn it, Cliff, I feel gruesome. I called Joyce and felt like an idiot, an intruder. There was nothing I could say."

"Did you?" he murmured. Strange that Joyce hadn't said anything about it, he thought. Then again, Joyce had said very little to him. "There isn't anything for you to say." He put his hands on her shoulders and felt the tension ripple. "This is something Joyce and her mother and the police have to deal with. It's nothing to do with you."

"I tell myself that," she said quietly. "Intellectually, I know it's true, but—" She turned, because she needed someone. Because, she admitted, she needed him. "It happened right outside. I'm involved, connected, whether I want to be or not. A man was murdered a few yards from my house. He was killed in a spot where I'd planned to put a nice quiet pond, and now—"

"And now," Cliff said, interrupting, "it's ten years later."

"Why should that matter?" she demanded. "My parents were killed ten years ago— Time doesn't make any difference."

"That," he countered, less gently than he'd intended, "had everything to do with you."

With a sigh, she allowed herself the weakness of resting her head against him. "I know how Joyce is feeling now. Everywhere I look, something draws me into this."

The more Maggie talked of Joyce, the less Cliff thought of the quiet brunette, and the more he thought of Maggie. His fingers tangled in her hair. It wasn't desire he felt now, but an almost fierce, protective urge he'd never expected. Perhaps there was something he could do, he decided, drawing her away.

"You didn't know William Morgan."

"No, but—"

"I did. He was a cold, ruthless man who didn't believe in words like compassion or generosity." Deliberately, he set Maggie aside and tended to the meat under the broiler himself. "Half the town would've cheered ten years ago if it hadn't been for Louella. She loved the old man. Joyce loved him, too, but both of them feared him every bit as much. The police won't have an easy time proving who killed him, and the town won't care. I detested him myself, for a lot of reasons."

She didn't like knowing that he could speak of a man's murder so calmly, so coldly. But then, as she'd told him herself before, they really didn't understand each other. To keep her hands busy, Maggie went back to the salad. "Joyce?" she asked casually.

He glanced at her sharply, then leaned on the counter again. "Yeah, for one. Morgan believed in discipline. Old-fashioned discipline. Joyce was like my kid sister. When I caught Morgan going at her with a belt when she was sixteen, I threatened to kill him myself."

He said it so casually Maggie's blood froze. He saw the doubts and the questions in her eyes when she looked at him.

"And so," Cliff added, "as the stories go, did half the population of Morganville. No one grieved when they fished William Morgan's car out of the river."

"No one has the right to take a life," Maggie said in a shaky voice. "Not their own or anyone else's."

He remembered that they had fished her husband's car out of the water, too. He remembered that the final verdict had been suicide. "You'd be better off not making comparisons," he said roughly.

"They seem to make themselves."

"What happened to Jerry Browning was a tragic waste of a life and of a talent. Do you plan on taking the blame for that, too?"

"I never took the blame," Maggie said wearily.

"Did you love him?"

Her eyes were eloquent, but her voice was steady. "Not enough."

"Enough to be faithful to him for six years," Cliff countered.

She smiled as her own words came back to her. "Yes, enough for that. Still, there's more to love than loyalty, isn't there?"

His hand was gentle again when he touched her face. "You said you hadn't taken the blame."

"Responsibility and blame are different things."

"No." He shook his head. "There's no responsibility or blame this time, either. Don't you think it's the height of egotism to feel responsible for someone else's actions?"

She started to snap at him, but the words hit home. "Maybe. Maybe it is." It wasn't easy, but she shook off the mood and smiled. "I think the hamburgers are done. Let's eat."

# *Chapter 7*

Maggie found the kitchen cozy with the smell of hot food and the patter of raindrops that had just begun to strike the windows. When she thought of it, she decided she'd never really experienced coziness before. Her parents had lived on a grand scale; huge, elegant rooms and huge, elegant parties, boisterous, eccentric friends. With her own home in Beverly Hills, Maggie had followed the same pattern. Extravagance might've been what she needed during that phase of her life, or it might've been a habit. She wasn't sure when it had begun to wear on her, any more than she was certain if she'd ever been as relaxed as she was at that moment, eating in her half-finished kitchen with a man she wasn't quite sure of.

He was strong, she mused. Perhaps she'd never allowed a strong man into her life. Her father had been strong, Maggie remembered. He'd been the type of man who could do and get precisely what he wanted simply because he wanted it. The strength hadn't been a physical one, but one of personality and will. But then, her mother had matched him with her own combination of grit and exuberance. Maggie had never seen a more perfect relationship than theirs.

Theirs had been an all-consuming, enduring love, with qualities of practicality, compassion and fire. They'd never competed, never envied each other's success. Support, she thought. Perhaps that had been the real key to the quality and lasting power of their relationship. Unquestioning mutual support. She hadn't found that in her own marriage, and she'd come to think her parents had been unique.

Something had happened to the balance in her relationship with Jerry. As he'd grown weaker, she'd grown stronger. Eventually, they'd come to a point where all the support had been on her side and all the need on his. Yet she'd stayed, because it had been impossible to forget that they'd been friends. Friends don't break promises.

She wondered, as she studied Cliff, what sort of friend he would be. And she wondered, though she tried not to, what he would be like as a lover.

"What're you thinking of?"

The question came so abruptly that Maggie almost overturned her glass. Quickly, she sorted out her thoughts and chose the least personal. She could hardly tell him what had been the last thing on her mind. "I was thinking," she began, picking up her wine again, "how cozy it is eating here in the kitchen. I'll probably demote the dining room to the last thing on my list."

"That's what you were thinking?" By the way he held her gaze, she knew he sensed there'd been other things.

"More or less." A woman who'd been interviewed and questioned all her life knew how to evade and dodge. Lifting the bottle, she filled

Cliff's glass again. "The Bordeaux's another present from my agent. Or another bribe," she added.

"Bribe?"

"He wants me to give up this mad scheme of camping out in the wilderness and come back to civilization."

"He thinks he can persuade you with puppies and French wine?"

With a bubbling laugh, Maggie sipped. "If I weren't so attached to this place, either one might've worked."

"Is that what you are?" Cliff asked thoughtfully. "Attached?"

At the question, her eyes stopped laughing, and her soft, wide mouth sobered. "In your business you should know that some things root quickly."

"Some do," he agreed. "And some that do can't acclimate to the new territory."

She tapped the side of her glass with a fingertip, wishing she understood why his doubts dug at her so deeply. "You don't have much faith in me, do you?"

"Maybe not." He shrugged as if to lighten a subject he wasn't so certain of any longer. "In any case, I'm finding it interesting to watch you make the adjustments."

She decided to go with his mood. "How'm I doing?"

"Better than I'd thought." He lifted his glass in a half toast. "But it's early yet."

She laughed, because arguing seemed like a waste of time. "Were you born cynical, Cliff, or did you take lessons?"

"Were you born an optimist?"

Both brows lifted to disappear under the fringe of sable bangs. "*Touché*," Maggie said. No longer interested in the meal, she studied him, finding that while his face was very much to her liking, she still couldn't judge him by his eyes. Too much control, she thought. A person would only get inside his head if he or she was invited. "You know," she began slowly, "after I'd stopped being annoyed, I decided I was glad you were coming by this evening." Now she grinned. "I don't know when I might've opened the wine otherwise."

This time he grinned. "I annoy you?"

"I think you're well aware of that," Maggie returned dryly. "And that for your own personal reasons it pleases you to do so."

Cliff tasted the wine again. It was warm and rich, reminding him of her mouth. "Actually, I do."

He said it so easily that Maggie laughed again. "Is it just me, or is annoying people a hobby of yours?"

"Just you." Over the rim of his glass, he studied her. She'd pinned her hair up in a loose Gibson style that accentuated her delicate, old-fashioned features. She wore some dark contouring shadow that made her eyes seem even larger, but her mouth was naked. This was a woman, Cliff thought, who knew how to accentuate her own looks to the best advantage, subtly, so that a man would be caught before he analysed what was Maggie and what was illusion. "I like your reactions," Cliff continued after a moment. "You don't like to lose your temper."

"So you like to provoke me until I do."

"Yeah." He smiled again. "That about sizes it up."

"Why?" she demanded in a voice filled with exasperated amusement.

"I'm not immune to you," Cliff said, so quietly her fingers tightened on the stem of her glass. "I wouldn't like to think you were immune to me."

She sat for a moment, stirred and baffled. Before her emotions could rise any closer to the surface, she stood and began to clear the table. "No, I'm not. Would you like more wine or some coffee?"

His hands closed over hers on the dishes. Slowly, he rose, his gaze fixed on her face. Maggie felt as though the kitchen had shrunk in size. Like Alice in the rabbit hole, she thought confusedly, unsure whether to sample that tempting little bottle or not. The patter of rain outside seemed to grow to a roar.

"I want to make love with you."

She wasn't a child, Maggie told herself. She was an adult, and men had wanted her before. She'd resisted temptations before. But had any ever been quite so alluring? "We've already been through this."

His hands tightened on hers when she tried to turn away. "But we never resolved it."

No, she couldn't turn away, or run away, from a man like this, Maggie realized. She'd have to stand her ground. "I was sure we had. Perhaps coffee would be best, since you have to drive this evening and I have to work."

Cliff took the dishes and set them back on the table. With her hands empty, Maggie found herself at a loss. She folded her arms under her breasts, a habit Cliff had discovered she used whenever she was upset or disturbed. At the moment, he didn't care which she was, as long as she wasn't unmoved.

"We haven't resolved it," he repeated, and plucked a pin from her hair. "We haven't begun to resolve it."

Though her eyes remained steady, she backed up when he stepped closer. It made him feel as though he were stalking her, an odd and thrilling sensation. "I really thought I'd made myself clear," Maggie managed, in what sounded to her like a firm, dismissive tone.

"It's clear when I touch you." Cliff backed her up against the counter, then pulled another pin from her hair. "It's clear when you look at me like you're looking at me now."

Maggie's heart began to pound at the base of her throat. She was weakening; she felt it in the heaviness of her limbs, the lightness in her head. Desire was temptation, and temptation a seduction in itself. "I didn't say I didn't want you—"

"No, you didn't," Cliff interrupted. When he drew out the next pin, her hair fell heavily to her shoulders and lay there, dark and tousled. "I don't think lying comes easily to you."

How could she have been so relaxed a few moments before and so tense now? Every muscle in her body was taut in the effort to combat what seemed to be inevitable. "No, I don't lie." Her voice was lower, huskier. "I said I didn't know you. I said you didn't understand me."

Something flashed into him. Perhaps it was rage; perhaps it was need. "I don't give a damn how little we know each other or how little we understand each other. I know I want you." He gathered her hair in one hand. "I only have to touch you to know you want me."

Her eyes grew darker. Why did it always seem her desire was mixed with anger and, though she detested it, a certain weakness she couldn't control? "Can you really believe it's that simple?"

He had to. For the sake of his own survival, Cliff knew, he had to keep whatever was between them purely physical. They'd make love through the night until they were exhausted. In the morning, the need and the bond would be gone. He had to believe it. Otherwise…

He didn't want to dwell on otherwise. "Why should it be complicated?" he countered.

The anger and the longing flowed through her. "Why indeed?" Maggie murmured.

The room had lost its cozy ambience. Now she felt she'd suffocate if she didn't escape it. Her eyes were stormy, his almost brutally calm, but she kept her gaze level on his while her thoughts raged. Why should she feel the need to rationalize, to romanticize? she asked herself. She wasn't an innocent young girl with misty dreams, but an adult, a widow, a professional woman who'd learned to live with reality. In reality, people took what they wanted, then dealt with the consequences. Now so would she.

"The bedroom's upstairs," she told him, and, brushing by him, walked out of the kitchen.

Disturbed, Cliff frowned after her. This was what he wanted, he thought. The lack of complications. Yet her abrupt acceptance had been so unexpected, so cool. No, he realized as he started after her, that wasn't what he wanted.

Maggie was at the base of the steps before he caught up with her. When she looked over her shoulder, he saw the fury in her eyes. The moment he took her arm, he felt the tension. This, he discovered, was what he wanted. He didn't want her cool, emotionless agreement or a careless acquiescence. He wanted to build that fury and tension until the passion that spawned them broke through. Before the night was over, he'd draw it all from her and purge himself, as well.

In silence, they climbed the stairs to the second floor.

The rain fell, strong and steady, against the windows and the newly seeded earth below. The sound made Maggie think of the subtle rhythmic percussion she'd imagined in the arrangement of the song she'd just completed. There was no moon to guide the way, so she moved from memory. Darkness was deep and without shadows. She didn't look when she entered the bedroom, but she knew Cliff was still beside her.

What now? she thought with sudden panic. What was she doing, bringing him here, to the single spot she considered purely private? He might learn more than she wanted before he left again, yet she might learn nothing more than she already knew. They wanted each other; it was unexplainable. It was undeniable.

As her nerves stretched tighter, Maggie was grateful for the dark. She didn't want him to see the doubts that would be clear on her face. As the need grew stronger, she knew she wouldn't have been able to conceal that, either. Darkness was better, she told herself, because it was anonymous. When he touched her, her body went rigid with a dozen conflicting emotions.

Feeling it, Cliff ran his hands over the slope of her shoulders, down to her lower back. He found he didn't want her to be too relaxed, to be too yielding. Not yet. He wanted to know she struggled against something deeper, something unnamed, even as he did.

"You don't want to give in to this," Cliff said quietly. "Or to me."

"No." Yet she felt the tremor, not fear but pleasure, course through her body when he slipped his hands under her thin wool sweater. "No, I don't."

"What choice is there?"

She could see his face through the gloom of darkness, close, very close, to hers. "Damn you," she whispered. "There's none at all."

He slid his hands up her naked back, through the neck opening of her sweater, until his fingers found her hair. "No, not for either of us."

His body was firm against hers. His voice, soft and low, was faintly edged with anger. She caught the scent of soap, sharp, unrepentantly male, that lingered on his skin. His face was mysterious, indistinct in the darkness. He might've been anyone. As Maggie felt the next fierce pull of desire, she almost wished he was.

"Make love with me," she demanded. A decision made quickly, freely, would leave no room for regrets. "Take me now. It's all either of us wants."

Was it? The question had barely formed in his mind when his mouth was on hers. Then there were no questions, just flame and flash and power. Understanding, if there had been any before, dimmed. Reason vanished. Sensation, and only sensation, ruled. While perhaps both of them had expected it, they were caught in a maelstrom in which neither of them had any control. Racked by it, they fell together onto the bed and let the fire rage.

He could find no gentleness to give her, but it seemed she neither demanded nor expected any. He wanted her naked but not vulnerable, soft but not yielding. If he had spoken the needs aloud, she could have been no more what he'd asked for. As she arched against him, her lips clung in a wild, urgent kiss that was only a prelude to passion. He pulled at her clothes, forgetting finesse, then caught his breath when, in an equal frenzy, she began to strip him.

Clothes were tossed aside as if they were meaningless. Her scent rose up from her skin, from her hair, clouding whatever logic he might have tried to regain. The mattress swayed and dipped as they rolled over it, mindless now of the rain, of the dark, of time and place.

Then they were naked, heated flesh to heated flesh. The desperation grew in each to have all there could be of the other. Whispered demands, labored breathing, moans and sighs of pleasure, drowned out the sound of falling rain. Her body was small and supple and surprisingly strong. All three aspects combined to drive him mad.

This was what it meant to be consumed. Maggie knew it as his hands skimmed over her, inciting thrill after thrill. She hungered, no, starved, for each new demand. Greedy for what pleasure he would give and what pleasure she would take, she allowed him whatever he wanted. She felt no shame, no hesitation, in tasting, in touching, in asking for more or in taking it.

If his body had been designed to her wish, it could have been no more perfect. She reveled in the leanness, the cords of muscle, the long, narrow bones that ran along his hips. Wherever, whenever, she touched, she could almost feel the blood throb under his skin.

She wanted to know he had no more control than she. She wanted to know they were both victims of their own combined power. The fuse that had been lit between them with a look was burning quickly. Desire was madness, and if the words she'd written were true, she'd cast aside her reason for it.

With a savageness they both craved, they came together, fighting to prolong an outrageous passion, greedy to capture that final flash of pleasure. She thought of whirlpools and high winds and the bellow of thunder. She felt the spin, the speed, and heard the roar. Then both her mind and body shuddered from the last violent surge.

Love? Maggie thought some dim time later, when her thoughts began to clear again. If this was making love, she'd been innocent all her life. Could something with so gentle a name have such a violent effect on the body? Hers was pulsing and throbbing as if she'd raced up one side of a mountain and fallen off the other. She'd written songs about love, songs about passion, yet she'd never fully understood her own words until now.

Until now, she thought, when the man who lay beside her had dared her to live her own fantasies. With him she'd found the answer to the dark, driving needs that gave the grit, or the wistfulness, to most of her music. She understood, but understanding opened the door to dozens of questions.

Maggie ran a hand up her own body, astonished at the lingering sense of power and of wonder. How long had she been waiting for this night to come? Perhaps it was possible for passion to lie dormant, unexplored, until it was triggered by a certain person at a certain time.

Maggie thought of the film her music would score. It had been that way for the female character. She'd been content with life, almost smug, until one day a man had entered it, a man she'd shared little common ground with, a man who'd ignited a spark that had changed everything. It hadn't mattered that the woman was intelligent, successful, independent. The man, merely by existing, had altered the scope and pattern of her life.

If the same thing was happening to her, there was still time to stop it before she, too, became so consumed by needs, so ruled by desire, that nothing would ever be the same again.

In the film, the relationship had spawned violence. Instinct told her that there was something between her and Cliff that could do the same. There was little moderation in either of them. It was extremes, she knew, that played havoc with human nature.

Maybe fate had brought her to this serene little plot of land with its undertones of violence. The same fate might have brought her to this taciturn, physical man who seemed connected with both the tranquillity and the danger. The question now was whether she was strong enough to deal with the consequences of each.

What, Maggie asked herself while she stared into the darkness, would happen next?

Because nothing was as he'd expected it, Cliff was silent. He'd wanted passion, but he'd never imagined the scope of it. He'd wanted what her song had whispered of, but the reality had been much more dramatic than any words or any melody. He'd been certain that once the tension between them had been released, once the lure had been accepted, the needs would lessen.

It was true his body was sated with a pleasure more intense than anything he'd known, but his mind— Cliff closed his eyes, wishing his mind would rest as easy. But it was too full of her. So full that he knew even a touch would set his body raging again. That kind of need was a shade too close to dependence for comfort. They had nothing to offer each other, he reminded himself, nothing but outrageous mutual desire.

And suddenly he remembered a line from her song. "Desire is madness."

If he could have stopped himself, he wouldn't have touched her again. He was already reaching for her.

"You're cold," he murmured, automatically drawing her against him to warm her.

"A bit." There was an awkwardness she didn't know how to alleviate and a need she didn't know how to explain.

"Here." He tugged the tangled spread over her, then pulled her close again. "Better?"

"Yes." Her body relaxed against his, even as her thoughts continued to race.

They lapsed into silence again, neither knowing quite how to deal with what had flared between them. Cliff listened to the rain beat against the window glass, adding to the sense of isolation. Even on a clear night, he knew, you would see no light from a neighboring house. "Are you having trouble staying out here alone?"

"Trouble?" Maggie hedged. She wanted to stay exactly as she was, wrapped close around him, warm and safe and untroubled. She didn't want to think now of staying in the big house alone, of sleeping alone.

"This place is more isolated than most around here." How soft she was, he thought. It brought him an odd sort of contentment to feel her hair lie against his shoulder. "A lot of people, even if they were raised here, would have trouble being this far back and alone, especially after everything that's happened."

No, she didn't want to talk about it. Maggie closed her eyes, reminding herself that she'd come here determined to take care of herself, to deal with whatever came. She drew a deep breath, but when she started to shift away, Cliff held her still.

"You are having trouble."

"No. No, not really." Her biggest problem at the moment was to keep her mind and body from wanting more of him. Opening her eyes again, she stared at the rain-drenched window. "I'll admit I've had a couple of restless nights since—well, since we started to dig the pond. It isn't easy knowing what happened in that gully ten years ago, and I have a very active imagination."

"Part of the job?" He turned toward her a bit more, so that her leg slid casually between his. Her skin was smooth as polished glass.

"I suppose." She laughed, but he thought he detected nerves in it. "One night I was certain I heard someone in the house."

He stopped stroking her hair, drawing her back far enough to see her eyes. "In the house?"

"Just my imagination," she said with a shrug. "Boards creaking in the attic, stealthy footsteps on the stairs, doors opening and closing. I worked myself up into quite a state."

He didn't like the sound of it, even in her dismissive tone of voice. "Don't you have a phone in this room?" Cliff demanded.

"Well, yes, but—"

"Why didn't you call the police?"

Maggie sighed and wished she'd never mentioned anything about it. He sounded like a cranky older brother scolding his scatterbrained sister. "Because I'd left the kitchen extension off the hook. I'd been trying to work that afternoon, and—" The word scatterbrained flowed back into her head. Embarrassed, she trailed off. "Anyway, it's better that I didn't call. I felt like an idiot in the morning in any case."

Imagination or not, Cliff reflected, she was still a woman alone, isolated, and everyone in a ten-mile radius knew it. "Are you locking your doors?"

"Cliff—"

"Maggie." He rolled until she was on her back and he was looking down at her. "Are you locking your doors?"

"I wasn't," she said, annoyed. "But after the sheriff came by, I—"

"Stan was here?"

A breath hissed out between her teeth. "Damn it, do you know how often you cut me off in the middle of a sentence?"

"Yes. When did Stan come by?"

"The day after the state police were here. He wanted to reassure me." She wasn't cold now, not with the way his body was pressed against hers. Desire began to stir again, not too quiet, not too slow. "He seems to know his job."

"He's been a good sheriff."

"But?" Maggie prompted, sensing more.

"Just a personal thing," Cliff murmured, shifting away again. Maggie felt the chill return immediately.

"Joyce," she said flatly, and started to rise. Cliff's arm came out to pin her down.

"You have a habit of saying little and implying a lot." His voice was cool now, his hold firm. "It's quite a talent."

"It seems we have little to say to each other."

"I don't have to explain myself to you."

She lay stiff and still. "I'm not asking you to."

"The hell you aren't." Angry, he sat up, drawing her with him so that the cover dropped away. Her skin was pale, her hair like a flood of night over her shoulders. Despite a strong will and a keen sense of privacy, he felt compelled to clarify. "Joyce's been like my sister. When she married Stan, I gave her away. I'm godfather to her oldest girl. It might be difficult for you to understand that kind of friendship."

It wasn't. It had been like that between herself and Jerry. The friendship had gradually deteriorated during marriage, because the marriage had been a mistake. "No, I understand it," Maggie said quietly. "I don't understand why you seem so concerned about her."

"That's my business."

"It certainly is."

He swore again. "Look, Joyce has been going through a difficult time. She never wanted to stay in Morganville. When she was a kid, she'd had ideas about going to the city and studying to be an actress."

"She wanted to act?"

"Pipe dreams, maybe." Cliff moved his shoulders. "Maybe not. She let them go when she married Stan, but she's never been happy staying in Morganville. One of the reasons she sold the house was so they'd have enough money to move. Stan won't budge."

"They could compromise."

"Stan doesn't understand how important it is to her to get away from here. She was eighteen when she married. Then she had three children over the next five years. She spent the first part of her life following her father's rules, the second caring for her children and her mother. A woman like you wouldn't understand that."

"I'm sick of that!" Maggie exploded, jerking away from him. "I'm sick to death of you putting me in some category. Pampered celebrity with no conception of how real people feel or live." Anger rocketed through her, so quick and powerful she never thought to repress it. "What kind of man are you, going to bed with a woman you haven't an ounce of respect for?"

Stunned by the sudden, passionate outburst, he watched her spring from the bed. "Wait a minute."

"No, I've made enough mistakes for one evening." She began to search for her clothes among those scattered on the floor. "You had your dinner and your sex," she said in a brittle tone. "Now get out."

Fury rose so that he had to fight it back. She was right, Cliff told himself. He'd come to take her to bed; that was all. Intimacy didn't always equal closeness. He wasn't interested in being close to her or in becoming involved with anything more than her body. Even as he thought it, the emptiness of it washed over him. The contentment he'd felt so briefly vanished. He could hear her unsteady breathing as she pulled on her sweater. Reaching for his clothes, he tried to concentrate on the sound of the rain instead.

"We're not finished, you and I," he murmured.

"Aren't we?" Enraged, aching, Maggie turned. She could feel the tears well in her eyes, but felt secure in the darkness. The sweater skimmed her thighs, leaving the length of her legs naked. She knew what he thought of her, and this time would give him the satisfaction of believing he was right. "We went to bed, and it was good for both of us," she said easily. "Not all one-night stands are as successful. You get a high rating as a lover, Cliff, if that helps your ego."

This time there was no controlling the temper that roared into him. Grabbing both her arms, he pulled her toward him. "Damn you, Maggie."

"Why?" she tossed back. "Because I said it first? Go home and curl up with your double standard, Cliff. I don't need it."

Everything she said hit home, and hit hard. If he stayed, he wasn't certain what he might do. Throttle her? It was tempting. Drag her back to bed and purge himself of the angry desire that pounded in him? More temptation. As he held her, he wasn't sure if it was he who was shaking or her, but he knew if he stayed, something volatile, perhaps irrevocable, would burst.

Dropping his hands, he walked from the room. "Lock your doors," he called out, and cursed her as he strode down the stairs.

Maggie wrapped her arms around herself and let the tears overflow. It was much too late for locks, she thought.

## *Chapter 8*

For the next few days, Maggie worked like a Trojan. Her kitchen floor was sealed, making it her first fully and successfully completed project. She added three fresh strips of wallpaper to her bedroom, found a rug for the music room and cleaned the trim in the downstairs hall.

In the evenings, she worked at her piano until she was too tired to see the keys or hear her own music. She kept her phone off the hook. All in all, she decided, the life of a recluse had its advantages. She was productive, and no one interfered with the flow of her days. It became almost possible to believe that was what she wanted and no more.

Perhaps she was pushing herself. She might admit that, but she wouldn't admit she did so to prevent herself from thinking about her night with Cliff. That had been a mistake. It wasn't wise to dwell on mistakes.

She saw no one, spoke to no one, and told herself she was content to go on that way indefinitely.

But of course complete solitude lasts only so long. Maggie was painting the window trim in the music room when she heard the sound of an approaching car. She debated whether she might just ignore the caller until he or she went away again. As a beginning recluse, it was certainly her right. Then she recognized the old Lincoln. Setting the paint bucket on the drop cloth at her feet, Maggie went to the front door to meet Louella Morgan.

She looked even more frail this time, Maggie mused. Her skin seemed almost translucent against the tidy white hair. It was an odd, somewhat eerie combination of youth and age. As Maggie watched, Louella looked over toward the gully. For a moment she seemed like a statue, unmoving, unblinking, unbreathing. When Maggie saw her take a step toward the fenced-off section, she walked outside.

"Good morning, Mrs. Morgan."

Louella glanced up, her eyes focusing slowly. The hand she lifted to pat at her hair shook lightly. "I wanted to come."

"Of course." Maggie smiled and hoped she was doing the right thing. "Please come in. I was about to fix some coffee."

Louella walked up the sagging steps Maggie had yet to contact Bog about. "You've made some changes."

Unsure which route to take, she decided on light, cheerful chatter. "Yes, inside and out. The landscapers work faster than I do." Killer stood in the doorway, snarling and backing up. Maggie hushed him as they went inside.

"This wallpaper was here when we moved in," Louella murmured, looking around the hall. "I always meant to change it."

"Did you?" Maggie led her gently toward the living room as she spoke. “Perhaps you could give me some suggestions. I haven’t quite made up my mind yet.”

“Something warm,” Louella said softly. “Something warm, with subtle color, so people would feel welcome. That’s what I wanted.”

“Yes, I’m sure that’s just what it needs.” She wanted to put her arm around the woman and tell her she understood. Perhaps it was kinder not to.

“A house like this should smell of lemon oil and flowers.”

“It will,” Maggie told her, wishing she could change the scent of dust and paint.

“I always felt it should be filled with children.” She gazed around the room with the kind of misty concentration that made Maggie think she was seeing it as it had been more than twenty years before. “Children give a house its personality, you know, more than its decorating. They leave their mark on it.”

“You have grandchildren, don’t you?” Maggie steered her toward the sofa.

“Yes, Joyce’s children. The baby’s in school now. Time goes so quickly for the young. You’ve looked at the pictures?” Louella asked suddenly.

“The pictures?” Maggie’s brow creased, then cleared. “Oh, yes, I’ve really only had a chance to glance at them. I’ve been a bit tied up.” Remembering, she walked to the mantel and retrieved the envelope. “Your roses looked beautiful. I’m not sure I’d have that kind of talent.”

Louella took the envelope and stared down at it. “Roses need love and discipline. Like children.”

Maggie decided against another offer of coffee. Instead, she sat down beside Louella. “Perhaps if we looked at them together it would help.”

"Old pictures." Louella opened the flap and drew them out. "There's so much to see in old pictures if you know where to look. Early spring," she murmured, looking down at the first snapshot. "You see, the hyacinths are blooming, and the daffodils."

Maggie studied the square, pristine black and white, but it was the man and small girl who caught her attention rather than the flowers. He was tall, broad in the chest, with a sharp-boned, lantern-jawed face. The suit he wore was severe and proper. Beside him, the little girl wore a frilly dress, ribboned at the waist with black strap shoes and a flowered bonnet.

It must've been Easter, Maggie concluded. The little girl smiled determinedly at the camera. Joyce would've been around four then, Maggie calculated, and perhaps a bit uncomfortable in the organdy and flounces. William Morgan didn't look cruel, she thought as she studied his set, unreadable face. He simply looked untouchable. She fought back a shudder and spoke lightly.

"I want to plant some bulbs myself. Things should be a little more settled by fall."

Louella said nothing as she turned over the next picture. This time Maggie was looking at a young Louella. The style of hair and dress told her the picture was more than twenty years old. The lopsided angle of the shot made her suspect that Joyce had taken it as a child.

"The roses," Louella murmured, running a finger over the picture where they grew in profusion. "Gone now, with no one to care for them."

"Do you have a garden now?"

"Joyce does." Louella set the picture aside and took up another. "I tend it now and then, but it isn't the same as having your own."

"No, it's not, but Joyce must be grateful for your help."

"She's never been easy in town," Louella said, half to herself. "Never easy. A pity she took after me rather than her father."

"She's lovely," Maggie told her, searching for something to say. "I hope to see more of her. Her husband suggested that we have dinner."

"Stan's a good man. Solid. He's always loved her." The sad, elusive smile touched her lips. "He's been kind to me."

When she turned over the next picture, Maggie felt her stiffen. She saw the smile freeze rather than fade. Looking down, she saw William Morgan and a young, perhaps teenaged Stan Agee. This more recent photo was in color, and the trees in the background were vibrant with fall. The two men were dressed in flannel shirts and caps, and each wore a drab-colored vest with what looked to Maggie like small weights around the hem. Each carried a shotgun.

Shells, not weights, Maggie realized as she looked at the vests again. They must've been hunting. And they stood, she noted, near the slope of the gully. Disturbed, she looked at the trees again, at the tapestry she wanted to see for herself.

"Joyce would've taken this," Louella murmured. "She hunted with her father. He taught her how to handle guns before she was twelve. It didn't matter that she hated them; she learned to please him. William looks pleased," Louella continued, though Maggie couldn't see it. "He liked to hunt this land. Now we know he died here. Here," she repeated, placing a palm over the picture. "Not three miles away, in the river. He never left his land. Somehow I think I always knew."

"Mrs. Morgan." Maggie set the pictures aside and laid a hand on her arm. "I know this must be difficult for you; it must be like going through it all over again. I wish there was something I could do."

Turning her head, Louella fixed Maggie with a long, unsmiling stare. "Put in your pond," she said flatly. "Plant your flowers. That's as it should be. The rest is over."

When she started to rise, Maggie found herself more disturbed by the emotionless reply than she would've been with a bout of tears. "Your pictures," she began helplessly.

"Keep them." Louella walked to the doorway before she turned. "I've no need for them anymore."

Should she have been depressed? Maggie wondered as she listened to the car drive away. Was her reaction normal empathy for another's tragedy, or was she allowing herself to become personally involved again? Over the last few days, she'd nearly convinced herself that the Morgan business had nothing to do with her. Now, after one brief contact, it was beginning again.

Yet it was more than a sense of involvement, Maggie admitted as she rubbed her arms to bring back warmth. There'd been something eerie in the way Louella had looked at the pictures. As if, Maggie reflected, she'd been putting the people in them to rest, though only one was dead.

Imagination again, she scolded herself. An overactive one. Yet hadn't there been something odd in the way Louella had studied that last snapshot? It had been as if she'd been searching for details, looking for something. With a frown, Maggie walked over and sifted through the pictures herself, stopping when she came to the color print.

There was William Morgan again, his hair a bit thinner, his eyes a bit sterner than they'd been in the Easter photo. Sheriff Agee stood beside him, hardly more than a boy, his build not quite filled out, his hair a little shaggy. He'd looked even more like a beachcomber in his youth, Maggie decided, though he held the gun as if he were very familiar with firearms. Looking at him, Maggie could easily see why Joyce had fallen for him hard enough to give up dreams of fame and fortune. He was young, handsome, with a trace of cocky sexuality around his mouth.

She could understand, too, why Joyce had feared and obeyed and struggled to please the man beside him. William Morgan looked straight at the camera, legs spread, the gun held in both hands. Cliff had described him as a hard, cold man. Maggie had no trouble believing him, but it didn't explain why Louella had been so disturbed by this one picture. Or why, Maggie added, she herself became uneasy when she looked at it.

Annoyed by her own susceptibility, she started to study the picture more closely when the rumble outside warned of another approaching vehicle.

*When it rains it pours,* she thought bad-temperedly. Tossing the picture carelessly on top of the others, she walked to the window. When Cliff's pickup came into view, the flare of excitement left her shaken. *Oh, no,* Maggie warned herself. *Not again. A woman who makes the same mistake twice deserves what she gets.* Determined, she picked up her brush and began to paint in long, hard strokes. Let him knock all he wanted, she thought with an angry toss of her head. She had work to do.

Minutes passed, but he didn't come to her door. Maggie continued to paint, telling herself it didn't matter to her what he was doing outside. When she tried to lean closer to the window to look through, paint smeared from the sill to her jeans. Swearing, she wiped at it and made it worse.

She didn't give a damn about Cliff Delaney, Maggie told herself. But she did care about having people wander around on her land. It was her right to go out and see what he was up to and order him away, she told herself as she set down her brush. If he were only checking on how her grass was growing, she fumed as she headed for the door, he should still have the courtesy to announce himself. By not announcing himself, he was denying her the satisfaction of ignoring him.

She yanked open the door but didn't, as she'd expected, see him bending over the little green sprouts that had begun to shoot up through the topsoil. Neither was he looking out over the plugs of phlox or the juniper shrubs on her front bank. Perhaps, Maggie thought with a frown, he'd gone around to check on the last project to be completed, the crown vetch on her eroding rear bank.

Annoyed that she hadn't thought of that in the first place, she started to turn back into the house when a movement near the gully caught her eye. For an instant, basic, primitive fear that slept in her awoke. She thought of ghouls and phantoms and legends of shades that never rest. In the next instant she recognized Cliff. As infuriated as she was embarrassed by her own reaction, she went to confront him.

As she drew closer, Maggie saw the willow, slender, small and tenderly green. Cliff was setting the ball of roots into a hole he'd dug out of the rocky soil with a pick and shovel. He stood perhaps six feet from the slope of the gully, his shirt tossed carelessly on the ground. She could see the muscles in his back ripple as he began to shovel dirt back into the hole. The twinge of her stomach told her that her reaction to him was no less powerful now than it had been before they'd made love.

Maggie straightened her shoulders and angled her chin. "What're you doing?"

Because he continued to shovel without breaking rhythm, she decided he'd known she was coming. "Planting a tree," Cliff said easily.

Her eyes narrowed dangerously. "I can see that. As far as I remember, I didn't order a willow from you."

"No." He knelt down to mound and smooth the dirt at the base of the tree. She watched his hands, knowing now what they could do on her body. It seemed he had the same talent with soil. "No charge."

Impatient with his nonanswers and with her own growing arousal, she folded her arms. "Why are you planting a tree I didn't buy?"

Satisfied that the willow was secure, he rose. Leaning casually on the shovel, he studied her. No, he hadn't gotten her out of his system, Cliff decided. Seeing her again didn't relieve the knots of tension he'd been living with for days. Somehow he'd known it wouldn't, but he'd had to try. "Some people might call it a peace offering," he told her at length, then watched her mouth open and close again.

Maggie looked at the tree. It was so young, so fragile, but one day she would see it in full sweep, spreading over her pond, and— She stopped, realizing that it was the first time she'd thought of going through with the pond since the discovery. He must have known that, just as he'd known the willow might be enough to make her see the beauty and serenity again. Most of her anger had drained before she remembered to hold on to any of it.

"A peace offering," she repeated, running a finger down one delicate leaf. "Is that what you call it?"

Her voice had been cool, but he saw that her eyes had already started to warm. He wondered how many strong men she'd slain with that one look. "Maybe." He sliced the shovel into the ground where it stood, tilting slightly to the left. "Got anything cold in there to drink?"

It was an apology, Maggie decided, perhaps the only kind a man like him could give. It only took her five seconds to decide to accept it. "Maybe," she said in an equal tone, then turned to walk back toward the house. A smile curved her lips when he fell into step beside her. "Your men did an excellent job," she continued while they circled around toward the rear of the house. "I'm anxious to see how the stuff over the retaining wall's going to look."

"Crown vetch," Cliff supplied before he stopped to check the job, as she'd suspected he would. "You should see something come through in four or five more days. It'll spread fast enough to cover this bank before summer's over." He kept his hands in his back pockets as he studied the work his men had done and thought of the woman beside him. "You've been busy?"

Maggie lifted a brow. "I suppose so. The house needs a lot of attention."

"Seen the paper?"

"No," she said, puzzled. "Why?"

Cliff shrugged, then walked ahead to the screen door to open it. "There was a big story on finding William Morgan buried on his old land. Land," he continued when Maggie moved by him into the kitchen, "recently purchased by a celebrated songwriter."

She turned sharply. "They had my name?"

"Yeah, it was mentioned—several times."

"Damn," she whispered, and, forgetting he'd asked for a drink, she dropped into a chair. "I'd wanted to avoid that." Half hopefully, she glanced up. "The local paper?"

Helping himself, Cliff went to the refrigerator and searched out a soda. "Morganville doesn't have a paper. There were stories in the *Frederick Post* and the *Herald Mail.*" As he twisted off the top, he nodded toward the phone sitting off the hook. "If you hadn't done that, you'd have already answered a flood of calls from reporters." And from himself, Cliff thought silently. In the past twenty-four hours, he'd called her a dozen times. He'd vacillated between being frantic and furious every time he'd gotten a busy signal. What kind of woman left her phone off the hook for hours at a time? One who was independent of the outside world, he mused, or one who was hiding from it. Lifting the bottle, he drank. "That your escape route these days?"

In defense, Maggie rose and slammed the receiver back in place. "I don't need to escape from anything. You said yourself that this whole business doesn't have anything to do with me."

"So I did." He examined the liquid left in the bottle. "Maybe you were escaping from something else." He shifted his gaze until it locked on hers. "Were you hiding from me, Maggie?"

"Certainly not." She swept over to the sink and began to scrub the paint splatters from her hands. "I told you, I've been busy."

"Too busy to answer the phone?"

"The phone's a distraction. If you want to start an argument, Cliff, you can just take your peace offering and—" The phone shrilled behind her so that she ended her suggestion with an oath. Before she could answer it herself, Cliff had picked up the phone.

"Yes?" He watched the fury spring into her eyes as he leaned on the counter. He'd missed that, he discovered, just as he'd missed the subtle sexiness of the scent she wore. "No, I'm sorry, Miss Fitzgerald isn't available for comment." He replaced the receiver while Maggie wiped her damp hands on her jeans.

"I can screen my own calls, thank you. When I want a liaison, I'll let you know."

He drank from the bottle again. "Just saving you some aggravation."

"I don't want you or anyone to save me aggravation," she fumed. "It's my aggravation, and I'll do whatever I want with it." He grinned, but before she could think of any retaliation, the phone rang again. "Don't you dare," she warned. Shoving him aside, she answered herself.

"Hello."

"Damn it, Maggie, you've been leaving the phone off the hook again."

She let out a huff of breath. A reporter might've been easier to deal with. "Hello, C.J. How are you?"

"I'll tell you how I am!"

Maggie drew the phone back from her ear and scowled at Cliff. "There's no need for you to hang around."

He took another long sip from the bottle before he settled back comfortably. "I don't mind."

"Maggie!" C.J.'s voice vibrated in her ear. "Who the hell are you talking to?"

"Nobody," she mumbled, deliberately turning her back on Cliff. "You were going to tell me how you were."

"For the past twenty-four hours I've been frantic trying to get through to you. Maggie, it's irresponsible to leave your phone off the hook when people're trying to reach you."

There was a bag of cookies on the counter. Maggie dug into it, then bit into one with a vengeance. "Obviously I left it off the hook so I couldn't be reached."

"If I hadn't gotten you this time, I was going to send a telegram, and I'm not even sure they deliver telegrams in that place. What the hell have you been doing?"

"I've been working," she said between her teeth. "I can't work when the phone's ringing off the wall and people are forever coming by. I moved out here to be alone. I'm still waiting for that to happen."

"That's a nice attitude," he tossed back. In Los Angeles, C.J. searched through his desk drawer for a roll of antacids. "You've got people all over the country worried about you."

"Damn it, people all over the country don't have to worry about me. I'm fine!"

"You sound fine."

With an effort, Maggie controlled her precarious temper. When she lost it with C.J., she invariably lost the bout, as well. "I'm sorry I snapped at you, C.J., but I'm tired of being criticized for doing what I want to do."

"I'm not criticizing you," he grumbled over the peppermint-flavored pill. "It's just natural concern. For God's sake, Maggie, who wouldn't be concerned after that business in the paper?"

She tensed and, without thinking, turned back to face Cliff. He was watching her intently, the neck of the bottle held loosely in his fingers. "What business in the paper?"

"About that man's—ah, what was left of that man being dug up on your property. Good God, Maggie, I nearly had a heart attack when I read it. Then, not being able to reach you—"

"I'm sorry." She dragged a hand through her hair. "I'm really sorry, C.J. I didn't think it would hit the papers, at least not out there."

"So what I didn't know wouldn't hurt me?"

She smiled at the offended tone of voice. "Yes, something like that. I'd've called you with the details if I'd realized the news would get that far."

"Get this far?" he retorted, unappeased. "Maggie, you know that anything with your name in it's going to hit the press on both sides of the Atlantic."

She began to rub one finger slowly up and down her right temple. "And you know that was one of the reasons I wanted to get out."

"Where you live isn't going to change that."

She sighed. "Apparently not."

"Besides, that doesn't have anything to do with what's happened now," C.J. argued. He pressed a hand to his nervous stomach and wondered if a glass of Perrier would calm him. Maybe scotch would be a better idea.

"I haven't seen the paper," Maggie began in an even tone, "but I'm sure the whole thing was blown out of proportion."

"Blown out of proportion?" Again, she had to move the receiver back from her ear. A few steps away, Cliff heard C.J.'s voice clearly. "Did you or did you not stumble over a pile of—of bones?"

She grimaced at the image. "Not exactly." She had to concentrate harder on keeping her voice calm. "Actually, it was the dog that found them. The police came right out and took over. I really haven't been involved." She saw Cliff lift a brow at her final statement but made no comment.

"Maggie, it said that man had been murdered and buried right there, only yards from your house."

"Ten years ago." She pressed her fingers more firmly against her temple.

"Maggie, come home."

She closed her eyes, because his voice held the kind of plea that was hard to resist. "C.J., I am home."

"Damn it, how am I supposed to sleep at night thinking of you alone out in the middle of nowhere? For God's sake, you're one of the most successful, wealthiest, most celebrated women in the world, and you're living in Dogpatch."

"If I'm successful, wealthy and celebrated, I can live wherever I want." She struggled against temper again. However he phrased it, whatever his tone, the concern was real. It was better to concentrate on that. "Besides, C.J., I have the vicious guard dog you sent me." She looked down to where Killer was sleeping peacefully at Cliff's feet. When she lifted her gaze, she found herself smiling into Cliff's face. "I couldn't be safer."

"If you hired a bodyguard—"

Now she laughed. "You're being an old woman again. The last thing I need's a bodyguard. I'm fine," she went on quickly before he could comment. "I've finished the score, I've a dozen ideas for new songs running around in my head, and I'm even considering another musical. Why don't you tell me how brilliant the score was?"

"You know it's brilliant," he mumbled. "It's probably the best thing you've done."

"More," she insisted. "Tell me more. My ego's starving."

He sighed, recognizing defeat. "When I played it for the producers, they were ecstatic. It was suggested that you come out and supervise the recording."

"Forget it." She began to pace to the sink and back again.

"Damn it, we'd come to you, but there's no studio in Hicksville."

"Morganville," she corrected mildly. "You don't need me for the recording."

"They want you to do the title song."

"What?" Surprised, she stopped her restless pacing.

"Now listen to me before you say no." C.J. straightened in his chair and put on his best negotiator's voice. "I realize you've always refused to perform or record, and I've never pressed you. But this is something I really think you should consider. Maggie, that song's dynamite, absolute dynamite, and nobody's going to be able to put into it what you did. After I played the tape, everyone in the room needed a cold shower."

Though she laughed, Maggie couldn't quite put the idea aside. "I can think of a half-dozen artists who could deliver that number, C.J. You don't need me."

"I can think of a dozen who could deliver it," he countered. "But not like you. The song needs you, Maggie. At least you could think about it."

She told herself she'd already refused him enough for one day. "Okay, I'll think about it."

"You let me know in a week."

"C.J.—"

"Okay, okay, two weeks."

"All right. And I'm sorry about the phone."

"You could at least get one of those hateful answering machines."

"Maybe. Take care of yourself, C.J."

"I always do. Just take your own advice."

"I always do. Bye." She hung up, heaving a long sigh. "I feel like I've just been taken to task by the school principal."

Cliff watched her pick up a folded dish towel, crumple it, then set it down again. "You know how to handle him."

"I've had plenty of practice."

"What's C.J. stand for?"

"Constant Jitters," she murmured, then shook her head. "No, to tell you the truth, I haven't any idea."

"Does he always give you a hard time?"

"I suppose." She picked up the dish towel again. "It seems the news hit the papers on the Coast. Then, when he couldn't reach me..." She trailed off, frowning out the window.

"You're tense."

She dropped the cloth over the edge of the sink. "No."

"Yes," Cliff corrected. "I can see it." Reaching out, he ran his hand down the side of her neck to the curve of her shoulder. "I can feel it."

The brush of his fingers made her skin hum. Slowly, she turned her head. "I don't want you to do that."

Deliberately, he took his other hand on a like journey, so that he could knead at the tension in both of her shoulders. Was it her nerves he sought to soothe or his own? "To touch you?" he said quietly. "It's difficult not to."

Knowing she was already weakening, Maggie lifted her hands to his wrists. "Put some effort into it," she advised as she tried to push him aside.

"I have for the past few days." His fingers pressed into her skin and released, pressed and released, in a rhythm that caused her bones to liquefy. "I decided it was a misdirection of energy when I could put the same effort into making love to you."

Her mind was starting to haze, her breath beginning to tremble. "We've nothing to give each other."

"We both know better than that." He lowered his head so that his lips could brush along the temple he'd seen her stroke while on the phone.

A sigh escaped before she stopped it. This wasn't what she wanted—it was everything she wanted. "Sex is—"

"A necessary and enjoyable part of life," Cliff finished before he moved his lips down to tease hers.

So this was seduction, Maggie thought as her mind began to float. This was arousal without will. She knew she wasn't resisting, but yielding, melting, submitting, just as she knew that when surrender was complete, her bridges would be in flames behind her.

"We'll only be two people sharing a bed," she murmured. "There's nothing else."

Whether it was a question or a statement, Cliff tried to believe it was true. If there was more, it wouldn't end, and he'd find himself tangled around a woman he barely understood for the rest of his life. If there were only needs, he could relinquish his control and race with them. If there was only desire, he could take whatever he wanted with no consequences. When she was softening and heating in his arms, what did he care for consequences?

"Let me feel you," he murmured against her lips. "I want your skin under my hands, smooth and hot, your heart pounding."

Anything, she thought dizzily. She'd give him anything, as long as he stayed close like this, as long as his mouth continued that dark, desperate, delirious seduction of her senses. He tugged her T-shirt over her head, then ran his hands down her sides, up again, so that the friction had her nearly mad for more. His shirt scraped against her taut nipples until his hands came between them to possess.

He could feel her heart beat now, and she could hear it pounding in her own head. Her thighs pressed against his with only two layers of thin, soft denim between. She could remember every slope and plane of his body, how it had felt warm and urgent and naked on hers.

He smelled of work and the outdoors, traces of sweat and turned earth. As the scent raced through her senses, she took her lips over his face and throat to draw in the taste.

Uncivilized, like the land that held them both. Alluring and not quite tamed, like the thick woods that surrounded them. If she thought at all, this is how she thought of the need that burned between them. There was danger in both, and pleasure and wonder. Throwing aside all reason, Maggie gave herself to it.

"Now," she demanded huskily. "I want you now."

With no sense of time or place, no hesitation, they lowered onto the floor. The struggle with clothes only added to the aura of desperation and unrelenting desire that sprang back whenever they touched. Warmth against warmth, they found each other.

When the phone shrilled on the wall beside them, neither heard. Whether it was by choice or the will of fate, there was nothing for either of them but each other.

A tremble, a moan, a rough caress, the scent and fury of passion; that was their world. Urgently and more urgently, they sought the taste and touch of each other, as if the hunger would never abate, as if neither would allow it to. The floor was hard and smooth beneath them. They rolled over it as if it were layered with feathers. Sunlight streamed in, falling over them. They explored all the secrets of the night.

Man for woman, woman for man—time had no place and place no meaning. Hot and open, his mouth found hers, and finding it, he burned with the need to possess her completely. His fingers dug into her hips as he shifted her on top of him so that her skin slid tantalizingly over his. He felt her throb, just as he felt the flood of passion beat against the weakened dam of his control. At the moment of joining, her body arched back in stunned pleasure. The pace was frenetic, leaving them both helpless and raging. On and on they drove each other, mercilessly, ruthlessly.

Through half-closed eyes, Cliff saw her shudder with the speed of the crest. Then he was swept up with her in the power of the ultimate heat dance.

# *Chapter 9*

Had hours passed, or was his sense of time still distorted? Cliff tried to gauge the hour by the slant of the sun through the window, but couldn't be sure. He felt more than rested; he felt vitalized. Turning his head, he watched Maggie as she slept beside him. Though his own actions were vague in his mind, like a half dream that blurs on awakening, he could remember carrying her upstairs where they'd tumbled into bed. Wrapped around each other, they'd fallen into an exhausted sleep. Yes, that part was vague, he mused, but the rest—

On the kitchen floor. He ran a hand over his face, uncertain if he was pleased or astonished. Cliff discovered he was both.

He'd made love to her on the kitchen floor like a frantic teenager in the first spin of desire. By the time a man of experience had reached his thirties, he should be able to show a bit more control, use a bit more finesse. Yet he'd had neither both times he'd made love with her. Cliff wasn't certain that would change if he'd loved her a hundred times. She had some power over him that went deep and triggered frenzy rather than style. And yet… Because she was asleep and unaware, he brushed the hair from her cheek so that he could see more of her face. Looking at her was becoming a habit he wasn't sure could be easily broken. Yet when they lay quiet like this, he was overwhelmed by a sense of protective tenderness. As far as he could remember, no other woman had elicited either response from him before. The knowledge wasn't comfortable.

Perhaps it was because when she slept as she did now, she looked frail, defenseless, small. He'd never been able to resist fragility. When she was in his arms, she was all fire and flare, with a power so potent she seemed indestructible. Challenges were something else he'd never been able to resist.

Just who was Maggie Fitzgerald? Cliff wondered while he traced the shape of her mouth with a fingertip. He wouldn't have said she was beautiful, yet her face had the power to both stun and haunt a man. He hadn't expected her to be kind or compassionate, yet he'd seen the qualities in her. He hadn't expected her to be self-sufficient, yet she was proving to be just that under an uneasy set of circumstances.

He frowned and unconsciously drew her closer. Maggie murmured but slept on. Though he'd told her that she had no connection with what had happened there ten years before, Cliff didn't like knowing she was alone in the big, remote house. Knowing Morganville was a quiet, settled town didn't change that. Even the quiet, the settled, had undercurrents. That had been made plain in the past two weeks.

Whoever had killed William Morgan had gone unpunished for a

decade. Whoever had murdered him had probably walked the streets of town, chatted outside the bank, cheered at Little League games. It wasn't a pleasant thought. Nor was it pleasant to conclude that whoever had killed once might do anything necessary to go on living a quiet, settled life in a town where everyone knew your name and your history. It might be a cliché about the murderer returning to the scene of the crime, but—

She woke up alone, her mind still disoriented. Was it morning? she wondered groggily. When she shifted, lifting both hands to push back her hair, she felt the sweet heaviness in her limbs that came from lovemaking. Abruptly awake, she looked over to see the bed beside her empty.

Perhaps she'd been dreaming. But when she felt the sheets beside her, they were still warm, and when she turned her face into the pillow, his scent lingered on the case.

They'd made love on the kitchen floor, she remembered with a reaction that directly paralleled Cliff's. But she also remembered quite clearly the sensation of being carried up the stairs, gently, as if she'd been something precious. It was a warm memory, different from the erotic scene that had preceded it. A memory like that was something she could hold on to during some long, restless night in the future.

But he'd left, saying nothing.

*Grow up, Maggie,* she ordered herself. *Be sensible.* From the beginning she'd known this wasn't romance but desire. The only thing she'd gain from dwelling on the first was pain. Romance was for the impractical, the vulnerable, the naive. Hadn't she spent a great deal of her time training herself to be none of those things?

He didn't love her; she didn't love him. There was a twinge in her stomach at the second denial that had her biting her lip. No, she insisted, she didn't love him. She couldn't afford to.

He was a hard man, though she'd seen some softer aspects of him. He was intolerant, impatient and more often rude than not. A woman didn't need to fix her heart on a man like that. In any case, he'd made it clear that he wanted her body, and her body only. Twice she'd made the decision to give it to him, so she had no right to regrets, even though he'd left without a word.

Maggie flung her arms over her eyes and refused to acknowledge the growing fear that she'd already given him more than her body, without either of them being aware of it.

Then she heard it, the soft creak directly overhead. Slowly, she lowered her arms, then lay still. When it came the second time, the panic fluttered in her throat. She was awake, it was midafternoon, and the sounds came from the attic, not her imagination.

Though she was shaking, she climbed quietly out of bed. This time she wouldn't cower in her room while someone invaded her home. This time, she thought, moistening her lips as she slipped into her T-shirt, she'd find out who it was and what they wanted. Cold and clearheaded, she took the poker from the fireplace and slipped into the hallway.

The attic stairs were to her right. When she saw that the door at the top was open, fear sliced through her again. It hadn't been opened since she'd moved in. Shaking, determined, she took a firmer grip on the poker and started up the stairs.

At the doorway, she paused, hearing the faint whisper of movement inside. She pressed her lips together, swallowed, then stepped inside.

"Damn it, Maggie, you could hurt someone with that thing."

She jumped back, banging smartly into the doorjamb. "What are you doing up here?" she demanded as Cliff scowled back at her.

"Just checking. When's the last time you were up here?"

She expelled a breath, releasing pent-up tension. "Never. It's far down on my lists of priorities, so I haven't been up since I moved in."

He nodded, taking another glance around. "Someone has."

For the first time, she looked into the room. As she'd suspected, it contained little more than dust and cobwebs. It was high enough that Cliff could stand upright with an inch or so to spare, though at the sides it sloped down with the pitch of the roof. There was an old rocker that might prove interesting after refinishing, a sofa that was hopeless, two lamps without shades and a large upright traveling chest.

"It doesn't look as though anyone's been up here for years."

"More like a week," Cliff corrected. "Take a look at this."

He walked toward the chest, and making a face at the layer of dust on the floor, Maggie padded after him in her bare feet. "So?" she demanded. "Joyce mentioned that there were some things up here she didn't have any use for. I told her not to bother with them, that I'd take care of hauling them out when I was ready."

"I'd say someone already took something out." Cliff crouched in front of the dust-covered chest, then pointed.

Annoyed, stifling the urge to sneeze, Maggie bent toward the dust-covered chest. Then she saw it. Just near the lock, and very faint, was the imprint of a hand. "But—"

Cliff grabbed her wrist before she could touch the imprint herself. "I wouldn't."

"Someone was here," she murmured. "I didn't imagine it." Struggling for calm, she looked back at Cliff. "But what could anyone have wanted up here, in this thing?"

"Good question." He straightened, but kept her hand in his.

She wanted to play it light. "How about a good answer?"

"I think we might see what the sheriff thinks."

"You think it has something to do with—the other thing."

Her voice was steady enough, but with his fingers on her wrist, he knew her pulse wasn't. "I think it's odd that everything's happening at once. Coincidences are curious things. You wouldn't be smart to let this one go."

"No." This wasn't ten years ago, she thought. This was now. "I'll call the sheriff."

"I'll do it."

She stopped in the doorway, bristling. "It's my house," she began.

"It certainly is," Cliff agreed mildly, then stunned her by running both hands up her naked thighs to her hips. "I don't mind looking at you half dressed, but it's bound to distract Stan."

"Very funny."

"No, very beautiful." While she stared, wide-eyed, he lowered his head and kissed her with the first true gentleness he'd shown. She didn't move or speak when he lifted his head again. Her eyes were still open. "I'll call the sheriff," Cliff said roughly. "You get some pants on."

Without waiting for her reply, he was heading down the steps, leaving her staring after him. Dazed, Maggie lifted a finger to trace over her own lips. That, she decided, had been as unexpected and as difficult to explain as anything else that had happened between them.

Utterly confused, Maggie left the poker tilted against the door and went back to her room. She couldn't have known he could kiss like that—tenderly, exquisitely. If she couldn't have known that, she couldn't have known that her heart could stop beating and her lungs could choke up. The totally different kiss had brought on a totally different reaction. This reaction, she knew, had left her without any form of defense.

A passionate, aggressive demand she could meet with passion and aggression of her own. There they were equal, and if she had no control, neither did he. Urgency would be met with urgency, fire with fire, but tenderness… What would she do if he kissed her like that again? And how long would she have to wait until he did? A woman could fall in love with a man who kissed like that.

Maggie caught herself. Some women, she corrected, hastily dragging on her jeans. Not her. She wasn't going to fall in love with Cliff Delaney. He wasn't for her. He wanted no more than—

Then she remembered that he hadn't left without a word. He hadn't left at all.

"Maggie!"

The voice from the bottom of the stairs had her jolting. "Yes." She answered him while she stared at her own astonished face in the mirror.

"Stan's on his way."

"All right, I'm coming down." In a minute, she added silently, in just a minute. Moving like someone who wasn't sure her legs could be trusted, she sat on the bed.

If she was falling in love with him, she'd better admit it now, while there was still time to do something about it. Was there still time? It washed over her that her time had been up days before, perhaps longer. Perhaps it had been up the moment he'd stepped out of his truck onto her land.

Now what? she asked herself. She'd let herself fall for a man she hardly knew, barely understood and wasn't altogether sure she liked a great deal of the time. He certainly didn't understand her and didn't appear to want to.

Yet he'd planted a willow in her yard. Perhaps he understood more than either of them realized. Of course, there couldn't be anything between them, really, she reminded herself hastily. They were poles apart in attitude. Still, for the moment, she had no choice but to follow her heart and hope that her mind would keep her somewhat level. As she rose, Maggie remembered fatalistically that it never had before.

It was quiet downstairs, but as soon as she came to the landing, she smelled coffee. She stood there a moment, wondering if she should be annoyed or pleased that Cliff was making himself at home. Unable to decide, she walked back to the kitchen.

"Want a cup?" Cliff asked as she entered. He was already leaning against the counter in his habitual position, drinking one of his own.

Maggie lifted a brow. "As a matter of fact, I would. Have any trouble finding what you needed?"

He ignored the sarcasm and reached in a cupboard for another cup. "Nope. You haven't eaten lunch."

"I generally don't." She came up behind him to pour the cup herself.

"I do," he said simply. With a naturalness Maggie thought bordered on arrogance, he opened the refrigerator and began to search through it.

"Just help yourself," she muttered before she scalded her tongue on the coffee.

"You'd better learn to stock up," Cliff told her when he found her supplies discouragingly slim. "It isn't unusual to get snowed in on a back road like this for a week at a time in the winter."

"I'll keep that in mind."

"You eat this stuff?" he asked, pushing aside a carton of yogurt.

"I happen to like it." She strode over, intending to slam the refrigerator door whether his hand was inside or not. Cliff outmaneuvered her by plucking out a single chicken leg, then stepping aside. "I'd just like to mention you're eating my dinner."

"Want a bite?" Apparently all amiability, he held out the drumstick. Maggie concentrated on keeping her lips from curving.

"No."

"Funny." Cliff took a bite and chewed thoughtfully. "Just coming into this kitchen seems to work up my appetite."

She shot him a look, well aware that she was now standing on the spot where they'd made wild love only a short time before. If he was trying to get a rise out of her, he was succeeding. If he was trying to distract her from what they'd discovered in the attic, he was succeeding, as well. Either way, Maggie found she couldn't resist him.

Deliberately, she took a step closer, running her hands slowly up his chest. It was time, she decided, to give him back a bit of his own. "Maybe I'm hungry, after all," she murmured, and, rising on her toes, brushed her lips teasingly over his.

Because he hadn't expected the move from her, Cliff did nothing. From the start he'd stalked and seduced. She was the lady, the crown princess with the wanton passion men often fantasize about on long, dark nights. Now, looking into those deep, velvet eyes, he thought her more of a witch. And who, he wondered as his blood began to swim, had been stalked and seduced?

She took his breath away—just the scent of her. She made his reason cloud—just the touch of her. When she looked at him like this, her eyes knowing, her lips parted and close, she was the only woman he wanted, the only woman he knew. At times like this, he wanted her with a fire that promised never to be banked. Quite suddenly and quite clearly, she terrified him.

"Maggie." He put a hand up to ward her off, to draw her closer; he'd never know, for the dog began to bark, and the rumble of a car laboring up the lane sounded from outside. Cliff dropped the hand to his side again. "That'll be Stan."

"Yes." She studied him with an open curiosity he wasn't ready to deal with.

"You'd better get the door."

"All right." She kept her gaze direct on his for another moment, rather pleased with the uncertainty she saw there. "You coming?"

"Yeah. In a minute." He waited until she had gone, then let out a long, uneasy breath. That had been too close for comfort. Too close to what, he wasn't certain, but he was certain he didn't like it. With his appetite strangely vanished, Cliff abandoned the drumstick and picked up his coffee. When he noticed his hands weren't quite steady, he downed the contents in one swallow.

Well, she certainly had enough to think about, Maggie mused as she walked down the hall. The sheriff was at her door again, Cliff was standing in her kitchen looking as though he'd been struck with a blunt instrument, and her own head was so light from a sense of—

was it power?—that she didn't know what might happen next. Her move to the country certainly hadn't been quiet. She'd never been more stimulated in her life.

"Miss Fitzgerald."

"Sheriff." Maggie scooped Killer up in one arm to quiet his barking.

"Quite a beast you've got there," he commented. Then, holding out a hand, he allowed the puppy to sniff it cautiously. "Cliff gave me a call," he continued. "Said it looked like somebody's broken into the house."

"That seems to be the only explanation." Maggie stepped back to struggle with both the puppy and the door. "Although it doesn't make any sense to me. Apparently someone was in the attic last week."

"Last week?" Stan took care of the door himself, then rested his hand lightly, it seemed negligently, on the butt of his gun. "Why didn't you call before?"

Feeling foolish, Maggie set the dog down, giving him an impatient nudge on the rear that sent him scampering into the music room. "I woke up sometime in the middle of the night and heard noises. I admit it panicked me at the time, but in the morning…" She trailed off and shrugged. "In the morning, I thought it'd been my imagination, so I more or less forgot the whole thing."

Stan listened, and his nod was both understanding and prompting. "And now?"

"I happened to mention it to Cliff this…ah…this morning," she finished. "He was curious enough to go up into the attic."

"I see." Maggie had the feeling he saw everything, very well.

"Stan." Cliff strode down the hall from the kitchen, looking perfectly at ease. "Thanks for coming by."

*I should've said that,* Maggie thought, but before she could open her mouth again, the men were talking around her.

"Just part of the job," Stan stated. "You're doing quite a job yourself on the grounds outside."

"They're coming along."

Stan gave him a crooked, appealing smile. "You've always liked a challenge."

They knew each other well enough that Cliff understood he referred to the woman, as well as her land. "Things would be dull without them," he said mildly.

"Heard you found something in the attic."

"Enough to make me think someone's been poking around."

"I'd better have a look."

"I'll show you," Maggie said flatly, then, sending Cliff a telling look, led the way upstairs.

When they came to the attic door, Stan glanced down at the poker still leaning against it. "Somebody could trip over that," he said mildly.

"I must have left it there before." Ignoring Cliff's grin, she picked it up and held it behind her back.

"Doesn't look like anyone's been up here in a long time," Stan commented as he brushed a cobweb away from his face.

"I haven't been up at all until today." Maggie shivered as a large black spider crawled sedately up the wall to her left. She hadn't admitted to anyone yet that the prospect of insects and mice was primarily what had kept her out. "There's been so much else to do in the house." Deliberately, she stepped farther away from the wall.

"Not much up here." Stan rubbed a hand over his chin. "Joyce and I cleared out everything we were interested in when she first inherited. Louella already had everything she wanted. If you haven't been up," he continued, peering slowly around, "how do you know anything's missing?"

"I don't. It's this." For the second time, Maggie crossed the dusty floor to the trunk. This time it was she who crouched down and pointed.

Stan bent down over her, close enough that she could smell the simple department-store aftershave he wore. She recognized it and, on a wave of nostalgia, remembered her mother's driver had worn it, too. For no other reason, her sense of trust in him was confirmed.

"That's curious," Stan murmured, careful not to smear the faint outline. "Did you open this?"

"Neither of us touched it," Cliff said from behind.

With another nod, Stan pushed the button on the latch. His other hand came up automatically, stopping just short of gripping the trunk in the same spot the handprint was. "Looks like somebody did." Cautiously, he put his hand on the closure and tugged. "Locked." Sitting back on his haunches, he frowned at the trunk. "Damn if I can remember what's in this thing or if there's a key. Joyce might know—more'n likely Louella, though. Still..." With a shake of his head, he straightened. "It doesn't make much sense for somebody to break in and take something out of this old trunk, especially now that the house is occupied for the first time in ten years." He looked back at Maggie. "Are you sure nothing's missing from downstairs?"

"No—that is, I don't think so. Almost everything I shipped out's still in crates."

"Wouldn't hurt to take a good look."

"All right." She started back toward the second floor, realizing she hoped something would be missing. That would make sense; that would be tangible. The faint handprint on the trunk and no explanation gave her a queasy feeling in the stomach. A cut-and-dried burglary would only make her angry.

With the two men following, she went into her bedroom, checking her jewelry first. Everything was exactly as it should've been. In the next bedroom were crates that at a glance she could see were untouched and unopened.

"That's all up here. There's more crates downstairs and some paintings I haven't had reframed yet."

"Let's take a look."

Going with the sheriff's suggestion, Maggie headed for the stairs again.

"I don't like it," Cliff said to Stan in an undertone. "And you don't think she's going to find anything missing downstairs."

"Only thing that makes sense is a burglary, Cliff."

"A lot of things haven't made sense since we started digging in that gully."

Stan let out a quiet breath, watching Maggie's back as she descended the steps. "I know, and a lot of times there just aren't any answers."

"Are you going to tell Joyce about this?"

"I might have to." Stan stopped at the base of the stairs, running a hand over the back of his neck as though there were tension or weariness there. "She's a strong woman, Cliff. I guess I didn't know just how strong until this business started. I know when we first got married, a lot of people thought I did it for her inheritance."

"Not anyone who knew you."

Stan shrugged. "Anyway, that died down after a while, died completely after I became sheriff. I guess there were times I wondered whether Joyce ever thought it."

"She'd have told me if she had," Cliff said bluntly.

With a half laugh, Stan turned to him. "Yes, she would've at that."

Maggie came back into the hall from the music room. "There's nothing missing in there, either. I've a few things in the living room, but—"

"Might as well be thorough," Stan told her, then strode across the hall and over the threshold. "Doing some painting?" he asked when he noticed the can and brush by the window.

"I'd planned to have all the trim done in here today," she said absently as she examined a few more packing boxes, "but then Mrs. Morgan stopped by, and—"

"Louella," Stan interrupted.

Because he was frowning, Maggie began to smooth it over. "Yes, though she didn't stay very long. We just looked over the pictures she'd lent me." Distracted, she picked up the stack. "Actually, I'd wanted to show these to you, Cliff. I wondered if you could tell me how to deal with getting some climbing roses like these started."

With the men flanking her, Maggie flipped through the snapshots.

"Louella certainly had a feel for making flowers look like they'd grown up on their own," she murmured. "I don't know if I have the talent for it."

"She always loved this place," Stan said. "She—" Then he stopped when she flipped to the color shot of himself and Morgan. "I'd forgotten about that one," he said after a moment. "Joyce took that the first day of deer season."

"Louella mentioned that she hunted."

"She did," Cliff put in, "because he wanted her to. Morgan had an—affection for guns."

And died by one, Maggie thought with a shudder. She turned the pictures facedown. "There's nothing missing anywhere that I can see, Sheriff."

He stared down at the pile of photos. "Well, then, I'll do a check of the doors and windows, see if anything's been forced."

"You can look," Maggie said with a sigh, "but I don't know if the doors were locked, and half the windows at least were open."

He gave her the look parents give children when they do something foolish and expected. "I'll just poke around, anyway. Never can tell."

When he'd gone out, Maggie flopped down on the sofa and lapsed into silence. As if he had nothing better to do, Cliff wandered to the clock on the mantel and began to wind it. Killer came out from under the sofa and began to dance around his legs. The tension in the room was palpable. Maggie had almost given up wondering if it would ever be resolved.

Why would anyone break into an old trunk that had been neglected for years? Why had Cliff been in on the discovery, just as he'd been in on the discovery in the gully? What had caused her to fall in love with him, and would this need between them fade, as flash fires had a habit of doing? If she could understand any of it, perhaps the rest would fall into place and she'd know what move to make.

"There doesn't seem to be any forced entry," Stan said as he came back into the room. "I'll go into town, file a formal report and get to work on this, but—" He shook his head at Maggie. "I can't promise anything. I'd suggest you keep your doors locked and give some more thought to those dead bolts."

"I'll be staying here for the next few days," Cliff announced, throwing Stan and Maggie into surprised silence. He continued as if he hadn't noticed the reaction his statement caused. "Maggie won't be alone, though it would seem that whatever was wanted in the house was taken."

"Yeah." Stan scratched his nose, almost concealing a grin. "I'd better get back. I'll just let myself out."

Maggie didn't rouse herself to say goodbye but stared at Cliff until the front door shut. "Just what do you mean, you'll be staying here?"

"We'll have to do some grocery shopping first. I can't live off what you keep in that kitchen."

"Nobody asked you to live off it," she said, springing to her feet. "And nobody asked you to stay here. I don't understand why I have to keep reminding you whose house and land this is."

"Neither do I."

"You told *him,*" she continued. "You just as good as announced to the town in general that you and I—"

"Are exactly what we are," Cliff finished easily. "You'd better get some shoes on, if we're going to town."

"I'm not going to town, and you're not staying here."

He moved so quickly she was caught completely off guard. His hands closed over both her arms. "I'm not letting you stay here alone until we know exactly what's going on."

"I've told you before I can take care of myself."

"Maybe you can, but we're not putting it to the test right now. I'm staying."

She gave him a long stare. The truth was, she didn't want to be alone. The truth was, she wanted him, perhaps too much for her own good. Yet he was the one insisting, she thought as her temper began to cool. Since he was insisting, perhaps he cared more than he was willing to admit. Maybe it was time she took a gamble on that.

"If I let you stay…" she began.

"I am staying."

"If I let you stay," she repeated coolly, "you have to cook dinner tonight."

He lifted a brow, and the grip on her arms relaxed slightly. "After sampling your cooking, you won't get any argument."

Refusing to be insulted, she nodded. "Fine. I'll get my shoes."

"Later." Before she knew what he was up to, they were tumbling back onto the sofa. "We've got all day."

# *Chapter 10*

Maggie considered it ironic that she'd just begun to become accustomed to living alone and she was no longer living alone. Cliff made the transition unobtrusively. No fuss, no bother. A brisk, rather subtle sense of organization seemed to be a part of his makeup. She'd always respected organized people—from a safe distance.

He left early each morning, long before she considered it decent for a person to be out of his bed. He was quiet and efficient and never woke her. Occasionally, when she groped her way downstairs later in the morning, she'd find a scrawled note next to the coffeepot.

"Phone was off the hook again," it might say. Or "Milk's low. I'll pick some up."

Not exactly love letters, Maggie thought wryly. A man like Cliff wouldn't put his feelings down on paper the way she was compelled to. It was just one more area of opposition between them.

In any case, Maggie wasn't certain Cliff had any feelings about her other than impatience and an occasional bout of intolerance. Though there were times she suspected she touched some of his softer edges, he didn't act much like a lover. He brought her no flowers, but she remembered he'd planted a willow tree. He gave her no smooth, clever phrases, but she remembered the look she'd sometimes catch in his eyes. He wasn't a poet, he wasn't a romantic, but that look, that one long, intense look, said more than most women ever heard.

Perhaps, despite both of them, she was beginning to understand him. The more she understood, the more difficult it became to control a steadily growing love. He wasn't a man whose emotions could be pushed or channeled. She was a woman who, once her feelings were touched, ran with them in whatever direction they went.

Though she'd lived in the house outside of Morganville for only a month, Maggie understood a few basics of small-town life. Whatever she did became common knowledge almost before she'd done it. Whatever it was she did would draw a variety of opinions that would lead to a general consensus. There were a few key people whose opinion could sway that consensus. Cliff, she knew, was one of them, if he chose to bother. Stan Agee and the postmistress were others. It didn't take her long to discover that Bog was another whose opinion was sought and carefully weighed.

The politics in Morganville might've been on a smaller scale than those in southern California's music industry, but Maggie saw that they ran in the same vein. In L.A., however, she'd been second-generation royalty, while here she was an outsider. An outsider, she knew, whose notoriety could be either scorned or accepted. To date, she'd been fortunate, because most of the key people had decided to accept. Thinking of small, close-knit towns, she realized she'd taken a chance on that acceptance by living with Cliff.

Not living with, Maggie corrected as she spread adhesive on her newly stripped bathroom floor. He wasn't living with her; he was staying with her. There was a world of difference between the two. He hadn't moved in, bag and baggage, nor had there been any discussion about the length of his stay. It was, she decided, a bit like having a guest whom you didn't feel obligated to entertain or impress.

Unnecessarily, and through his own choice, he'd opted to be her bodyguard. And at night, when the sun went down and the woods were quiet, her body was his. He accepted her passion, her hungers and desires. Perhaps, just perhaps, one day he might accept her emotions, which raged just as hot, and just as high. First he had to come to understand her as she was beginning to understand him. Without that, and the respect that went with it, emotions and desires would wither and die.

Maggie set the next square of tile into position, then sat back to judge the outcome. The stone-patterned ceramic was rustic and would leave her free to use an infinite range of color combinations. She wanted nothing in her home to be too restricted or regimented, just as she wanted to do most of the changes and improvements herself.

Looking at the six pieces of tile she'd installed, Maggie nodded. She was becoming quite handy these days. Though her pansies had never recovered, they were her only major failure.

Pleased and ready for more, Maggie debated whether to mix up another batch of adhesive or to start the next wall of paper in her bedroom. There was only a wall and a half left to cover, she remembered; then it would be time to make a decision on curtains. Priscillas, cafés,

Cape Cods... Nothing monumental, most people would say, she mused, but then she'd always left such things up to decorators before. Now, if something didn't work, she had no one to blame but herself.

With a laugh, she reached into the box of tiles again, swearing halfheartedly as she scraped her finger against a sharp edge. The price of being your own handyman, Maggie decided, going to the sink to run water over the cut. Maybe it was time to turn in the tiles for wallpaper and paste.

When the dog began to bark, she knew that either project would have to wait. Resigned, she turned off the tap just as the sound of a car reached her. Going to the tiny latticed window, she watched Lieutenant Reiker pull around the last curve.

Why was he back? she wondered, frowning. There couldn't possibly be any more information she could give him. When he didn't approach the house immediately, Maggie stayed where she was. He walked along the path of flagstone Cliff's crew had set just that week. When he reached the end, he didn't turn toward the porch, but looked out over the gully. Slowly, he drew out a cigarette, then lit it with a short wooden match. For several moments he just stood there, smoking and watching the dirt and rocks as if they had the answers he wanted. Then, before she could react, he turned and looked directly up at the window where she stood. Feeling like an idiot, she started down to meet him.

"Lieutenant." Maggie went cautiously down the porch steps and onto the sturdy new flagstone.

"Miss Fitzgerald." He flipped the cigarette stub into the tangle of brush near the gully. "Your place is coming along. Hard to believe what it looked like a few weeks ago."

"Thank you." He looked so harmless, so pleasant. She wondered if he carried a gun in a shoulder holster under his jacket.

"Noticed you planted a willow over there." But he looked at her, not at the gully. "It shouldn't be much longer before you can have your pond put in."

Like Reiker, Maggie didn't look toward the gully. "Does that mean the investigation's almost over?"

Reiker scratched along the side of his jaw. "I don't know if I'd say that. We're working on it."

She bit back a sigh. "Are you going to search the gully again?"

"I don't think it's going to come to that. We've been through it twice now. Thing is—" He stopped, shifting his weight to ease his hip. "I don't like loose ends. The more we look into this thing, the more we find. It's hard to tie up ends that've been dangling for ten years."

Was this a social call or an official one? she wondered, trying not to be annoyed. Maggie could remember how embarrassed he'd been when he'd asked for her autograph. At the moment, she didn't need a fan. "Lieutenant, is there something I can do?"

"I wondered if you'd had anyone coming around, someone you know, maybe someone you don't know."

"Coming around?"

"The murder happened here, Miss Fitzgerald, and the more we dig, the more people we find who had reason to kill Morgan. A lot of them still live in town."

She folded her arms under her breasts. "If you're trying to make me uneasy, Lieutenant, you're doing a good job."

"I don't want to do that, but I don't want to keep you in the dark, either." He hesitated, then decided to go with his instincts. "We discovered that Morgan withdrew twenty-five thousand cash from his bank account on the day he disappeared. His car was found, now his body's been found, but the money's never showed up."

"Twenty-five thousand," Maggie murmured. A tidy sum, even tidier ten years ago. "You're telling me you think the money was the motive for murder?"

"Money's always a motive for murder, and it's a loose end. We're checking a lot of people out, but it takes time. So far, nobody around here's ever flashed that kind of money." He started to reach for another cigarette, then apparently changed his mind. "I've got a couple of theories..."

She might've smiled if her head wasn't beginning to ache. "And you'd like to tell me?"

"Whoever killed Morgan was smart enough to cover his tracks. He might've been smart enough to know that coming up with twenty-five thousand dollars wouldn't go unnoticed in a town like this. Maybe, just maybe, he panicked and got rid of the money. Or maybe he hid it so he could wait a good long time, until any rumors about Morgan had died down; then it'd just be waiting for him."

"Ten years is a very long time, Lieutenant."

"Some people're more patient than others." He shrugged. "It's just a theory."

But it made her think. The attic, and the trunk and the handprint. "The other night—" she began, then stopped.

"Something happen the other night?" he prompted.

It was foolish not to tell him, to feel as though, if she did, she would be forging another link in the chain that bound her to everything that had happened. He was, after all, in charge of the investigation. "Well, it seems someone broke in and took something out of a trunk in the attic. I didn't realize it until days later; then I reported it to Sheriff Agee."

"That was the thing to do." His gaze lifted to the dormer window. "He come up with anything?"

"Not really. He did find a key. That is, his wife found one somewhere. He came back and opened the trunk, but it was empty."

"Would you mind if I had a look myself?"

She wanted it over, yet it seemed every step she took brought her in deeper. "No, I don't mind." Resigned, Maggie turned to lead him into the house. "It seems odd that anyone would hide money in the attic, then wait until someone was living here to claim it."

"You bought the place almost as soon as the sign was posted," Reiker reminded her.

"But it was nearly a month before I'd moved in."

"I heard Mrs. Agee kept quiet about the sale. Her husband didn't like the idea."

"You hear a lot of things, Lieutenant."

He gave her the slow, half-embarrassed smile he'd given her when he'd asked for her autograph. "I'm supposed to."

Maggie lapsed into silence until they reached the second floor. "The attic's up here. For what it's worth, I haven't found anything missing in the house."

"How'd they get in?" he asked as he began to climb the steeper, more narrow staircase.

"I don't know," she mumbled. "I wasn't locking my doors."

"But you are now?" He looked back over his shoulder.

"Yes, I'm locking them."

"Good." He went directly to the trunk, and, crouching down, studied the lock. The handprint had faded back to dust. "You say Mrs. Agee had the key?"

"Yes, or one of them. It seems this trunk belonged to the last people who rented the house, an old couple. The woman left it here after her husband died. Apparently there were at least two keys, but Joyce could only find one of them."

"Hmm." Reiker opened the now-unlocked trunk and peered inside, much as he'd peered into the gully. And it, Maggie thought, was just as empty now.

"Lieutenant, you don't really think there's a connection between this and—what you're investigating?"

"I don't like coincidences," he muttered, echoing Cliff's earlier statement. "You say the sheriff's looking into it?"

"Yes."

"I'll talk to him before I head back. Twenty-five thousand doesn't take up much room," he said. "It's a big trunk."

"I don't understand why anyone would let it sit in one for ten years."

"People're funny." He straightened, grunting a little with the effort. "Of course, it's just a theory. Another is that Morgan's mistress took the money and ran."

"His mistress?" Maggie repeated blankly.

"Alice Delaney," Reiker said easily. "She'd been having an affair with Morgan for five or six years. Funny how people'll talk once you get them started."

"Delaney?" Maggie said it quietly, hoping she'd heard incorrectly.

"That's right. As a matter of fact, it's her son who's been doing your landscaping. Coincidences," he repeated. "This business is full of them."

Somehow she managed to remain composed as they walked back downstairs. She spoke politely when he told her again how much he admired her music. Maybe she even smiled when she closed the door on him. When she was alone, Maggie felt her blood turn to ice, then drain.

Cliff's mother had been Morgan's mistress for years; then she'd disappeared, right after his death? Cliff would've known. Everyone would've known, she thought, and covered her face with both hands. What had she fallen into, and how would she ever get out again?

Maybe he was going crazy, but Cliff was beginning to think of the long, winding drive up the hill as going home. He'd never have believed he could consider the old Morgan place as home. Not with the way he'd always felt about William Morgan. Nor would he have believed the woman who lived there could make him think that way. It seemed a great deal was happening that he could neither stop nor harness. Yet staying with Maggie had been his own choice, just as leaving again would be—when he was ready. From time to time he found he needed to remind himself that he could and would leave again.

Yet when she laughed, the house was so warm. When she was angry, it was so full of energy. When she sang—when she worked in the music room in the evening, Cliff thought. When the woods were quiet, before the moon had risen, she'd play. She'd sing snatches of words, sentences, phrases, as she composed. Long before she'd finished, he'd find himself in a frenzy of need. He wondered how she worked hour after hour, day after day, with such passion and feeling driving her.

It was the discipline, Cliff decided. He'd never expected her to be so disciplined about her music. The talent he'd admired all along, but in the few days he'd lived with her, he'd learned that she drove herself hard in the hours she worked.

A contrast, Cliff decided. It was an implausible contrast to the woman who jumped sporadically from one project to another in that big, dusty house. She left walls half papered, ceilings half painted. There were crates and boxes everywhere, most of which hadn't been touched. Rolls of supplies were tucked into every corner. He'd say her work on the house was precise, even creative, to the point where she'd leave off for something new.

She wasn't like anyone he'd ever known, and he realized that somewhere along the way he'd begun to understand her. It had been easier when he could dismiss her as a spoiled Hollywood princess who'd bought a dilapidated country house on a whim or for a publicity stunt. He knew now that she'd bought the house for no other reason than she'd loved it.

Perhaps she was a bit spoiled. She tended to give orders a little too casually. When she didn't get her own way, she tended to bristle or to freeze up. Cliff grinned. The same could be said of himself, he admitted.

To give Maggie her due, she hadn't run from the trouble or unpleasantness that had begun so shortly after she'd moved in. If he'd seen another woman stick as Maggie was sticking, he'd have said she'd indeed taken root. Cliff still had his doubts. Perhaps he fostered them purposely, because if he believed Maggie Fitzgerald would stay in Morganville, he might have to admit he wanted her to. He might have to admit that coming home every night to a woman who made him laugh and fume and throb wasn't something he'd give up without a fight.

He drove the last few yards, then stopped at the edge of the drive. The phlox was blooming on the bank. The new grass was like a green shadow over the soil. Maggie's petunias were a splash of color.

They'd both put part of themselves into the land already, he realized. Perhaps that in itself was a bond that would be difficult to break. Even as he stepped out of the truck, he wanted her, just the scent, just the softness of her. There was nothing he could do to change it.

There was no music. Cliff frowned as he slowly climbed the front steps. Maggie was always at her piano at this time of day. There were times he'd come back earlier and work on the yard himself. He'd know it was five o'clock, because that's when the music would begin, and it would continue for no less than an hour, often longer. Cliff looked at his watch: 5:35. Uneasy, he turned the knob on the front door.

Of course it was unlocked, he thought, annoyed. He'd left her a note that morning, telling her none of his crew would be there that day and to keep the doors locked. Senseless woman, he thought as he shoved the door open. Why couldn't she get it through her head that she was completely isolated here? Too many things had happened, and simply by living in this house, she was in the center of them.

Quiet. Too damn quiet, Cliff realized as annoyance began to fade into anxiety. The dog wasn't barking. The house had that echoing, empty feeling almost everyone can sense but can't explain. Though instinct told him no one was there, he began to go from room to room, calling her. Her name bounced back off the walls in his own voice and taunted him.

Where the hell was she, Cliff demanded as he took the stairs two at a time to check the second floor. He didn't like to admit that he could feel panic at nothing more than coming home to an empty house, but panic was exactly what he felt. Every day that week he'd been sure he'd had a crew, or part of one, working outside until he'd been there. He hadn't wanted her left alone, but because he couldn't explain it, Cliff had broken the ritual that day. And now he couldn't find her.

"Maggie!" Desperately, he searched the second floor, not even certain what he expected, or wanted, to find. He'd never experienced this kind of raw, basic fear. He only knew the house was empty and his woman was gone. A pair of her shoes sat carelessly in the center of the bedroom rug. A blouse was tossed negligently over a chair. The earrings he'd watched her take off the night before still lay on the dresser, beside a silver-backed brush engraved with her mother's initials. The room held her scent; it always did.

When he saw the new tiles in the bathroom, he tried to calm himself. In her helter-skelter way, she'd started a new project. But where in the hell—

Then, in the bowl of the sink, he saw something that stopped his heart. Against the pristine white porcelain were three drops of blood. He stared while panic swirled through him, making his head swim and his skin ice.

From somewhere outside, the dog began to bark frantically. Cliff was racing down the steps, not even aware that he called her name again and again.

He saw her as soon as he burst through the back door. She was coming slowly through the woods to the east, the dog dancing around her legs, leaping and nipping. She had her hands in her pockets, her head down. His mind took in every detail while the combination of fear and relief made his legs weak.

He ran toward her, seeing her head lift as he called her again. Then he had her in his arms, holding tight, closing his eyes and just feeling her, warm and whole and safe. He was too overcome with emotions that had no precedent to notice that she stood stiff and unyielding against him.

He buried his face in the soft luxury of her hair. "Maggie, where've you been?"

This was the man she'd thought she was beginning to understand. This was the man she was beginning to love. Maggie stared straight ahead over his shoulder to the house beyond. "I went for a walk."

"Alone?" he demanded irrationally, drawing her back. "You went out alone?"

Everything turned cold; her skin, her manner, her eyes. "It's my land, Cliff. Why shouldn't I go out alone?"

He caught himself before he could rage that she should've left him a note. What was happening to him? "There was blood in the sink upstairs."

"I cut my finger on a tile."

He found he wanted to rage at her for that. She had no business hurting herself. "You're usually playing this time of day," he managed.

"I'm not locked into a routine any more than I'm locked into the house. If you want a placid little female who's waiting to fall at your

TRANSLink 131230
TRANSLink
SINGLE
ADULT
DCU08341 18:37 077100
700 L 18
ZONES 14-18
TRANSFER UNTIL
08:37PM
TUE 09 MAR 10
Public Transport
Tax Invoice
ABN 46097411749
$6.00 (Incl GST)

National Security Hotline 1800 123 400

TRANSLink 13 12 30

**Conditions of Travel**

This ticket is issued subject to the Transport Operations (Passenger Transport) Act 1994 and the Translink Conditions of Travel

Passengers must be in possession of a valid ticket at all times, and must produce their ticket and valid concession card on request.

**For all conditions of travel visit www.translink.com.au**

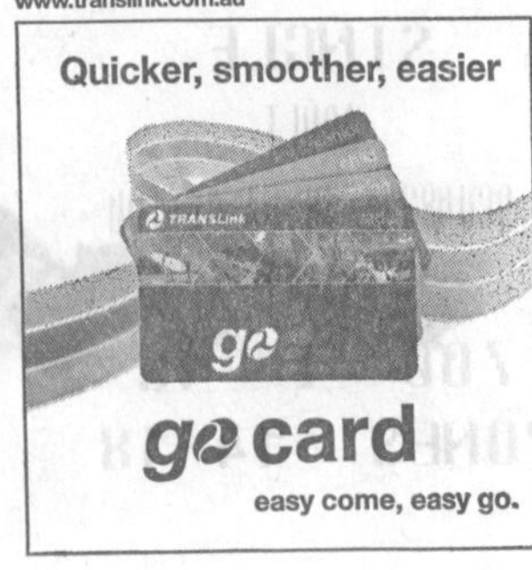


**Conditions of Travel**

This ticket is issued subject to the Transport Operations (Passenger Transport) Act 1994 and the Translink Conditions of Travel

Passengers must be in possession of a valid ticket at all times, and must produce their ticket and valid concession card on request.

**For all conditions of travel visit www.translink.com.au**

National Security Hotline 1800 123 400

TRANSLink 13 12 30

feet every night when you come home, you'd better look somewhere else." Leaving him staring, she broke away and went into the house.

Calmer but more confused, Cliff went into the kitchen to see her pouring a drink. Scotch, he noted, another first. With his mind a bit clearer, he could see that the normal color was absent from her cheeks and that her shoulders were stiff with tension. This time he didn't go to her or touch her.

"What's happened?"

Maggie swirled the scotch once before she swallowed.

She found it too warm, too strong, but she sipped again. "I don't know what you mean." The kitchen was too small. Maggie took the glass and went out. The air was warm and soft. Outside there were no walls or ceilings to make her feel closed in. Circling around, she sat down on the spread of new grass. She'd sit here in the summer, Maggie thought, and read—Byron, if that was her mood. She'd let the sun fall over her, the silence cloak her, and read until she slept. Maggie continued to look out over the woods when Cliff's shadow slanted over her.

"Maggie, what's wrong with you?"

"I'm having a mood," she said flatly. "You'd expect spoiled celebrities to have moods, wouldn't you?"

Keeping his temper in check, Cliff sat down beside her, then took her chin in his hand. He waited until their eyes had met and held. "What?"

She'd known she'd have to tell him. It was the not knowing what there would be afterward that left her insides cold and knotted. "Lieutenant Reiker was here today," she began, but carefully removed Cliff's hand from her face.

Cliff swore, cursing himself for leaving her alone. "What'd he want?"

Maggie shrugged and sipped at the scotch again. "He's a man who doesn't like loose ends. Apparently he's been finding quite a number. It seems William Morgan withdrew twenty-five thousand dollars from his bank account on the day he was murdered."

"Twenty-five thousand?"

He sounded surprised, Maggie noted. Genuinely surprised. She recognized his expression, that thoughtful, narrow-eyed look that meant he was considering all the details and angles. How could she be certain of anything any longer? "The money was never recovered. One of Reiker's theories is that the murderer hid it away, patiently waiting until people forgot about Morgan."

Cliff's eyes sharpened. Automatically, he turned his head and looked back to the house. "Here?"

"Possibly."

"Ten years is a damn long time to sit on twenty-five thousand," Cliff muttered. Still, he didn't care for loose ends, either. "Did you tell him about the trunk in the attic?"

"Yes, he had a look at it himself."

He touched her shoulder, just his fingertips, so lightly that the touch offered whatever support she might want to take. "It's upset you." Maggie said nothing, nor did she look at him. Tension began to work at his own muscles. "There's more."

"There's always more," Maggie said quietly. Now she looked at him; she had to. "He mentioned that Morgan's mistress had disappeared right after his death." She felt Cliff's fingers tighten convulsively on her shoulder just as she felt the waves of anger.

"She wasn't his mistress," Cliff said tightly. "My mother might've been foolish enough to fall in love with a man like Morgan, she might've been unwise enough to sleep with him, but she wasn't his mistress."

"Why didn't you tell me before?" Maggie demanded. "Why did you wait until I found out this way?"

"It doesn't have anything to do with you or with anything that's happened here." As restless anger swarmed in him, he rose.

"Coincidences," Maggie said quietly, but Cliff turned and stared down at her. "Weren't you the one who said not to trust coincidences?"

He was trapped, by an old anger and by a pair of depthless brown eyes. Again he found himself compelled to explain what he'd never explained before. "My mother was lonely and very vulnerable after my father died. Morgan knew how to exploit that. I was living outside of D.C. at the time. If I'd been here, I might've stopped it." Resentment welled up and was controlled. "He knew how to play on weaknesses, and he played on my mother's. When I found out they were lovers, I wanted to kill him."

He said it as he had once before, coldly, calmly. Maggie swallowed on a dry throat. "She was already too involved for anything to be done, deluded into believing she loved him, or maybe she did love him. Other intelligent women had. She'd been friends with Louella for years, but that didn't matter. When they found his car in the river, she snapped."

It was painful to look back on it, but Maggie's solemn brown eyes insisted he go on. "She didn't disappear; she came to me. She was frantic, and for the first time since she'd become involved with Morgan, she was seeing clearly again. Shame affects different people in different ways. My mother broke all ties with Morganville and everyone in it. She knew her relationship with Morgan wasn't a secret, and now that it was over, she simply couldn't face the gossip. She's still in D.C. She has a new life, and I don't want any of this to touch her."

Was he always so unflaggingly protective of the women in his life? Maggie wondered. Joyce, his mother... Where, she wondered, did she fit in? "Cliff, I understand how you feel. My mother was one of the most precious people in my life, too. But there might not be anything you can do about it. They're reconstructing what happened ten years ago, and your mother has a part in it."

But that wasn't all she was thinking, Cliff realized. Deliberately, he sat down beside her, struggling to keep the tension from his fingers when he took her shoulders. "You're wondering how much a part I might've had in it."

"Don't." She tried to stand, but he held her still.

"It's possible that I could've shot Morgan to end a destructive relationship with my mother."

"You hated him."

"Yes."

Her eyes never left his. They looked deep, searching. Logic might implicate him; his own temperament might make him suspect. Maggie stared into the smoky gray of his eyes and believed what she saw. "No," she murmured, drawing him against her. "No, I understand you too well."

Her faith—the warm flood of it—almost destroyed him. "Do you?"

"Maybe too well," she murmured. "I was so frightened before." Closing her eyes, she drew in the familiar scent of him. He was real, he was solid, and for as long as she could hold on, he was hers. "Not now, not now that you're here."

He could feel the pull, that slow, gentle pull. If he wasn't careful, he'd soon forget there was anything or anyone but her in his life. "Maggie." His fingers were already tangling in her hair. "You shouldn't trust without questions."

"It isn't trust with questions," she countered. She wanted it to be only the two of them, with the rest of the world locked out, forgotten. Framing his face with her hands, she drew his mouth down to hers.

She'd expected fire, aggression, but his lips were soft and sweet. Confused, moved, Maggie drew back to stare at him. The eyes that had fascinated her from the beginning held hers as seconds edged closer to a minute. She was lost in the mists and the smoke. Without a word, he brought her close again.

With his eyes on hers, he lightly traced the shape of her face with a fingertip. This, he discovered, was the only face he ever needed to see again. Lightly, he outlined the shape of her lips. These, he knew, were the only lips he'd ever need to taste. With a gentleness he'd shown to no other lover, he laid her back. This was the only body he ever wanted to possess.

Tenderness left her stunned, weak. His mouth lingered on hers, but with such poignancy, the kiss alone made her bones liquefy. The grass was cool beneath her, the sun warm. Swimming in emotion, Maggie closed her eyes while his lips traveled over her face.

Had she ever been touched like this before? As if she were spun glass, his hands stroked over her. As if she were the rarest of delicacies, his lips tasted. And she was helplessly caught in the silken web that was more love than passion.

"Cliff—"

She might've told him, if his lips hadn't captured hers with a sweetness that left her speechless.

He'd never felt a stronger need to savor. It was as if each moment could be stretched to an hour as long as they lay together in the fragrant spring grass. The color in her cheeks was delicate; the sunlight combed through her hair. The look in her eyes was one no man could resist. It told him as clearly as words that she was his. He had only to claim. Knowing it, he moved only more slowly and touched only more reverently.

He undressed her while his kisses continued to hold her in the honey-steeped prison of pleasure. When she was naked, he watched how the sun streamed over her skin. Her large, expressive eyes were half closed. He could feel the pliancy in her body when, with a sigh, she lifted her hands to help him undress.

The raw, primitive need she so often incited in him didn't rise up. Instead, she drew out the softer emotions he normally held back. He wanted only to please her.

Gently, he lowered his mouth to her breast. He could hear her heartbeat increase in pace as he lingered there with his tongue tracing, his teeth nibbling. The tip grew taut, so that when he drew it into his mouth, he heard her breath shudder out, then catch again. Her hand moved through his hair as she lay back, saturated with sensation.

Her body was like a treasure to be discovered and admired before possession. Slowly, almost leisurely, he took those moist kisses and gentle hands over it, stopping, lingering, when he felt her shuddering response. He knew she was steeped in that dim, heavy world where passions hover around the edges and desires lick temptingly, like tiny tongues of fire. He wanted to keep her there for hours or days or years.

Her thighs were slender and long and pearl white. He loitered there, nudging them both closer, still closer to the edge. But not yet.

She'd forgotten where she was. Though her eyes were half opened, she saw nothing but mists and dreams. She could feel, oh, yes, she could feel each stroke of his hand, each warm brush of lips. She could hear gentle murmurs, quiet sighs that might've been his or hers. There was no reason to ever feel or hear anything else. She was slowly, inevitably, being drawn through the sweetness and into the heat. She began to crave it.

He felt the change in her body, heard the change in the breaths that whispered through her lips. He swept his mouth farther up her thigh, but still he didn't hurry. She would have all he had to give before they were finished.

She arched, catapulted with the sudden intensity of pleasure. She crested, quickly, shatteringly, with an abandonment of self and will. He wanted, demanded, just that. Before she could settle, he drove her up again until the madness once more began to creep into both of them. Cliff held it off, almost delirious with the knowledge that he could give her what a woman might only dream of. Her body was alive with sensations only he could bring to her. Her mind was swirling with thoughts of only him.

Knowing it, reveling in it, he slipped into her, taking her with a tenderness that lasted and lasted and lasted.

## *Chapter 11*

Saturday morning, Maggie decided she could lie there, half dozing, until it was Saturday afternoon. She could feel the weight of Cliff's arm across her waist, his warm breath fluttering over her cheek. Without opening her eyes, she snuggled closer, wallowing in lazy contentment.

If she'd been certain he could be so gentle, she'd have fallen in love with him willingly. But how satisfying it was to have discovered it after her heart had already been lost. He had such emotion in him. Perhaps he was cautious with it, but she could love him much more comfortably knowing it was there and that now and again, unexpectedly, it would reach out to her.

No, it wasn't flowery phrases she wanted, but his stability. She didn't need smooth charm. When a woman found a man who was capable of such passion and such tenderness, she'd be a fool to want to change him in any way. Maggie Fitzgerald, she thought with a little satisfied smile, was no fool.

"What're you smiling at?"

Opening her eyes, Maggie looked directly into Cliff's. Because his were alert and direct, she knew he'd been awake for some time. She tried to blink away the mists and smiled again. "It feels good," she murmured, snuggling even closer. "You feel good."

He ran a hand down her back, over her hip and thigh. Yes, it felt very good. "Soft," Cliff said quietly. "So soft and smooth." He wondered how he'd gone so many years without being able to touch her like this, when she was lazy and warm and naked. He felt no tension in her, none of the subtle little signs he'd grown so adept at spotting. The need was very strong in him to keep that tension away for as long as he could. She'd walked unwittingly into a whirlpool, and somehow he was connected with it. If it was only for a day, he'd keep the problems at bay.

He rolled, pressed her down into the mattress so that she laughingly murmured a complaint. "Are you going to cook breakfast?" he demanded.

Maggie pillowed her head on her hands, giving him arrogant look for arrogant look. "You don't like my cooking."

"I've decided to be tolerant this morning."

"Have you?" She arched a brow. "How lucky for me."

"Floppy bacon and sloppy eggs," he told her before he nuzzled at her neck.

She shifted, enjoying the rough feel of the night's growth of beard against her skin. "What?"

"I don't like my bacon too crisp—" he nipped at the pulse in her throat "—or my eggs too set."

With a sigh, she closed her eyes again. She wanted to bottle this moment, so that she could take it out again whenever she needed to feel content. "I like my bacon so crisp it crumbles, and I don't like eggs at all."

"They're good for you." Cliff took his lips up her throat to nibble at her ear. "Might put some meat on you." As he spoke, he took his hand down her side again.

"Complaining?"

"Uh-uh." He ran his hand back up again so that his fingers brushed the side of her breast. "Though you do tend toward the lean side. We could build you up with three square meals a day and some exercise."

"No one needs three meals a day," she began, a bit huffily. "And as for exercise—"

"Do you like to dance?"

"Yes, but I—"

"Not much muscle," he noted, pinching her arm. "How's your endurance?"

She gave him a saucy look. "You should know."

With a laugh, he pressed his lips to hers. "You've a very quick, very wicked mind."

"Thanks."

"Now, about dancing. Ever been in a contre line?"

"A what?"

"I thought so." He shook his head, then shifted so that he could look down at her with pity. "Country dancing, Maggie."

Her brows drew together. "Square dancing?"

"No." It was time to educate the lady, Cliff decided, and drew her up to a sitting position. Her hair flowed wildly over her shoulders, the way he liked it best. "Square dancing's more formal, more regimented, than country dancing, but there'd be traditional music and a caller."

Maggie ran a finger up his chest. "Swing your partner and do-si-do?"

He felt the little thrill inch along his skin behind the trail of her finger. Did she know it? he wondered. From the smile that hovered on her lips, he thought she knew it very well. "Among other things."

Maggie linked her hands around his neck and let her head fall back so that she could look at him from beneath lowered lashes. "I'm sure it's all very fascinating, but I don't know why we're doing all this talking when you could be kissing me."

For an answer he gave her a long, searing kiss that left her breathless and pleased. "Because," he said, and nipped at her ear, "I want to go dancing with you."

Sighing, content, Maggie enjoyed the sensation of feeling her own blood begin to sizzle. "Where and when?"

"Tonight, in the park outside of town."

"Tonight?" She opened one eye. "Dancing in the park?"

"It's a tradition." He laid her back again but kept himself propped up so that his hand was free to skim her body. "A sort of Founder's Day celebration combined with rites of spring. Most of the town'll show. There'll be dancing till midnight, then a potluck supper. Then…" He cupped her breast, enjoying the way her eyes clouded when he brushed a fingertip over the point. "There's dancing till dawn for anybody who can handle it."

"Until dawn?" Intrigued and already hopelessly aroused, Maggie arched under him.

"You've danced until dawn before, I imagine."

He'd said the wrong thing or used the wrong tone, because her body stiffened. No, he didn't want to bring up their differences now. At the moment, he could hardly recognize them. He lay down beside her and cradled her in his arms. "We could watch the sun come up," he murmured. "And the stars go out."

She lay against him, but her mind was clear now. The doubts had returned. "You never mentioned this to me before."

"I didn't think you'd be much interested in country dances and potluck suppers. I guess I realized I was wrong."

It was another kind of apology. Maggie accepted this one as easily as she had the first. Smiling again, she tilted her head back from him. "Are you asking me for a date?"

He liked it when her eyes held that half-teasing, half-challenging light. "Looks like it."

"I'd love to."

"Okay." Her hair fell onto his shoulder. Absently, he twisted the end around his finger. "Now, about breakfast."

She grinned, lowering her mouth to his. "We'll have it for lunch."

She didn't know what she expected, but Maggie looked forward to an evening out, away from the house, an evening to spend with other people. After her brief stab at being a hermit, she'd discovered that she could indeed take total command of her own needs. Being able to live with herself for long periods of time simply showed her that she didn't always have to in order to prove her independence. Perhaps she hadn't been attempting to learn anything with the dramatic change in her lifestyle, but she'd learned something, anyway. She could take charge of the tiny details of day-to-day living that she'd always left to others, but she didn't have to cut herself off from everyone to do it.

No, she didn't know what to expect, perhaps a quaint little festival with tinny music and warm lemonade in paper cups. She didn't expect to be particularly impressed. She certainly didn't expect to be enchanted.

The line of cars that sloped down the winding drive to the park surprised her. She'd thought most of the people in town would simply walk. When she mentioned it to Cliff, he shrugged and negotiated his pickup into a spot behind a yellow van.

"They come from all over the county, and from as far away as D.C. and Pennsylvania."

"Really?" Pursing her lips, she climbed out of the truck into the warm, clear night. There'd be a full moon, though the sun was just beginning to set. She wondered if the town had planned it that way or if it had been the luck of the draw. Either way, it was one more thing to be enjoyed. Putting her hand in Cliff's, she began to walk with him to the crest of the hill.

As she watched, the sun dropped lower behind the mountains in the west. She'd seen the sun sink gloriously into the sea and been awed by the colors and brilliance of sunsets in the snow-covered Alps. She'd seen the desert vibrate with color at dusk and cities glow with twilight. Somehow, watching the gold and mauve and pink layer over what were hardly more than foothills of a great range, she was more deeply affected. Perhaps it was foolish, perhaps it was fanciful, but she felt more a part of this place, more involved with the coming of this night, than she'd been of any other. On impulse, she threw her arms around Cliff's neck and held on.

Laughing, he put his hands on her hips. "What's this for?"

"It feels good," she said, echoing her morning words.

Then with a bang that shattered the silence, the music burst out. As a musician, she recognized each individual instrument—violin, banjo, guitar, piano. As a music lover, she felt her excitement leap.

"It's fabulous!" she exclaimed, drawing quickly away. "Absolutely fabulous. Hurry, I have to see." Maggie grabbed his hand and raced the rest of the way up the hill.

Her first impression was of a maze of people, two hundred, perhaps two hundred fifty, crowded together in a covered pavilion. Then she saw they were in lines, six, no, eight, she realized after a quick count. There would be a line of men facing a line of women, and so on, until they simply ran out of room. And they were moving to the music in a system that looked both confusing and fluid.

Some of the women wore skirts that flared out as they dipped, swayed or spun. Others wore jeans. Men's attire was no more consistent and no more formal than the women's. Some of the dancers wore sneakers, while a great many more wore what seemed to be old-fashioned black leather shoes that tied and had thick, sturdy heels. Still others wore what looked like oriental slippers with a single strap across the instep. It didn't seem to matter what was worn; everyone moved. Petticoats flashed, heels stomped, laughter rang out.

A woman stood at the edge of a small wooden stage in front of the band and belted out instructions in a singsong voice. Maggie might not have understood most of the words, but she understood rhythm. Already she was itching to try it herself.

"But how do they know what do to?" she shouted over the music. "How do they understand her?"

"It's a sequence of moves repeated over and over," Cliff told her. "Once you've got the sequence down, you don't even need a caller; she just adds to it."

A sequence, Maggie mused, and tried to find it. At first, she only saw bodies moving in what seemed a helter-skelter pattern, but gradually she began to see the repetition. Counting off the beats, she concentrated on one couple while trying to anticipate their next move. It pleased her to be able to find the sequence, just as the music pleased her ear and the swirling colors pleased her eye. She could smell a mixture of colognes, men's and women's, and the bursting fragrance of the spring flowers that skirted the pavilion.

As the sun dropped lower, the lights, strung overhead, spilled over the dancers. The floor vibrated under her feet so that she felt she was already dancing herself. With Cliff's arm around her, she watched with the undiluted fascination of discovering something new and exciting. She recognized the postmistress. The rather severe-looking middle-aged woman spun by like a dervish and flirted like a young girl.

Flirtation was part of it, Maggie realized as she began to watch faces instead of feet and bodies. Eye contact was essential, as were the saucy smiles she noted and the quick head tosses. It was, as perhaps dances had always been, a kind of mating ritual.

He hadn't thought she'd be fascinated or excited, but he recognized both in the look in her eyes. It gave Cliff overwhelming pleasure to know he'd brought that to her. Her face was flushed, her body already moving to the beat, and her eyes were everywhere at once. She didn't make him think of Maggie Fitzgerald, star baby and glamorous celebrity, but of Maggie, a woman he could hold on to and dance with until the sun came up again.

When the music ended, Maggie burst into raucous applause with everyone else. Laughing, her face tilted back, she grabbed his hand. "I have to try the next one, even if I make a fool of myself."

"Just listen to the calls and follow the music," he said simply as the lines began to form again. "They always run through the dance once before the music starts."

She listened as the next dance sequence was explained by the caller. Though she didn't understand half of the terms, Maggie tried to link them in her mind with the moves that followed. As Cliff guided her slowly through the paces, she enjoyed the sense of camaraderie and the lack of inhibitions around her.

Though she could sense that she was being watched with speculation and interest, Maggie refused to be perturbed by it. They had a right to look, she decided. It was, after all, the first time she'd participated in a town function, and she was being partnered by a man everyone seemed to know.

"This one's called, 'Whiskey before Breakfast,'" the caller sang out. "If you've tried it, you know it ain't as good for you as dancing." She stomped her foot on the platform, one, two, three, and the music began.

The dance was fast and exuberant. Maggie was caught up in the moves before she'd fully registered them. Right, then left; join left hands with your corner and turn around twice. Pass through. Balance and swing.

The first time Cliff whirled her around, she felt the rush of air on her face and laughed.

"Watch my eyes," he warned. "Or you'll be too dizzy to stand up."

"I like it!" she tossed back, then "Whoops!" as she botched the next step and hurried to keep up with the rest of the line.

She didn't mind the sense of confusion or the crowd. Shoulders bumped, feet tangled, her waist was gripped, and she was whirled around by people she'd never met. Teenagers danced with grandmothers. Ladies in frilly dresses swirled with men in jeans with bandannas in their back pockets. Obviously anyone was welcome to line up and dance, and Maggie had already noticed that women picked men for partners just as often as men picked women. It was a free-for-all, and the rules were loose.

As the steps became more repetitive and more instinctive, she began to enjoy it even more. Her steps became more animated, her concentration less focused on the moves and more on the music. She could see why it drove people to dance. Feet couldn't be still with that rhythm jangling out. She knew, as Cliff grabbed her and swung her in fast circles, that she could've danced for hours.

"That's it," he said, laughing as she clung to him.

"Already?" She was breathless but not nearly finished. "It was wonderful, but too short. When do we do another?"

"Any time you like."

"Now," she told him, sliding in as new lines formed.

She was fitting in as if she'd been to country dances in rural parks all her life. Perhaps he shouldn't have been surprised; she'd proved him wrong time and time again in his preconception of her. Yet in other ways, Cliff mused, he'd been right. She had an elegance that was too ingrained to be missed, whether she was scraping linoleum or lying in his arms. There was a polish that came from affluence and classy schools that set her apart from the other women around her. For days he'd been telling himself that it was that difference that attracted him as much as it put his back up. He couldn't explain the reason for either. He couldn't explain now, as he watched her begin the next dance as if she'd been moving to the call all her life, why she made him uneasy.

Circumstances, he told himself, and turned her back and around in a butterfly swing. The circumstances almost from the moment they'd met had been uneasy. That was bound to affect the way he felt when he looked at her—when he thought of her. And he thought of her, Cliff admitted, more often than he should; he looked at her less often than he wanted to.

Living with her for the past few days had given him the odd sensation of having something he hadn't known he'd wanted. There was something just a little too appealing about waking each morning with her warm beside him, about coming home to Maggie and her music. It would be wiser, much wiser, if he remembered those differences between them. No real common ground, he told himself again. But when she whirled into his arms, laughing, it was as though he'd been waiting for her.

The first few dances were a blur of color and sound and music. Maggie let herself go, realizing it had been weeks since she'd felt this free of tension and trouble. She'd danced in trendy clubs with celebrities, twirled in ballrooms with royalty, but she knew she'd never had as much simple fun as she was having now, following the caller and the fiddle.

As she turned to her next partner, she found her hand gripped by Stan Agee. Without his badge and gun, he might've been an attractive athlete in his prime. For a reason Maggie couldn't analyze, she tensed immediately on contact.

"Glad to see you're out, Miss Fitzgerald."

"Thank you." Determined not to give in to the mood, she smiled, lifting a hand to his shoulder as he began the spin. She caught his scent, the familiar department-store cologne, but it didn't soothe her.

"You catch on fast."

"It's wonderful. I can't believe I've missed it all my life." Out of the corner of her eye, she saw Cliff spinning with Joyce. The tension wouldn't dissolve.

"Save out a dance for me," he ordered before they whirled back to their original partners for the next step.

The moment he touched her, Cliff felt the rigidity of her muscles. "What's wrong?"

"Nothing." It was nothing, Maggie told herself, because she couldn't explain it. But now, as she swirled and turned from one pair of arms to another, it came to her that each time she danced with someone, she might be dancing with a murderer. How was she to know? It could be anyone—the real estate agent who'd sold her the house, the butcher who'd recommended the pork chops only the day before, the postmistress, the bank teller. How was she to know?

Maggie's mind began to whirl. For an instant, her eyes locked on Lieutenant Reiker's as he stood on the sidelines, watching. Why here, she asked herself as she was snatched up and spun again. Why would he come here? Perhaps he was watching her—but why? Protecting her—from what?

Then she was in Cliff's arms again, grateful that her feet could follow the mindless repetition of the dance while her thoughts raced in dozens of directions. Hadn't Cliff said people came from all over to this all-night festival? Maybe Reiker was a country-dance enthusiast. More likely, she thought grimly, he'd wanted to see all the townspeople together, observe, dissect. She shuddered. It was his job, she reminded herself. He was only doing his job. But how she wished he'd go away.

There was Louella, seeming to float through the dance. Rather than verve, she had a restrained dignity in her movements that was both lovely and uncomfortable to watch. Lovely, Maggie realized, because Louella had the grace of a natural dancer. Uncomfortable—though she wasn't able to put her finger on it, Maggie sensed there was something beneath the restraint that struggled for release.

Fanciful, she berated herself. She was being foolish and fanciful, imagining things that weren't there. But the feeling of discomfort was persistent. She was being watched, she knew. By Reiker? Stan Agee, Joyce, Louella? By everyone, Maggie thought. They all knew one another; they'd all known William Morgan. She was the outsider who'd uncovered what had been dead and buried for a decade. Logic indicated that at least one of them would resent her for that—perhaps all of them.

Suddenly, the music was too loud, the steps were too fast and the air was too full of scent.

Then she was caught up in Bog's short, wiry arms and spun at a breathless pace. "You're a good spinner, Miss Maggie," he told her, grinning and showing several gaps instead of teeth. "One helluva spinner."

Looking down into his homely, wrinkled face, she broke into a grin of her own. She was being ridiculous. No one resented her. Why should they? She wasn't involved in a tragedy that was ten years old. It was time she stopped looking beneath the surface and accepted things as she saw them. "I love to spin!" she shouted to Bog, leaning back into it. "I could spin for hours."

He gave a cackling laugh and released her for the next sequence.

The music built, but it no longer seemed too loud. The tempo increased, but she could've danced faster and faster. When it was over, she had her hands linked around Cliff's neck and was laughing.

There was no tension in her now, but there had been. He thought he understood the reason. Deliberately, he steered her away from the Agees and Louella. "I could use a beer."

"Sounds perfect. I'd like to watch another one, anyway. It's the best show in town."

"You want a beer?"

Maggie glanced up, brow lifted. "Aren't I allowed?"

He shrugged and passed a man in overalls a dollar. "You just don't look like the beer type."

"You type too easily," Maggie countered, watching as beer was tapped from a wooden keg into paper cups.

"Maybe," he murmured as she sipped at the froth. "You're having a good time?"

"Yes." She laughed over the rim. The beer was lukewarm, but it was wet. Her foot was already tapping. They'd added a mandolin, she noticed. The sound was sweet and old-fashioned. "Didn't you think I would?"

"I thought you'd enjoy the music." He leaned against the wall so that he could see her with the dancers at her back. "I thought you needed to get out. But I didn't expect you to take to all this as if you'd been born doing it."

She lowered her half-empty cup and gave him a solemn smile. "When are you going to stop putting me in that shiny glass cage, Cliff? I'm not a delicate hothouse flower or a spoiled Hollywood bitch. I'm Maggie Fitzgerald, and I write music."

The look held for a long time while the music pulsed around them. "I think I know who you are." Lifting a hand, he ran the back of it down her cheek. "I think I know Maggie Fitzgerald. It might've been safer for both of us with you in that glass cage."

She felt the heat rise. It only took a touch. "We'll have to see, won't we?" With one brow still lifted in question, she touched her cup to his. "To new understanding?"

"All right." He cradled her chin in his hand before he kissed her. "We'll give it a shot."

"Miss Fitzgerald?"

Maggie turned to see a short man in his early twenties running a felt hat around and around in his hands. Until that moment, she'd been so intent on Cliff that she hadn't noticed the music had stopped. "You're the piano player." Her eyes lit, and the smile that could stun so unexpectedly curved on her lips. "You're wonderful."

He'd been nervous before; now he was overwhelmed. "I just— Thank you," he managed, staring at her with his soul in his eyes.

She doesn't even know it, Cliff realized. She wasn't aware that she could make a man want to grovel. Sipping his beer, he watched the piano player try to find his voice again.

"I couldn't believe it when I heard you were here."

"I live here," she told him simply.

The way she said it, so matter-of-factly, had Cliff looking at her again. She'd said it before, countless times in countless ways, but he realized now he hadn't listened. Yes, she lived here. She'd chosen to live here just as he had. It hardly mattered where she'd lived or how she'd lived before. She was here now because she'd chosen to be. And she was staying. For the first time, he fully believed it.

"Miss Fitzgerald..." The piano player crushed the brim of his hat in his fingers, torn between pleasure and anxiety. "I just wanted you to know it's great having you here. We don't want to push you into anything, but if you'd like to play anything, anything at all—"

"Are you asking?" she interrupted.

The boy stumbled over uncertain ground. "We just wanted you to know that if you'd like—"

"I don't know any of the songs," she told him, taking a last sip of beer. "Do you trust me to improvise?"

His mouth dropped open. "Are you kidding?"

She laughed and handed her cup to Cliff. "Hang on to this."

He shook his head, leaning back against the wall as she walked to the stage with the piano player. She had a habit of giving orders, he mused. Then he thought of the look of stunned admiration in the boy's eyes. Maybe it was worth it.

She played for an hour. It was, she discovered, as much fun making the music as it was dancing to it. She enjoyed the challenge of the unfamiliar music and the freewheeling style. Before she'd gone through the second number, Maggie had decided to write one of her own.

From the vantage point of the stage, she could see the dancers. She saw Louella again, partnered by Stan. Automatically, she searched the crowd for Joyce and found her, facing Cliff. As if she'd known he'd be there, her gaze was drawn to the left. Reiker leaned against a post, smoking, watching the dancers.

Who? Maggie wondered. Who is he watching? As the lines merged and shifted, she couldn't be sure, only that the direction of his gaze rested on where Stan danced with Louella and Cliff with Joyce.

If he saw one of them as a murderer, it didn't show in his eyes. They were calm and steady and made Maggie's stomach queasy. Deliberately, she turned her head and concentrated on the music.

"I didn't expect to lose my partner to a piano," Cliff said when the music paused again.

Maggie sent him an arch look. "You didn't appear to lack for any."

"A lone man's easy prey around here." Grabbing her hand, he drew her to her feet. "Hungry?"

"Is it midnight already?" Maggie pressed a hand to her stomach. "I'm starving."

They piled their plates high, though the light was so dim it was impossible to tell what they were eating until it was tasted. They sat on the grass under a tree and chatted easily to the people who passed by. It was easy, Maggie thought. They were just people drawn to one place by music. Again she felt a sense of camaraderie and connection. Leaning back, Maggie scanned the crowd.

"I don't see Louella."

"Stan would've taken her home," Cliff said between bites. "She never stays past midnight. He'll come back."

"Mmm." Maggie sampled what turned out to be Waldorf salad.

"Miss Fitzgerald."

Maggie set down her fork as Reiker crouched down beside her. "Lieutenant."

"I enjoyed your playing." He gave her the quiet smile that had her cursing her reaction to him. "I've listened to your music for years, but I never expected to be able to hear you play."

"I'm glad you liked it." She knew she should leave it at that, but felt compelled to go on. "I haven't noticed you dancing."

"Me?" The smile turned sheepish. "No, I don't dance. My wife, now, she likes to come."

Maggie felt herself relax. So the explanation had been a simple one, an innocent one. "Most people who appreciate music like to dance."

"I'd like to. My feet don't." His gaze shifted to Cliff. "I want to thank you for your cooperation. It might help us tie up a few loose ends."

"Whatever I can do," Cliff said briskly. "We'd all like this business tied up."

Reiker nodded, then, with some effort, rose. "I hope you'll play some more before the night's over, Miss Fitzgerald. It's a real pleasure listening to you."

When he was gone, Maggie let out a long breath. "It isn't fair that he makes me uncomfortable. He's only doing his job." She began to pick at her food again when Cliff remained silent. "What did he mean by cooperation?"

"I contacted my mother. She's coming up Monday to give a statement."

"I see. That must be difficult for her."

"No." Cliff shrugged it off. "It was ten years ago. It's behind her. It's behind all of us," he added quietly, "but one."

Maggie closed her eyes on a shudder. She wouldn't think of it now, not tonight. "Dance with me again," she insisted when the musicians began to tune. "There are hours yet before dawn."

She never tired, even after the moon began to set. The music and the movement gave her the release she needed for nervous energy. Some dancers faded; others became only more exuberant as the night grew later. The music never stopped.

As the sky began to lighten, there were no more than a hundred dancers left on their feet. There was something mystical, something powerful, in watching the sun rise from behind the mountains while the music poured onto the air. As the light grew rosy with the new day, the last waltz was called.

Cliff folded Maggie in his arms and circled the floor. He could feel the life vibrate from her—exciting, strong. Once she'd stopped, he thought as he gathered her closer, she'd sleep for hours.

She moved with him, snug against him. Her heartbeat was steady, her hair soft. He watched the colors spread over the mountains to the east. Then she tilted back her head and smiled at him.

And when he realized he was in love with her, Cliff was stunned and speechless.

## *Chapter 12*

Maggie might've noticed Cliff's abrupt withdrawal if she hadn't been so full of the night and the music. "I can't believe it's over. I've hours more dancing in me."

"You'll be asleep before you're home," Cliff told her, but made certain he wasn't touching her. He must be crazy, falling in love with a woman like her. She couldn't decide whether to hang wallpaper or lay tile. She gave orders. She wore silk under her jeans. He must be crazy.

But she could dance with him through the night. There was a ridge of strength and courage under the delicate features. She made music that was part heaven and part sin. Hadn't he known, and hadn't he fought so hard, because he'd known almost from the first that she was a woman he'd never get out of his mind?

Now she was climbing into the cab of his pickup and resting her head against his shoulder as if it belonged there. It did belong there.

Though the acceptance didn't come easily to him, Cliff put his arm around her, drawing her closer. She belonged there.

"I don't know when I've had such a good time." The energy was draining out of her swiftly. Through sheer will, Maggie kept her eyes open.

"The music's still running around in your head."

She tilted her head so that she could see his profile. "I think you are beginning to understand me."

"Some."

"Some's enough." She yawned hugely. "It was fun playing tonight. You know, I've always avoided performing, mainly because I knew it would only open the door for more comparisons. But tonight..."

Cliff frowned, not certain if he liked the drift. "You're thinking of performing?"

"No, not on a regular basis. If I'd had a drive to do it, I'd have done it long before this." She shifted into a more comfortable position. "But I've decided to take C.J.'s advice and do the title song for *Heat Dance*. It's a compromise, a recording rather than a performance. And I do feel rather personally toward that song."

"You decided this tonight?"

"I've been leaning toward it for quite a while. It seems foolish to live by rules so strict you can't do something you really want to do. I really want to do that song." As her head began to droop, she noticed they were turning into her lane. "It'll mean flying back to L.A. for a few days for the taping, which'll thrill C.J." She gave a sleepy laugh. "He'll pull out every trick in the book to keep me from coming back."

Cliff felt the panic in his chest. He pulled the truck up at the end of the drive and set the brake. "I want you to marry me."

"What?" Half asleep, Maggie shook her head, certain she'd misunderstood.

"I want you to marry me," Cliff repeated, but this time he took her shoulders so that she wasn't slumped down in the seat any longer. "I don't care if you record a dozen songs. You're going to marry me before you go back to California."

To say she was stunned would've been an immeasurable understatement. Maggie stared at him as if one of them had lost his mind. "I must be a little foggy at the moment," she said slowly. "Are you saying you want to marry me?"

"You know damn well what I'm saying." It was too much to know the fear of losing her just when he'd realized he couldn't live without her. He couldn't be calm; he couldn't be rational; he couldn't let her go without a pledge that she'd come back. "You're not going to California until you marry me."

Trying to clear her mind, Maggie drew back. "Are you talking about my doing a recording, or are we talking marriage? One has to do with my business, the other with my life."

Frustrated that she was calm when he couldn't be, Cliff dragged her back. "From now on, your life is my business."

"No." That sounded too familiar. "No, I don't want someone looking out for me, if that's what you mean. I won't take that kind of responsibility again, or that kind of guilt."

"I don't know what the hell you're talking about," Cliff exploded. "I'm telling you you're going to marry me."

"That's just it—you can't *tell* me!" She jerked away from him, and the sleepiness in her eyes had turned to fire. "Jerry told me we were getting married, and I went along because it seemed like the thing to do. He was my best friend. He'd helped me get over the death of my parents, encouraged me to write again. He wanted to take care of me." Maggie dragged a hand through her hair. "And I let him, until things started going downhill and he couldn't even take care of himself. I couldn't help him then. The pattern had been set, and I couldn't help him. Not again, Cliff. I won't be put in that glass cage again."

"This has nothing to do with your first marriage and nothing to do with cages," Cliff tossed back. "You can damn well take care of yourself, but you're going to marry me."

Her eyes narrowed into slits as she held down her own uncertain temper. "Why?"

"Because I'm telling you."

"Wrong answer." With a toss of her head, she was out of the truck and had slammed the door. "You can go cool off or go sleep it off or whatever you want," she told him coldly. "I'm going to bed." Turning on her heel, she strode up the shaky front steps to the door. As she turned the handle, she heard the sound of his truck descending the hill. *Let him go,* Maggie told herself before she could turn around and call him back. *You can't let yourself be pushed around that way.* When a man thinks he can order a woman to marry him, he deserves exactly what she'd given him, Maggie decided. A good swift kick in the ego. Imagine bringing up marriage out of the blue that way, she thought as she shoved open the front door. Marriage, not love. He dangled marriage at her as though it were a carrot at the end of a stick. She wasn't biting. If he wanted her, really wanted her, he'd have to do a hell of a lot better.

I love you. She leaned her head against the door and told herself she wouldn't cry. That's all it would've taken; that's all he'd needed to say. Understanding. No, she decided as she straightened again, they were still a long way from understanding each other.

Why wasn't the dog barking, she wondered grumpily as she pushed the door shut again. Terrific watchdog he'd turned out to be. Annoyed, she turned toward the steps, planning on a hot bath and a long sleep, when a scent stopped her. Candle wax, Maggie thought, puzzled. Roses? Odd, she thought. Her imagination was good, but not good enough to conjure up scents. She crossed toward the living room and stopped in the doorway.

Louella sat very straight and very prim in a high-backed chair. Her hands were neatly folded in the lap of the same misty-gray dress she'd worn for dancing. Her skin was so pale that the shadows under her eyes looked like bruises. The eyes themselves seemed to stare straight through Maggie. On the table beside her there were candles burning, the tapers hardly more than stubs now, with the wax pooled heavily on the base of the holders. A vase of fresh roses sat nearby, so that the breeze through the open window carried the scent through the room.

After the first shock, Maggie tried to bring her thoughts to order. It had been obvious from the first that Louella wasn't completely well. She'd have to be handled gently, Maggie thought, and so she approached her as one might a wounded bird.

"Mrs. Morgan," she said quietly, then cautiously touched a hand to her shoulder.

"I've always liked candlelight." Louella spoke in her calm, soft voice. "So much prettier than a lamp. I'd often burn candles in the evening."

"They're lovely." Maggie kept her tone gentle as she knelt beside her. "But it's morning now."

"Yes." Louella looked blankly at the sun-filled window. "I often sit up through the night. I like the sounds. The woods make such music at night."

Perhaps if she'd thought it through, Maggie wouldn't have questioned. She would simply have led Louella out to her car and driven her home. But she didn't think it through. "Do you often come here at night, Mrs. Morgan?"

"Sometimes I'll drive," she said dreamily. "Sometimes, if the night's as clear and warm as this, I'll walk. I used to walk a great deal as a girl. Joyce used to love to toddle on the paths in the woods when she was just a baby."

Maggie moistened her lips. "Do you come back here often, Mrs. Morgan, at night?"

"I know I should stay away. Joyce has told me so all along. But—" Louella sighed, and the small, sad smile touched her mouth. "She has Stan. Such a good man—they take care of each other. That's what marriage is, you know, loving and taking care of each other."

"Yes." Helplessly, Maggie watched as Louella's hands grew agitated in her lap.

"William wasn't a loving man. He just wasn't made that way. I wanted Joyce to have a loving man, like Stan." She lapsed into silence, closing her eyes and breathing shallowly so that Maggie thought she slept. Deciding it was best to call the Agees, she started to rise, when Louella's hand closed over hers.

"I followed him here that night," she whispered. Now her eyes were intense, fully focused. Maggie's mouth went dry.

"Followed him?"

"I didn't want anything to happen. Joyce loved him so."

Maggie struggled to keep her voice low and even, her eyes steady. "You followed your husband here?"

"William was here," Louella told her. "He was here, and he had the money. I knew he was going to do something dreadful, something he'd have gotten away with because of who he was. There had to be an end to it." Her fingers tightened convulsively on Maggie's, then relaxed just as abruptly as her head fell back. "Of course, the money couldn't be buried with him. I thought, no, if they find him, they shouldn't find the money. So I hid it."

"Here," Maggie managed. "In the attic."

"In the old trunk. I forgot all about it," Louella said as fatigue washed through her voice. "Forgot until a few weeks ago, when they dug in the gully. I came and took the money out and burned it, as I should've burned it ten years ago."

Maggie looked down at the hand that lay limply on hers. It was frail, the blue veins showing sharply against the thin ivory skin. Could that hand have pulled a trigger, sending a bullet into a man? Maggie shifted her gaze to Louella's face and saw it was now serene in sleep.

What do I do? Maggie asked herself as she laid Louella's hand carefully back in her lap. Call the police? Maggie looked at the peacefully sleeping, fragile figure in the chair. No, she couldn't; she didn't have the steel for it. She'd call Joyce.

She went to the phone and asked the operator for Joyce's number. There was no answer at the Agee house. Maggie sighed and glanced over her shoulder into the living room at Louella, who was still sleeping. She hated to do it, but she had to call Lieutenant Reiker. When she couldn't get hold of him, either, she left a message with his office.

Coming back into the living room, Maggie gasped as a figure moved toward her. "Oh, you frightened me."

"Sorry." Stan looked with concern from Maggie to his mother-in-law. "I came in the back. The dog's sleeping pretty heavily in the kitchen. Looks like Louella might've given him part of a sleeping pill to keep him quiet."

"Oh." Maggie made an instinctive move toward the kitchen.

"He's all right," Stan assured her. "He'll just be a little groggy when he wakes up."

"Sheriff—Stan," she decided, hoping the lack of formality would make it easier for him. "I was just about to call you. I think Louella's been here most of the night."

"I'm sorry." He rubbed his own sleep-starved eyes. "She's been getting steadily worse since this business started. Joyce and I don't want to put her in a home."

"No." Concerned, she touched his arm. "But she told me she wanders at night, and—" Maggie broke off and circled the room. Could she tell him what Louella had said? He was her son-in-law, but he was still the sheriff. The badge and the gun he wore reminded her.

"I heard what she told you, Maggie."

She turned, her eyes filled with compassion and concern. "What should we do? She's so fragile. I can't bear to be a part of having her punished for something that happened so long ago. And yet, if she killed…" With her conscience tearing her in different directions, she turned again.

"I don't know." Stan looked at Louella while he rubbed the back of his neck. "What she told you doesn't have to be true."

"But it makes sense," Maggie insisted. "She knew about the money. If she'd hid it in the trunk, then forgotten about it, blocked it out because it reminded her—" Maggie shook her head and forced herself to continue. "Stan, it's the only explanation for the break-in here." She covered her face with her hands as her sense of right and wrong battled. "She needs help," Maggie said abruptly. "She doesn't need police or lawyers. She needs a doctor."

Relief ran over Stan's face. "She'll get one. The best one Joyce and I can find."

Shaky, uncertain, Maggie rested a hand on the table. "She's devoted to you," she murmured. "She always speaks so highly of you, of how you love Joyce. I think she'd do anything she could to keep both of you happy."

As she spoke, Maggie's gaze was drawn down to where her palm rested—on the color snapshot of Morgan and Stan, near the gully. It would all be laid to rest now, she thought as she stared down at the photo. Louella had suffered enough, been punished enough for—

Distracted, she narrowed her eyes and looked closer. Why it came to her now, Maggie would never know, but she remembered Reiker's words. "We found a ring, too, an old ring with a lot of fancy carving and three small diamond chips...Joyce Agee identified it as her father's."

But in the picture William Morgan wasn't wearing the ring. Stan Agee was.

She looked up, her eyes dry and clear with the knowledge.

He didn't have to look at the picture under her hand. He'd already seen. "You should've let it go, Maggie."

She didn't stop to think, to reason; she only reacted. In a dead run, she headed for the front door. The move was so unexpected, she was into the hall with her hand on the knob before he'd taken the first step. As the door stuck, she cursed it, cursed her own inefficiency for not having it seen to weeks before. As she started to tug a second time, Stan's hand closed over her arm.

"Don't." His voice was low and strained. "I don't want to hurt you. I have to think this through."

With her back to the door, Maggie stared at him. She was alone in the house with a murderer. Alone, she thought desperately, except for a fragile old woman who loved him enough to have shielded him for ten years. Maggie watched him rest his hand on the butt of his gun.

"We'd better sit down."

Cliff drank his second cup of coffee and wished it was bourbon. If he'd tried to make a fool of himself over a woman, he could've done no better. Drinking in the strong, bitter taste, he scowled down at the laminated counter in the café. The scent of frying eggs and sausage did nothing for his appetite.

How could he have botched it so badly? What woman in her right mind, he asked himself, would respond favorably to a shouted, angry proposal? Maggie had given him the heave-ho, and now that he'd cooled off a bit, he couldn't blame her.

Still, he wasn't one of the fancy crowd she'd run with in L.A., he reminded himself. He wasn't going to change his manners for her any more than he expected her to change for him. She'd chosen to change her life before he'd been a part of it.

Chosen, Cliff thought again, cursing himself. She'd chosen her home, and he'd never seen anyone put down roots so quickly. He shouldn't have panicked at the mention of the recording in L.A. She'd be back. The land was as important to her as it was to him. Perhaps that had been their first bond, though they both insisted they'd had no common ground.

She'd be back, Cliff told himself again. He'd been an idiot to think bullying her into marriage would assure that. Maggie wouldn't be bullied, and she was here to stay. Those were two of the reasons he loved her.

He should have told her that, he thought, pushing the unwanted coffee aside. He could have found the words to tell her he'd been in love with her for weeks and that at dawn, with the morning light spilling over her face, he'd realized it. It had taken his breath away, stolen his senses, made him weak. He could've found the words to tell her.

Straightening from the counter, he checked his watch. She'd had an hour's sleep. Cliff decided a woman didn't need any more than that for a proper proposal of marriage. He tossed the money on the counter and began to whistle.

He continued to whistle as he took the road through town, until Joyce dashed into the street and frantically hailed him.

"Oh, Cliff!"

Though he'd stopped the car in the middle of the street, he was halfway out of it as he spoke. "What is it, one of the kids?"

"No, no." Struggling for calm, Joyce gripped his arms. She, too, hadn't changed from the dance, but the hair she'd worn up was now escaping its pins and falling in clumps. "It's my mother," she managed after a moment. "She hasn't been in bed all night—and Stan, I can't find Stan anywhere."

"We'll find Louella." Cliff brushed the hair from her face as he'd done since she'd been a child. "She might have been restless and gone for a walk. With the excitement last night—"

"Cliff." Joyce gripped his arms tighter. "I think she went out to the old place. I'm dead sure of it; it wouldn't be the first time."

He thought of Maggie with a little ripple of unease. "Maggie's home," he said soothingly. "She'll look out for her."

"She's been getting worse." Joyce's breath began to shudder. "Oh, Cliff, I thought I was doing the right thing, the only thing."

"What're you talking about?"

"I lied to the police. I lied before I'd thought it through, but I know I'd do the same thing again." She pressed her fingers to her eyes briefly, then dropped them. When she looked at Cliff now, she looked at him with a surface calm that was deadly. "I know who killed my father. I've known for weeks. Mother—it seems Mother's known for ten years."

"Get in," he ordered. He was thinking of Maggie now, of Maggie alone in the house, surrounded by woods. "Tell me while we drive."

Maggie's back was stiff and straight as she sat on a low bench. Moving only her eyes, she watched Stan pace the room. She wanted to believe he wouldn't hurt her. But he'd killed once, ten years before. Now he'd have to deal with her or pay for it.

"I never wanted Joyce to sell this house." He paced to the window, then back to the center of the room. "I never wanted it. The money meant nothing to me. Her money—her father's money—never has. How could I've guessed she'd get it into her head to put it on the market when I was out of town?"

He ran a hand over his shirt and left faint streaks. He's sweating, Maggie noted. It didn't help her nerves.

"She lied to the police about the ring."

Maggie moistened her lips. "She loves you."

"She didn't know—I'd never told her all these years. Then, when I finally had to, she stood by me. A man can't ask for more than that." He paced again, so that the soles of his shoes hitting hardwood and rug were the only sounds. "I didn't murder him," Stan said flatly. When he looked at Maggie, his eyes were glazed with fatigue. "It was an accident."

She gripped that, clung to that. "Then if you go to the police and explain—"

"Explain?" Stan cut her off. "Explain that I killed a man, buried him and drove his car into the river?" He rubbed the heels of his hands over his face. "I was only twenty," he began. "Joyce and I'd been in love for two years. Morgan had already made it clear that there couldn't be anything between us, so we saw each other in secret. When Joyce found out she was pregnant, there couldn't be any more secrets."

He leaned against the window and stared into the room. "We should've known there was something wrong when he took it so well, but we were both so relieved, both so thrilled at the idea of being married and starting a family, that we never caught on. He told us to keep it quiet for a few weeks while he arranged for the wedding."

Maggie remembered the stern face from the photograph. "But he didn't mean it."

"No, both of us were too wrapped up in each other to remember what kind of man he was." Stan kept moving in the same line, to the window, back to the center of the room, to the window again. "He said he was having trouble with groundhogs up at his old place. I was young and eager to do anything to keep on the right side of him. I told him I'd bring my shotgun one evening after work and take care of them."

He saw Maggie shudder and glance at the pistol on his hip. "It was dusk when he drove up. I didn't expect him. When he got out of the car, I remember thinking he looked like an undertaker, all in black with shiny shoes. He was carrying a little metal box that he set down on the stump of a tree near the gully. He didn't waste any time," Stan continued. "He told me outright that he'd never let a small-town nobody like me marry his daughter. He said he was going to send her away. Sweden or somewhere. She'd have the baby and give it away. He didn't expect me to keep quiet for nothing. He told me he had twenty-five thousand in the box. I was to take it and disappear."

So the twenty-five thousand had been payoff money, blackmail. Yes, she could believe that the man in the photo had thought money would ensure anything.

"I got frantic. I couldn't believe he was threatening to take away everything I'd ever wanted. He could've done it, too." Stan wiped at the sweat that beaded on his upper lip. "He would've done it without a second thought. I shouted at him. I told him he wasn't going to take Joyce and our baby away from me. I told him we'd go away, we didn't need his filthy money. He opened the cash box and showed me all those bills, as if it would tempt me. I knocked it out of his hands."

His breath was coming quickly now, heavily, as if he were reliving that moment—the anger, the despair. Maggie felt her pity well up to tangle with her fear.

"He never lost his temper. Never once. He just bent down and scooped the money back in the box. He thought I wanted more. He never understood, wasn't capable of understanding. When it got to the point where he saw I wasn't going to take the money and go away, he picked up my gun just as calmly as he'd picked up the box. I knew, as sure as I'd ever know anything, that he'd kill me where I stood and he'd get away with it. Somehow he'd get away with it. All I could think was that I'd never see Joyce again, never hold our baby. I grabbed for the gun—it went off over my shoulder. We started struggling."

He was panting now, his eyes glazed. Maggie could visualize the struggle between man and boy as clearly as if it were happening in front of her eyes. She shut them. Then she saw the scene in the film she'd scored in which overpowering need had erupted into irrevocable violence. But this was real and needed no music to spark the drama.

"He was strong—that old man was strong. I knew I'd be dead if I didn't get the gun away. Somehow—" Stan dragged both his hands up his face and into his hair. "Somehow I had it in my hands and was falling back. I'll never forget—it was like a dream, a nightmare. I was falling back, and the gun went off."

She could picture it, all too clearly. Both sympathetic and afraid, Maggie dared to speak. "But it was an accident, self-defense."

He shook his head as his hands dropped back to his side, back, she noted with a tremor, near the gun on his hip. "I was twenty, scraping pennies. I'd just killed the most important man in town, and there was twenty-five thousand dollars in a box next to his body. Who'd have believed me? Maybe I panicked, maybe I did the only sensible thing, but I buried him and his money in the gully, then sent his car into the river."

"Louella..." Maggie began.

"I didn't know she'd followed me. I guess she knew Morgan better than anyone and understood he'd never let me marry Joyce. I didn't know she'd watched everything from the woods. Maybe if I had, things would've been different. It seemed she never really came out of the shock of losing her husband; now I understand better. She'd seen it all—then, for some reason of her own, she'd dug out the cash box and hidden it in the house. I guess she was protecting me all these years."

"And Joyce?"

"She never knew." Stan shook his head and tugged at the collar of his shirt as if it were too tight. "I never told her. You have to understand. I love Joyce. I've loved her since she was a girl. There's nothing I wouldn't do for her if I could. If I'd told her everything, everything he'd threatened to do and what had happened, she might have thought—she might not have believed it was an accident. I couldn't have lived with that. For years I've done everything I could to make up for what happened in that gully. I dedicated myself to the law, to the town. I've been the best father, the best husband, I know how to be."

He picked up the color snapshot and crushed it in his hand. "That damn picture. Damn ring. I was so wired up I didn't notice I'd lost it until days afterward. My grandfather's ring." He rubbed a hand over his temple. "Ten years later it's dug up with Morgan. Do you know how I felt when I learned that Joyce had identified it as her father's? She knew," he said passionately. "She knew it was mine, but she stood behind me. She never questioned me, and when I told her everything, she never doubted me. All these years—I've lived with it all these years."

"You don't have to live with it anymore." Maggie spoke calmly, though her heart was in her throat. He was strung so tight she couldn't gauge when he might snap or what he might do. "People respect you, know you. Louella saw everything. She'd testify."

"Louella's on the edge of a complete breakdown. Who knows if she'd be capable of making a coherent sentence if all this comes out? I have to think of Joyce, of my family, of my reputation." A muscle began to jerk in his cheek as he stared at Maggie. "There's so much at stake," he whispered. "So much to protect."

She watched his hand hover over the butt of his gun.

Cliff started up the steep lane at full speed, spitting gravel. Joyce's breathless story told him one vital thing. Maggie was caught in the middle of violence and passion that had simmered underground for ten years. If it erupted today, she'd be alone—alone because he'd been a fool. As he rounded the top curve, a man stepped into the path of the car, forcing him to brake. Swearing, Cliff stormed out of the car.

"Mr. Delaney," Reiker said mildly. "Mrs. Agee."

"Where's Maggie?" Cliff demanded, and would've moved past him if Reiker hadn't stopped him with a surprisingly strong grip.

"She's inside. At the moment, she's fine. Let's keep it that way."

"I'm going up."

"Not yet." He gave Cliff a long, steely look before he turned to

Joyce. "Your mother's inside, Mrs. Agee. She's fine, sleeping. Your husband's in there, too."

"Stan." Joyce looked toward the house, taking an instinctive step forward.

"I've been keeping a close eye on things. Your husband told Miss Fitzgerald everything."

Cliff's blood iced. "Damn it, why haven't you gotten her out?"

"We're going to get her out. We're going to get them all out. Quietly."

"How do you know he won't hurt her?"

"I don't—if he's pushed. I want your help, Mrs. Agee. If your husband loves you as much as he says, you're the key." He looked toward the house. "He'd have heard the car. Better let him know you're here."

Inside the house, Stan had Maggie by the arm, holding her close as he stood at the window. She could feel his muscles jumping, hear his breath whistling. As terror washed over her, she closed her eyes and thought of Cliff. If he'd come back, everything would be all right. If he came back, the nightmare would end.

"Someone's out there." Stan jerked his head toward the open window, and his free hand opened and closed on the butt of his gun. "I can't let you talk to anyone. You have to understand. I can't risk it."

"I won't." His fingers dug into her arm so that the pain kept her head clear. "Stan, I want to help you. I swear I only want to help. If you hurt me, it'll never be over."

"Ten years," he muttered, straining to see any movement outside. "Ten years and he's still trying to ruin my life. I can't let him."

"Your life will be ruined if you do anything to me." *Be logical,* Maggie told herself as waves of panic threatened to overtake her. *Be calm.* "It wouldn't be an accident this time, Stan. This time you'd be a murderer. You'd never make Joyce understand."

His fingers tightened until she had to dig her teeth into her lower lip to keep from crying out. "Joyce stood behind me."

"She loves you. She believes in you. But if you hurt me, everything would change."

She felt him tremble. The grip on her arm loosened fractionally. As Maggie watched, Joyce walked up over the rise toward the house. At first, she thought she was hallucinating; then she heard Stan's breath catch. He saw her, too.

"Stan." Joyce's hand moved on her throat, as if she could make her voice stronger. "Stan, please come out."

"I don't want you involved in this." Stan's fingers were like iron on Maggie's arm again.

"I am involved. I've always been involved. I know everything you did you did for me."

"Damn it." He pressed his face against the window glass, pounding one fist steadily against the frame. "He can't ruin everything we've built."

"No, he can't." Joyce came closer to the house, measuring each step. In all the years she'd known her husband, she'd never heard despair in his voice. "Stan, he can't touch us now. We're together. We'll always be together."

"They'll take me away from you. The law." He squeezed his eyes tighter. "I've done my best by the law."

"Everyone knows that. Stan, I'll be with you. I love you. You're everything to me, my whole life. Please, please, don't do anything I'd be ashamed of."

Maggie felt him tense as he straightened from the window. The muscle was still working in his cheek. There was a line of sweat over his lip he no longer bothered to wipe away. He stared out the window, at Joyce, then over at the gully.

"Ten years," he whispered. "But it's still not over."

His fingers worked sporadically on Maggie's arm. Numb with fear, she watched as he drew the gun out of its holster. His eyes met hers, cold, clear blue, without expression. Perhaps she would've begged for her life, but she knew, as any prey knows, that mercy comes at the hunter's whim.

His expression never changed as he set the gun down on the sill and released her arm. Maggie felt her blood begin to pump again, fast and hot. "I'm going outside," Stan said flatly, "to my wife."

Weak with relief, Maggie sank down on the piano stool. Without even the energy to weep, she buried her face in her hands.

"Oh, Maggie." Then Cliff's arms were around her, and she could feel the hard, fast beat of his heart. "That was the longest ten minutes of my life," he murmured as he began to run wild kisses over her face. "The longest."

She didn't want explanations. He was here; that was enough. "I kept telling myself you'd come. It kept me sane."

"I shouldn't have left you alone." He buried his face in her hair and drew in the scent.

She held him tighter. "I told you I could take care of myself."

He laughed, because she was in his arms and nothing had changed. "Yes, you did. It's over now." He framed her face in his hands so that he could study it. Pale, he noticed. The eyes were shadowed but steady. His Maggie was a woman who could take care of herself.

"Reiker was outside, long enough to get the drift of what was going on. He's taking all three of them."

She thought of Louella's pale face, Stan's anguished eyes, Joyce's trembling voice. "They've been punished enough."

"Maybe." He ran his hands up her arms, just to assure himself she was whole and safe. "If he'd hurt you—"

"He wouldn't have." She shook her head and clung again. "He couldn't have. I want the pond, Cliff," she said fiercely. "I want you to put in the pond quickly, and I want to see the willow draping over it."

"You'll have it." He drew her back again. "And me? Will you have me, Maggie?"

She took a deep breath, letting his fingers rest on her face again. Again, she thought. She would try again and see if he understood. "Why should I?"

His brows drew together, but he managed to swallow the oath that came to mind. Instead, he kissed her, hard and long. "Because I love you."

She let out a trembling breath. She was indeed home. "That was the right answer."

* * * * *

# One Man's Art

## *Chapter 1*

Gennie knew she'd found it the moment she passed the first faded clapboard building. The village, pragmatically and accurately called Windy Point, at last captured her personal expectations for a coastal Maine settlement. She'd found her other stops along the rugged, shifting coastline scenic, picturesque, at times postcard perfect. Perhaps the perfection had been the problem.

When she'd decided on this working vacation, she'd done so with the notion of exploring a different aspect of her talent. Where before, she'd always fancified, mystified, relying on her own bent toward illusions, she'd made a conscious decision to stick to realism, no matter how stark. Indeed, her trunk was laden with her impressions of rock and sea and earth on canvas and sketch pads, but…

There was something more about Windy Point. Or perhaps it was something less. There was no lushness here or soft edges. This was hard country. There were no leafy shade trees, but a few stunted fir and spruce, gnarled and weather-beaten. The road had more than its fair share of bumps.

The village itself, though it wasn't precisely tumbledown, had the air of old age with all its aches and pains. Salt and wind had weathered the buildings, picking away at the paint, scarring the windows. The result wasn't a soft wash, but a toughness.

Gennie saw a functional beauty. There were no frivolous buildings here, no gingerbread. Each building served its purpose—dry goods, post office, pharmacy. The few houses along the main road held that implacable New England practicality in their sturdy shape and tidy size. There might be flowers, adding a surprisingly gay and smiling color against the stern clapboard, but she noted nearly every home had a well-tended vegetable patch at the rear or the side. The petunias might be permitted to grow a bit unruly, but the carrots were tidily weeded.

With her car window down she could smell the village. It smelled quite simply of fish.

She drove straight through first, wanting a complete impression of the main street. She stopped by a churchyard where the granite markers were rather stern and the grass was high and wild, then turned to drive back through again. It wasn't a large town and the road was rather narrow, but she had a sense of spaciousness. You wouldn't bump into your neighbor here unless you meant to. Pleased, Gennie pulled up in front of the dry goods store, guessing this would be the hub of Windy Point's communications network.

The man sitting in an old wooden rocker on the stoop didn't stare, though she knew he'd seen her drive through and backtrack. He continued to rock while he repaired a broken lobster trap. He had the tanned brown face of the coast, guarded eyes, thinning hair and gnarled strong hands. Gennie promised herself she'd sketch him just like that. She stepped from the car, grabbing her purse as an afterthought, and approached him.

"Hello."

He nodded, his hands still busy with the wooden slats of the trap. "Need some help?"

"Yes." She smiled, enjoying the slow, thick drawl that somehow implied briskness. "Perhaps you can tell me where I can rent a room or a cottage for a few weeks."

The shopkeeper continued to rock while he summed her up with shrewd, faded eyes. City, he concluded, not altogether disdainfully. And South. Though he was a man who considered Boston South, he pegged her as someone who belonged in the humid regions below the Mason-Dixon line. She was neat and pretty enough, though he felt her dark complexion and light eyes had a substantially foreign look. Then again, if you went much farther south than Portland, you were talking foreign.

While he rocked and deliberated, Gennie waited patiently, her rich black hair lifting from her shoulders and blowing back in the salt-scented breeze. Her experience in New England during the past few months had taught her that while most people were fair-minded and friendly enough, they generally took their time about it.

Didn't look like a tourist, he thought—more like one of those fairy princesses his granddaughter read about in her picture books. The delicate face came to a subtle point at the chin and the sweep of cheekbones added hauteur. Yet she smiled, softening the look, and her eyes were the color of the sea.

"Don't get many summer people," he said at length. "All gone now anyhow."

He wouldn't ask, Gennie knew. But she could be expansive when it suited her purpose. "I don't think I qualify as summer people, Mr...."

"Fairfield—Joshua Fairfield."

"Genvièye Grandeau." She offered a hand which he found satisfactorily firm in his work-roughened one. "I'm an artist. I'd like to spend some time here painting."

An artist, he mused. Not that he didn't like pictures, but he wasn't sure he completely trusted the people who produced them. Drawing was a nice hobby, but for a job...still, she had a good smile and she didn't slouch. "Might be there's a cottage 'bout two miles out. Widow Lawrence ain't sold it yet." The chair creaked as he moved back and forth. "Could be she'll rent it for a time."

"It sounds good. Where can I reach her?"

"'Cross the road, at the post office." He rocked for another few seconds. "Tell her I sent you over," he decided.

Gennie gave him a quick grin. "Thank you, Mr. Fairfield."

The post office was hardly more than a counter and four walls. One of the walls was taken up with slots where a woman in a dark cotton dress deftly sorted mail. She even *looks* like a Widow Lawrence, Gennie thought with inner pleasure as she noted the neat circular braid at the back of the woman's head.

"Excuse me."

The woman turned, giving Gennie a quick, birdlike glance before she came over to the counter. "Help you?"

"I hope so. Mrs. Lawrence?"

"Ayah."

"Mr. Fairfield told me you might have a cottage to rent."

The small mouth pursed—the only sign of facial movement. "I've a cottage for sale."

"Yes, he explained that." Gennie tried her smile again. She wanted the town—and the two miles distance from it the cottage would give her. "I wonder if you'd consider renting it for a few weeks. I can give you references if you'd like."

Mrs. Lawrence studied Gennie with cool eyes. She made her own references. "For how long?"

"A month, six weeks."

She glanced down at Gennie's hands. There was an intricate gold twist of a ring, but it was on the wrong finger. "Are you alone?"

"Yes." Gennie smiled again. "I'm not married, Mrs. Lawrence. I've been traveling through New England for several months, painting. I'd like to spend some time here at Windy Point."

"Painting?" the widow finished with another long look.

"Yes."

Mrs. Lawrence decided she liked Gennie's looks—and that she was a young woman who didn't run on endlessly about herself. And fact was fact. An empty cottage was a useless thing. "The place is clean and the plumbing's good. Roof was fixed two years back, but the stove's got a temperament of its own. There's two bedrooms but one of 'em stands empty."

This is painful for her, Gennie realized, though the widow's voice stayed even and her eyes were steady. She's thinking about all the years she lived there.

"Got no close neighbors, and the phone's been taken out. Could be you could have one put in if you've a mind to."

"It sounds perfect, Mrs. Lawrence."

Something in Gennie's tone made the woman clear her throat. It had been sympathy and understanding quietly offered. After a moment she named a sum for the month's rent, far more reasonable than Gennie had expected. Characteristically she didn't hesitate, but went with her instincts.

"I'll take it."

The first faint flutter of surprise showed on the widow's face. "Without seeing it?"

"I don't need to see it." With a brisk practicality Mrs. Lawrence admired, Gennie pulled a checkbook out of her purse and dashed off the amount. "Maybe you can tell me what I'll need in the way of linen and dishes."

Mrs. Lawrence took the check and studied it. "Genevieve," she murmured.

"Genviève," Gennie corrected, flowing easily over the French. "After my grandmother." She smiled again, softening that rather ruthless fairy look. "Everyone calls me Gennie."

An hour later Gennie had the keys to the cottage in her purse, two boxes of provisions in the back seat of her car and directions to the cottage in her hand. She'd passed off the distant, wary stares of the villagers and had managed not to chuckle at the open ogling of a scrawny teenager who'd come into the dry goods store while she was mulling over a set of earthenware dishes.

It was dusk by the time she was ready to set out. The clouds were low and unfriendly now, and the wind had picked up. It only added to the sense of adventure. Gennie set out on the narrow, bumpy road that led to the sea with a restless inner excitement that meant something new was on the horizon.

She came by her love of adventure naturally. Her great-great-grandfather had been a pirate—an unapologetic rogue of the sea. His ship had been fast and fierce, and he had taken what he wanted without qualm. One of Gennie's treasures was his logbook. Philippe Grandeau had recorded his misdeeds with flair and a sense of irony she'd never been able to resist. She might have inherited a strong streak of practicality from the displaced aristocrats on her mother's side, but Gennie was honest enough to know she'd have sailed with the pirate Philippe and loved every minute of it.

As her car bounced along the ruts, she took in the scenery, so far removed from her native New Orleans it might have been another planet. This was no place for long lazy days and riotous nights. In this rocky, windswept world, you'd have to be on your toes every minute. Mistakes wouldn't be easily forgiven here.

But she saw more than hard land and rock. Integrity. She sensed it in the land that vied continually with the sea. It knew it would lose, inch by minute inch, century after endless century, but it wasn't giving in. Though the shadows lengthened with evening, she stopped, compelled to put some of her impressions on paper.

There was an inlet some yards from the road, restless now as the storm approached. As Gennie pulled out a sketchbook and pencil, she caught the smell of decaying fish and seaweed. It didn't make her wrinkle her nose; she understood that it was part of the strange lure that called men forever to the sea.

The soil was thin here, the rocks worn smooth. Near the road were clumps of wild blueberry bushes, pregnant with the last of the summer fruit. She could hear the wind—a distinctly feminine sound—sighing and moaning. She couldn't see the sea yet, but she could smell it and taste it in the air that swirled around her.

She had no one to answer to, no timetable to keep. Gennie had long since taken her freedom for granted, but solitude was something else. She felt it here, near the little windswept inlet, along the narrow, impossible road. And she held it to her.

When she was back in New Orleans, a city she loved, and she soaked up one of those steamy days that smelled of the river and humanity, she would remember passing an hour in a cool, lonely spot where she might have been the only living soul for miles.

Relaxed, but with that throb of excitement just buzzing along her skin, she sketched, going into much more detail than she had intended when she'd stopped. The lack of human noises appealed to her. Yes, she was going to enjoy Windy Point and the little cottage very much.

Finished, she tossed her sketchbook back in the car. It was nearly dark now or she might have stayed longer, wandered closer to the water's edge. Long days of painting stretched ahead of her…and who knew what else a month could bring? With a half smile, she turned the key in the ignition.

When she got only a bad-tempered rattle, she tried again. She was rewarded with a wheeze and a groan and a distinctly suspicious clunk. The car had given her a bit of trouble in Bath, but the mechanic there had tightened this and fiddled with that. It had been running like a top ever since. Thinking of the jolting road, Gennie decided that what could be tightened could just as easily be loosened again. With a mildly annoyed oath, she got out of the car to pop the hood.

Even if she had the proper tools, which she didn't think included the screwdriver and flashlight in her glove compartment, she would hardly know what to do with them. Closing the hood again, she glanced up and down the road. Deserted. The only sound was the wind. It was nearly dark, and by her calculations she was at the halfway point between town and the cottage. If she hiked back, someone was bound to give her a lift, but if she went on she could probably be in the cottage in fifteen minutes. With a shrug, she dug her flashlight out of the glove compartment and did what she usually did. She went forward.

She needed the light almost immediately. The road was no better to walk on than to drive on, but she'd have to take care to keep to it unless she wanted to end up lost or taking a dunking in an inlet. Ruts ran deeply here, rocks worked their way up there, so that she wondered how often anyone actually traveled this stretch.

Darkness fell swiftly, but not in silence. The wind whipped at her hair, keeping up its low, keening sound. There were wisps of fog at her feet now which she hoped would stay thin until she was indoors. Then she forgot the fog as the storm burst out, full of fury.

Under other circumstances, Gennie wouldn't have minded a soaking, but even her sense of adventure was strained in the howling darkness where her flashlight cut a pitiful beam through the slashing rain. Annoyance was her first reaction as she continued to trudge along the uneven road in thoroughly wet sneakers. Gradually annoyance became discomfort and discomfort, unease.

A flash of lightning would illuminate a cropping of rocks or stunted bush, throwing hard, unfriendly shadows. Even a woman possessing a pedestrian imagination might have had a qualm. Gennie had visions of nasty little elves grinning out of the cloaking darkness.

Humming tunelessly to stave off panic, she concentrated on the beam of her flashlight.

So I'm wet, Gennie told herself as she dragged dripping hair out of her eyes. It's not going to kill me. She gave another uneasy glance at the side of the road. There was no dark, Gennie decided, like the dark of the countryside. And where was the cottage? Surely she'd walked more than a mile by now. Halfheartedly she swung the light in a circle. Thunder boiled over her head while the rain slapped at her face. It would take a minor miracle to find a dark, deserted cottage with only the beam of a household flashlight.

Stupid, she called herself while she wrapped her arms tightly around her chest and tried to think. It was always stupid to set out toward the unknown when you had a choice. And yet she would always do so. There seemed to be nothing left but find her way back to the car and wait out the storm there. The prospect of a long wet night in a compact wasn't pleasant, but it had it all over wandering around lost in a thunderstorm. And there was a bag of cookies in the car, she remembered while she continued to stroke the flashlight back and forth, just in case there was—something out there. With a sigh, she gave one last look down the road.

She saw it. Gennie blinked rain out of her eyes and looked again. A light. Surely that was a light up ahead. A light meant shelter, warmth, company. Without hesitation, Gennie headed toward it.

It turned out to be another mile at best, while the storm and the road worsened. Lightning slashed the sky with a wicked purple light, tossing out a brief eerie glow that made the darkness only deeper when it faded. To keep from stumbling, she was forced to move slowly and keep her eyes on the ground. She began to be certain she'd never be dry or warm again. The light up ahead stayed steady and true, helping her to resist glancing over her shoulder too often.

She could hear the sea now, beating violently on rocks and shale. Once in a flash of lightning, she thought she saw the crest of angry waves, white-capped and turbulent in the distance. Even the rain smelled of the sea now—an angry, vengeful one. She wouldn't—couldn't—allow herself to be frightened, though her heart was beating fast from more than the two-mile walk. If she admitted she was frightened, she would give in to the urge to run and would end up over a cliff, in a ditch, or in some soundless vacuum.

The sense of displacement was so great, she might have simply sat on the road and wept had it not been for the steady beam of light sending out the promise of security.

When Gennie saw the silhouette of the building behind the curtain of rain she nearly laughed aloud. A lighthouse—one of those sturdy structures that proved man had some sense of altruism. The guiding light hadn't come from the high revolving lens but from a window. Gennie didn't question, but quickened her pace as much as she dared. Someone was there—a gnarled old man perhaps, a former seaman. He'd have a bottle of rum and talk in brief salty sentences. As a new bolt of lightning slashed across the sky, Gennie decided she already adored him.

The structure seemed huge to her—a symbol of safety for anyone lost and storm-tossed. It looked stunningly white under the play of her flashlight as she searched the base for a door. The window that was lit was high up, the top of three on the side Gennie approached.

She found a door of thick rough wood and beat on it. The violence of the storm swallowed the sound and tossed it away. Nearer to panic than she wanted to admit, Gennie pounded again. Could she have come so far, got so close, and then not be heard? The old keeper was in there, she thought as she beat on the door, probably whistling and whittling, perhaps idling away the evening putting a ship into a bottle.

Desperate, Gennie leaned against the door, feeling the hard, wet wood against her cheek as well as the side of her fist as she continued to thud against it. When the door opened, she went with it, overbalancing. Her arms were gripped hard as she pitched forward.

"Thank God!" she managed. "I was afraid you wouldn't hear me." With one hand she dragged her sopping hair out of her face and looked up at the man she considered her savior.

The one thing he wasn't was old. Nor was he gnarled. Rather he was young and lean, but the narrow, tanned face of planes and angles might have been a seafaring one—in her great-great-grandfather's line. His hair was as dark as hers, and as thick, with that careless windblown effect a man might get if he stood on the point of a ship. His mouth was full and unashamedly sensual, the nose a bit aristocratic in the rugged face. His eyes were a deep, deep brown under dark brows. They weren't friendly, Gennie decided, not even curious. They were simply annoyed.

"How the hell did you get here?"

It wasn't the welcome she had expected, but her trek through the storm had left her a bit muddled. "I walked," she told him.

"Walked?" he repeated. "In this? From where?"

"A couple of miles back—my car stalled." She began to shiver, either with chill or with reaction. He'd yet to release her, and she'd yet to recover enough to demand it.

"What were you doing driving around on a night like this?"

"I—I'm renting Mrs. Lawrence's cottage. My car stalled, then I must have missed the turnoff in the dark. I saw your light." She heaved a long breath and realized abruptly that her legs were shaking. "Can I sit down?"

He stared at her for another minute, then with something like a grunt nudged her toward a sofa. Gennie sank down on it, dropped her head back, and concentrated on pulling herself together.

And what the hell was he supposed to do with her? Grant asked himself. Brows lowered, he stared down at her. At the moment she looked like she'd keel over if he breathed too hard. Her hair was plastered to her head, curling just a bit and dark as the night itself. Her face wasn't fine or delicate, but beautiful in the way of medieval royalty—long bones, sharp features. A Celtic or Gallic princess with a compact athletic little body he could see clearly as her clothes clung to it.

He thought the face and body might be appealing enough, under certain circumstances, but what had thrown him for an instant when she'd looked up at him had been her eyes. Sea green, huge, and faintly slanted. Mermaid's eyes, he'd thought. For a heartbeat, or perhaps only half of that, Grant had wondered if she'd been some mythical creature who'd been tossed ashore in the storm.

Her voice was soft and flowing, and though he recognized it as Deep South, it seemed almost a foreign tongue after the coastal Maine cadence he'd grown used to. He wasn't a man to be pleased with having a magnolia blossom tossed on his doorstep. When she opened her eyes and smiled at him, Grant wished fervently he'd never opened the door.

"I'm sorry," Gennie began, "I was barely coherent, wasn't I? I suppose I wasn't out there for more than an hour, but it seemed like days. I'm Gennie."

Grant hooked his thumbs in the pockets of his jeans and frowned at her again. "Campbell, Grant Campbell."

Since he left it at that and continued to frown, Gennie did her best to pick things up again. "Mr. Campbell, I can't tell you how relieved I was when I saw your light."

He stared down at her another moment, thinking briefly that she looked familiar. "The turnoff for the Lawrence place's a good mile back."

Gennie lifted a brow at the tone. Did he actually expect her to go back outside and stumble around until she found it? She prided herself on being fairly even-tempered for an artist, but she was wet and cold, and Grant's unfriendly, scowling face tripped the last latch. "Look, I'll pay you for a cup of coffee and the use of this—" she thumped a hand on the sofa and a soft plume of dust rose up "—thing for the night."

"I don't take in lodgers."

"And you'd probably kick a sick dog if he got in your way," she added evenly. "But I'm not going back out there tonight, Mr. Campbell, and I wouldn't advise trying to toss me out, either."

That amused him, though the humor didn't show in his face. Nor did he correct her assumption that he had meant to shove her back into the storm. The statement had been simply meant to convey his displeasure and the fact that he wouldn't take her money. If he hadn't been annoyed, he might have appreciated the fact that soaking wet and slightly pale, she held her own.

Without a word he walked over to the far side of the room and crouched to rummage through a scarred oak cabinet. Gennie stared straight ahead, even as she heard the sound of liquid hitting glass.

"You need brandy more than coffee at the moment," Grant told her, and shoved the glass under her nose.

"Thank you," Gennie said in an icy tone southern women are the champions of. She didn't sip, but drank it down in one swallow, letting the warmth shock her system back to normal. Distantly polite, she handed the empty glass back to him.

Grant glanced down at it and very nearly smiled. "Want another?"

"No," she said, frigid and haughty, "thank you."

I have, he mused wryly, been put in my place. Princess to peasant. Considering his option, Grant rocked back on his heels. Through the thick walls of the lighthouse, the storm could be heard whipping and wailing. Even the mile ride to the Lawrence place would be wild and miserable, if not dangerous. It would be less trouble to bed her down where she was than to drive her to the cottage. With an oath that was more weary than pungent he turned away.

"Well, come on," he ordered without looking back, "you can't sit there shivering all night."

Gennie considered—seriously considered—heaving her purse at him.

The staircase charmed her. She nearly made a comment on it before she stopped herself. It was iron and circular, rising up and up the interior. Grant stepped off onto the second level which Gennie calculated was a good twenty feet above the first. He moved like a cat in the dark while she held on to the rail and waited for him to hit the light switch.

It cast a dim glow and many shadows over the bare wood floor.

He passed through a door on the right into what she discovered were his sleeping quarters—small, not particularly neat, but with a curvy antique brass bed Gennie fell instantly in love with. Grant went to an old chifforobe that might have been beautiful with refinishing. Muttering to himself, he routed around and unearthed a faded terrycloth robe.

"Shower's across the hall," he said briefly, and dumped the robe in Gennie's arms before he left her alone.

"Thank you very much," she mumbled while his footsteps retreated back down the stairs. Chin high, eyes gleaming, she stalked across the hall and found herself charmed all over again.

The bath was white porcelain and footed with brass fixtures he obviously took the time to polish. The room was barely more than a closet, but somewhere in its history it had been paneled in cedar and lacquered. There was a pedestal sink and a narrow little mirror. The light was above her, operated by a pull string.

Stripping gratefully out of her cold, wet clothes, Gennie stepped into the tub and drew the thin circular curtain. In an instant, she had hot water spraying out of the tiny shower head and warming her body. Gennie was certain paradise could have felt no sweeter, even when it was guarded by the devil.

In the kitchen Grant made a fresh pot of coffee. Then, as an afterthought, he opened a can of soup. He supposed he'd have to feed her. Here, at the back of the tower, the sound of the sea was louder. It was a sound he was used to—not so he no longer heard it, but so he expected to. If it was vicious and threatening as it was tonight, Grant acknowledged it, then went about his business.

Or he would have gone about his business if he hadn't found a drenched woman outside his door. Now he calculated he'd have to put in an extra hour that night to make up for the time she was costing him. With his first annoyance over, Grant admitted it couldn't be helped. He'd give her the basic hospitality of a hot meal and a roof over her head, and that would be that.

A smile lightened his features briefly when he remembered how she had looked at him when she'd sat dripping on his sofa. The lady, he decided, was no pushover. Grant had little patience with pushovers. When he chose company, he chose the company of people who said what they thought and were willing to stand by it. In a way, that was why Grant was off his self-imposed schedule.

It had barely been a week since his return from Hyannis Port where he'd given away his sister, Shelby, in her marriage to Alan MacGregor. He'd discovered, uncomfortably, that the wedding had made him sentimental. It hadn't been difficult for the MacGregors to persuade him to stay on for an extra couple of days. He'd liked them, blustery old Daniel in particular, and Grant wasn't a man who took to people quickly. Since childhood he'd been cautious, but the MacGregors as a group were irresistible. And he'd been weakened somewhat by the wedding itself.

Giving his sister away, something that would have been his father's place had he lived, had brought such a mix of pain and pleasure that Grant had been grateful to have the distraction of a few days among the MacGregors before he returned to Windy Point—even to the extent of being amused by Daniel's not so subtle probing into his personal life. He'd enjoyed himself enough to accept an open-ended invitation to return. An invitation even he was surprised that he intended to act on.

For now there was work to be done, but he resigned himself that a short interruption wouldn't damage his status quo beyond repair. As long as it remained short. She could bunk down in the spare room for the night, then he'd have her out and away in the morning. He was nearly in an amiable mood by the time the soup started to simmer.

Grant heard her come in, though the noise from outside was still fierce. He turned, prepared to make a moderately friendly comment, when the sight of her in his robe went straight to his gut.

Damn, she was beautiful. Too beautiful for his peace of mind. The robe dwarfed her, though she'd rolled the frayed sleeves nearly to the elbow. The faded blue accented the honey-rich tone of her skin. She'd brushed her damp hair back, leaving her face unframed but for a few wayward curls that sprung out near her temples. With her eyes pale green and the dark lashes wet, she looked to him more than ever like the mermaid he'd nearly taken her for.

"Sit down," he ordered, furiously annoyed by the flare of unwelcome desire. "You can have some soup."

Gennie paused a moment, her eyes skimming up and down his back before she sat at the rough wooden table. "Why, thank you." His response was an unintelligible mutter before he thumped a bowl in front of her. She picked up the spoon, not about to let pride get in the way of hunger. Though surprised, she said nothing when he sat opposite her with a bowl of his own.

The kitchen was small and brightly lit and very, very quiet. The only sound came from the wind and restless water outside the thick walls. At first Gennie ate with her eyes stubbornly on the bowl in front of her, but as the sharp hunger passed she began to glance around the room. Tiny certainly, but with no wasted space. Rough oak cabinets ringed the walls giving generous room for supplies. The counters were wood as well, but sanded and polished. She saw the modern conveniences of a percolator and a toaster.

He took better care of this room, she decided, than he did the rest of the house. No dishes in the sink, no crumbs or spills. And the only scents were the kitcheny aromas of soup and coffee. The appliances were old and a bit scarred, but they weren't grimy.

As her first hunger ebbed, so did her anger. She had, after all, invaded his privacy. Not everyone offered hospitality to a stranger with smiles and open arms. He had scowled, but he hadn't shut the door in her face. And he had given her something dry to wear and food, she added as she did her best to submerge pride.

With a slight frown she skimmed her gaze over the tabletop until it rested on his hands. Good God, she thought with a jolt, they were beautiful. The wrists were narrow, giving a sense not of weakness but of graceful strength and capability. The backs of his hands were deeply tanned and unmarred, long and lean, as were his fingers. The nails were short and straight. Masculine was her first thought, then delicate came quickly on the tail of it. Gennie could picture the hands holding a flute just as easily as she could see them wielding a saber.

For a moment she forgot the rest of him in her fascination with his hands, and her reaction to them. She felt the stir but didn't suppress it. She was certain any woman who saw those romantic, exquisite hands would automatically wonder just what they would feel like on her skin. Impatient hands, clever. They were the kind that could either rip the clothes off a woman or gently undress her before she had any idea what was happening.

When a thrill Gennie recognized as anticipation sprinted up her spine, she caught herself. What was she thinking of! Even her imagination had no business sneaking off in that direction. A little dazed by the feeling that wouldn't be dismissed, she lifted her gaze to his face.

He was watching her—coolly, like a scientist watching a specimen. When she'd stopped eating so suddenly, he'd seen her eyes go to his hands and remain there with her lashes lowered just enough to conceal their expression. Grant had waited, knowing sooner or later she'd look up. He'd been expecting that icy anger or frosty politeness. The numb shock on her face puzzled him, or more accurately intrigued him. But it was the vulnerability that made him want her almost painfully. Even when she had stumbled into the house, wet and lost, she hadn't looked defenseless. He wondered what she would do if he simply got up, hauled her to her feet and dragged her up into his bed. He wondered what in the hell was getting into him.

They stared at each other, each battered by feelings neither of them wanted while the rain and the wind beat against the walls, separating them from everything civilized. He thought again that she looked like some temptress from the sea. Gennie thought he'd have given her rogue of an ancestor a run for his money.

Grant's chair legs scraped against the floor as he pushed back from the table. Gennie froze.

"There's a room on the second level with a bunk." His eyes were hard and dark with suppressed anger—his stomach knotted with suppressed desire.

Gennie found that her palms were damp with nerves and was infuriated. Better to be infuriated with him. "The couch down here is fine," she said coldly.

He shrugged. "Suit yourself." Without another word, he walked out. Gennie waited until she heard his footsteps on the stairs before she pressed a hand to her stomach. The next time she saw a light in the dark, she told herself, she'd run like hell in the opposite direction.

## *Chapter 2*

Grant hated to be interrupted. He'd tolerate being cursed, threatened or despised, but he never tolerated interruptions. It had never mattered to him particularly if he was liked, as long as he was left alone to do as he chose. He'd grown up watching his father pursue the goodwill of others—a necessary aspect in the career of a senator who had chosen to run for the highest office in the country.

Even as a child Grant knew his father was a man who demanded extreme feelings. He was loved by some, feared or hated by others, and on a campaign trail he could inspire a fierce loyalty. He had been a man who would go out of his way to do a favor—friend or stranger—it had never mattered. His ideals had been high, his memory keen, and his flair for words admirable. Senator Robert Campbell had been a man who had felt it his duty to make himself accessible to the public. Right up to the moment someone had put three bullets into him.

Grant hadn't only blamed the man who had held the gun, or the profession of politics, as his sister had done. In his own way Grant had blamed his father. Robert Campbell had given himself to the world, and it had killed him. Perhaps it was as a direct result that Grant gave himself to no one.

He didn't consider the lighthouse a refuge. It was simply his place. He appreciated the distance it gave him from others, and enjoyed the harshness and the harmony of the elements. If it gave him solitude, it was as necessary to his work as it was to himself. He required the hours, even the days, of aloneness. Uninterrupted thought was something Grant considered his right. No one, absolutely no one, was permitted to tamper with it.

The night before he'd been midway through his current project when Gennie's banging had forced him to stop. Grant was perfectly capable of ignoring a knock on the door, but since it had broken his train of thought, he had gone down to answer—with the idea of strangling the intruder. Gennie might consider herself lucky he'd only resorted to rudeness. A hapless tourist had once found himself faced with an irate Grant, who had threatened to toss him into the ocean.

Since it had taken Grant the better part of an hour after he'd left Gennie in the kitchen to get his mind back on his work, he'd been up most of the night. Interruptions. Intrusions. Intolerable. He'd thought so then, and now as the sun slanted in the window and onto the foot of his bed, he thought so again.

Groggy after what amounted to almost four hours sleep, Grant listened to the voice that drifted up the stairwell. She was singing some catchy little tune you'd hear every time you turned on the radio—something Grant did every day of his life, just as religiously as he turned on the TV and read a dozen newspapers. She sang well, in a low-pitched, drumming voice that turned the cute phrasing into something seductive. Bad enough she'd interrupted his work the night before, now she was interrupting his sleep.

With a pillow over his head, he could block it out. But, he discovered, he couldn't block out his reaction to it. It was much too easy in the dark, with the sheet warm under his chest, to imagine her. Swearing, Grant tossed the pillow aside and got out of bed to pull on a pair of cutoffs. Half asleep, half aroused, he went downstairs.

The afghan she'd used the night before was already neatly folded on the sofa. Grant scowled at it before he followed Gennie's voice into the kitchen.

She was still in his robe, barefoot, with her hair waving luxuriously down her back. He'd like to have touched it to see if those hints of red that seemed to shimmer through the black were really there or just a trick of the light.

Bacon sizzled in a pan on the stove, and the coffee smelled like heaven.

"What the hell are you doing?"

Gennie whirled around clutching a kitchen fork, one hand lifting to her heart in reflex reaction. Despite the discomfort of the sofa, she'd woken in the best of moods—and starving. The sun was shining, gulls were calling, and the refrigerator had been liberally stocked. Gennie had decided Grant Campbell deserved another chance. As she'd puttered in his kitchen, she'd made a vow to be friendly at all costs.

He stood before her now, half naked and obviously angry, his hair sleep-tumbled and a night's growth of beard shadowing his chin.

Gennie gave him a determined smile. "I'm making breakfast. I thought it was the least I could do in return for a night's shelter."

Again he had the sensation of something familiar about her he couldn't quite catch. His frown only deepened. "I don't like anyone messing with my things."

Gennie opened her mouth, then shut it again before anything nasty could slip out. "The only thing I've broken is an egg," she said mildly as she indicated the bowl of eggs she intended to scramble. "Why don't you do us both a favor? Get a cup of coffee, sit down, and shut up." With an almost imperceptible toss of her head, she turned her back on him.

Grant's brows rose not so much in surprise as in appreciation. Not everyone could tell you to shut up in a butter-melting voice and make it work. He had the feeling he wasn't the first person she'd given the order to. With something perilously close to a grin, he got a mug and did exactly what she said.

She didn't sing anymore as she finished making the meal, but he had the feeling she would've muttered bad-temperedly if she hadn't wanted him to think she was unaffected by him. In fact, he was certain there was a good bit of muttering and cursing going on inside her head.

As he sipped coffee the grogginess gave way to alertness, and hunger. For the first time he sat in the tiny kitchen while a woman fixed his breakfast. Not something he'd want to make a habit of, Grant mused while he watched her—but then again, it wasn't an unpleasant experience.

Still clinging to silence, Gennie set plates on the table, then followed them with a platter of bacon and eggs. "Why were you going to the old Lawrence place?" he asked as he served himself.

Gennie sent him a narrowed-eyed glare. So now we're going to make polite conversation, she thought and nearly ground her teeth. "I'm renting it," she said briefly, and dashed salt on her eggs.

"Thought the Widow Lawrence had it up for sale."

"She does."

"You're a little late in the season for renting a beach cottage," Grant commented over a mouthful of eggs.

Gennie gave a quick shrug as she concentrated on her breakfast. "I'm not a tourist."

"No?" He gave her a long steady look she found both deft and intrusive. "Louisiana, isn't it? New Orleans, Baton Rouge?"

"New Orleans." Gennie forgot annoyance long enough to study him in turn. "You're not local, either."

"No," he said simply, and left it at that.

Oh, no, she thought, he wasn't going to start a conversation, then switch it off when it suited him. "Why a lighthouse?" she persisted. "It's not operational, is it? It was the light from the window I followed last night, not the beacon."

"Coast Guard takes care of this stretch with radar. This station hasn't been used in ten years. Did you run out of gas?" he asked before she realized he'd never answered the why.

"No. I'd pulled off the side of the road for a few minutes, then when I tried to start the car again, it just made a few unproductive noises." She shrugged and bit into a slice of bacon. "I guess I'll have to get a tow truck in town."

Grant made a sound that might have been a laugh. "You might get a tow truck up at Bayside, but you're not going to find one at Windy Point. I'll take a look at it," he told her as he finished off his breakfast. "If it's beyond me, you can get Buck Gates from town to come out and get it started."

She studied him for nearly thirty seconds. "Thank you," Gennie said warily.

Grant rose and put his plate in the sink. "Go get dressed," he ordered. "I've got work to do." For the second time he left Gennie alone in the kitchen.

Just once, she thought as she stacked her plate on top of his, she'd like to get in the last word. Giving the belt of Grant's robe a quick tug, she started out of the room. Yes, she'd go get dressed, Gennie told herself. And she'd do it quickly before he changed his mind. Rude or not, she'd accept his offer of help. Then as far as she was concerned, Grant Campbell could go to the devil.

There wasn't any sign of him on the second floor when she slipped into the bathroom to change. Gennie stripped out of the robe and hung it on a hook on the back of the door. Her clothes were dry, and she thought she could ignore the fact that her tennis shoes were still a bit cold and damp. With luck she could be settled into the cottage within the hour. That should leave her the best of the afternoon for sketching. The idea kept Gennie's spirits high as she made her way back downstairs. Again there was no sign of Grant. After a brief fight with the heavy front door, Gennie went outside.

It was so clear she nearly caught her breath. Whatever fog or fury had visited that place the night before had been swept clean. The places on the earth where the air really sparkled were rare, she knew, and this was one of them. The sky was blue and cloudless, shot through with the yellow light of the sun. There was some grass on this side of the lighthouse, tough and as wild as the few hardy flowers that were scattered through it. Goldenrod swayed in the breeze announcing the end of summer, but the sun shone hotly.

She could see the narrow rut of a road she'd traveled on the night before, but was surprised by the three-story farmhouse only a few hundred yards away. That it was deserted was obvious by the film of dirt on the windows and the waist-high grass, but it wasn't dilapidated. It would have belonged to the keeper and his family, Gennie concluded, when the lighthouse was still functional. They would have had a garden and perhaps a few chickens. And there would have been nights when the wind howled and the waves crashed that the keeper would have stayed at his station while his family sat alone and listened.

The white paint was faded, but the shutters hung true. She thought it sat on its hill waiting to be filled again.

There was a sturdy little pickup near the base of the slope which she assumed was Grant's. Because he was nowhere in sight, Gennie wandered around the side of the lighthouse, answering the call of the sea.

This time Gennie did catch her breath. She could see for miles, down the irregular coastline, over to tiny islands, and out to the distant horizon. There were boats on the water, staunch, competent little boats of the lobstermen. She knew she would see no chrome and mahogany crafts here, nor should she. This was a place of purpose, not idle pleasure. Strength, durability. That's what she felt as she looked out into blue-green water that frothed white as it flung itself at the rocks.

Seaweed floated in the surf, gathering and spreading with the movement of the water. The sea had its way with everything here. The rocks were worn smooth by it, and the ledges rose showing colors from gray to green with a few muted streaks of orange. Shells littered the shoreline, flung out by the sea and yet to be trampled under a careless foot. The smell of salt and fish was strong. She could hear the toll of the bell buoys, the hollow hoot of the whistling markers, the distant putter of the lobster boats and the mournful cry of gulls. There was nothing, no sound, no sight, no smell, that came from anything other than that endless, timeless sea.

Gennie felt it—the pull, the tug that had called men and women to it from the dawn of time. If humanity had truly sprung from there, perhaps that was why they were so easily lured back to it. She stood on the ledge above the narrow, rocky beach and lost herself in it. Danger, challenge, peace; she felt them all and was content.

She didn't hear Grant come behind her. Gennie was too caught up in the sea itself to sense him, though he watched her as a minute stretched to two and two into three. She looked right there, he thought and could have cursed her for it. The land was his, this small, secluded edge of land that hovered over the sea.

He wouldn't claim to own the sea, not even when it rose high at noon to lick at the verge of his land, but this slice of rock and wild grass belonged to him, exclusively. She had no right to look as though she belonged—to make him wonder if the cliff would ever be only his again.

The wind plastered her clothes against her, as the rain had done the night before, accenting her slim, athletic body with its woman's roundness. Her hair danced frantically and free while the sun teased out those touches of fire in the ebony that seemed to hint of things he was nearly ready to test. Before he realized what he was doing, Grant took her arm and swung her to face him.

There was no surprise in her face as she looked at him, but excitement—and an arousal he knew came from the sea. Her eyes mirrored it and tempted.

"I wondered last night why anyone would choose to live here." She tossed the hair from her eyes. "Now I wonder how anyone lives anywhere else." She pointed to a small fishing boat at the end of the pier. "Is that yours?"

Grant continued to stare at her, realizing abruptly he'd nearly hauled her against him and kissed her—so nearly he could all but taste her mouth against his. With an effort he turned his head in the direction she pointed. "Yes, it's mine."

"I'm keeping you from your work." For the first time, Gennie gave him the simple gift of a real smile. "I suppose you'd have been up at dawn if I hadn't gotten in the way."

With an unintelligible mutter as an answer, Grant began to propel her toward his pickup. Sighing, Gennie gave up her morning vow to be friendly as a bad bet. "Mr. Campbell, do you have to be so unpleasant?"

Grant stopped long enough to shoot her a look—one Gennie would have sworn was laced with amused irony. "Yes."

"You do it very well," she managed as he began to pull her along again.

"I've had years of practice." He released her when they reached the truck, then opened his door and got in. Without comment, Gennie skirted the hood and climbed in the passenger side.

The engine roared into life, a sound so closely associated with towns and traffic, Gennie thought it a sacrilege. She looked back once as he started down the bumpy road and knew instantly she would paint—had to paint—that scene. She nearly stated her intention out loud, then caught a glimpse of Grant's frowning profile.

The hell with him, Gennie decided. She'd paint while he was out catching lobsters or whatever he caught out there. What he didn't know wouldn't hurt her, in this case. She sat back in the seat, primly folded her hands, and kept quiet.

Grant drove a mile before he started to feel guilty. The road was hardly better than a ditch, and at night it would have been a dark series of ruts and rocks. Anyone walking over that stretch in a storm had to have been exhausted, miserable. Anyone who hadn't known the way would have been half terrified as well. He hadn't exactly dripped sympathy and concern. Still frowning, he took another quick look at her as the truck bounced along. She didn't look fragile, but he never would have believed she'd walked so far in that weather along a dark, rutted road.

He started to form what Gennie would have been astonished to hear was an apology when she lifted her chin. "There's my car." Her voice was distantly polite again—master to servant this time. Grant swallowed the apology.

He swung toward her car, jostling Gennie in her seat a bit more than was absolutely necessary. Neither of them commented as he switched off the engine and climbed out. Grant popped the hood of her car, while Gennie stood with her hands in the back pockets of her jeans.

He talked to himself, she noticed, softly, just under his breath, as he fiddled with whatever people fiddled with under hoods of cars. She supposed it was a natural enough thing for someone who lived alone at the edge of a cliff. Then again, she thought with a grin, there were times in the thickly populated *Vieux Carré* when she found herself the very best person to converse with.

Grant walked back to his truck, pulling a toolbox out of the back of the cab. He rummaged around, chose a couple of different-sized wrenches, and returned to dive under her hood again. Pursing her lips, Gennie moved behind him to peer over his shoulder. He seemed to know what he was about, she decided. And a couple of wrenches didn't seem so complicated. If she could just… She leaned in closer, automatically resting her hand on his back to keep her balance.

Grant didn't straighten, but turned, his arm brushing firmly across her breast with the movement. It could easily happen to strangers in a crowded elevator and hardly be noticed. Both of them felt the power of contact, and the surge of need.

Gennie would have backed up if she hadn't so suddenly found herself staring into those dark, restless eyes—feeling that warm, quick breath against her lips. Another inch, she thought, just another inch and it would be his mouth on hers instead of just the hint of it. Her hand had slipped to his shoulder, and without her realizing it, her fingers had tightened there.

Grant felt the pressure, but it was nothing compared to what had sprung up at the back of his neck, the base of his spine, the pit of his stomach. To take what was within his reach might relieve the pressure, or it might combust it. At the moment Grant wasn't certain what result he'd prefer.

"What are you doing?" he demanded, but this time his voice wasn't edged with anger.

Dazed, Gennie continued to stare into his eyes. She could see herself in there, she thought numbly. When did she get lost in there? "What?"

They were still leaning into the car, Gennie with her hand on his shoulder, Grant with one hand on a bolt, the other on a wrench. He had only to shift his weight to bring them together. He nearly did before he remembered how uncomfortably right she had looked standing on his land gazing out to sea.

*Touch this one, Campbell, and you're in trouble, the kind of trouble a man doesn't walk away from whistling a tune.*

"I asked what you were doing," he said in the same quiet tone, but his gaze slid down to her mouth.

"Doing…? What *had* she been doing? "I—ah—I wanted to see how you fixed it so…" His gaze swept up and locked on hers again, scattered every coherent thought.

"So?" Grant repeated, enjoying the fact that he could confuse her.

"So…" His breath whispered over her lips. She caught herself running her tongue along them to taste it. "So if it happens again I could fix it."

Grant smiled—slowly, deliberately. Insolently? Gennie wasn't sure, but her heart rose to her throat and stuck there. However he smiled, whatever his intent, it added a wicked, irresistible charm to his face. She thought it was a smile a barbarian might have given his woman before he tossed her over his shoulder and took her into some dark cave. Just as slowly, he turned away to begin working with the wrench again.

Gennie backed up and let out a long, quiet breath. That had been close—too close. To what, she wasn't precisely sure, but to something no smart woman would consider safe. She cleared her throat. "Do you think you can fix it?"

"Hmm."

Gennie took this for the affirmative, then stepped closer, this time keeping to the side of the hood. "A mechanic looked at it a couple weeks ago."

"Think you're going to need new plugs soon. I'd have Buck Gates take a look if I were you."

"Is he a mechanic? At the service station?"

Grant straightened. He wasn't smiling now, but there was amusement in his eyes. "There's no service station in Windy Point. You need gas, you go down to the docks and pump it. You got car trouble, you see Buck Gates. He repairs the lobster boats—a motor's a motor." The last was delivered in an easy Down East cadence, with a hint of a smile that had nothing to do with condescension. "Start her up."

Leaving her door open, Gennie slid behind the wheel. A turn of the key had her engine springing cheerfully to life. Even as she let out a relieved sigh, Grant slammed the hood into place. Gennie cut the engine again as he walked back to his truck to replace his tools.

"The Lawrence cottage's about three quarters of a mile up on the left. You can't miss the turnoff unless you're hiking through a storm in the middle of the night with only a flashlight."

Gennie swallowed a chuckle. Don't let him have any redeeming qualities, she pleaded. Let me remember him as a rude, nasty man who just happens to be fatally sexy. "I'll keep that in mind."

"And I wouldn't mention that you'd spent the night at Windy Point Station," he added easily as he slipped the toolbox back into place. "I have a reputation to protect."

This time she bit her lip to hold back a smile. "Oh?"

"Yeah." Grant turned back, leaning against the truck a moment as he looked at her again. "The villagers think I'm odd. I'd slip a couple notches if they found out I hadn't just shoved you back outside and locked the door."

This time she did smile—but only a little. "You have my word, no one will hear from me what a Good Samaritan you are. If anyone should happen to ask, I'll tell them you're rude, disagreeable and generally nasty."

"I'd appreciate it."

When he started to climb back into the truck, Gennie reached for her wallet. "Wait, I haven't paid you for—"

"Forget it."

She hooked her hand on the door handle. "I don't want to be obligated to you for—"

"Tough." Grant started the engine. "Look, move your car, I can't turn around with you in my way."

Eyes narrowed, she whirled away. So much for gratitude, she told herself. So the villagers thought he was odd, she mused as she slammed the car door. Perceptive people. Gennie started down the road at a cautious speed, making it a point not to look into the rearview mirror. When she came to the turnoff, she veered left. The only sign of Grant Campbell was the steady hum of his truck as he went on. Gennie told herself she wouldn't think of him again.

And she didn't as she drove down the straight little lane with black-eyed Susans springing up on either side. The sound of his truck was a distant echo, soon lost. Without any trees to block the view, Gennie saw the cottage almost immediately, and was charmed. Small certainly, but it didn't evoke images of seven dwarfs heigh-hoing. Gennie immediately had a picture of a tidy woman in a housedress hanging out the wash, then a rough-featured fisherman whittling on the tiny porch.

It had been painted blue but had weathered to a soft blue-gray. A one-story boxlike structure, it had a modest front porch facing the lane and, she was to discover, another screened porch looking out over the inlet. A pier that looked like it might be a bit shaky stretched out over the glassily calm water. Someone had planted a willow near the shore, but it wasn't flourishing.

Gennie turned off the engine and was struck with silence. Pleasant, peaceful—yes, she could live with this, work with this. Yet she discovered she preferred the thrash and boom of the sea that Grant had outside his front door.

Oh, no, she reminded herself firmly, she vowed not to think of him. And she wouldn't. After stepping from the car, Gennie hefted the first box of groceries and climbed the plank stairs to the front door. She had to fight with the lock a moment, then it gave a mighty groan and yielded.

The first thing Gennie noticed was tidiness. The Widow Lawrence had meant what she said when she had stated the cottage was clean. The furniture was draped in dustcovers but there was no dust. Obviously, she came in regularly and chased it away. Gennie found the idea touching and sad. The walls were painted a pale blue, and the lighter patches here and there indicated where pictures had hung for years. Carrying her box of supplies, Gennie wandered toward the back of the house and found the kitchen.

The sense of order prevailed here as well. Formica counters were spotless, the porcelain sink gleamed. A flick of the tap proved the plumbing was indeed cooperative. Gennie set down the box and went through the back door onto the screened porch. The air was warm and moist, tasting of the sea. Someone had repaired a few holes in the screen and the paint on the floor was cracked but clean.

Too clean, Gennie realized. There was no sign of life in the cottage, and barely any echo of the life that had once been there. She would have preferred the dusty disorder she had found in Grant's lighthouse. Someone *lived* there. Someone vital. Shaking her head, she pushed him to the back of her mind. Someone lived here now—and in short order the house would know it. Quickly she went back to her car to unpack.

Because she traveled light and was inherently organized, it took less than two hours for Gennie to distribute her things throughout the house. Both bedrooms were tiny, and only one had a bed. When Gennie made it up with the linens she had bought, she discovered it was a feather bed. Delighted, she spent some time bouncing on it and sinking into it. In the second bedroom she stowed her painting gear. With the dustcovers removed and a few of her own paintings hung on the faded spots, she began to feel a sense of home.

Barefoot and pleased with herself, she went out to walk the length of the pier. A few boards creaked and others shook, but she decided the structure was safe enough. Perhaps she would buy a small boat and explore the inlet. She could do as she pleased now, go where she liked. Her ties in New Orleans would pull her back eventually, but the wanderlust which had driven her north six months before had yet to fade.

Wanderlust, she repeated as her eyes clouded. No, the word was guilt—or pain. It was still following her, perhaps it always would. It's been more than a year, Gennie thought as she closed her eyes. Seventeen months, two weeks, three days. And she could still see Angela. Perhaps she should be grateful for that—for the fact that her artist's memory could conjure up her sister's face exactly as it had been. Young, beautiful, vibrant. But on the other side of the coin, it was too easy to see Angela lifeless and broken—the way her sister had looked after she'd killed her.

*Not your fault*. How many times had she heard that?

*It wasn't your fault, Gennie. You can't blame yourself.*

Oh, yes, I can, she thought with a sigh. If I hadn't been driving.... If my reflexes had been quicker.... If I'd only seen that car running the red light.

There was no going back, and Gennie knew it. The times the helpless guilt and grief flooded her were fewer now, but no less painful. She had her art, and sometimes she thought that alone had saved her sanity after her sister's death. All in all this trip had been good for her—by taking her away from the memories that were still too close, and by letting her concentrate on painting for painting's sake.

Art had become too much like a business to her in the past few years. She'd nearly lost herself in the selling and showings. Now it was back to basics—she needed that. Oil, acrylic, watercolor, charcoal; and the canvases that waited to be filled.

Perhaps the hard realism of losing her sister had influenced her to seek the same hard realism in her work. It might have been her way of forcing herself to accept life, and death. Her abstracts, the misty quality of her painting had always given the world she created a gentle hue. Not quite real but so easy to believe in. Now she was drawn to the plain, the ev|eryday. Reality wasn't always pretty, but there was a strength in it she was just beginning to understand.

Gennie drew in a deep breath. Yes, she would paint this—this quiet, settled little inlet. There'd be a time for it. But first, now, she needed the challenge and power of the ocean. A glance at her watch showed her it was noon. Surely he would be out on his boat now, making up the time she had cost him that morning. She could have three or four hours to sketch the lighthouse from different angles without him even knowing. And if he did, Gennie added with a shrug, what difference would it make? One woman with a sketch pad could hardly bother him. In any case, he could just bolt himself up inside and ignore her if he didn't like it. Just as she intended to ignore him.

Grant's studio was on the third level. More precisely, Grant's studio *was* the third level. What had been three cubbyhole rooms had been remodeled into one with good natural light, strongest from the north. Glass-topped cabinets, called taborets, held an assortment of tools, completely organized. Fountain pens, ballpoints, knives, sable brushes, a wide variety of pencils and erasers, bow compass, T square. An engineer or architect would have recognized several of the tools and approved the quality. Matte paper was already taped down to his drawing board.

On the whitewashed wall he faced hung a mirror and a framed reprint of *The Yellow Kid*, a cartoon strip nearly a hundred years old. On the other side of the room was a sophisticated radio and a small color TV. The stack of newspapers and magazines in the corner was waist-high. The room had the sense of practical order Grant bothered with in no other aspect of his life.

He worked without hurry this morning. There were times he worked frantically, not because of a deadline—he was always a month ahead of schedule—but because his own thoughts pushed at him. At times he would take a week or perhaps two to simply gather ideas and store them. Other times, he would work through the night as those same ideas fretted to be put down with pen and ink.

He'd finished the project he'd been working on in the early hours of the morning. Now a new angle had been pushing at him, one he didn't seem to be able to resist. Grant rarely resisted anything that applied to his art. Already he had scaled the paper, striking diagonal lines with the blue pencil that wouldn't photograph. He knew what he wanted, but the preparation came first, those finite, vital details no one would ever notice in the few seconds it took to view his work.

When the paper was set and scaled, divided into five sections double the size they would be when reproduced, he began to sketch lightly. Doodling really, he brought his main character to life with a few loops and lines. The man was quite ordinary. Grant had insisted he be when he had created what his sister called his alter ego ten years before. An ordinary man, perhaps a bit scruffy, with a few features—the nose, the puzzled eyes—a bit exaggerated. But Grant's Macintosh was easily recognizable as someone you might pass on the street. And barely notice.

He was always too thin so that his attempts at dressing sharply never quite came off. He carried the air of someone who knew he was going to be put upon. Grant had a certain fondness for his general ineptitude and occasional satirical remarks.

Grant knew all of his friends—he'd created them as well. Not precisely a motley crew, but very close. Well-meaning dreamers, smart alecks. They were the shades of the people Grant had known in college—friends and acquaintances. Ordinary people doing ordinary things in an unusual way. That was the theme of his craft.

He'd given birth to Macintosh in college, then had left him in a closet while he had pursued art in a more traditional manner for almost three years. Perhaps he would have been successful; the talent had been there. But Grant had discovered he was much happier sketching a caricature than painting a portrait. In the end Macintosh had won. Grant had hauled him back out of the closet, and at the end of seven years the slightly weary, bleary-eyed character appeared in every major newspaper in the country seven days a week.

People followed his life and times over coffee, on the subway, on buses, and in bed. Over a million Americans opened their newspapers and looked to see just what he was up to that day before they had to face their own.

As a cartoonist, Grant knew it was his responsibility to amuse, and to amuse quickly, with a few short sentences and simple drawings. The strip would be looked at for ten or twelve seconds, chuckled over, then tossed aside. Often to line a bird cage. Grant had few illusions. It was the chuckle that was important, the fact that for those few seconds, he had given people something to laugh at—something to relate to. In *Macintosh*, Grant looked for the common experience, then twisted it.

What he wanted, what he insisted on having, was the right to do so, and the right to be left alone to do it. He was known to the public only by his initials. His contract with United Syndicate specifically stated his name would never be used in conjunction with the strip, nor would he grant any interviews or do any guest spots. His anonymity was as much a part of his price as his annual income.

Still using only the pencil, he began on the second section—Macintosh mumbling as the thudding on the door interrupted his newest hobby. Stamp collecting. Grant had gotten two full weeks out of this particular angle—Macintosh's bumbling attempts, his friends' caustic comments about his terminal boredom. Macintosh had fussed with his stamps and wondered if he'd finally hit a gold mine as the television had droned on behind him on the latest increase in the first-class mail service.

Here, he would open his door to be faced with a wet, bad-tempered siren. Grant didn't have any trouble drawing Gennie. In fact, he felt making her a character would put her firmly in perspective. She'd be just as ridiculous, and as vulnerable, as the rest of the people in his world. He'd begin to think of her as a character instead of a woman—flesh, blood, soft, fragrant. He didn't have any room for a woman, but he always had room for a character. He could tell them when to come, when to go, what to say.

He named her Veronica, thinking the more sophisticated name suited her. Deliberately, he exaggerated the tilt of her eyes and the lush sensuality of her mouth. Since the setting was Washington, D.C., rather than coastal Maine, Grant gave her a flat tire on the way home from a White House function. Macintosh goggled at her. Grant captured this by giving himself several stunned stares in the mirror above the drawing board.

He worked for two hours, perfecting the storyline—the situation, the setup, the punchline. After changing her tire and practicing macho lines to impress her, Macintosh ended up with five dollars, a stutter, and soaked shoes as Veronica zoomed out of his life.

Grant felt better when the sketches were done. He'd put Gennie just where he wanted—driving away. Now he would detail his work with India ink and brush. Solid black would accent or focus, the Benday patterns—zones of dots or lines—would give the gray areas.

Detailing Macintosh's room was simple enough; Grant had been there a thousand times. But it still took time and precision. Balance was crucial, the angles and positioning in order to draw the reader's attention just where you wanted it for the few seconds they would look at the individual panel. His supply of patience was consumed by his work, giving him little for the other areas of his life. The strip was half finished and the afternoon waning before he stopped to rest his hand.

Coffee, he thought, stretching his back and shoulders as he noticed the ache. And food. Breakfast had been too long ago. He'd grab something and take a walk down on the beach. He still had two papers to read and a few hours of television. Too much could happen in a day for him to ignore either form of communication. But the walk came first, Grant decided as he moved idly to the window. He needed some fresh air....

The hand he had lifted to rub at the back of his neck dropped. Leaning closer, he narrowed his eyes and stared down. It was bad enough when he had to deal with the occasional stray tourist, he thought furiously. A few curt words sent them away and kept them away. But there was no mistaking, even at this height, that thick ebony hair.

Veronica had yet to drive out of his life.

# Chapter 3

It was beautiful, no matter what angle you chose or how the light shifted. Gennie had a half-dozen sketches in her pad and knew she could have a half-dozen more without catching all the aspects of that one particular jut of land. Look at the colors in the rocks! Would she ever be able to capture them? And the way the lighthouse stood there, solid, indomitable. The whitewash was faded here and there, the concrete blocks pockmarked with time and salt spray. That only added to the humanity of it. Man's strike for safety against the mercurial sea.

There would have been times the sea would have won, Gennie mused. Because man was fallible. There would have been times the lighthouse would have won. Because man was tenacious. Pitted together they spoke of harmony, perseverance, sweat, and strength.

She lost track of the time she had sat there, undisturbed, disturbing no one. Yet she knew she could go on sitting as long as the sun gave enough light. There were so few places in New Orleans where she could go to paint without the distractions of curiosity seekers or art buffs. When she chose to paint in the city, she was invariably recognized, and once recognized, watched or questioned.

Even when she went out—into the bayou, along a country road, she was often followed. She'd grown used to working around that and to saving most of her serious work for her studio. Over the years she'd nearly forgotten the simple freedom of being able to work outdoors, having the advantage of smelling and tasting what you drew while you drew it.

The past six months had given her something she hadn't been aware she'd looked for—a reminder of what she had been before success had put its limitations on her.

Content, half dreaming, she sketched what she saw and felt, and needed nothing else.

"Damn it, what do you want now?"

To her credit, Gennie didn't jolt or drop her sketch pad. She'd known Grant was around somewhere as his boat hadn't been moved. And she'd already decided he wasn't going to spoil what she'd found here. She was arrogant enough to feel it her right to be there to paint what her art demanded she paint. Thinking he was rather casual about his trade as a fisherman, she turned to him.

He was furious, she thought mildly. But she'd hardly seen him any other way. She decided he was suited to the out-of-doors—the sun, the wind, and the sea. Perhaps she'd do a sketch or two of him before she was finished. Tilting her head back, Gennie studied him as she would any subject that interested her.

"Good afternoon," she said in her best plantation drawl.

Knowing he was being measured and insulted might have amused him under different circumstances. At the moment it made him yearn to give her a hefty shove off her rock. All he wanted was for her to go away, and stay away—before he gave in to the urge to touch her.

"I asked you what you wanted."

"No need for you to bother. I'm just taking some preliminary sketches." Gennie kept her seat on the contorted rock near the verge of the cliff and shifted back to sea. "You can just go on with whatever you were doing."

Grant's eyes narrowed to dark slits. Oh, she was good at this, he thought. Dismissing underlings. "You're on my land."

"Mmm-hmm."

The idea of helping her off the rock became more appealing. "You're trespassing."

Gennie sent him an indulgent glance over her left shoulder. "You should try barbed wire and land mines. Nothing like a land mine to make a statement. Not that I can blame you for wanting to keep this little slice of the world to yourself, Grant," she added as she began to sketch again. "But I'm going to leave it exactly as I found it—no pop cans, no paper plates, no cigarette butts."

Even lifted over the roar of the sea, her voice held a mild, deliberately placating tone designed to set nerve ends on edge. Grant came very close to grabbing her by the hair and dragging her to her feet when he was distracted by her pencil moving over the paper. What he saw halted the oath on the tip of his tongue.

It was more than good, too true to life for a mere excellent. With dashes and shading, she was capturing the swirl of the sea on rock, the low swoop of gulls and the steady endurance of the lighthouse. In the same way, she'd given the sketch no hint of quiet beauty. It was all hard edges, chips, flaws, and simplicity. It wouldn't make a postcard, nor would it make a soothing touch of art over a mantel. But anyone who'd ever stood on a point where sea battled shore would understand it.

Frowning in concentration rather than anger, Grant bent closer. Hers weren't the hands of a student; hers wasn't the soul of an amateur. In silence Grant waited until she had finished, then immediately took the sketchbook from her.

"Hey!" Gennie was halfway off her rock.

"Shut up."

She did, only because she saw he wasn't going to hurl her work into the sea. Settling back on her rock, she watched Grant as he flipped through her pages. Now and again he stopped to study one sketch a bit longer than the others.

His eyes were very dark now, she noted, while the wind blew his hair over his forehead and away again. There was a line, not of temper but of intensity, between his brows. His mouth was unsmiling, set, Gennie thought, to judge. It should have amused her to have her work critiqued by a reclusive fisherman. Somehow it didn't. There was a faint ache behind her temple she recognized as tension. She'd felt that often enough before every one of her showings.

Grant's eyes skimmed over the page and met hers. For a long moment there was only the crash of the surf and the distant bell of a buoy. Now he knew why he'd had that nagging sense of having seen her before. But her newspaper pictures didn't do her justice. "Grandeau," he said at length. "Genvième Grandeau."

At any other time she wouldn't have been surprised to have had her work or her name recognized. Not in New York, California, Atlanta. But it was intriguing to find a man at some forgotten land's end who could recognize her work from a rough sketch in a notepad.

"Yes." She stood then, combing her hair back from her forehead with her hand and holding it there. "How did you know?"

He tapped the sketchbook on his palm while his eyes stayed on hers. "Technique is technique whether it's sketches or oils. What's the toast of New Orleans doing in Windy Point?"

The dry tone of the question annoyed her enough that she forgot how easily he had recognized her work. "I'm taking a year's sabbatical." Rising, she held out her hand for her pad.

Grant ignored the gesture. "An odd place to find one of the country's most...social artists. Your work's in art papers almost as often as your name's in the society section. Weren't you engaged to an Italian count last year?"

"He was a baron," she corrected coolly, "and we weren't engaged. Do you fill your time between catches reading the tabloids?"

The flash of temper in her eyes made him grin. "I do quite a bit of reading. And you," he added before she could think of some retort, "manage to get yourself in the *New York Times* almost as often as you get yourself in the tabloids and the glossies."

Gennie tossed her head in a gesture so reminiscent of royal displeasure, his grin widened. "It seems some live and others only read about life."

"You do make good copy, Genvième." He couldn't resist, and hooked his thumbs in his pockets as new ideas for Veronica raced through his mind. It seemed inevitable that she would come back and drive Macintosh crazy for a while. "You're a favorite with the paparazzi."

Her voice remained cool and distant, but she began to tap her pencil against the rock. "I suppose they have to make their living like anyone else."

"I seem to recall something about a duel being fought in Brittany a couple of years ago."

A smile lit her face, full of fun, when he hadn't expected it. "If you believe that, I have a bridge in New York you might be interested in."

"Don't spoil my illusions," Grant said mildly. The smile wasn't easy to resist, he discovered, not when it was genuine and touched with self-deprecating humor.

"If you'd rather believe tripe," she said graciously, "who am I to argue?"

Better to keep digging at her than to dwell too long on that smile. "Some tripe's fascinating in its way. There was a film director before the count—"

"Baron," Gennie reminded him. "The count you're thinking of was French, and one of my first patrons."

"You've had quite a selection of…patrons."

She continued to smile, obviously amused. "Yes. Are you an art buff or do you just like gossip?"

"Both," he told her easily. "Come to think of it, there hasn't been a great deal about your—adventures—in the press for the last few months. You're obviously keeping your sabbatical very low key. The last thing I recall reading was…"

He remembered then and could have cut out his tongue. The car accident—her sister's death—a beautiful and intrusive wire-service photo of Genvièνe Grandeau at the funeral. Devastation, shock, grief; that much had been clear even through the veil she had worn.

She wasn't smiling now, but looking at him with a mask of placid blankness. "I'm sorry," he said.

The apology nearly buckled her knees. She'd heard those words so many times before, from so many different people, but they'd never struck her with such simple sincerity. From a stranger, Gennie thought as she turned toward the sea again. It shouldn't mean so much coming from a stranger.

"It's all right." The wind felt so cool, so vital. It wasn't the place to dwell on death. If she had to think of it, she would think of it when she was alone, when there was silence. Now she could breathe deep and drink in the sea, and the strength. "So you spend your leisure time reading all the gossip in this wicked world. For a man who's so interested in people, you chose a strange place to live."

"Interested in them," Grant agreed, grateful that she was stronger than she looked. "That doesn't mean I want to be around them."

"You don't care for people, then." When she turned back, the smile was there again, teasing. "The tough recluse. In a few years you might even make crusty."

"You can't be crusty until you're fifty," he countered. "It's an unwritten law."

"I don't know." Gennie stuck her pencil behind her ear and tilted her head. "I wouldn't think you'd bother with laws, unwritten or otherwise."

"Depends," he said simply, "on whether they're useful or not."

She laughed. "Tell me…" She glanced down to the sketchbook Grant still held. "Do you like the sketches?"

He gave a short laugh. "I don't think Genvième Grandeau needs an unsolicited critique."

"Genvième has a tremendous ego," Gennie corrected. "Besides, it's not unsolicited if I ask for it."

Grant gave her a long, steady look before answering. "Your work's always very moving, very personal. The publicity attached to it isn't necessary."

"I believe, from you, that's a compliment," Gennie considered. "Are you going to give me free rein to paint here, or am I going to have to fight you every step of the way?"

He frowned again, and his face settled into the lines so quickly, Gennie swallowed a laugh. "Why here, precisely?"

"I was beginning to think you were perceptive," Gennie said with a sigh. She made a sweep with her hand, wide, graceful, encompassing. "Can't you see it? It's life and it's death. It's a war that never ends, one we'll never see the outcome of. I can put that on canvas—only a part of it, a small, small slice. But I can do it. I couldn't resist if I wanted to."

"The last thing I want here is a bunch of eager reporters or a few displaced European noblemen."

Gennie lifted a brow, at once haughty and amused. It was the casual superiority of the look, Grant told himself, that made him want to drag her to the ground and prove to them both she was only a woman. "I think you take your reading too seriously," she told him in an infuriatingly soft drawl. "But I could give my word, if you like, that I won't phone the press or any of the two dozen lovers you seem to think I have."

"Don't you?" His banked temper came out in sarcasm. Gennie met it coolly.

"That's none of your business. However," she continued, "I could sign a contract in blood—yours preferably—and pay you a reasonable fee, since it's your lighthouse. I'm going to paint here, with your cooperation or without it."

"You seem to have a disregard for property rights, Genviève."

"You seem to have a disregard for the rights of art."

He laughed at that, a sound that was appealing, masculine, and puzzling. "No," he said after a moment, "as it happens, I feel very strongly about the rights of the artist."

"As long as it doesn't involve you."

He sighed, a sound she recognized as frustrated. His feelings about art and censorship were too ingrained to allow him to bar her way. And he knew, even as he stood there, that she was going to give him a great deal of trouble. A pity she hadn't chosen Penobscot Bay. "Paint," he said briefly. "And stay out of my way."

"Agreed." Gennie stepped up on the rock and looked out to sea again. "It's your rocks I want, your house, your sea." The lazily feminine smile touched her lips as she turned to him again. "But you're quite safe, Grant. I haven't any designs on you."

It was bait, they both knew it. But he nibbled anyway. "You don't worry me, Genviève."

"Don't I?" *What are you doing?* her common sense demanded. She ignored it. He thought she was some kind of twentieth-century siren. Why not humor him? With the aid of the rock she was a few inches above him. His eyes were narrowed against the sun as he looked up at her, hers were wide and smiling. With a laugh, she rested her hands on his shoulders. "I could have sworn I did."

Grant considered simply yanking her from the rock and into his arms. He ignored the stab of desire that came so quickly then left a nagging ache. She was taunting him, damn her, and she would win if he wasn't careful. "It's your ego again," he told her. "You're not the type that appeals to me."

Anger flashed into her eyes again, making her nearly irresistible. "Does any?"

"I prefer a softer type," he said, knowing her skin would be soft enough to melt if he gave in and put his hands on her. "Quieter," he lied. "Someone a bit less aggressive."

Gennie struggled not to lose her temper completely and slug him. "Ah, you prefer women who sit silently and don't think."

"Who don't flaunt their—attributes." This time his smile was taunting. "I don't have any trouble resisting you."

The bait was cast again, and this time Gennie swallowed it whole. "Really? Let's see about that."

She brought her mouth down to his before she had a chance to consider the consequences. Her hands were still on his shoulders, his still in his pockets, but the contact of lips brought on a full-scale explosion. Grant felt it rocket through him, fierce and fast, while his fingers balled into fists.

What in God's name was this? he demanded while he used every ounce of control not to bring her body against his. Instinctively he knew that would be the end for him. He had only to weather this one assault on his system, and it would be over.

Why didn't he back away? He wasn't chained. Grant told himself to, ordered himself to, then stood helpless while her mouth moved over his. Dozens, dozens of images and fantasies rained in his head until he nearly drowned in them. Witch, he thought as his mind hazed. He'd been right about her all along. He felt the ground tilt under his feet, the roar of the sea fill his brain. Her taste, warm, mysterious, spiced with woman, seeped into everything. And even that wasn't enough. For a moment he believed that there could be more than everything, a step just beyond what men knew. Perhaps women understood it. He felt his body tense as though he'd been shot. Perhaps this woman did.

In some part of his brain, he knew that for one brief moment he was completely vulnerable.

Gennie drew away quickly. Grant thought he felt the hands still on his shoulders tremble lightly. Her eyes were dazed, her lips parted not in temptation but in astonishment. Through his own shock, he realized she'd been just as moved as he, and just as weakened by it.

"I—I have to go," she began, then bit her lip as she realized she was stuttering again—a habit she seemed to have developed in the past twenty-four hours. Forgetting her sketch pad, she stepped off the rock and prepared to make an undignified dash for her car. In the next instant she was whirled around.

His face was set, his breathing unsteady. "I was wrong." His voice filled her head, emptying it of everything else. "I have a great deal of trouble resisting you."

What had she done, Gennie wondered frantically, to both of them? She was trembling—she never trembled. Frightened? Oh, God, yes. She could face the storm and the dark now with complete confidence. It was nothing compared to this. "I think we'd better—"

"So do I," he muttered as he hauled her against him. "But it's too late now."

In the next instant his mouth covered hers, hard, undeniable. But she would deny it, Gennie told herself. She had to or be swallowed up. How had she ever thought she understood emotions, sensations? Translating them with paints was nothing compared with an onslaught of experience. He poured through her until she wasn't certain she'd ever be free of him.

She lifted her hands to push him away. She drew him yet closer. His fingers gripped her hair, not gently. The savageness of the cliff, the sea, the wind, tore into both of them and ruled. He tugged her head back, perhaps to pretend he was still in command. Her lips parted, and her tongue raced to meet his.

Is this what she'd always ached to feel? Gennie wondered. This wild liberation, this burning, searing need? She'd never known what it was like to be so filled with another's taste that you could remember no others. She'd known he had this kind of strength in him, had sensed it from the first. But to feel it now, to know she was caught up in it was such a conflicting emotion—power and weakness—that she couldn't tell one from the other.

His skin was rough, scraping against hers as he slanted his mouth to a new angle. Feeling the small, intimate pain, she moaned from the sheer pleasure of it. His hands were still in her hair, roaming, gripping, tangling, while their mouths met in mutual assault.

Let yourself go. It was an order that came from somewhere deep inside of her. Let yourself feel. Helpless, she obeyed.

She heard the gulls, but the sound seemed romantic now, no longer mournful. The sea beat against the land. Power, power, power. She knew the full extent of it as her lips clung to Grant's. The edge of the cliff was close, she knew. One step, two, and she would be over, cartwheeling into space to be brought up short by the hard earth of reality. But those few seconds of giddy freedom would be worth the risk. Her sigh spoke of yielding and of triumph.

Grant swore, the sound muffled against her lips before he could force himself to break away from her. This was exactly what he had sworn wouldn't happen. He'd done enough fishing to know when he was being reeled in. He didn't have time for this—that's what he told himself as he looked down at Gennie. Her face was soft, flushed with passion, her hair trailing down to be tugged at by the wind as she kept her head tilted back. His lips ached to press against that slender, golden throat. It was her eyes, half closed and gleaming with the ageless power of woman, that helped him resist. It was a trap he wouldn't be caught in no matter which of them baited it.

His voice was low when he spoke, and as furious as his eyes. "I might want you. I might even take you. But it'll be when I'm damn good and ready. You want to call the tune, play the games, stick with your counts and your barons." Grant whirled away, cursing both of them.

Too stunned to move, Gennie watched him disappear inside the lighthouse. Was that all it had meant to him? she thought numbly. Just any man, any woman, any passion? Hadn't he felt that quicksilver pain that had meant unity, intimacy, destiny? Games? How could he talk of games after they had… Closing her eyes, she ran an unsteady hand through her hair.

No, it was her fault. She was making something out of nothing. There was no unity between two people who didn't even know each other, and intimacy was just a handy word to justify the needs of the physical. She was being fanciful again, turning something ordinary into something special because it was what she wanted.

Let him go. She reached down to pick up her sketch pad and found the pencil Grant had dislodged from her hair. Let him go, and concentrate on your work, she ordered herself. It was the scene that carried you away, not the content. Careful not to look back, she walked to her car.

Her hands didn't stop trembling until she reached the lane to the cottage. This was better, she thought as she listened to the quiet lap of water and the gentle sounds of swallows coming back to nest for the evening. There was peace here, and the light was easy. This was what she should paint instead of the turbulence of the ocean and the ruggedness of rocks. This was where she should stay, soaking up the drifting solitude of still water and calm air. When you challenged the tempestuousness of nature, odds were you lost. Only a fool continued to press against the odds.

Suddenly weary, Gennie got out of the car and wandered down to the pier. At the end she sat down on the rough wood to let her feet dangle over the side. If she stayed here, she'd be safe.

She sat in silence while the sun lowered in the sky. It took no effort to feel the lingering pressure of Grant's lips on hers. She'd never known a man to kiss like that—forceful, consuming, yet with a trace of vulnerability. Then again, she wasn't as experienced as Grant assumed.

She dated, she socialized, she enjoyed men's company, but as her art had always come first, her more intimate relationships were limited. Classes, work, showings, traveling, parties: almost everything she'd ever done for almost as long as she could remember had been connected with her art, and the need to express it.

Certainly she enjoyed the social benefits, the touches of glitter and glamor that came her way after days and weeks of isolation. She didn't mind the image the press had created, because it seemed rather unique and bohemian. She didn't mind taking a bit of glitz here and there after working herself to near exhaustion in silence and solitude. At times the Genvième the papers tattled about amused or impressed her. Then it would be time for the next painting. She'd never had any trouble tucking the socialite away from the artist.

Wouldn't the press be shocked, Gennie mused, to learn that Genvième Grandeau of the New Orleans Grandeaus, successful artist, established socialite, and woman of the world had never had a lover?

With a half laugh, she leaned back on her elbows. She'd been wedded to her art for so long, a lover had seemed superfluous. Until… Gennie started to block out the thought, then calling herself a coward, finished it out. Until Grant Campbell.

Staring up at the sky, she let herself remember those sensations, those feelings and needs he'd unlocked in her. She would have made love with him without a thought, without a moment's hesitation. He'd rejected her.

No, it was more than that, Gennie remembered as anger began to rise again. Rejection was one thing, painful, humiliating, but that hadn't been all of it. Grant had dumped his arrogance on top of rejection—that was intolerable.

He'd said he'd *take* her when *he* was ready. As if she were a—a chocolate bar on a store counter. Her eyes narrowed, pale green with fury. We'll see about that, Gennie told herself. We'll just see about that!

Standing, she brushed off the seat of her pants with one clean swipe. No one rejected Genvième Grandeau. And no one took her. It was games he wanted, she thought as she stalked toward the cottage, it would be games he'd get.

# *Chapter 4*

She wasn't going to be chased away. Gennie told herself that with a grim satisfaction as she packed her painting gear the next morning. *No one* chased her away—especially a rude, arrogant idiot. Grant Campbell was going to find her perched on his doorstep—in a manner of speaking—until she was good and ready to move on.

The painting, Gennie mused as she checked her brushes. Of course the painting was of first importance, but…while she was about it, she thought with a tight smile, she would take a bit of time to teach that man a lesson. Oh, he deserved one. Gennie tossed the hair out of her eyes as she shut the lid on her paint box. No one, in all of her experience, deserved a good dig in the ribs as much as Grant Campbell. And she was just the woman to give it to him.

So he thought she wanted to play games. Gennie snapped the locks on the case a bit violently, so that the sound echoed like two shots through the empty cottage. She'd play games all right—her games, her rules.

Gennie had spent twenty-six years watching her grandmother beguile and enchant the male species. An amazing woman, Gennie thought now with an affectionate smile. Beautiful and vibrant in her seventies, she could still twist a man of any age around her finger. Well, she was a Genviève, too. She stuck her hands on her hips. And Grant Campbell was about to take a short walk off a high cliff.

Take me, will he? she thought, seething all over again with the memory. Of all the impossible gall. When *he's* ready? Making a low sound in her throat, she grabbed a paint smock. She'd have Grant Campbell crawling at her feet before she was through with him!

The anger and indignation Gennie had nursed all night made it easy to forget that sharp, sweet surge of response she'd felt when his mouth had been on hers. It made it easy to forget the fact that she'd wanted him—blindly, urgently—as she'd never wanted any man before. Temper was much more satisfying than depression, and Gennie rolled with it. She'd take her revenge coolly; it would taste better that way.

Satisfied that her gear was in order, Gennie walked through the cottage to her bedroom. Critically, she studied herself in the mirror over the old bureau. She was artist enough to recognize good bone structure and coloring. Perhaps suppressed anger suited her, she considered, as it added a faint rose flush to the honey tone of her skin.

As grimly as a warrior preparing for battle, she picked up a pot of muted green eyeshadow. When you had an unusual feature, she thought as she smudged it on her lids, you played it up. The result pleased her—a bit exotic, but not obvious. Lightly, she touched her lips with color—not too much, she reflected, just enough to tempt. With a lazy smile, she dabbed her scent behind her ears. Oh, she intended to tempt him all right. And when he was on his knees, she'd stroll blithely away.

A pity she couldn't wear something a bit sexier, she thought as she pursed her lips and turned sideways in the mirror. But the painting did come first, after all. One couldn't wear something slinky to sit on a rock. The jeans and narrow little top would have to do. Pleased with the day's prospects, Gennie started back for her gear when the sound of an approaching car distracted her.

Her first thought was Grant, her first reaction a flood of nerves. Annoyed, Gennie told herself it was simply the anticipation of the contest that had her heart pounding. When she went to the window, she saw it wasn't Grant's pickup, but a small, battered station wagon. The Widow Lawrence stepped out, neat and prim, carrying a covered plate. Surprised, and a bit uncomfortable, Gennie opened the door to her landlady.

"Good morning." She smiled, trying to ignore the oddness of inviting the woman inside a cottage where she had lived, slept, and worked for years.

"See you're up and about." The widow hovered at the threshold with her tiny, dark eyes on Gennie's face.

"Yes." Gennie would have taken her hand instinctively if the widow hadn't been gripping the plate with both of them. "Please, come in, Mrs. Lawrence."

"Don't want to bother you. Thought maybe you'd like some muffins."

"I would." Gennie forgot her plans for an early start and opened the door wider. "Especially if you'd have some coffee with me."

"Wouldn't mind." The widow hesitated almost imperceptibly, then stepped inside. "Can't stay long, I'm needed at the post office." But her gaze skimmed over the room as she stood in front of the door.

"They smell wonderful." Gennie took the plate and headed back toward the kitchen, hoping to dispel some of the awkwardness. "You know, I can never drum up much energy for cooking when it's only for me."

"Ayah. There's more pleasure when you've a family to feed."

Gennie felt another well of sympathy, but didn't offer it. She faced the stove as she measured out coffee in the little pot she'd bought in town. The widow would be looking at her kitchen, Gennie thought, and remembering.

"You settled in all right, then."

"Yes." Gennie took two plates and set them on the narrow drop-leaf table. "The cottage is just what I needed. It's beautiful, Mrs. Lawrence." She hesitated as she took down cups and saucers, then turned to face the woman again. "You must have hated to leave here."

Mrs. Lawrence shifted her shoulders in what might have been a shrug. "Things change. Roof hold up all right in the storm the other night?"

Gennie gave her a blank look, but caught herself before she said she hadn't been there to notice. "I didn't have any trouble," she said instead. Gennie saw the gaze wander around the room. Perhaps it would be best if she talked about it. Everyone had told Gennie that about Angela, but she hadn't believed them then. Now she began to wonder if it would help to talk about a loss instead of submerging it.

"Did you live here long, Mrs. Lawrence?" She brought the cups to the table as she asked, then went for the cream.

"Twenty-six years," the woman said after a moment. "Moved in after my second boy was born. A doctor he is, a resident in Bangor." Stiff New England pride showed in the jut of her chin. "His brother's got himself a job on an oil rig—couldn't keep away from the sea."

Gennie came to join her at the table. "You must be very proud of them."

"Ayah."

"Was your husband a fisherman?"

"Lobsterman." She didn't smile, but Gennie heard it in her voice. "A good one. Died on his boat. Stroke they tell me." She added a dab of cream to her coffee, hardly enough to change the color. "He'd've wanted to die on his boat."

She wanted to ask how long ago, but couldn't. Perhaps the time would come when she would be able to speak of the loss of her sister in such simple terms of acceptance. "Do you like living in town?"

"Used to it now. There be friends there, and this road..." For the first time, Gennie saw the wisp of a smile that made the hard, lined face almost pretty. "My Matthew could curse this road six ways to Sunday."

"I believe it." Tempted by the aroma, Gennie removed the checkered dishcloth from the plate. "Blueberry!" She grinned, pleased. "I saw wild blueberry bushes along the road from town."

"Ayah, they'll be around a little while more." She watched, satisfied as Gennie bit into one. "Young girl like you might get lonely away out here."

Gennie shook her head as she swallowed. "No, I like the solitude for painting."

"You do the pictures hanging in the front room?"

"Yes, I hope you don't mind that I hung them."

"Always had a partiality for pictures. You do good work."

Gennie grinned, as pleased with the simple statement as she would have been with a rave review. "Thank you. I plan to do quite a bit of painting around Windy Point—more than I had expected at first," she added, thinking of Grant. "If I decided to stay an extra few weeks—"

"You just let me know."

"Good." Gennie watched as the widow broke off a small piece of muffin. "You must know the lighthouse..." Still nibbling, Gennie toyed with exactly what information she wanted and how to get it.

"Charlie Dees used to keep that station," Mrs. Lawrence told her. "Him and his missus had it since I was a girl. Use radar now, but my father and his father had that light to keep them off the rocks."

There were stories here, Gennie thought. Ones she'd like to hear, but for now it was the present keeper who interested her.

"I met the man who lives there now," she said casually over the rim of her coffee cup. "I'm going to do some painting out there. It's a wonderful spot."

The widow's stiff straight brows rose. "You tell him?"

So they knew him in town, Gennie thought with a mental sniff. "We came to an...agreement of sorts."

"Young Campbell's been there near on to five years." The widow speculated on the gleam in Gennie's eyes, but didn't comment on it. "Keeps to himself. Sent a few out-of-towners on their way quick enough."

"No doubt," Gennie murmured. "He's not a friendly sort."

"Stays out of trouble." The widow gave Gennie a quick, shrewd look. "Nice-looking boy. Hear he's been out with the men on the boats a time or two, but does more watching than talking."

Confused, Gennie swallowed the last of the muffin. "Doesn't he fish for a living?"

"Don't know what he does, but he pays his bills right enough."

Gennie frowned, more intrigued than she wanted to be. "That's odd, I got the impression..." Of what? she asked herself. "I don't suppose he gets a lot of mail," she hazarded.

The widow gave her wispy smile again. "Gets his due," she said simply. "I thank you for the coffee, Miss Grandeau," she added, rising. "And I'm happy to have you stay here as you please."

"Thank you." Knowing she had to be satisfied with the bare snips of information, Gennie rose with her. "I hope you'll come back again, Mrs. Lawrence."

Nodding, the widow made her way back to the front door. "You let me know if you have any problems. When the weather turns, you'll be needing the furnace. It's sound enough mind, but noisier than some."

"I'll remember. Thanks."

Gennie watched her walk to her car and thought about Grant. He wasn't one of them, she mused, but she had sensed a certain reserved affection for him in Mrs. Lawrence's tone. He kept to himself, and that was something the people of Windy Point would respect. Five years, she thought as she wandered back for her paints. A long time to seclude yourself in a lighthouse...doing what?

With a shrug, she gathered her gear. What he did wasn't her concern. Making him crawl a bit was.

The only meal Grant ate with regularity was breakfast. After that, he grabbed what he wanted when he wanted—or when his work permitted. He'd eaten at dawn only because he couldn't sleep, then had gone out on his boat only because he couldn't work. Gennie, tucked into bed two miles away, had managed to interfere with his two most basic activities.

Normally, he would have enjoyed the early run at sea, catching the rosy light with the fishermen and facing the chill dawn air. He would try his luck, and if it was good, have his catch for dinner. If it was bad, he'd broil a steak or open a can.

He hadn't enjoyed his outing this morning, because he had wanted to sleep—then he'd wanted to work. His mood hadn't been tuned to fishing, and the diversion hadn't been a success. The sun had still been low in the sky when he'd returned.

It was high now, but Grant's mood was little better than it had been. Only the discipline he'd imposed on himself over the years kept him at his drawing board, perfecting and refining the strip he'd started the day before.

She'd thrown him off schedule, he thought grimly. And she was running around inside his head. Grant often let people do just that, but they were *his* people, and he controlled them. Gennie refused to stay in character.

Genvième, he thought, as he meticulously inked in Veronica's long, lush hair. He'd admired her work, its lack of gimmickry, its basic class. She painted with style, and the hint, always the hint of a raging passion underneath a misty overlay of fancy. Her paintings asked you to pretend, to imagine, to believe in something lovely. Grant had never found any fault with that.

He remembered seeing one of her landscapes, one of the bayou scenes that often figured prominently in her showings. The shadows had promised secrets, the dusky blue light a night full of possibilities. There'd been a fog over the water that had made him think of muffled whispers. The tiny house hanging over the river hadn't seemed ramshackle, but lovely in a faded, yesterday way. The serenity of the painting had appealed to him, the clever lighting she'd used had amused him. He could remember being disappointed that the work had already been sold. He wouldn't have even asked the price.

The passion that often lurked around the edges of her works was a subtle contrast to the serenity of her subjects. The fancy had always been uppermost.

She got enough passion in her personal life, he remembered as his mouth tightened. If he hadn't met her, hadn't touched her, he would have kept to the opinion that ninety percent of the things printed about her were just what she had said. Tripe.

But now all he could think was that any man who could get close to Genviève Grandeau would want her. And that the passion that simmered in her paintings, simmered in her equally. She knew she could make a slave out of a man, he thought, and forced himself to complete his drawing of Veronica. She knew it and enjoyed it.

Grant set down his brush a moment and flexed his fingers. Still, he had the satisfaction of knowing he'd turned her aside.

Turned her aside, hell, he thought with a mirthless laugh. If he'd done that he wouldn't be sitting here remembering how she'd been like a fire in his arms—hot, restless, dangerous. He wouldn't be remembering how his mind had gone blank one instant and then had been filled—with only her.

A siren? By God, yes, he thought savagely. It was easy to imagine her smiling and singing and luring a man toward some rocky coast. But not him. He wasn't a man to be bewitched by a seductive voice and a pair of alluring eyes. After his parting shot, he doubted she'd be back in any case. Though he glanced toward the window, Grant refused to go to it. He picked up his brush and worked for another hour, with Gennie teasing the back of his mind.

Satisfied that he had finished the strip on schedule after all, Grant cleaned his brushes. Because the next one was already formed in his mind, his mood was better. With a meticulousness that carried over into no other area of his life, he set his studio to rights. Tools were replaced in a precise manner in and on the glass-topped cabinet beside him. Bottles and jars were wiped clean, tightly capped, and stored. His copy would remain on the drawing board until well dried.

Taking his time, Grant went down to rummage in the kitchen for some food while he kept the portable radio on, filling him in on whatever was going on in the outside world.

A mention of the Ethics Committee, and a senator Grant could never resist satirizing, gave him an angle for another strip. It was true that his use of recognizable names and faces, often in politics, caused some papers to place his work on the editorial page. Grant didn't care where they put it, as long as his point got across. Caricaturing politicians had become a habit when he'd been a child—one he'd never had the least inclination to break.

Leaning against the counter, idly depleting a bag of peanut butter cookies, Grant listened to the rest of the report. An awareness of trends, of moods, of events was as essential to his art as pen and ink. He'd remember what he'd need when the time came to use it. For now it was filed and stored in the back of his mind and he wanted air and sunshine.

He'd go out, Grant told himself, not because he expected to see Gennie—but because he expected not to.

Of course, she was there, but he wanted to believe the surge he felt was annoyance. It was always annoyance—never pleasure—that he felt when he found someone infringing on his solitude.

It wouldn't be much trouble to ignore her.... The wind had her hair caught in its dragging fingers, lifting it from her neck. He could simply go the other way and walk north on the beach.... The sun slanted over the skin of her bare arms and face and had it gleaming. If he turned his back and moved down the other side of the cliff, he'd forget she was even there.

Swearing under his breath, Grant went toward her.

Gennie had seen him, of course, the moment he stepped out. Her brush had only hesitated for a moment before she'd continued to paint. If her pulse had scrambled a bit, she told herself it was only the anticipation of the battle she was looking forward to engaging in—and winning. Because she knew she couldn't afford to keep going now that her concentration was broken, she tapped the handle of her brush to her lips and viewed what she'd done that morning.

The sketch on the canvas gave her precisely what she wanted. The colors she'd already mixed satisfied her. She began to hum, lightly, as she heard Grant draw closer.

"So..." Gennie tilted her head, as if to study the canvas from a different angle. "You decided to come out of your cave."

Grant stuck his hands in his pockets and deliberately stood where he couldn't see her work. "You didn't strike me as the kind of woman who asked for trouble."

Barely moving the angle of her head, Gennie slid her eyes up to his. Her smile was very faint, and very taunting. "I suppose that makes you a poor judge of character, doesn't it?"

The look was calculated to arouse, but knowing it didn't make any difference. He felt the first kindling of desire spread low in his stomach. "Or you a fool," he murmured.

"I told you I'd be back, Grant." She allowed her gaze to drift briefly to his mouth. "Generally I try to—follow through. Would you like to see what I've done?"

He told himself he didn't give a hang about the painting or about her. "No."

Gennie moved her mouth into a pout. "Oh, and I thought you were such an art connoisseur." She set down her brush and ran a hand leisurely through her hair. "What are you, Grant Campbell?" Her eyes were mocking and alluring.

"What I choose to be."

"Fortunate for you." She rose. Taking her time, she drew off the short-sleeved smock and dropped it on the rock beside her. She watched his face as his eyes traveled over her, then ran a lazy finger down his shirtfront. "Shall I tell you what I see?" He didn't answer, but his eyes stayed on hers. Gennie wondered if she pressed her hand to his heart if the beat would be fast and unsteady. "A loner," she continued, "with the face of a buccaneer and the hands of a poet. And the manners," she added with a soft laugh, "of a lout. It seems to me that the manners are all you've had the choice about."

It was difficult to resist the gleam of challenge in her eyes or the promise in those soft, full lips that smiled with calculated feminine insolence. "If you like," Grant said mildly while he kept the hands that itched to touch her firmly in his pockets.

"I can't say I do." Gennie walked a few steps away, close enough to the cliff edge so that the spray nearly reached her. "Then again, your manners add a rather rough-and-ready appeal." She glanced over her shoulder. "I don't suppose a woman always wants a gentleman. You wouldn't be a man who looks for a lady."

With the sea behind her, reflecting the color of her eyes, she looked more a part of it than ever. "Is that what you are, Genviève?"

She laughed, pleased with the frustration and fury she read in his eyes. "It depends," she said, deliberately mimicking him, "on whether it's useful or not."

Grant came to her then but resisted the desire to shake her until her teeth rattled. Their bodies were close, so that little more than the wind could pass between them. "What the hell are you trying to do?"

She gave him an innocent stare. "Why, have a conversation. I suppose you're out of practice."

He glared, narrow-eyed, then turned away. "I'm going for a walk," he muttered.

"Lovely." Gennie slipped her arm through his. "I'll go with you."

"I didn't ask you," Grant said flatly, stopping again.

"Oh." Gennie batted her eyes. "You're trying to charm me by being rude again. It's so difficult to resist."

A grin tugged at his mouth before he controlled it. There was no one he laughed at more easily than himself. "All right, then." There was a gleam in his eyes she didn't quite trust. "Come on."

Grant walked swiftly, without deference to the difference in their strides. Determined to make him suffer before the afternoon was over, Gennie trotted to keep up. After they'd circled the lighthouse, Grant started down the cliff with the confidence of long experience.

Gennie took a long look at the steep drop, at the rock ledges Grant walked down with no more care than if they'd been steps. Below, the surf churned and battered at the shoreline. She wasn't about to be intimidated, Gennie reminded herself. He'd just love that. Taking a deep breath, she started after him.

For the first few feet her heart was in her throat. She'd really make him suffer if she fell and broke her neck. Then she began to enjoy it. The sea grew louder with the descent. Salt spray tingled along her skin. Doubtless there was a simpler way down, but at the moment she wouldn't have looked for it.

Grant reached the bottom in time to turn and see Gennie scrambling down the last few feet. He'd wanted to believe she'd still be up on the cliff, yet somehow he'd known better. She was no hot-house magnolia no matter how much he'd like to have tossed her in that category. She was much too vital to be admired from a distance.

Instinctively, he reached for her hand to help her down. Gennie brushed against him on the landing, then stood, head tilted back, daring him to do something about it. Her scent rushed to his senses. Before, she'd only smelled of the rain. This was just as subtle, but infinitely more sensuous. She smelled of night in the full light of the afternoon, and of all those whispering, murmuring promises that bloomed after sundown.

Infuriated that he could be lured by such an obvious tactic, Grant released her. Without a word he started down the narrow, rocky beach where the sea boomed and echoed and the gulls screamed. Smug and confident with her early success, Gennie moved with him.

Oh, I'm getting to you, Grant Campbell. And I haven't even started.

"Is this what you do with your time when you're not locked in your secret tower?"

"Is this what you do with your time when you're not hitting the hot spots on Bourbon Street?"

Tossing back her hair, Gennie deliberately slipped her arm through his again. "Oh, we talked enough about me yesterday. Tell me about Grant Campbell. Are you a mad scientist conducting terrifying experiments under secret government contract?"

He turned his head, then gave her an odd smile. "At the moment I'm stamp collecting."

That puzzled her enough that she forgot the game and frowned. "Why do I feel there's some grain of truth in that?"

With a shrug, Grant continued to walk, wondering why he didn't shake her off and go on his way alone. When he came here, he always came alone. Walks along this desolate, rocky beach were the only time other than sleep that he allowed his mind to empty. There where the waves crashed like thunder and the ground was hard and unforgiving was his haven against his own thoughts and self-imposed pressure. He'd never allowed anyone to join him there, not even his own creations. He wanted to feel the sense of intrusion he'd expected with Gennie at his side; instead he felt something very close to contentment.

"A secret place," Gennie murmured.

Distracted, Grant glanced down at her. "What?"

"This." Gennie gestured with her free hand. "This is a secret place." Bending she picked up a shell, pitted by the ocean, dried like a bone in the sun. "My grandmother has a beautiful old plantation house filled with antiques and silk pillows. There's a room off the attic upstairs. It's gloomy and dusty. There's a broken rocker in there and a box full of perfectly useless things. I could sit up there for hours." Bringing her gaze back to his, she smiled. "I've never been able to resist a secret place."

Grant remembered, suddenly and vividly, a tiny storeroom in his parents' home in Georgetown. He'd closeted himself in there for hours at a stretch with stacks of comic books and a sketch pad. "It's only a secret if nobody knows about it."

She laughed, slipping her hand into his without any thought. "Oh, no, it can still be a secret with two—sometimes a better secret." She stopped to watch a gull swoop low over the water. "What are those islands out there?"

Disturbed, because her hand felt as though it belonged in his, Grant scowled out to sea. "Hunks of rock mostly."

"Oh." Gennie sent him a desolate look. "No bleached bones or pieces of eight?"

The grin snuck up on him. "There be talk of a skull that moans when a storm's brewing," he told her, slipping into a thick Down East cadence.

"Whose?" Gennie demanded, ready for whatever story he could conjure.

"A seaman's," Grant improvised. "He lusted after his captain's woman. She had the eyes of a sea-witch and hair like midnight." Despite himself Grant took a handful of Gennie's while the rest tossed in the wind. "She tempted him, made him soft, wicked promises if he'd steal the gold and the longboat. When he did, because she was a woman who could drive a man to murder with a look, she went with him." Grant felt her hair tangle around his fingers as though it had a life of its own.

"So he rowed for two days and two nights, knowing when they came to land he'd have her. But when they spotted the coast, she drew out a saber and lopped off his head. Now his skull sits on the rocks and moans in frustrated desire."

Amused, Gennie tilted her head. "And the woman?"

"Invested her gold, doubled her profits, and became a pillar of the community."

Laughing, Gennie began to walk with him again. "The moral seems to be never trust a woman who makes you promises."

"Certainly not a beautiful one."

"Have you had your head lopped off, Grant?"

He gave a short, appreciative laugh. "No."

"A pity." She sighed. "I suppose that means you make a habit of resisting temptation."

"It's not necessary to resist it," he countered. "As long as you keep one eye open."

"There's no romance in that," Gennie complained.

"I've other uses for my head, thanks."

She shot him a thoughtful look. "Stamp collecting?"

"For one."

They walked in silence again while the sea crashed close beside them. On the other side the rocks rose like a wall. Far out on the water there were dots of boats. That one sign of humanity only added to the sense of space and aloneness.

"Where did you come from?" she asked impulsively.

"The same place you did."

It took her a minute, then she chuckled. "I don't mean biologically. Geographically."

He shrugged, trying not to be pleased she had caught on so quickly. "South of here."

"Oh, well that's specific," she muttered, then tried again. "What about family? Do you have family?"

He stopped to study her. "Why?"

With an exaggerated sigh, Gennie shook her head. "This is called making friendly conversation. It's a new trend that's catching on everywhere."

"I'm a noncomformist."

"No! Really?"

"You do that wide-eyed, guileless look very well, Genviève."

"Thank you." She turned the shell over in her hand, then looked up at him with a slow smile. "I'll tell you something about my family, just to give you a running start." She thought for a moment, then hit on something she thought he'd relate to. "I have a cousin, a few times removed. I've always thought he was the most fascinating member of the family tree, though you couldn't call him a Grandeau."

"What would you call him?"

"The black sheep," she said with relish. "He did things his own way, never giving a damn about what anyone thought. I heard stories about him from time to time—though I wasn't meant to—and it wasn't until I was a grown woman that I met him. I'm happy to say we took to each other within minutes and have kept in touch over the last couple of years. He'd lived his life by his wits, and done quite well—which didn't sit well with some of the more staid members of the family. Then he confounded everyone by getting married."

"To an exotic dancer."

"No." She laughed, pleased that he was interested enough to joke. "To someone absolutely suitable—intelligent, well bred, wealthy—" She rolled her eyes. "The black sheep, who'd spent some time in jail, gambled his way into a fortune, had outdone them all." With a laugh, Gennie thought of the Comanche Blade. Cousin Justin had indeed outdone them all. And he didn't even bother to thumb his nose.

"I love a happy ending," Grant said dryly.

With her eyes narrowed, Gennie turned to him. "Don't you know that the less you tell someone, the more they want to know? You're better off to make something up than to say nothing at all."

"I'm the youngest of twelve children of two South African missionaries," he said with such ease, she very nearly believed him. "When I was six, I wandered into the jungle and was taken in by a pride of lions. I still have a penchant for zebra meat. Then when I was eighteen, I was captured by hunters and sold to a circus. For five years I was the star of the sideshow."

"The Lion Boy," Gennie put it.

"Naturally. One night during a storm the tent caught fire. In the confusion I escaped. Living off the land, I wandered the country—stealing a few chickens now and again. Eventually an old hermit took me in after I'd saved him from a grizzly."

"With your bare hands," Gennie added.

"I'm telling the story," he reminded her. "He taught me to read and write. On his deathbed he told me where he'd buried his life savings—a quarter million in gold bullion. After giving him the Viking funeral he'd requested, I had to decide whether to be a stockbroker or go back to the wilderness."

"So you decided against Wall Street, came here, and began to collect stamps."

"That's about it."

"Well," Gennie said after a moment. "With a boring story like that, I can see why you keep it to yourself."

"You asked," Grant pointed out.

"You might have made something up."

"No imagination."

She laughed then and leaned her head on his shoulder. "No, I can see you have a very literal mind."

Her laugh rippled along his skin, and the casual intimacy of her head against his shoulder shot straight down to the soles of his feet. He should shake her off, Grant told himself. He had no business walking here with her and enjoying it. "I've got things to do," he said abruptly. "We can go up this way."

It was the change in his tone that reminded Gennie she'd come there for a purpose, and the purpose was not to wind up liking him.

The way up was easier than the way down, she noted as he turned toward what was now a slope rather than a cliff. Though his fingers loosened on hers, she held on, shooting him a smile that had him muttering under his breath as he helped her climb. Thinking quickly, she stuck the shell in her back pocket. When they neared the top, Gennie held her other hand out to him. With her eyes narrowed a bit against the sun, her hair flowing down her back, she looked up at him. Swearing, Grant grabbed her other hand and hauled her up the last few feet.

On level ground she stayed close, her body just brushing his as their hands remained linked. His breath had stayed even during the climb, but now it came unsteadily. Feeling a surge of satisfaction, Gennie gave him a slow, lazy smile.

"Going back to your stamps?" she murmured. Deliberately, she leaned closer to brush her lips over his chin. "Enjoy yourself." Drawing her hands from his, Gennie turned. She'd taken three steps before he grabbed her arm. Though her heart began to thud, she looked over her shoulder at him. "Want something?" she asked in a low, amused voice.

She could see it on his face—the struggle for control. And in his eyes she could see a flare of desire that had her throat going dry. No, she wasn't going to back down now, she insisted. She'd finish out the game. When he yanked her against him, she told herself it wasn't fear she felt, it wasn't passion. It was self-gratification.

"It seems you do," she said with a laugh, and slid her hands up his back.

When his mouth crushed down on hers, her mind spun. All thoughts of purpose, all thoughts of revenge vanished. It was as it had been the first time—the passion, and over the passion a rightness, and with the rightness a storm of confused needs and longings and wishes. Opening to him was so natural she did so without thought, and with a simplicity that made him groan as he drew her closer.

His tongue skimmed over her lips then tangled with hers as his hands roamed to mold her hips. Strong hands—she'd known they'd be strong. Her skin tingled with the image of being touched without barriers even as her mouth sought to take all he could give her through a kiss alone. She strained against him, offering, demanding, and it seemed he couldn't give or take fast enough to satisfy either of them. His mouth ravaged, but hers wouldn't surrender. What she drew out of him excited them both.

It wasn't until she began to feel the weakness that Gennie remembered to fear. This wasn't what she'd come for... Was it? No, she wouldn't believe she'd come to feel this terrifying pleasure, this aching, gnawing need to give what she'd never given before. Panic rose and she struggled against it in a way she knew she'd never be able to struggle against desire. She had to stop him, and herself. If he held her much longer, she would melt, and melting, lose.

Drawing on what was left of her strength she pulled back, determined not to show either the passion or the fear that raced through her. "Very nice," she murmured, praying he wouldn't notice how breathless her voice was. "Though your technique's a bit—rough for my taste."

His breath came quick and fast. Grant didn't speak, knowing if he did madness would pour out. For the second time she'd emptied him out then filled him again with herself. Need for her, raw, exclusive, penetrating, ripped through him as he stared into her eyes and waited for it to abate. It didn't.

He was stronger than she was, he told himself as he gathered her shirtfront in his hand. Her heart thudded against his knuckles. There was nothing to stop him from... He dropped his hand as though she'd scalded him. No one pushed him to that, he thought furiously while she continued to stare up at him. No one.

"You're walking on dangerous ground, Genvième," he said softly.

She tossed back her head. "I'm very sure-footed." With a parting smile, she turned, counting each step as she went back to her canvas. Perhaps her hands weren't steady as she packed up her gear.

Perhaps her blood roared in her ears. But she'd won the first round. She let out a deep breath as she heard the door to the lighthouse slam shut.

The first round, she repeated, wishing she wasn't looking forward quite so much to the next one.

# *Chapter 5*

Grant managed to avoid Gennie for three days. She came back to paint every morning, and though she worked for hours, she never saw a sign of him. The lighthouse was silent, its windows winking blankly in the sun.

Once his boat was gone when she arrived and hadn't returned when she lost the light she wanted. She was tempted to go down the cliff and walk along the beach where he had taken her. She found she could have more easily strolled into his house uninvited than gone to that one particular spot without his knowledge. Even had she wanted to paint there, the sense of trespassing would have forbidden it.

She painted in peace, assured that since she had gotten her own back with Grant she wouldn't think of him. But the painting itself kept him lodged in her mind. She would never be able to see that spot, on canvas or in reality, and not see him. It was his, as surely as if he'd been hewed from the rocks or tossed up by the sea. She could feel the force of his personality as she guided her brush, and the challenge of it as she struggled to put what should have only been nature's mood onto canvas.

But it wouldn't only be nature's, she discovered as she painted sea and surf. Though his form wouldn't be on the canvas, his substance would. Gennie had always felt a particle of her own soul went into each one of her canvases. In this one she would capture a part of Grant's as well. Neither of them had a choice.

Somehow knowing it drove her to create something with force and muscle. The painting excited her. She knew she'd been meant to paint that view, and to paint it well. And she knew when it was done, she would give it to Grant. Because it could never belong to anyone else.

It wouldn't be a token of affection, she told herself, or an offer of friendship. It was simply something that had to be done. She'd never be able, in good conscience, to sell that canvas. And if she kept it herself, he'd haunt her. So before she left Windy Point, she would make him a gift of it. Perhaps, in her way, she would then haunt him.

Her mornings were filled with an urgency to finish it, an urgency she had to block again and again unless she miss something vital in the process. Gennie knew it was imperative to move slowly, to absorb everything around her and give it to the painting. In the afternoons she forced herself to pack up so that she wouldn't work longer than she should and ignore the changing light.

She sketched her inlet and planned a watercolor. She fretted for morning so that she could go back to the sea.

Her restlessness drove her to town. It was time to make some sketches there, to decide what she would paint and in what medium.

She told herself she needed to see people again to keep her mind from focusing so continually on Grant.

In the midafternoon, Windy Point was sleepy and quiet. Boats were out to sea, and a hazy summer heat shimmered in the air. She saw a woman sitting on her porch stringing the last of the season's beans while a toddler plucked at the clover in the yard.

Gennie parked her car at the end of the road and began to walk. She could sketch the buildings, the gardens. She could gather impressions that would bring them to life again when she began to paint. This was a different world from the force at Windy Point Station, different yet from the quiet inlet behind her cottage, but they were all connected. The sea touched all of them in different ways.

She wandered, glad she had come though the voices she heard were voices of strangers. It was a town she'd remember more clearly than any of the others she'd visited on her tour of New England. But it was the sea that continued to tug at her underneath it all—and the man who lived there.

When would she see him again? Gennie wondered, forced to admit that she missed him. She missed the scowl and the curt words, the quick grin and surprising humor, the light of amused cynicism she caught in his eyes from time to time. And though it was the hardest to admit, she missed that furious passion he'd brought to her so suddenly.

Leaning against the side of a building, she wondered if there would be another man somewhere who would touch her that way. She couldn't imagine one. She'd never looked for a knight in armor—they were simply too much trouble, expecting a helpless damsel in return. Helpless she would never be, and chivalry, for the most part, got in the way of an intelligent relationship. Grant Campbell, Gennie mused, would never be chivalrous, and a helpless female would infuriate him.

Remembering their first meeting, she chuckled. No, he didn't care to be put out by a lady in distress anymore than she cared to be one. She supposed, on both parts, it went back to a fierce need for independence.

No, he wasn't looking for a lady, and while she hadn't been looking for a knight, she hadn't been searching out ogres, either. Gennie thought Grant came very close to fitting into that category. While she enjoyed men's company, she didn't want one tangling up her life—at least not until she was ready. And she certainly didn't want to be involved with an ogre—they were entirely too unpredictable. Who knew when they'd just swallow you whole?

Shaking her head, she glanced down, surprised to see that she'd not only been thinking of Grant, but had been sketching him. Lips pursed, Gennie lifted the pad for a critical study. A good likeness, she decided. His eyes were narrowed a bit, dark and intense on the point of anger. His brows were lowered, forming that faint vertical line of temper between them. She'd captured that lean face with its planes and shadows, the aristocratic nose and unruly hair. And his mouth…

The little jolt of response wasn't surprising, but it was unwelcomed. She'd drawn his mouth as she'd seen it before it came down on hers—the sensuousness, the ruthlessness. Yes, she could taste that stormy flavor even now, standing in the quiet town with the scent of fish and aging flowers around her.

Carefully closing the book, Gennie reminded herself she'd be much better off sticking to the buildings she'd come to draw. With the pencil stuck behind her ear, Gennie crossed the road to go into the post office. The skinny teenager she remembered from her first trip through the town turned to goggle at her when she entered. As she walked up to the counter, she smiled at him, then watched his Adam's apple bob up and down.

"Will." Mrs. Lawrence plunked letters down on the counter. "You'd best be getting Mr. Fairfield his mail before you lose your job."

"Yes, ma'am." He scooped at the letters while he continued to stare at Gennie. When he dropped the lot of them on the floor, Gennie bent to help him and sent him into a blushing attack of stutters.

"Will Turner," Mrs. Lawrence repeated with the pitch of an impatient schoolteacher. "Gather up those letters and be on your way."

"You missed one, Will," Gennie said kindly, then handed the envelope to him as his jaw went slack. Face pink, eyes glued to hers, Will stumbled to the door and out.

Mrs. Lawrence gave a dry chuckle. "Be lucky he doesn't fall off the curb."

"I suppose I should be flattered," Gennie considered. "I don't remember having that effect on anyone before."

"Awkward age for a boy when he starts noticing females is shaped a bit different."

With a laugh, Gennie leaned on the counter. "I wanted to thank you again for coming by the other day. I've been painting out at the lighthouse and haven't been into town."

Mrs. Lawrence glanced down at the sketchbook Gennie had set on the counter. "Doing some drawing here?"

"Yes." On impulse, Gennie opened the book and flipped through.

"It was the town that interested me right away—the sense of permanence and purpose."

Cool-eyed, the widow paged through the book while Gennie nibbled on her lip and waited for the verdict. "Ayah," she said at length. "You know what you're about." With one finger, she pushed back a sheet, then studied Gennie's sketch of Grant. "Looks a bit fierce," she decided as the wispy smile touched her mouth.

"*Is* a bit for my thinking," Gennie countered.

"Ayah, well there be a woman who like a touch of vinegar in a man." She gave another dry chuckle and for once her eyes were more friendly than shrewd. "I be one of them." With a glance over Gennie's shoulder, the widow closed the book. "Afternoon, Mr. Campbell."

For a moment Gennie goggled at the widow much as Will had goggled at her. Recovering, she laid a hand on the now closed book.

"Afternoon, Mrs. Lawrence." When he came to stand at the counter beside her, Gennie caught the scent of the sea on him. "Genviève," he said, giving her a long, enigmatic look.

He'd wondered how long he could stand it before he saw her up close again. There'd been too many times in the past three days that he hadn't been able to resist the urge to go to his studio window and watch her paint. All that had stopped him from going down to her was the knowledge that if he touched her again, he'd be heading down a road he'd never turn back from. As yet he was uncertain what was at the end of it.

A picture of the blushing, stuttering teenager ran through her mind and straightened Gennie's spine. "Hello, Grant." When she smiled, she was careful to bank down the warmth and make up for it with mockery. "I thought you were hibernating."

"Been busy," he said easily. "Didn't know you were still around." That gave him the satisfaction of seeing annoyance dart into her eyes before she controlled it.

"I'll be around for some time yet."

Mrs. Lawrence slid a thick bundle of mail on the counter, then followed it with a stack of newspapers. Gennie caught the Chicago return address of the top letter and the banner of the *Washington Post* before Grant scooped everything up. "Thanks."

With a frown between her brows, Gennie watched him walk out. There must have been a dozen letters *and* a dozen newspapers. Letters from Chicago, a Washington paper for a man who lived on a deserted cliff outside a town that didn't even boast a stoplight. What in the hell…

"Fine-looking young man," Mrs. Lawrence commented behind Gennie's back.

With a mumbled answer, Gennie started for the door. "Bye, Mrs. Lawrence."

Mrs. Lawrence tapped a finger on the counter thinking there hadn't been such tugging and pulling in the air since the last storm. Maybe another one was brewing.

Puzzled, Gennie began to walk again. It wasn't any of her business why some odd recluse received so much mail. For all she knew, he might only come into town to pick it up once a month…but that had been yesterday's paper. With a brisk shake of her head, she struggled against curiosity. The real point was that she'd been able to get a couple shots in—even if he'd had a bull's-eye for her.

She loitered at the corner, doing another quick sketch while she reminded herself that instead of thinking of him, she should be thinking what provisions she needed before she headed back to the cottage.

But she was restless again. The sense of order and peace she'd found after an hour in town had vanished the moment he'd walked into the post office. She wanted to find that feeling again before she went back to spend the night alone.

Aimlessly, she wandered down the road, pausing now and then at a store window. She was nearly to the edge of town when she remembered the churchyard. She'd sketch there until she was tired enough to go home.

A truck rattled by, perhaps the third vehicle Gennie had seen in an hour. After waiting for it, she crossed the road. She passed the small, uneven plot of the cemetery, listening to the quiet. The grass was high enough to bend in the breeze. Overhead a flock of gulls flew by, calling out on their way to the sea.

The paint on the high fence was rusted and peeling. Queen Anne's lace grew stubbornly between the posts. The church itself was small and white with a single stained-glass panel at the V of the roof. Other windows were clear glass and paned, and the door itself was sturdy and scarred with time. Gennie walked to the side and sat where the grass had been recently tended. She could smell it.

Fleetingly she wondered how it was possible one tiny scrap on the map could have so much that demanded to be painted. She could easily spend six months there rather than six weeks and never capture all she wanted to.

The restlessness evaporated as she began to sketch. Perhaps she wouldn't be able to transfer everything into oils or watercolor before she left, but she'd have the sketches. In months to come, she could use them to go back to Windy Point when she felt the need for it.

She'd turned over the page to start a second sketch when a shadow fell over her. A quick fluctuation of her pulse, a swift warmth on her skin. She knew who stood behind her. Shading her eyes, she looked up at Grant. "Well," she said lightly, "twice in one day."

"Small town." He gestured toward her pad. "You finished out at the station?"

"No, the light's wrong this time of day for what I want there."

It was annoyance he was supposed to feel, not relief. Casually, he dropped to the grass beside her. "So now you're going to immortalize Windy Point."

"In my own small way," she said dryly, and started to sketch again. Was she glad he had come? Hadn't she known, somehow, he would? "Still playing with stamps?"

"No, I've taken up classical music." He only smiled when she turned to study him. "You'd have been reared on that, I imagine. A little Brahms after dinner."

"I favored Chopin." She tapped her pencil on her chin. "What did you do with your mail?"

"I stowed it."

"I didn't notice your truck."

"I brought the boat." Taking the sketchbook, he flipped through to the front.

"For someone who's so keen on privacy," she began heatedly, "you have little respect when it belongs to someone else."

"Yeah." Unceremoniously, he shoved her hand away when she reached for the pad. While she simmered, Grant went through the book, pausing, then going on until he came to the sketch of himself. He studied it a moment, wordlessly, then surprised Gennie by grinning. "Not bad," he decided.

"I'm overwhelmed by your flattery."

He considered her a moment, then acted on impulse. "One deserves another."

Plucking the pencil out of her fingers, he turned the pages over until he came to a blank one. To her astonishment, he began to draw with the easy confidence of long practice. Mouth open, she stared at him while he whistled between his teeth and looped lines and curves onto the paper. His eyes narrowed a moment as he added some shading, then he tossed the book back into her lap. Gennie gave him a long, last stare before she looked down.

It was definitely her—in clever, merciless caricature. Her eyes were slanted—exaggerated, almost predatory, her cheekbones an aristocratic slash, her chin a stubborn point. With her mouth just parted and her head tilted back, he'd given her the expression of royalty mildly displeased. Gennie studied it for a full ten seconds before she burst into delighted laughter.

"You pig!" she said and laughed again. "I look like I'm about to have a minion beheaded."

He might have been saved if she'd gotten angry, been insulted. Then he could have written her off as vain and humorless and not worth his notice—at least he could have tried. Now with her laughter bouncing on the air and her eyes alive with it, Grant stepped off the cliff.

"Gennie." He murmured her name as his hand reached up to touch her face. Her laughter died.

What she would have said if her throat hadn't closed, she didn't know. She thought the air went very still very suddenly. The only movement seemed to be the fingers that brushed the hair back from her face, the only sound her own uneven breath. When he lowered his face toward hers, she didn't move but waited.

He hesitated, though the pause was too short to measure, before he touched his mouth to hers. Gentle, questioning, it sent a line of fire down her spine. For him, too, she realized, as his fingers tightened, briefly, convulsively, on her neck before they relaxed again. He must be feeling, as she did, that sudden urgent thrust of power that was followed by a dazed kind of weakness.

Floating…were people meant to float like this? Limitless, mindless. How could she have known one man's lips could bring such an endless variety of sensations when touched to hers? Perhaps she'd never been kissed before and only thought she had. Perhaps she had only imagined another man casually brushing her mouth with his. Because this was real.

She could taste—warm breath. She could feel—lips soft, yet firm and knowing. She could smell—that subtle scent on him that meant wind and sea. She could see—his face, blurred and close when her lashes drifted up to assure her. And when he moaned her name, she heard him.

Her answer was to melt, slowly, luxuriously against him. With the melting came a pain, unexpected and sharp enough to make her tremble. How could there be pain, she wondered dazedly, when her body was so truly at peace? Yet it came again on a wave that rocked her. Some lucid part of her mind reminded her that love hurt.

But no. She tried to shake off the pain, and the knowledge it brought her even as her lips clung to his. She wasn't falling in love, not now, not with him. That wasn't what she wanted…. What did she want? *Him.*

The answer came so clearly, so simply. It drove her into panic.

"Grant, no." She drew away, but the hand on her face slid to the back of her neck and held her still.

"No, what?" His voice was very quiet, with rough edges.

"I didn't intend—we shouldn't be—I didn't… Oh!" She shut her eyes, frustrated that she could be reduced to stammering confusion.

"Why don't you run that by me again?"

The trace of humor in his voice had her springing to her feet. She wasn't lightheaded, she told herself. She'd simply sat too long and rose too quickly. "Look, this is hardly the place for this kind of thing."

"What kind of thing?" he countered, rising, too, but with a lazy ease that moved muscle by muscle. "We were only kissing. That's more popular than making friendly conversation. Kissing you's become a habit." He reached out for her hair, then let it drift through his spread fingers. "I don't break them easily."

"In this case—" she paused to even her breathing "—I think you should make an exception."

He studied her, trying to make light of something that had struck him down to the bone. "You're quite a mix, Genviève. The practiced seductress one minute, the confused virgin the next. You know how to fascinate a man."

Pride moved automatically to shield her. "Some men are more easily fascinated than others."

"True enough." Grant wasn't sure just what emotion was working through him, but he knew it wasn't comfortable. "Damn if I won't be glad to see the last of you," he muttered.

Listening to the sound of his retreating footsteps, Gennie bent to pick up her sketchbook. By some malicious coincidence, it had fallen open to Grant's face. Gennie scowled at it. "And I'll be glad to see the last of you." She closed the book, made a business of brushing off her jeans, and started to leave the churchyard with quiet dignity.

The hell with it!

"Grant!" She raced down the steps to the sidewalk and tore after him. "Grant, wait!"

With every sign of impatience, he turned and did so. "What?"

A little breathless, she stopped in front of him and wondered what it was she wanted to say. No, she didn't want to see the last of him. If she didn't understand why yet, she felt she was at least entitled to a little time to find out.

"Truce," she decided and held out a hand. When he only stared at her, she gave a quick huff and swallowed another morsel of pride. "Please."

Trapped by the single word, he took the offered hand. "All right." When she would have drawn her hand away, he tightened his grip. "Why?"

"I don't know," Gennie told him with fresh impatience. "Just a wild urge to see if I can get along with an ogre." At the ironic lift of his brow, she sighed. "All right, that was just a quick slip. I take it back."

Idly, he twisted the thin gold chain she wore around his finger. "So, what now?"

What now indeed? Gennie thought as even the brush of his knuckles had her skin humming. She wasn't going to give in to it—but she wasn't going to jump like a scared rabbit either. "Listen, I owe you a meal," she said impulsively. "I'll pay you back, that way we'll have a clean slate."

"How?"

"I'll cook you dinner."

"You've already cooked me breakfast."

"That was your food," Gennie pointed out. Already planning things out, she looked past him into town. "I'll need to pick up a few things."

Grant studied her, considering. "You going to bring them to the lighthouse?"

Oh, no, she thought immediately. She knew better than to trust herself with him there, that close to the sea and the power. "To my cottage. There's a little brick barbecue out back if you like steaks."

What's going on in her mind? he wondered as he watched secret thoughts flicker in her eyes. He knew he'd never be able to resist finding out. "I've been known to choke down a bite or two in my time."

"Okay." She gave a decisive nod and took his hand. "Let's go shopping."

"Wait a minute," Grant began as she pulled him down the sidewalk.

"Oh, don't start complaining already. Where do I buy the steaks?"

"Bayside," Grant said dryly, and brought her up short.

"Oh."

Grinning at her expression, he draped an arm around her shoulder. "Once in a while Leeman's Market gets in a few good cuts of meat."

Gennie shot him a suspicious look. "From where?"

Still grinning, Grant pushed open the market door. "I love a mystery."

Gennie wasn't certain she was amused until she found there was indeed a steak—only one, but sizable enough for two people—and that it was from a nearby farm, authorized and licensed. Satisfied with this, and a bag of fresh salad greens, Gennie drew Grant outside again.

"Okay, now where can I buy a bottle of wine?"

"Fairfield's," he suggested. "He carries the only spirits in town. If you're not too particular about the label."

As they started across the road, a boy biked by, shooting Grant a quick look before he ducked his chin on his chest and pedaled away.

"One of your admirers?" Gennie asked dryly.

"I chased him and three of his friends off the cliffs a few weeks back."

"You're a real sport."

Grant only grinned, remembering his first reaction had been fury at having his peace interrupted, then fear that the four careless boys would break their necks on the rocks. "Ayah," he said, recalling with pleasure the acid tongue-lashing he'd doled out.

"Do you really kick sick dogs?" she asked as she caught the gleam in his eye.

"Only on my own land."

Heaving a hefty sigh, Gennie pushed open the door of Fairfield's store. Across the room, Will immediately dropped the large pot he'd been about to stock on a shelf. Red to the tips of his ears, he left it where it was. "Help you?" His voice cracked painfully on the last word.

"I need a bag of charcoal," Gennie told him as she crossed the room. "And a bottle of wine."

"Charcoal's in the back," he managed, then took a step in retreat as Gennie came closer. His elbow caught a stack of cans and sent them crashing. "What—what size?"

Torn between laughter and sympathy, Gennie swallowed. "Five pounds'll be fine."

"I'll get it." The boy disappeared, and Gennie caught Fairfield's voice demanding what the devil ailed him before she was forced to press a hand to her mouth to hold back the laughter.

Thinking of Macintosh's reaction to Veronica, Grant felt a wave of empathy. "Poor kid's going to be mooning like a puppy for a month. Did you have to smile at him?"

"Really, Grant. He can't be more than fifteen."

"Old enough to break out in a sweat," he commented.

"Hormones," she murmured as she found Fairfield's sparse selection of wine. "They just need time to balance."

Grant's gaze drifted down and focused as she bent over. "It should only take thirty or forty years," he muttered.

Gennie found a domestic burgundy and plucked it from the bottom shelf. "Looks like we feast after all."

Will came back with a bag of charcoal and almost managed not to trip over his own feet. "Brought you some starter, too, in case..." He broke off as his tongue tied itself into knots.

"Oh, thanks." Gennie set the wine on the counter and reached for her wallet.

"You gotta be of age to buy the wine," Will began. Gennie's smile widened and his blush deepened. "Guess you are, huh?"

Unable to resist, Gennie gestured to Grant. "He is."

Enraptured, Will stared at Gennie until she gently asked what the total was. He came to long enough to punch out numbers on the little adding machine, send it into clanking convulsions, and begin again.

"It be five-oh-seven, with—" a long sigh escaped "—tax."

Gennie resisted the urge to pat his cheek and counted out the change into his damp palm. "Thank you, Will."

Will's fingers closed over the nickel and two pennies. "Yes, ma'am."

For the first time the boy's eyes left Gennie's. Grant was struck with a look of such awe and envy, he wasn't sure whether to preen or apologize. In a rare gesture of casual affection, he reached over and squeezed Will's shoulder. "Makes a man want to sit up and beg, doesn't she?" he murmured when Gennie reached the door.

Will sighed. "Ayah." Before Grant could turn, Will plucked at his sleeve. "You gonna have dinner with her and everything?"

Grant lifted a brow but managed to keep his composure. *Everything,* he reminded himself, meant different things to different people. At the moment it conjured up rather provocative images in his brain. "Things are presently unsettled," he murmured, using one of Macintosh's stock phrases. Catching himself, he grinned. "Yeah, we're going to have dinner." And something, he added as he strolled out after Gennie.

"What was all that about?" she demanded.

"Man talk."

"Oh, I beg your pardon."

The way she said it—very antebellum and disdainful—made him laugh and pull her into his arms to kiss her in full view of all of Windy Point. As the embrace lingered on, Grant caught the muffled crash from inside Fairfield's. "Poor Will," he murmured. "I know just how he feels." Humor flashed into his eyes again. "I better start around in the boat if we're going to have dinner...and everything."

Confused by his uncharacteristic lightheartedness, Gennie gave him a long stare. "All right," she said after a moment. "I'll meet you there."

# *Chapter 6*

It was foolish to feel like a girl getting ready for a date. Gennie told herself that as she unlocked the door to the cottage. She'd told herself the same thing as she'd driven away from town…and as she'd turned down the quiet lane.

It was a spur of the moment cookout—two adults, a steak, and a bottle of burgundy that may or may not have been worth the price. A person would have to look hard to find any romance in charcoal, lighter fluid and some freshly picked greens from a patch in the backyard. Not for the first time, Gennie thought it a pity her imagination was so expansive.

It had undoubtedly been imagination that had brought on that rush of feeling in the churchyard. A little unexpected tenderness, a soft breeze and she heard bells. Silly.

Gennie set the bags on the kitchen counter and wished she'd bought candles. Candlelight would make even that tidy, practical little kitchen seem romantic. And if she had a radio, there could be music...

Catching herself, Gennie rolled her eyes to the ceiling. What was she thinking of? She'd never had any patience with such obvious, conventional trappings in the first place, and in the second place she didn't *want* a romance with Grant. She'd go halfway toward making a friendship—a very careful friendship—with him, but that was it.

She'd cook dinner for him because she owed him that much. They'd have conversation because she found him interesting despite the thorns. And she'd make very, very certain she didn't end up in his arms again. Whatever part of her longed for a repeat of what had happened between them in the churchyard would have to be overruled by common sense. Grant Campbell was not only basically unpleasant, he was just too complicated. Gennie considered herself too complex a person to be involved with anyone who had so many layers to him.

Gennie grabbed the bag of charcoal and the starter and went into the side yard to set the grill. It was so quiet, she mused, looking around as she ripped the bag open. She'd hear Grant coming long before she saw him.

It was the perfect time for a ride on the water, with the late afternoon shadows lengthening and the heat draining from the day. The light was bland as milk now, and as soothing. She could hear the light lap-slap of water against the pier and the rustle of insects in the high grass on the bank. Then, barely, she heard the faint putt of a distant motor.

Her nerves gathered together so quickly, Gennie nearly dropped the five pounds of briquettes on the ground. When she'd finished being exasperated with herself, she laughed and poured a neat pile of charcoal into the barbecue pit. So this was the coolly sophisticated Genviève Grandeau, she thought wryly; established member of the art world and genteel New Orleans society, about to drop five pounds of charcoal on her toes because a rude man was going to have dinner with her. How the mighty have fallen.

With a grin, she rolled the bag up and dropped it on the ground. So what? she asked herself before she strolled down to the pier to wait for him.

Grant took the turn into the inlet at a speed that sent water spraying high. Laughing, Gennie stretched on her toes and waved, wishing he were already there. She hadn't realized, not until just that moment, how much she'd dreaded spending the evening alone. And yet, there was no one she wanted to spend it with but him. He'd infuriate her before it was over, she was certain. She was looking forward to it.

He cut back the motor so that it was a grumble instead of a roar, then guided the boat alongside the pier. When the engine shut off completely, silence snapped back—water lapping and wind in high grass.

"When are you going to take me for a ride?" Gennie demanded when he tossed her a line.

Grant stepped lightly onto the pier and watched as she deftly secured the boat. "Was I going to?"

"Maybe you weren't, but you are now." Straightening, she brushed her hands on the back of her jeans. "I was thinking about renting a little rowboat for the inlet, but I'd much rather go out to sea."

"A rowboat?" He grinned, trying to imagine her manning oars.

"I grew up on a river," she reminded him. "Sailing's in my blood."

"Is that so?" Idly, Grant took her hand, turning it over to examine the palm. It was smooth and soft and strong. "This doesn't look as if it's hoisted too many mainsails."

"I've done my share." For no reason other than she wanted to, Gennie locked her fingers with his. "There've always been seamen in my family. My great-great-grandfather was a…freelancer."

"A pirate." Intrigued, Grant caught the tip of her hair in his hand then twirled a lock around his finger. "I get the feeling you think more of that than the counts and dukes scattered through your family tree."

"Naturally. Almost anyone can find an aristocrat somewhere if they look hard enough. And he was a very good pirate."

"Good-hearted?"

"Successful," she corrected with a wicked smile. "He was almost sixty when he retired in New Orleans. My grandmother lives in the house he built there."

"With money plucked from hapless merchants," Grant finished, grinning again.

"The sea's a lawless place," Gennie said with a shrug. "You take your chances. You might get what you want—" now she grinned as well "—or you could get your head lopped off."

"It might be smarter to keep you land-locked," Grant murmured, then tugging on the hair he held, brought her closer.

Gennie put a hand to his chest for balance, but found her fingers straying up. His mouth was tempting, very tempting as it lowered toward hers. It would be smarter to resist, she knew, but she rose on her toes to meet it with her own.

With barely any pressure, he kept his lips on hers, as if unsure of his moves, unsure just how deeply he dared plunge this time. He could have swept her against him; she could have drawn him closer with no more than a sigh. Yet both of them kept that slight, tangible distance between them, as a barrier—or a safety hatch. It was still early enough for them to fight the current that was drawing them closer and closer to the point of no return.

They moved apart at the same moment and took a small, perceptible step back.

"I'd better light the charcoal," Gennie said after a moment.

"I didn't ask before," Grant began as they started down the pier. "But do you know how to cook one of those things?"

"My dear Mr. Campbell," Gennie said in a fluid drawl, "you appear to have several misconceptions about southern women. I can cook on a hot rock."

"And wash shirts in a fast stream."

"Every bit as well as you could," Gennie tossed back. "You might have some advantage on me in mechanical areas, but I'd say we're about even otherwise."

"A strike for the woman's movement?"

Gennie narrowed her eyes. "Are you about to say something snide and unintelligent?"

"No." Picking up the can of starter fluid, he handed it to her. "As a sex, you've had a legitimate gripe for several hundred years which has been handled one way as a group and another individually. Unfortunately there's still a number of doors that have to be battered down by women as a whole while the individual woman occasionally unlocks one with hardly a sound. Ever hear of Winnie Winkle?"

Fascinated despite herself, Gennie simply stared at him. "As in Wee Willie?"

Grant laughed and leaned against the side of the barbecue. "No. *Winnie Winkle, the Breadwinner,* a cartoon strip from the twenties. It touched on women's liberation several decades before it became a household word. Got a match?"

"Hmmm." Gennie dug in her pocket. "Wasn't that a bit before your time?"

"I did some research on—social commentary in college."

"Really?" Again, she sensed a grain of truth that only hinted at the whole. Gennie lit the soaked charcoal, then stepped back as the fire caught and flames rose. "Where did you go?"

Grant caught the first whiff, a summer smell he associated with his childhood. "Georgetown."

"They've an excellent art department there," Gennie said thoughtfully.

"Yeah."

"You did study art there?" Gennie persisted.

Grant watched the smoke rise and the haze of heat that rippled the air. "Why?"

"Because it's obvious from that wicked little caricature you drew of me that you have talent, and that you've had training. What are you doing with it?"

"With what?"

Gennie drew her brows together in frustration. "The talent and the training. I'd have heard of you if you were painting."

"I'm not," he said simply.

"Then what are you doing?"

"What I want. Weren't you going to make a salad?"

"Damn it, Grant—"

"All right, don't get testy. I'll make it."

As he started toward the back door, Gennie swore again and grabbed his arm. "I don't understand you."

He lifted a brow. "I didn't ask you to." He saw the frustration again, but more, he saw hurt, quickly concealed. Why should he suddenly feel the urge to apologize for his need for privacy? "Gennie, let me tell you something." In an uncharacteristic gesture, he stroked his knuckles gently over her cheek. "I wouldn't be here right now if I could stay away from you. Is that enough for you?"

She wanted to say yes—and no. If she hadn't been afraid of what the words might trigger, she would have told him she was already over her head and sinking fast. Love, or perhaps the first stirrings of love that she had felt only a short time before, was growing swiftly. Instead, she smiled and slipped her hands into his.

"I'll make the salad."

It was as simple as she'd told herself it could be. In the kitchen they tossed together the dewy fresh greens and argued over the science of salad making. Meat smoked and sizzled on the grill while they sat on the grass and enjoyed the last light of the afternoon of one of the last days of summer.

Lazy smells...wet weeds, cook smoke. A few words, an easy silence. Gennie bound them up and held them close, knowing they'd be important to her on some rainy day when she was crowded by pressures and responsibilities. For now, she felt as she had when she'd been a girl and August had a few precious days left and school was light-years away. Summer always seemed to have more magic near its end.

Enough magic, Gennie mused, to make her fall in love where there was no rhyme or reason.

"What're you thinking?" Grant asked her.

She smiled and stretched her head back to the sky one last time. "That I'd better tend to that steak."

He grabbed her arm, toppling her onto her back before she could rise. "Uh-uh."

"You like it burnt?"

"Uh-uh, that's not what you were thinking," he corrected. He traced a finger over her lips, and though the gesture was absent, Gennie felt the touch in every pore.

"I was thinking about summer," she said softly. "And that it always seems to end before you're finished with it."

When she lifted her hand to his cheek, he took her wrist and held it there. "The best things always do."

As he stared down at her she smiled in that slow, easy way she had that sent ripples of need, flurries of emotion through him. All thought fled as he lowered his mouth to hers. Soft, warm, ripe, her lips answered his, then drew and drew until everything he was, felt, wished for, was focused there. Bewitched, beguiled, bedazed, he went deeper, no longer sure what path he was on, only that she was with him.

He could smell the grass beneath them, sweet and dry; a scent of summer like the smoke that curled above their heads. He wanted to touch her, every inch of that slimly rounded body that had tormented his dreams since the first moment he'd seen her. If he did once, Grant knew his dreams would never be peaceful again. If her taste alone—wild fruit, warm honey—could so easily take over his mind, what would the feel of her do to him?

His need for her was like summer—or so he told himself. It had to end before he was finished.

Lifting his head he looked down to see her eyes, faintly slanted, barely open. Without guards, she'd bring him to his knees with a look. Cautiously, he drew away then pulled her to her feet.

"We'd better get that steak off before we have to make do with salad."

Her knees were weak. Gennie would have sworn such things happened only in fiction, yet here she was throbbingly alive with joints that felt like water. Turning, she stabbed the steak with a kitchen fork to lift it to the platter.

"The fat's in the fire," she murmured.

"I was thinking the same thing myself," Grant said quietly before they walked back into the house.

By unspoken agreement, they kept the conversation light as they ate. Whatever each had felt during that short, enervating kiss was carefully stored away.

*I'm not looking for a relationship,* their minds rationalized separately.

*We're not suited to each other in the first place.... There isn't time for this.*

*Good God, I'm* not *falling in love.*

Shaken, Gennie lifted her wine and drank deeply while Grant scowled down at his plate.

"How's your steak?" she asked him for lack of anything else.

"What? Oh, it's good." Pushing away the uncomfortable feeling, Grant began to eat with more enthusiasm. "You cook almost as well as you paint," he decided. "Where'd you learn?"

Gennie lifted a brow. "Why, at my mammy's knee."

He grinned at the exaggerated drawl. "You've got a smart mouth, Genvièe." Lifting the bottle, he poured more wine into the sturdy water glasses she'd bought in town. "I was thinking it odd that a woman who grew up with a house full of servants could grill a steak." He grinned, thinking of Shelby, who'd considered cooking a last resort.

"In the first place," she told him, "cookouts were always considered a family affair. And in the second, when you live alone you learn, or you live in restaurants."

He couldn't resist poking at her a bit as he sat back with his wine. "You've been photographed in or around every restaurant in the free world."

Not to be baited, Gennie mirrored his pose, watching him over the rim as she drank. "Is that why you get a dozen newspapers? So you can read how people live while you hibernate?"

Grant thought about it a moment. "Yeah." He didn't suppose he could have put it better himself.

"Don't you consider that an arrogant sort of attitude?"

Again he pondered on it, studying the dark red wine in his water glass. "Yeah."

Gennie laughed despite herself. "Grant, why don't you like people?"

Surprised, he looked back at her. "I do, individually in some cases, and as a whole. I just don't want them crowding me."

He meant it, she realized as she rose to stack the plates. There was just no understanding him. "Don't you ever have the need to rub elbows? Listen to a babble of voices?"

He'd had his share of elbows and voices before he'd been seventeen, Grant thought ruefully. But… No, he supposed it wasn't quite true. There were times he needed a heavy dose of humanity with all its flaws and complications; for his work and for himself. He thought of his week with the MacGregors. He'd needed that, and them, though he hadn't fully realized it until he'd settled back into his own routine.

"I have my moments," he murmured. He automatically began to clear the table as Gennie ran hot water in the sink. "No dessert?"

She looked over her shoulder to see that he was perfectly serious. He packed away food like a truck driver, yet there wasn't an ounce of spare flesh on him. Nervous energy? Metabolism? With a shake of her head, Gennie wondered why she persisted in trying to understand him. "I have a couple of fudge bars in the freezer."

Grant grinned and took her at her word. "Want one?" he asked as he ripped the thin white paper from the ice cream stick.

"No. Are you eating that because you want it or because it gets you out of drying these?" She stacked a plate into the drainer.

"Works both ways."

Leaning on the counter, he nibbled on the bar. "I could eat a carton of these when I was a kid."

Gennie rinsed another plate. "And now?"

Grant took a generous bite. "You only have two."

"A polite man would share."

"Yeah." He took another bite.

With a laugh, Gennie flicked some water into his face. "Come on, be a sport."

He held out the bar, pausing a half inch in front of her lips. Up to her elbows in soapy water, Gennie opened her mouth. Grant drew the bar away, just out of reach. "Don't get greedy," he warned.

Sending him an offended look, Gennie leaned forward enough to nibble delicately on the chocolate, then still watching him took a bite large enough to chill her mouth.

"Nasty," Grant decided, frowning at what was left of his fudge bar as Gennie laughed.

"You can have the other one," she said kindly after she'd swallowed and then dried her hands. "I just don't have any willpower when someone puts chocolate under my nose."

Deliberately, Grant ran his tongue over the bar. "Any other… weaknesses?"

As the heat expanded in her stomach, she wandered toward the porch door. "A few." She sighed as the call of swallows announced dusk. "The days are getting shorter," she murmured.

Already the lowering sun had the white clouds edged with pink and gold. The smoke from the grill struggled skyward, thinning. Near the bank of the inlet was a scrawny bush, its sparse leaves hinting of autumn red.

When Grant's hands came to her shoulders, she leaned back toward him instinctively. Together, in silence, they watched the approach of evening.

He couldn't remember the last time he'd shared a sunset with anyone, when he'd felt the desire to. Now it seemed so simple, so frighteningly simple. Would he think of her now whenever he watched the approach of evening?

"Tell me about your favorite summer," he asked abruptly.

She remembered a summer spent in the south of France and another on her father's yacht in the Aegean. Smiling, she watched the clouds deepen to rose. "I stayed with my grandmother for two weeks once while my parents had a second honeymoon in Venice. Long, lazy days with bees humming around honeysuckle blossoms. There was a big old oak outside my bedroom window just dripping with moss. Some nights I'd climb out the window to sit on a branch and look at the stars. I must have been twelve," she remembered. "There was a boy down at the stables." She laughed suddenly with her back comfortably nestled against Grant's chest. "Oh, Lord, he was a bit like Will, all sharp, awkward edges."

"You were crazy about him."

"I'd spend hours mucking out stalls and grooming horses just to get a glimpse of him. I wrote pages and pages about him in my diary and one very mushy poem."

"And kept it under your pillow."

"Apparently you've had a nodding acquaintance with twelve-year-old girls."

He thought of Shelby and grinned, resting his chin on the top of her head. Her hair smelled as though she'd washed it with rain-drenched wildflowers. "How long did it take you to get him to kiss you?"

She laughed. "Ten days. I thought I'd discovered the answer to the mysteries of the universe. I was a woman."

"No female's more sure of that than a twelve-year-old."

She smiled into the dimming sky. "More than a nodding acquaintance it appears," she commented. "One afternoon I found Angela giggling over my diary and chased her all over the house. She was..." Gennie stiffened as the grief washed over her, wave after tumultuous wave. Before Grant could tighten his hold, she had moved away from him to stare through the patched screen into twilight. "She was ten," Gennie continued in a whisper. "I threatened to shave her head if she breathed a word about what was in that diary."

"Gennie."

She shook her head as she felt his hand brush through her hair. "It'll be dark soon. You can already hear the crickets. You should start back."

He couldn't bear to hear the tears in her voice. It would be easier to leave her now, just back away. He told himself he had no skill when it came to comforting. His hands massaged gently on her shoulders. "There's a light on the boat. Let's sit down." Ignoring her resistance, Grant drew her to the porch glider. "My grandmother had one of these," he said conversationally as he slipped an arm around her and set it into creaking motion. "She had a little place on Maryland's Eastern Shore. A quiet little spot with land so flat it looked like it'd been laid out with a ruler. Ever been to the Chesapeake?"

"No." Deliberately, Gennie relaxed and closed her eyes. The motion was easy, his voice curiously soothing. She hadn't known he could speak in such quiet, gentle tones.

"Soft-shell crabs and fields of tobacco." Already he could feel the tautness in her shoulders easing. "We had to take a ferry to get to her house. It wasn't much different than this cottage except it was two stories. My father and I could go across the street and fish. I caught a trout once using a piece of Longhorn cheese as bait."

Grant continued to talk, ramble really, recounting things he'd forgotten, things he'd never spoken of aloud before. Unimportant things that droned quietly on the air while the light softened. For the moment it seemed to be the right thing, the thing she needed. He wasn't certain he had anything else to give.

He kept the motion of the glider going while her head rested against his shoulder and wondered how he'd never noticed just how peaceful dusk could be when you shared it with someone.

Gennie sighed, listening more to his tone than his words. She let herself drift as the chirp of crickets grew more insistent.... Dreams are often no more than memories.

"Oh, Gennie, you should have been there!" Angela, golden and vibrant, turned in her seat to laugh while Gennie maneuvered through the traffic of downtown New Orleans. The streets were damp with a chilly February rain, but nothing could dampen Angela. She was sunlight and spring flowers.

"I'd rather have been there than freezing in New York," Gennie returned.

"You can't freeze when you're basking in the limelight," Angela countered, twisting a bit closer to her sister.

"Wanna bet?"

"You wouldn't have missed that showing for a dozen parties."

No, she wouldn't have, Gennie thought with a smile. But Angela... "Tell me about it."

"It was so much fun! All that noise and music. It was so crowded, you couldn't take a step without bumping into someone. The next time Cousin Frank throws a bash on his houseboat you have to come."

Gennie sent Angela a quick grin. "It doesn't sound like I was missed."

Angela laughed, the quick bubble that was irresistible. "Well, I got a little tired of answering questions about my talented sister."

Gennie gave a snort as she stopped at a light. She could see the hazy red glow as the windshield wipers moved briskly back and forth. "They just use that as a line to get to you."

"Well, there was someone..." When Angela trailed off, Gennie turned to look at her. So beautiful, she thought. Gold and cream with eyes almost painfully alive and vivid.

"Someone?"

"Oh, Gennie." Excitement brought a soft pink to her cheeks."He's gorgeous. I could hardly make a coherent sentence when he started to talk to me."

"You?"

"Me," Angela agreed, laughing again. "It felt like someone had drained off half my brain. And now... Well, I've been seeing him all week. I think—ta-da—this is it."

"After a week?" Gennie countered.

"After five seconds. Oh, Gennie, don't be practical. I'm in love. You have to meet him."

Gennie shifted into first as she waited for the light to change. "Do I get to size him up?"

Angela shook back her rich gold hair and laughed as the light turned green. "Oh, I feel wonderful, Gennie. Absolutely wonderful!"

The laugh was the last thing Gennie heard before the squeal of brakes. She saw the car skidding toward them through the intersection. In the dream it was always so slow, second by terrifying second, closer and closer. Water spewed out from the tires and seemed to hang in the air.

There wasn't time to breathe, there wasn't time to react or prevent before there was the sound of metal striking metal, the explosion of blinding lights. Terror. Pain. And darkness.

"*No!*" She jerked upright, rigid with fear and shock. There were arms around her, holding her close…safe. Crickets? Where had they come from? The light, the car. Angela.

Gasping for breath, Gennie stared out at the darkened inlet while Grant's voice murmured something comforting in her ear.

"I'm sorry." Pushing away, she rose, lifting nervous hands to her hair. "I must have dozed off. Poor company," she continued in a jerky voice. "You should have given me a jab, and—"

"Gennie." He stood, grabbing her arm. "Stop it."

She crumbled. He hadn't expected such complete submission and had no defense against it. "Don't," he murmured, stroking her hair as she clung to him. "Gennie, don't cry. It's all right now."

"Oh, God, it hasn't happened in weeks." She buried her face against his chest as the grief washed over her as fresh as the first hour. "At first, right after the accident, I'd go through it every time I closed my eyes."

"Come on." He kissed the top of her head. "Sit down."

"No, I can't—I need to walk." She held him tight another moment, as if gathering her strength. "Can we walk?"

"Sure." Bringing her to his side, Grant opened the screen door. For a time he was silent, his arm around her shoulders as they skirted the inlet and walked aimlessly. But he knew he needed to hear as much as she needed to tell. "Gennie, talk to me."

"I was remembering the accident," she said slowly, but her voice was calmer now. "Sometimes when I'd dream of it, I'd be quick enough, swerve out of the way of that car and everything was so different. Then I'd wake up and nothing was different at all."

"It's a natural reaction," he told her, though the thought of her being plagued by nightmares began to gnaw at his gut. He'd lived through a few of his own. "They'll fade after a while."

"I know. It hardly ever happens anymore." She let out a long breath and seemed steadier for it. "When it does, it's so clear. I can see the rain splattering on the windshield right before the wipers whisk it away. There're puddles near the curbs, and Angela's voice is so—vital. She was so beautiful, Grant, not just her face, but her. She never outgrew sweetness. She was telling me about a party she'd been to where she'd met someone. She was in love, bubbling over with it. The last thing she said was that she felt wonderful, absolutely wonderful. Then I killed her."

Grant took her shoulders, shaking her hard. "What the hell kind of craziness is that?"

"It was my fault," Gennie returned with deadly calm. "If I'd seen that car, if I'd seen it just seconds earlier. Or if I'd *done* something, hit the brakes, the gas, anything. The impact was all on her side. I had a mild concussion, a few bruises, and she…"

"Would you feel better if you'd been seriously injured?" he demanded roughly. "You can mourn for her, cry for her, but you can't take the blame."

"I was driving, Grant. How do I forget that?"

"You don't forget it," he snapped back, unnerved by the dull pain in her voice. "But you put it in perspective. There was nothing you could have done, you know that."

"You don't understand." She swallowed because the tears were coming and she'd thought she was through with them. "I loved her so much. She was part of me—a part of me I needed very badly. When you lose someone who was vital to your life, it takes a chunk out of you."

He did understand—the pain, the need to place blame. Gennie blamed herself for exposing her sister to death. Grant blamed his father for exposing himself. Neither way changed the loss. "Then you have to live without that chunk."

"You can't know what it's like," she began.

"My father was killed when I was seventeen," he said, saying the words he would rather have avoided. "I needed him."

Gennie let her head fall against his chest. She didn't offer sympathy, knowing he wanted none. "What did you do?"

"Hated—for a long time. That was easy." Without realizing it, he was holding her against him again, gaining comfort as well as giving it. "Accepting's tougher. Everyone does it in different ways."

"How did you?"

"By realizing there was nothing I could have done to stop it." Drawing her away a little, he lifted her chin with his hand. "Just as there was nothing you could have done."

"It's easier, isn't it, to tell yourself you could have done something than to admit you were helpless?"

He'd never thought about it—perhaps refused to think about it. "Yeah."

"Thank you. I know you didn't want to tell me that even more than I didn't want to tell you. We can get very selfish with our grief—and our guilt."

He brushed the hair away from her temples. He kissed her cheeks where tears were still drying and felt a surge of tenderness that left him shaken. Defenseless, she made him vulnerable. If he kissed her now, really kissed her, she'd have complete power over him. With more effort than he'd realized it would take, Grant drew away from her.

"I have to get back," he said, deliberately putting his hands in his pockets. "Will you be all right?"

"Yes, but—I'd like you to stay." The words were out before she realized she'd thought them. But she wouldn't take them back. Something flared in his eyes. Even in the dim light she saw it. Desire, need, and something quickly banked and shuttered.

"Not tonight."

The tone had her brows drawing together in puzzlement. "Grant," she began, and reached for him.

"Not tonight," he repeated, stopping the motion of her outstretched hand.

Gennie put it behind her back as if he'd slapped it. "All right." Her pride surged forward to cover the hurt of fresh rejection. "I appreciated the company." Turning, she started back to the house.

Grant watched her go, then swore, taking a step after her. "Gennie."

"Good night, Grant." The screen door swung shut behind her.

# *Chapter 7*

She was going to lose it. Gennie cast a furious look at the clouds whipping in from the north, and swore. Damn, she was going to lose the light and she wasn't ready. The energy was pouring through her, flowing from her mind and heart to her hand in one of the rare moments an artist recognizes as *right*. Everything, everything told her that something lasting, something important would spring onto the canvas that morning; she had only to let herself go with it. But to go with it now, she had to race against the storm.

Gennie knew she had perhaps thirty minutes before the clouds would spoil her light, an hour before the rain closed out everything. Already a distant thunder rumbled over the sound of crashing waves. She cast a defiant look at the sky. By God, she would beat it yet!

The impetus was with her, an urgency that said today—it's going to happen today. Whatever she'd done before—the sketches, the preliminary work, the spread of paint on canvas—was just a preparation for what she would create today.

Excitement rippled across her skin with the wind. And a frustration. She seemed to need them both to draw from. Maybe a storm was brewing in her as well. It had seemed so since the night before when her mood had fluctuated and twisted, with Grant, without him. The last rejection had left her numb, ominously calm. Now her emotions were raging free again—fury, passion, pride, and torment. Gennie could pour them into her art, liberating them so that they wouldn't fester inside her.

Need him? No, she needed neither him nor anyone, she told herself as she streaked her brush over the canvas. Her work was enough to fill her life, cleanse her wounds. It was always fresh, always constant. As long as her eyes could see and her fingers could lift pencil or brush, it would be with her.

It had been her friend during her childhood, a solace during the pangs of adolescence. It was as demanding as a lover, and as greedy for her passion. And it was passion she felt now, a vibrant, physical passion that drove her forward. The moment was ripe, and the electricity in the air only added to the sense of urgency that shimmered inside her.

Now! it shouted at her. The time for merging, soul and heart and mind was now. If not now, it would be never. The clouds raced closer. She vowed to beat them.

Skin cool with anticipation, blood hot, Grant came outside. Like a wolf, he'd scented something in the air and had come in search of it. He'd been too restless to work, to tense too relax. Something had been driving at him all morning, urging him to move, to look, to find.

He'd told himself it was the approach of the storm, the lack of sleep. But he'd known, without understanding, that each of those things was only a part of the whole. Something was brewing, brewing in more than that cauldron of a sky.

He was hungry without wanting to eat, dissatisfied without knowing what he would change. Restless, reckless, he'd fretted against the confines of his studio, all walls and glass. Instinct had led him out to seek the wind and the sea. And Gennie.

He'd known she'd be there, though he'd been convinced that he'd closed his mind to even the thought of her. But now, seeing her, he was struck, just as surely as the north sky was struck with the first silver thread of lightning.

He'd never seen her like this, but he'd known. She stood with her head thrown back in abandon to her work, her eyes glowing green with power. There was a wildness about her only partially due to the wind that swept up her hair and billowed the thin smock she wore. There was strength in the hand that guided the brush so fluidly and yet with such purpose. She might have been a queen overlooking her dominion. She might have been a woman waiting for a lover. As his blood quickened with need, Grant thought she was both.

Where was the woman who'd wept in his arms only hours before? Where was the fragility, the defenselessness that had terrified him? He'd given her what comfort he could, though he knew little of soothing tearful women. He'd spoken of things he hadn't said aloud in fifteen years—because she'd needed to hear them and he, for some indefinable reason, had needed to say them. And he'd left her because he'd felt himself being sucked into something unknown, and inevitable.

Now, she looked invulnerable, magnificent. This was a woman no man would ever resist, a woman who could choose and discard lovers with a single gesture. It wasn't fear he felt now, but challenge, and with the challenge a desire so huge it threatened to swallow him.

She stopped painting on a roll of thunder then looked up to the sky in a kind of exaltation. He heard her laugh, once, with an arousing defiance that had him struggling with a fresh slap of desire.

Who in God's name was she? he demanded. And why, in heaven and hell, couldn't he stay away?

The excitement that had driven her to finish the painting lingered. It was done, Gennie thought with a breathless triumph. And yet…there was something more. Her passion hadn't been diffused by the consummation of woman and art, but spun in her still; restless, waiting.

Then she saw him, with the sea and the storm at his back. The wind blew wilder. Her blood pounded with it. For a long moment they only stared at each other while thunder and lightning inched closer.

Ignoring him, and the flash of heat that demanded she close the distance between them, Gennie turned back to the canvas. This and only this was what called to her, she told herself. This and only this was what she needed.

Grant watched her pack her paints and brushes. There was something both regal and defiant about the way she had turned her back on him and gone about her business. Yet there was no denying that jolt of recognition he had felt when their gazes had locked. Under his feet the ground shook with the next roll of thunder. He went to her.

The light shifted, dimming as clouds rolled over the sun. The air was so charged, sparks could be felt along the skin. Gennie packed up her gear with deft, steady hands. She'd beaten the storm that morning. She could beat anything.

"Genviève." She wasn't Gennie now. He'd seen Gennie in the churchyard, laughing with young, fresh delight. It had been Gennie who had clung to him, weeping. This woman's laugh would be low and seductive, and she would shed no tears at all. Whichever, whoever she was, Grant was drawn to her, irrevocably.

"Grant." Gennie closed the lid on her paint case before she turned. "You're out early."

"You've finished."

"Yes." The wind blew his hair wildly around his face, and while the face was set, his eyes were dark and restless. Gennie knew her own emotions matched his like two halves of the same coin. "I've finished."

"You'll go now." He could see the flush of triumph on her face and the moody, unpredictable green of her eyes.

"From here?" She tossed her head as her gaze shifted to the sea. The waves were swelling higher, and no boat dared test them now. "Yes. I have other things I want to paint."

It was what he wanted. Hadn't he wanted to be rid of her from the very first? But Grant said nothing as the grumbling thunder rolled closer.

"You'll have your solitude back." Gennie's smile was light and mocking. "That's what's most important to you, isn't it? And I've gotten what I needed here."

His eyes narrowed, but he wasn't certain of the origin of his temper. "Have you?"

"Have a look," she invited with a gesture of her hand.

He hadn't wanted to see the painting, had deliberately avoided even a glance at it. Now her eyes dared him and the flick of her wrist was too insolent to deny. Hooking his thumbs in his pockets, Grant turned toward the canvas.

She saw too much of what he needed there, what he felt. The power of limitless sea, the glory of space and unending challenge. She'd scorned muted colors and had chosen bold. She'd forsaken delicacy for muscle. What had been a blank canvas was now as full of force as the turbulent Atlantic, and as full of secrets. The secrets there were nature's, as the strength and solidity of the lighthouse were man's. She'd captured both, pitting them against each other even while showing their timeless harmony.

The painting moved him, disturbed him, pulled at him, as much as its creator.

Gennie felt the tension build up at the base of her neck as Grant only frowned at the painting. She knew it was everything she'd wanted it to be, felt it was perhaps the best work she'd ever done. But it was his—his world, his force, his secrets that had dominated the emotions she'd felt when she'd painted it. Even as she'd finished, the painting had stopped being hers and had become his.

Grant took a step away from the painting and looked out to sea. The lightning was closer; he saw it shimmer dangerously behind the dark, angry clouds. He seemed to have lost the words, the phrases that had always come so easily to him. He couldn't think of anything but her, and the need that had risen up to work knots in his stomach. "It's fine," he said flatly.

He could have struck her and hurt her no less. Her small gasp was covered by the moan of the wind. For a moment Gennie stared at his back while pain rocketed through her. Rejection...would she never stop setting herself up for his rejection?

Pain altered to anger in the space of seconds. She didn't need his approval, his pleasure, his understanding. She had everything she needed within herself. In raging silence she slipped the canvas into its carrying case, then folded her easel. Gathering her things together, she turned toward him slowly.

"Before I go, I'd like to tell you something." Her voice was cool over flowing vowels. "It isn't often one finds one's first impression was so killingly accurate. The first night I met you, I thought you were a rude, arrogant man with no redeeming qualities." The wind blew her hair across her eyes and with a toss of her head she sent it flying back so that she could keep her icy gaze on his. "It's very gratifying to learn just how right I was...and to be able to dislike you so intensely." Chin high, Gennie turned and walked to her car.

She jerked up the trunk of her car and put her equipment and canvas in, perversely glad to flow with the fury that consumed her. When Grant's hand closed over her arm, she slammed the trunk closed and whirled around, ready to battle on any terms, any grounds. Blind with her own emotions, she didn't notice the heat in his eyes or the raggedness of his breathing.

"Do you think I'm just going to let you walk away?" he demanded. "Do you think you can walk into my life and take and not leave anything behind?"

Her chest was heaving, her eyes brilliant. With calculated disdain, she looked down at the fingers that circled her arm. "Take your hand off me," she told him, spacing her words with insolent precision.

Lightning shot across the sky as they stared at each other, cold white heat against boiling gray and angry purple. The deafening roar of thunder drowned out Grant's oath. The moment stood poised, crackling, then swirled like the wind that screamed in triumph.

"You should have taken my advice," he said between his teeth, "and stuck with your counts and barons." Then he was pulling her across the tough grass, against the wind.

"What the hell do you think you're doing?"

"What I should have done the minute you barged into my life."

Murder? Gennie stared at the cliffs and the raging sea below. God knew he looked ready for it at that moment—and perhaps he would have liked her to believe he was capable of tossing her over the edge. But she knew what the violence in him meant, where it would lead them both. She fought him wildly as he pulled her toward the lighthouse.

"You must be mad! Let me go!"

"I must be," he agreed tightly. Lightning forked again, opening the sky. Rain spewed out.

"I said take your hands off me!"

He whirled to her then, his face sculptured and shadowed in the crazed light of the storm. "It's too late for that!" he shouted at her. "Damn it, you know it as well as I do. It was too late from the first minute." Rain poured over them, pounding and warm.

"I won't be dragged into your bed, do you hear me!" She grabbed his soaking shirt with her free hand while her body vibrated with fury and with wanting. "I won't be dragged anywhere. Do you think you can just suddenly decide you need a lover and haul me off?"

His breath was raging in and out of his lungs. The rain pouring down his face only accented the passionate darkness of his eyes. She was sleek and wet. A siren? Maybe she was, but he'd already wrecked on the reef. "Not any lover." He swung her against him so that their wet clothes fused then seemed to melt away. "You. Damn it, Gennie, you know it's you."

Their faces were close, their eyes locked. Each had forgotten the storm around them as the tempest within took over. Heart pounded against heart. Need pounded against need. Full of fear and triumph, she threw her head back.

"Show me."

Grant crushed her closer so that not even the wind could have forced its way between. "Here," he said roughly. "By God, here and now."

His mouth took hers madly, and she answered. Unleashed, the passion drove them far past sanity, beyond the civilized and into the dark tunnel of chaotic desire. His lips sped across her face, seeking to devour all that could be consumed and more. When his teeth scraped over the cord of her neck, Gennie moaned and drew him with her to the ground.

Raw, keening wind, hard, driving rain, the pound and crash of the stormy sea. They were nothing in the face of this tempest. Grant forgot them as he pressed against her, feeling every line and curve as though he'd already torn the clothes from her. Her heart pounded. It seemed as if it had worked its way inside his chest to merge with his.

Her body felt like a furnace. He hadn't known there could be such heat from a living thing. But alive she was, moving under him, hands seeking, mouth greedy. The rain sluicing over them should have cooled the fire, yet it stoked it higher so that the water might have sizzled on contact.

He knew only greed, only ageless need and primitive urges. She'd bewitched him from the first instant, and now, at last, he succumbed. Her hands were in his hair, bringing his mouth back to hers again and again so that her lips could leave him breathless, arouse more hunger.

They rolled on the wet grass until she was on top of him, her mouth ravaging his with a strength and power only he could match. In a frenzy, she dragged at his shirt, yanking and tugging until it was over his head and discarded. With a long, low moan she ran her hands over him. Grant's reason shattered.

Roughly, he pushed her on her back, cutting off her breath as lightning burst overhead. Ignoring buttons, he pulled the blouse from her, desperate to touch what he had denied himself for days. His hands slid over her wet skin, kneading, possessing, hurrying in his greed for more. And when she arched against him, agile and demanding, he buried his mouth at her breast and lost himself.

He tasted the rain on her, laced with summer thunder and her own night scent. Like a drowning man he clung to her as he sank beneath the depths. He knew what it was to want a woman, but not like this. Desire could be controlled, channeled, guided. So what was it that pounded in him? His fingers bruised her, but he was unaware in his desperation to take all and take it quickly.

When he dragged the jeans down her hips, he felt both arousal and frustration as they clung to her skin and those smooth, narrow curves. Struggling with the wet denim, he followed its inching progress with his mouth, thrilling as Gennie arched and moaned. His teeth scraped over her hip, down her thigh to the inside of her knee as he pulled the jeans down her, then left them in a heap.

Mindlessly, he plunged his tongue into her and heard her cry out with the wind. Heat suffused him. Rain fell on his back unfelt, ran from his hair onto her skin but did nothing to wash away the passion that drove them both closer and closer to the peak.

Then they were both fighting with his jeans, hands tangling together while their lips fused again. The sounds coming low from her throat might have been his name or some new spell she was weaving over him. He no longer cared.

Lightning illuminated her face once, brilliantly—the slash of cheekbone, the eyes slanted and nearly closed, the soft full lips parted and trembling with her breathing. At that moment she was witch, and he, willingly bewitched.

With his mouth against the hammering pulse in her throat, he plunged into her, taking her with a violent kind of worship he didn't understand. When she stiffened and cried out, Grant struggled to find both his sanity and the reason. Then she was wrapped around him drawing him into the satin-coated darkness.

Breathless, dazed, empty, Grant lay with his face buried in Gennie's hair. The rain still fell, but until that moment he didn't realize that it had lost its force. The storm was passed, consumed by itself like all things of passion. He felt the hammer-trip beat of her heart beneath him, and her trembles. Shutting his eyes, he tried to gather his strength and the control that meant lucidity.

"Oh, God." His voice was rough and raw. The apology wouldn't come; he thought it less than useless. "Why didn't you tell me?" he murmured as he rolled from her to lie on his back against the wet grass. "Damn it, Gennie, why didn't you tell me?"

She kept her eyes closed so that the rain fell on her lids, over her face and throbbing body. Was this how it was supposed to be? she wondered. Should she feel so spent, so enervated while her skin hummed everywhere, everywhere his hand had touched it? Should she feel as though every lock she had, had been broken? By whom, him or her, it didn't matter. But her privacy was gone, and the need for it. Yet now, hearing the harsh question—accusation?—she felt a ripple of pain sharper than the loss of innocence. She said nothing.

"Gennie, you let me think you were—"

"What?" she demanded, opening her eyes. The clouds were still dark, she saw, but the lightning was gone.

Cursing himself, Grant dragged a hand through his hair. "Gennie, you should have told me you hadn't been with a man before." And how was it possible, he wondered, that she'd let no man touch her before? That he was the first…the only.

"Why?" she said flatly, wishing he would go, wishing she had the strength to leave. "It was my business."

Swearing, he shifted, leaning over her. His eyes were dark and angry, but when she tried to pull away, he pinned her. "I don't have much gentleness," he told her, and the words were unsteady with feeling. "But I would have used all I had, I would have tried to find more, for you." When she only stared at him, Grant lowered his forehead to hers. "Gennie…"

Her doubts, her fears, melted at that one softly murmured word. "I wasn't looking for gentleness then," she whispered. Framing his face with her hands, she lifted it. "But now…" She smiled, and watched the frown fade from his eyes.

He dropped a kiss on her lips, soft, more like a whisper, then rising, lifted her into his arms. Gennie laughed at the feeling of weightlessness and ease. "What're you doing now?"

"Taking you inside so you can warm up, dry off and make love with me again—maybe not in that order."

Gennie curled her arms around his neck. "I'm beginning to like your ideas. What about our clothes?"

"We can salvage what's left of them later." He pushed open the door of the lighthouse. "We won't be needing them for quite a while."

"Definitely liking your ideas." She pressed her mouth against his throat. "Are you really going to carry me up those stairs?"

"Yeah."

Gennie cast a look at the winding staircase and tightened her hold. "I'd just like to mention it wouldn't be terribly romantic if you were to trip and drop me."

"The woman casts aspersions on my machismo."

"On your balance," she corrected as he started up. She shivered as her wet skin began to chill, then abruptly laughed. "Grant, did it occur to you what those assorted piles of clothes would look like if someone happened by?"

"They'd probably look a great deal like what they are," he considered. "And it should discourage anyone from trespassing. I should have thought of it before—much better than a killer-dog sign."

She sighed, partially from relief as they reached the landing. "You're hopeless. Anyone would think you were Clark Kent."

Grant stopped in the doorway to the bathroom to stare at her. "Come again?"

"You know, concealing a secret identity. Though you're anything but mild-mannered," she added as she toyed with a damp curl that hung over his ear. "You've set up this lighthouse as some kind of Fortress of Solitude."

The long intense look continued. "What was Clark Kent's Earth mother's name?"

"Is this a quiz?"

"Do you know?"

She arched a brow because his eyes were so suddenly serious. "Martha."

"I'll be damned," he murmured. He laughed, then gave her a quick kiss that was puzzlingly friendly considering they were naked and pressed together. "You continue to surprise me, Genviève. I think I'm crazy about you."

The light words went straight to her heart and turned it over. "Because I know Superman's adoptive mother's first name?"

Grant nuzzled his cheek against her, the first wholly sweet gesture she'd ever seen in him. In that one instant she was lost, as she'd never been lost before. "For one thing." Feeling her tremble, Grant drew her closer. "Come on, into the shower; you're freezing."

He stepped into the tub before he set her down, then still holding her close, pressed his mouth to hers in a long, lingering kiss. With the storm, with the passion, she'd felt invulnerable. Now, no longer innocent, no longer unaware, the nerves returned. Only a short time before she had given herself to him, perhaps demanded that he take her, but now she could only cling while her mind reeled with the wonder of it.

When the water came on full and hot, she jolted, gasping. With a low laugh, Grant stroked a hand intimately over her hip. "Feel good?"

It did, after the initial shock, but Gennie tilted back her head and eyed him narrowly. "You might have warned me."

"Life's full of surprises."

Like falling in love, she thought, when you hadn't the least intention of doing so. Gennie smiled, finding her arms had wound around his neck.

"You know..." He traced his tongue lightly over her mouth. "I'm getting used to the taste—and the feel of you wet. It's tempting just to stay right here for the next couple of hours."

She nuzzled against him when he ran his hands down her back. Strong hands, toughened in contrast to the elegance of their shape. There were no others she could ever imagine touching her.

With the steam rising around him, and Gennie soft and giving in his arms, Grant felt that rushing, heady desire building again. His muscles contracted with it—tightening, preparing.

"No, not this time," he murmured, pressing his mouth to her throat. This time he would remember her fragility and the wonder of being the only man to ever possess her. Whatever tenderness he had, or could find in himself, would be for her.

"You should dry off." He nibbled lightly at her lips before he drew her away. She was smiling, but her eyes were uncertain. As he turned off the water he tried to ignore the very real fear her vulnerability brought to him. Taking a towel from the rack, he stroked it over her face. "Here, lift your arms."

She did, laying her hands on his shoulders as he wrapped the towel around her. Slowly, running soft, undemanding kisses over her face, he drew the towel together to knot it loosely at her breasts. Gennie closed her eyes, the better to soak up the sensation of being pampered.

Using a fresh towel, Grant began to dry her hair. Gently, lazily, while her heart began to race, he rubbed the towel over it. "Warm?" he murmured, dipping his head to nibble at her ear. "You're trembling."

How could she answer when her heart was hammering in her throat? Heat was creeping into her, yet her body shivered with anticipation, uncertainties, longings. He had only to touch his mouth to hers to know that for that moment, for always, she was his.

"I want you," he said softly. "I wanted you right from the start." He skimmed his tongue over her ear. "You knew that."

"Yes." The word came out breathlessly, like a sigh.

"Do you know how much more I want you now than I did even an hour ago?" His mouth covered hers before she could answer. "Come to bed, Gennie."

He didn't carry her, but took her hand so that they could walk together into the thin gray light of his room. Her pulses pounded. The first time there had been no thought, no doubts. Desire had ruled her and the power had flowed. Now her mind was clear and her nerves jumping. She knew now where he could take her with a touch, with a taste. The journey was as much feared as it was craved.

"Grant—"

But he barely touched her, only cupping her face as they stood beside the bed. "You're beautiful." His eyes were on hers, intense, searching. "The first time I saw you, you took my breath away. You still do."

As moved by the long look and soft words as she had been by the tempestuous kisses, she reached up to take his wrists. "I don't need the words unless you want to give them. I just want to be with you."

"Whatever I tell you will be the truth, or I won't tell you at all." He leaned toward her, touching his mouth to hers, but nibbling only, testing the softness, lingering over that honey-steeped taste. As he took her deep with tenderness, his fingers moved over her face, skimming, stroking. Gennie's head went light while her body grew heavy. She barely felt the movement when they lowered to the bed.

Then it seemed she felt everything—the tiny nubs in the bedspread, the not quite smooth, not quite rough texture of Grant's palms, the thin mat of hair on his chest. All, she felt them all, as if her skin had suddenly become as soft and sensitive as a newborn's. And he treated her as though she were that precious with the slow, whisper-light kisses he brushed over her face and the hands that touched her—arousing, but stopping just short of demand.

The floating weightlessness she had experienced in the churchyard drifted back over her, but now, with the shivering excitement of knowledge. Aware of where they could lead each other, Gennie sighed. This time the journey would be luxurious, lazy and loving.

The light through the window was thin, misty gray from the clouds that still hid the sun. It cast shadows and mysteries. She could hear the sea—not the deafening, titanic roar, but the echo and the promise of power. And when he murmured to her, it was like the sea, with its passionate pull and thrust. The urgency she had felt before had become a quiet enjoyment. Though the needs were no less, there was a comfort here, an unquestioning trust she'd never expected to feel. He would protect if she needed him, cherish in his own fashion. Beneath the demands and impatience was a man who would give unselfishly where he cared. Discovering that was discovering everything.

Touch me—don't ever stop touching me. And he seemed to hear her silent request as he caressed, lingered, explored. The pleasure was liquid and light, like a lazy river, like rain misting. Her mind was so clouded with him, only him, she no longer thought of her body as separate, but a part of the two that made one whole.

Soft murmurs and quiet sighs, the warmth that only flesh can bring to flesh. Gennie learned of him—the man he showed so rarely to anyone. Sensitivity, because it was not his way, was all the sweeter. Gentleness, so deeply submerged, was all the more arousing.

She hardly knew when her pliancy began to kindle to excitement. But he did. The subtle change in her movements, her breathing, had a shiver of pleasure darting down his spine. And he drew yet more pleasure in the mere watching of her face in the gloomy light. A flicker of passion reminded him that no one had ever touched her as he did. And no one would. For so long he'd taken such care not to allow anyone to get too close, to block off any feelings of possession, to avoid being possessed. Though the proprietary sensation disturbed him, he couldn't fight it. She was his. Grant told himself it didn't yet mean he was hers. Yet he could think of no one else.

He ran kisses over her slowly, until his mouth brushed then loitered at her shoulder. And when he felt her yield, completely, unquestioningly, he took her once, gasping, to the edge. On her moan, he pressed his lips to hers, wanting to feel the sound as well as hear it.

Mindless, boneless, burning, Gennie moved with him, responding to the agonizingly slow pace by instinct alone. She wanted to rush, she wanted to stay in that cloudy world of dreams forever. Now, and only now, did she fully understand why the coming together of two separate beings was called making love.

She opened to him, offering everything. When he slipped inside her she felt his shudder, heard the groan that was muffled against her throat. His breath rasped against her ear but he kept the pace exquisitely slow. There couldn't be so much—she'd never known there could be—but he showed her.

She drifted down a tunnel with soft melting edges. Deeper and lusher it grew until her whole existence was bound there in the velvet heat that promised forever. Reason peeled away layer by layer so that her body was guided by senses alone. He was trembling—was she? As her hands glided over his shoulders she could feel the hard, tense muscles there while his movements were gentle and easy. Through the mists of pleasure she knew he was blocking off his own needs for hers. A wave of emotion struck her that was a hundred times greater than passion.

"Grant." His name was only a whisper as her arms tightened around him. "Now. Take me now."

"Gennie." He lifted his face so that she had a glimpse of dark, dark eyes before his mouth met hers. His control seemed to snap at the contact and he swallowed her gasps as he rushed with her to the peak.

There were no more thoughts nor the need for any.

# Chapter 8

With a slow stretch and a long sigh, Gennie woke. Ingrained habit woke her early and quickly. Her first feeling of disorientation faded almost at once. No, the sun-washed window wasn't hers, but she knew whose it was. She knew where she was and why.

The morning warmth had a new texture—body to body, man to woman, lover to lover. Simultaneous surges of contentment and excitement swam through her to chase away any sense of drowsiness. Turning her head, Gennie watched Grant sleep.

He sprawled, taking up, Gennie discovered to her amusement, about three-fourths of the bed. During the night, he had nudged her to within four inches of the edge. His arm was tossed carelessly across her body—not loverlike, she thought wryly, but because she just happened to be in his space. He had most of her pillow. Against the plain white, his face was deeply tanned, shadowed by the stubble that grew on his jaw. Looking at him, Gennie realized he was completely relaxed as she had seen him only once before—on their walk along the beach.

What drives you, Grant? she wondered as she gave in to the desire to toy with the tips of his rumpled hair. What makes you so intense, so solitary? And why do I want so badly to understand and share whatever secrets you keep?

With a fingertip, carefully, delicately, Gennie traced down the line of his jaw. A strong face, she thought, almost hard, and yet occasionally, unexpectedly the humor and sensitivity would come into his eyes. Then the hardness would vanish and only the strength would remain.

Rude, remote, arrogant; he was all of those things. And she loved him—despite it, perhaps because of it. It had been the gentleness he had shown her that had allowed her to admit it, accept it, but it had been true all along.

She longed to tell him, to say those simple, exquisite words. She'd shared her body with him, given her innocence and her trust. Now she wanted to share her emotions. Love, she believed, was meant to be given freely, without conditions. Yet she knew him well enough to understand that step would have to be taken by him first. His nature demanded it. Another man might be flattered, pleased, even relieved to have a woman state her feelings so easily. Grant, Gennie reflected, would feel cornered.

Lying still, watching him, she wondered if it had been a woman who had caused him to isolate himself. Gennie felt certain it had been pain or disillusionment that had made him so determined to be unapproachable. There was a basic kindness in him which he hid, a talent he apparently wasn't using and a warmth he hoarded. Why? With a sigh, she brushed the hair from his forehead. They were his mysteries; she only hoped she had the patience to wait until he was ready to share them.

Warm, content, Gennie snuggled against him, murmuring his name. Grant's answer was an unintelligible mutter as he shifted onto his stomach and buried his face in the pillow. The movement cost Gennie a few more precious inches of mattress.

"Hey!" Laughing, she shoved against his shoulder. "Move over."

No response.

You're a romantic devil, Gennie thought wryly, then pressing her lips to that unbudgeable shoulder, slipped out of the bed. Grant immediately took advantage of all the available space.

A loner, Gennie thought, studying him as he lay crosswise over the twisted sheets. He wasn't a man used to making room for anyone. With a last thoughtful glance, Gennie walked across the hall to shower.

Gradually the sound of running water woke him. Hazy, Grant lay still, sleepily debating how much effort it would take to open his eyes. It was his ingrained habit to put off the moment of waking until it could no longer be avoided.

With his face buried in the pillow, he could smell Gennie. It brought dreamy images to him, images sultry but not quite formed. There were soft, fuzzy-edged pictures that both aroused and soothed.

Barely half awake, Grant shifted enough to discover he was alone in bed. Her warmth was still there—on the sheets, on his skin. He lay steeped in it a moment, not certain why it felt so right, not trying to reason out the answers.

He remembered the feel of her, the taste, the way her pulse would leap under the touch of his finger. Had there ever been a woman who had made him want so badly? Who could make him comfortable one moment and wild the next? How close was he to the border between want and need, or had he already crossed it?

They were more questions he couldn't deal with—not now while his mind was still clouded with sleep and with Gennie. He needed to shake off the first and distance himself from the second before he could find any answers.

Groggy, Grant sat up, running a hand over his face as Gennie came back in.

"Morning." With her hair wrapped in a towel and Grant's robe belted loosely at her waist, Gennie dropped onto the edge of the bed. Linking her hands behind his neck, she leaned over and kissed him. She smelled of his soap and shampoo—something that made the easy kiss devastatingly intimate. Even as this began to soak into him, she drew away to give him a friendly smile. "Awake yet?"

"Nearly." Because he wanted to see her hair, Grant pulled the towel from her head and let it drop to the floor. "Have you been up long?"

"Only since you pushed me out of bed." She laughed when his brows drew together. "That's not much of an exaggeration. Want some coffee?"

"Yeah." As she rose, Grant took her hand, holding it until her smile became puzzled. What did he want to say to her? Grant wondered. What did he want to tell her—or himself? He wasn't certain of anything except the knowledge that whatever was happening inside him was already too far advanced to stop.

"Grant?"

"I'll be down in a minute," he mumbled, feeling foolish. "I'll fix breakfast this time."

"All right." Gennie hesitated, wondering if he would say whatever he'd really meant to say, then she left him alone.

Grant remained in bed a moment, listening to the sound of her footsteps on his stairs. Her footsteps—his stairs. Somehow, the line of demarcation was smearing. He wasn't certain he'd be able to lie in his bed again without thinking of her curled beside him.

But he'd had other women, Grant reminded himself. He'd enjoyed them, appreciated them. Forgotten them. Why was it he was so certain there was nothing about Gennie he'd forget? Nothing, down to that small, faint birthmark he'd found on her hip—a half moon he could cover with his pinkie. Foolishly it had pleased him to discover it—something he knew no other man had seen or touched.

He was acting like an idiot, he told himself—enchanted by the fact that he was her first lover, obsessed with the idea of being her last, her only. He needed to be alone for a while, that was all, to put his feelings back in perspective. The last thing he wanted was to start tying strings on her, and in turn, on himself.

Rising, he rummaged in his drawers until he found a pair of cutoffs. He'd fix breakfast, send her on her way, then get back to work.

But when he reached the bottom of the stairs, he smelled the coffee, heard her singing. Grant was struck with a powerful wave of *déjà vu*. He could explain it, he told himself he could explain it because it had been just like this the first morning after he'd met her. But it wasn't that—that was much, much too logical for the strength of the feeling that swamped him. It was more than an already seen—it was a sensation of rightness, of always, of pleasure so simple it stung. If he walked into that kitchen a hundred times, year after year, it would never seem balanced, never seem whole, unless she was waiting for him.

Grant paused in the doorway to watch her. The coffee was hot and ready as she stretched up for the mugs that he could reach easily. The sun shot light into her hair, teasing out those deep red hints until they shimmered, flame on velvet. She turned, catching her breath in surprise when she saw him, then smiling.

"I didn't hear you come down." She swung her hair behind her shoulder as she began to pour coffee. "It's gorgeous out. The rain's got everything gleaming and the ocean's more blue than green. You wouldn't know there'd ever been a storm." Taking a mug in each hand, she turned back to him. Though she'd intended to cross to him, the look in his eyes stopped her. Puzzlement quickly became tension. Was he angry? she wondered. Why? Perhaps he was already regretting what had happened. Why had she been so foolish as to think what had been between them had been as special, as unique for him as it had been for her?

Her fingers tightened on the handles. She wouldn't let him apologize, make excuses. She wouldn't cause a scene. The pain was real, physically real, but she told herself to ignore it. Later, when she was alone, she would deal with it. But now she would face him without tears, without pleas.

"Is something wrong?" Was that her voice, so calm, so controlled?

"Yeah, something's wrong."

Her fingers held the mugs so tightly she wondered that the handles didn't snap off. Still, it kept her hands from shaking. "Maybe we should sit down."

"I don't want to sit down." His voice was sharp as a slap but she didn't flinch. She watched as he paced to the sink and leaned against it, muttering and swearing. Another time the Grantlike gesture would have amused her, but now she only stood and waited. If he was going to hurt her, let him do it quickly, at once, before she fell apart. He whirled, almost violently, and stared at her accusingly. "Damn it, Gennie, I've had my head lopped off."

It was her turn to stare. Her fingers went numb against the stoneware. Her pulse seemed to stop long enough to make her head swim before it began to race. The color drained from her face until it was like porcelain against the glowing green of her eyes. On another oath, Grant dragged a hand through his hair.

"You're spilling the coffee," he muttered, then stuck his hands in his pockets.

"Oh." Gennie looked down foolishly at the tiny twin puddles that were forming on the floor, then set down the mugs. "I'll—I'll wipe it up."

"Leave it." Grant grabbed her arm before she could reach for a towel. "Listen, I feel like someone's just given me a solid right straight to the gut—the kind that doubles you over and makes your head ring at the same time. I feel that way too often when I look at you." When she said nothing, he took her other arm and shook. "In the first place I never asked to have you walk into my life and mess up my head. The last thing I wanted was for you to get in my way, but you did. So now I'm in love with you, and I can tell you, I'm not crazy about the idea."

Gennie found her voice, though she wasn't quite certain what to do with it. "Well," she managed after a moment, "that certainly puts me in my place."

"Oh, she wants to make jokes." Disgusted, Grant released her to storm over to the coffee. Lifting a mug, he drained half the contents, perversely pleased that it scalded his throat. "Well, laugh this off," he suggested as he slammed the mug down again and glared. "You're not going anywhere until I figure out what the hell I'm going to do about you."

Struggling against conflicting emotions of amusement, annoyance, and simple wonder, she put her hands on her hips. The movement shifted the too-big robe so that it threatened to slip off of one shoulder. "Oh, really? So you're going to figure out what to do about me, like I was an inconvenient head cold."

"Damned inconvenient," he muttered.

"You may not have noticed, but I'm a grown woman with a mind of my own, accustomed to making my own decisions. You're not going to *do* anything about me," she told him as her temper began to overtake everything else. She jabbed a finger at him, and the gap in the robe widened. "If you're in love with me, that's your problem. I have one of my own because I'm in love with you."

"Terrific!" he shouted at her. "That's just terrific. We'd both have been better off if you'd waited out that storm in a ditch instead of coming here."

"You're not telling me anything I don't already know," Gennie retorted, then spun around to leave the room.

"Just a minute." Grant had her arm again and backed her into the wall. "You're not going anywhere until this is settled."

"It's settled!" Tossing her hair out of her face, she glared at him. "We're in love with each other and I wish you'd go jump off that cliff. If you had any finesse—"

"I don't."

"Any sensitivity," she continued, "you wouldn't announce that you were in love with someone in the same tone you'd use to frighten small children."

"I'm not in love with someone!" he shouted at her, infuriated because she was right and he couldn't do a thing about it. "I'm in love with you, and damn it, I don't like it."

"You've made that abundantly clear." She straightened her shoulders and lifted her chin.

"Don't pull that regal routine on me," Grant began. Her eyes sharpened to dagger points. Her skin flushed majestically. Abruptly he began to laugh. When she tossed her head back in fury, he simply collapsed against her. "Oh, God, Gennie, I can't take it when you look at me as though you were about to have me tossed in the dungeon."

"Get off of me, you ass!" Incensed, insulted, she shoved against him, but he only held her tighter. Only quick reflexes saved him from a well-aimed knee at a strategic point.

"Hold on." Still chuckling, he pressed his mouth to hers. Then as abruptly as his laughter had begun, it stilled. With the gentleness he so rarely showed, his hands came up to frame her face, and she was lost. "Gennie." With his lips still on hers he murmured her name so that the sound of it shivered through her. "I love you." He combed his fingers through her hair, drawing her head back so that their eyes met. "I don't like it, I may never get used to it, but I love you." With a sigh, he brought her close again. "You make my head swim."

With her cheek against his chest, Gennie closed her eyes. "You can take time to get used to it," she murmured. "Just promise you won't ever be sorry it happened."

"Not sorry," he agreed on a long breath. "A little crazed, but not sorry." As he ran a hand down her hair, Grant felt a fresh need for her, softer, calmer than before but no less vibrant. He nuzzled into her neck because he seemed to belong there. "Are you really in love with me, or did you say that because I made you mad?"

"Both. I decided this morning I'd have to bend to your ego and let you tell me first."

"Is that so?" With his brows drawn together, he tilted her head back again. "My ego."

"It tends to get in the way because it's rather oversized." She smiled, sweetly. In retaliation, he crushed his mouth to hers.

"You know," he managed after a moment. "I've lost my appetite for breakfast."

Smiling again, she tilted her face back to his. "Have you really?"

"Mmm. And I don't like to mention it..." He took his fingertips to the lapel of the robe, toying with it before he slid them down to the belt. "But I didn't say you could use my robe."

"Oh, that was rude of me." The smile became saucy. "Would you like it back now?"

"No hurry." He slipped his hand into hers and started toward the steps. "You can wait until we get upstairs."

From his bedroom window, Grant watched her drive away. It was early afternoon now, and the sun was brilliant. He needed some distance from her—perhaps she needed some from him as well. That's what he told himself even while he wondered how long he could stay away.

There was work waiting for him in the studio above his head, a routine he knew was directly connected to the quality and quantity of his output. He needed that one strict discipline in his life, the hours out of the day and night that were guided by his creativity and his drive. Yet how could he work when his mind was so full of her, when his body was still warm from hers?

Love. He'd managed to avoid it for so many years, then he had thoughtlessly opened the door. It had barged in on him, Grant reflected, uninvited, unwelcomed. Now he was vulnerable, dependent—all the things he'd once promised himself he'd never be again. If he could change it, he was sure he would. He had lived by his own rules, his own judgment, his own needs for so long he wasn't certain he was willing or able to make the compromises love entailed.

He would end up hurting her, Grant thought grimly, and the pain would ricochet back on him. That was the inevitable fate of all lovers. What did they want from each other? Shaking his head, Grant turned from the window. For now, time and affection were enough, but that would change. What would happen when the demands crept in, the strings? Would he bolt? He had no business falling in love with someone like Gennie, whose life-style was light-years away from the one he had chosen, whose very innocence made her that much more susceptible to hurt.

She'd never be content to live with him there on his isolated finger of land, and he'd never ask her to. He couldn't give up his peace for the parties, the cameras, the social whirl. If he'd been more like Shelby…

Grant thought of his sister and her love for crowds, people, noise. Each of them had compensated in their own way for the trauma of losing their father in such a hideous, public fashion. But after fifteen years, the scars were still there. Perhaps Shelby had healed more cleanly, or perhaps her love for Alan MacGregor was strong enough to overcome that nagging fear. The fear of exposure, of losing, of depending.

He remembered Shelby's visit to him before she made her decision to marry Alan. She'd been miserable, afraid. He'd been rough on her because he'd wanted to hold her, to let her weep out the memories that haunted them both. He'd spoken the truth because the truth was what she'd needed to hear, but Grant wasn't certain he could live by it.

*"Are you going to shut yourself off from life because of something that happened fifteen years ago?"*

He'd asked her that, scathingly, when she'd sat in his kitchen with her eyes brimming over. And he remembered her angry, intuitive, *"Haven't you?"*

In his own way he had, though his work and the love of it kept him permanently connected with the world. He drew for people, for their pleasure and entertainment, because in a fashion perhaps only he himself understood, he liked them—their flaws and strengths, their foolishness and sanity. He simply wouldn't be crowded by them. And he'd refused, successfully until Gennie, to be too deeply involved with anyone on a one to one level. It was so simple to deal with humanity on a general scope. The pitfalls occurred when you narrowed it down.

Pitfalls, he thought with a snort. He'd fallen into a big one. He was already impatient to have her back with him, to hear her voice, to see her smile at him.

She'd be setting up now for the watercolor she'd told him she was going to begin. Maybe she'd still be wearing the shirt Grant had lent her. Her own had been torn beyond repair. Without effort, he could picture her setting up her easel near the inlet. Her hair would be brushed away from her face to fall behind her. His shirt would be hanging past her hips....

And while she was getting her work done, he was standing around mooning like a teenager. On a sound of frustration, Grant strode into the hall just as the phone began to ring. He started to ignore it, something he did easily, then changed his mind and loped down the stairs. He kept only one phone, in the kitchen, because he refused to be disturbed by anything while he was in his studio or in his bed. Grant snatched the receiver from the wall and leaned against the doorway.

"Yeah?"

"Grant Campbell?"

Though he'd only met the man once, Grant had no trouble identifying the voice. It was distinctive, even without the slight slur it cast on the *Campbell*. "Hello, Daniel."

"You're a hard man to reach. Been out of town?"

"No." Grant grinned. "I don't always answer the phone."

The snort Daniel gave caused Grant's grin to widen. He could imagine the big MacGregor sitting in his private tower room, smoking one of his forbidden cigars behind his massive desk. Grant had caricatured him just that way, then had slipped the sketch to Shelby during her wedding reception. Absently he reached for a bag of corn chips on the counter and ripped them open.

"How are you?"

"Fine. More than fine." Daniel's booming voice took on hints of pride and arrogance. "I'm a grandfather—two weeks ago."

"Congratulations."

"A boy," Daniel informed him, taking a satisfied puff on his thick, Cuban cigar. "Seven pounds, four ounces, strong as a bull. Robert MacGregor Blade. They'll be calling him Mac. Good stock." He took a deep breath that strained the buttons on his shirt. "The boy has my ears."

Grant listened to the rundown on the newest MacGregor with a mixture of amusement and affection. His sister had married into a family that he personally found irresistible. He knew pieces of them would be popping up in his strip for years to come. "How's Rena?"

"Came through like a champ." Daniel bit down on his cigar. "Of course, I knew she would. Her mother was worried. Females."

He didn't mention it was he who had insisted on chartering a plane the minute he'd learned Serena had gone into labor. Or that he had paced the waiting room like a madman while his wife, Anna, had calmly finished the embroidery on a baby blanket.

"Justin stayed with her the whole time." There was just a touch of resentment in the words—enough to tell Grant the hospital staff had barred the MacGregor's way into the delivery room. And probably hadn't had an easy time of it.

"Has Shelby seen her nephew yet?"

"Off on their honeymoon during the birthing," Daniel told him with a wheezy sigh. It was difficult for him to understand why his son and daughter-in-law hadn't canceled their plans to be on hand for such a momentous occasion. "But then, she and Alan are making up for it this weekend. That's why I called. We want you to come down, boy. The whole family's coming, the new babe, too. Anna's fretting to have all the children around again. You know how women are."

He knew how Daniel was, and grinned again. "Mothers need to fuss, I imagine."

"Aye, that's it. And with a new generation started, she'll be worse than ever." Daniel cast a wary eye at his closed door. You never knew when someone might be listening. "Now, then, you'll come, Friday night."

Grant thought of his schedule and did some quick mental figuring. He had an urge to see his sister again, and the MacGregors. More, he felt the need to take Gennie to the people whom, without knowing why, he considered family. "I could come down for a couple of days, Daniel, but I'd like to bring someone."

"Someone?" Daniel's senses sharpened. He leaned forward with the cigar smoldering in his hand. "Who might this someone be?"

Recognizing the tone, Grant crunched on a corn chip. "An artist I know who's doing some painting in New England, in Windy Point at the moment. I think she'd be interested in your house."

*She,* Daniel thought with an irrepressible grin. Just because he'd managed to comfortably establish his children didn't mean he had to give up the satisfying hobby of matchmaking. Young people needed to be guided in such matters—or shoved along. And Grant—though he was a Campbell—was by way of being family....

"An artist...aye, that's interesting. Always room for one more, son. Bring her along. An artist," he repeated, tapping out his cigar. "Young and pretty, too, I'm sure."

"She's nearly seventy," Grant countered easily, crossing his ankles as he leaned against the wall. "A little dumpy, has a face like a frog. Her paintings are timeless, tremendous emotional content and physicality. I'm crazy about her." He paused, imagining Daniel's wide face turning a deep puce. "Genuine emotion transcends age and physical beauty, don't you agree?"

Daniel choked, then found his voice. The boy needed help, a great deal of help. "You come early Friday, son. We'll need some time to talk." He stared hard at the bookshelf across the room. "Seventy, you say?"

"Close. But then true sensuality is ageless. Why just last night she and I—"

"No, don't tell me," Daniel interrupted hastily. "We'll have a long talk when you get here. A long talk," he added after a deep breath. "Has Shelby met— No, never mind," he decided. "Friday," Daniel said in a firmer tone. "We'll see about all this on Friday."

"We'll be there." Grant hung up, then leaning against the doorjamb, laughed until he hurt. That should keep the old boy on his toes until Friday, Grant thought. Still grinning, he headed for the stairs. He'd work until dark—until Gennie.

# Chapter 9

Gennie had never known herself to be talked into anything so quickly. Before she knew what was happening, she was agreeing to pack her painting gear and a suitcase and fly off to spend a weekend with people she didn't know.

Part of the reason, she realized when she had a moment to sort it out, was that Grant was enthusiastic about the MacGregors. She learned enough about him in little more than a week to know that he rarely felt genuine affection for anyone—enough affection at any rate to give up his precious privacy and his time. She had agreed primarily because she simply wanted to be where he was, next because she was caught up in his pleasure. And finally because she wanted to see him under a different set of circumstances, interacting with people, away from his isolated spot on the globe.

She would meet his sister. The fact that he had one had come as a surprise. Though she admitted it was foolish, Gennie had had a picture of Grant simply popping into the world as an adult, by himself, already prepared to fight for the right to his place and his privacy.

Now she began to wonder about his childhood—what had formed him? What had made him into the Grant Campbell she knew? Had he been rich or poor, outgoing or introverted? Had he been happy, loved, ignored? He rarely talked about his family, his past…for that matter, of his present.

Oddly, because the answers were so important, she couldn't ask the questions. Gennie found she needed that step to come from him, as proof of the love he said he felt. No, perhaps proof was the wrong word, she mused. She believed he loved her, in his way, but she wanted the seal. To her, there was no separating trust from love, because one without the other was just an empty word. She didn't believe in secrets.

From childhood until her sister's death, Gennie had had that one special person to share everything with—all her doubts, insecurities, wishes, dreams. Losing Angela had been like losing part of herself, a part she was only beginning to feel again. It was the most natural thing in the world for her to give that trust and affection to Grant. Where she loved, she loved without boundaries.

Beneath the joy she felt was a quiet ache that came from knowing he had yet to open to her. Until he did, Gennie felt their future extended no further than the moment. She forced herself to accept that, because the thought of the moment without him was unbearable.

Grant glanced over as he turned onto the narrow cliff road that led to the MacGregor estate. He glimpsed Gennie's profile, the quiet expression, the eyes dreamy and not quite happy. "What're you thinking?"

She turned her head, and with her smile the wisp of sadness vanished. "That I love you."

It was so simple. It made his knees weak. Needing to touch her, Grant pulled onto the shoulder of the road and stopped. She was still smiling when he cupped her face in his hands, and her lashes lowered in anticipation of the kiss.

Softly, with a reverence he never expected to feel, he brushed his lips over her cheeks, first one, then the other. Her breath caught in her throat to lodge with her heart. His rare spurts of gentleness never failed to undo her. Anything, everything he might have asked of her at that moment, she would have given without hesitation. The whisper of his lashes against her skin bound her to him more firmly than any chain.

Her name was only a sigh as he trailed kisses over her closed lids. With her tremble, his thoughts began to swirl. What was this magic she cast over him? It glittered one instant, then pulsed the next. Was it only his imagination, or had she always been there, waiting to spring into his life and make him a slave? Was it her softness or her strength that made him want to kill or to die for her? Did it matter?

He knew it should. When a man got pulled in too deeply—by a woman, an ideal, a goal—he became vulnerable. Then the instinct for survival would take second place. Grant had always understood this was what had happened to his father.

But now all he could grasp was that she was so soft, so giving. His.

Lightly, Grant touched his lips to hers. Gennie tilted back her head and opened to him. His fingers tightened on her, his breath quickened, rushing into her mouth just before his tongue. The transition from gentle to desperate was too swift to be measured. Her fingers tangled in his hair to drag him closer while he ravished a mouth more demanding than willing. Caught in the haze, Gennie thought her passion rose higher and faster each time he touched her until one day she would simply explode from a mere look.

"I want you." She felt the words wrench from her. As they slipped from her mouth into his, he crushed her against him in a grip that left all gentleness behind. His lips savaged, warred, absorbed, until they were both speechless. With an inarticulate murmur, Grant buried his face in her hair and fought to find reason.

"Good God, in another minute I'll forget it's still daylight and this is a public road."

Gennie ran her fingers down the nape of his neck. "I already have."

Grant forced the breath in and out of his lungs three times, then lifted his head. "Be careful," he warned quietly. "I have a more difficult time remembering to be civilized than doing what comes naturally. At this moment I'd feel very natural dragging you into the back seat, tearing off your clothes and loving you until you were senseless."

A thrill rushed up and down her spine, daring her, urging her. She leaned closer until her lips were nearly against his. "One should never go against one's nature."

"Gennie..." His control was so thinly balanced, he could already feel the way her body would heat and soften beneath his. Her scent contradicted the lowering sun and whispered of midnight. When she slid her hands up his chest, he could hear his own heartbeat vibrate against her palm. Her eyes were clouded, yet somehow they held more power. Grant couldn't look away from them. He saw himself a prisoner, exulting in the weight of the chains.

Just as the scales tipped away from reason, the sound of an approaching engine had him swearing and turning his head. Gennie looked over her shoulder as a Mercedes pulled to a halt beside them. The driver was in shadows, so that she had only the impression of dark, masculine looks while the passenger rolled down her window.

A cap of wild red hair surrounding an angular face poked out the opening. The woman leaned her arms on the base of the window and grinned appealingly. "You people lost?"

Grant sent her a narrow-eyed glare, then astonished Gennie by reaching out and twisting her nose between his first two fingers. "Scram."

"Some people just aren't worth helping," the woman stated before she gave a haughty toss of her head and disappeared back inside. The Mercedes purred discreetly, then disappeared around the first curve.

"Grant!" Torn between amusement and disbelief, Gennie stared at him. "Even for you that was unbelievably rude."

"Can't stand busybodies," he said easily as he started the car again.

She let out a gusty sigh as she flopped back against the cushions. "You certainly made that clear enough. I'm beginning to think it was a miracle you didn't just slam the door in my face that first night."

"It was a weak moment."

She slanted a look at him, then gave up. "How close are we? You might want to run off the cast of characters for me so I'll have an idea who…" She trailed off. "Oh, God."

It was incredible, impossible. Wonderful. Stark gray in the last lights of the sun, it was the fairy castle every little girl imagined herself trapped in. It would take a valiant knight to free her from the high stone walls of the tower. That it was here, in this century of rockets and rushing was a miracle in itself.

The structure jutted and spread, and quite simply dominated the cliff on which it stood. No ivy clung to its walls. What ivy would dare encroach? But there were flowers—wild roses, blooms in brambles, haunting colors that stubbornly shouted of summer while the nearby trees were edged with the first breath of fall.

Gennie didn't simply want to paint it. She had to paint it in essentially the same way she had to breathe.

"I thought so," Grant commented.

Dazed, Gennie continued to stare. "What?"

"You might as well have a brush in your hand already."

"I only wish I did."

"If you paint this with half the insight and the power you used in your study of the cliffs and lighthouse, you'll have a magnificent piece of work."

Gennie turned to him then, confused. "But I—you didn't seem to think too much of the painting."

He snorted as he negotiated the last curve. "Don't be an idiot."

It never occurred to him that she would need reassurance. Grant knew his own skills, and accepted with a shrug the fact that he was considered one of the top in his field. What others thought mattered little, because he knew his own capabilities. He assumed Gennie would feel precisely the same about herself.

If he had known the agony she went through before each of her showings, he would have been flabbergasted. If he had known just how much he had hurt her by his casual comment the day she had finished the painting, he would have been speechless.

Gennie frowned at him, concentrating. "You did like it, then?"

"Like what?"

"The painting," she snapped impatiently. "The painting I did in your front yard."

With their minds working at cross purposes, Grant didn't hear the insecurity in the demand. "Just because I don't paint," he began curtly, "doesn't mean I have to be slugged over the head with genius to recognize it."

They lapsed into silence, neither one certain of the other's mood, or their own.

If he liked the painting, Gennie fumed, why didn't he just say so instead of making her drag it out of him?

Grant wondered if she thought *serious* art was the only worthwhile medium. What the hell would she have to say if he told her he made his living by depicting people as he saw them through cartoons? Funny papers. Would she laugh or throw a fit if she caught a glimpse of his Veronica in the New York *Daily* in a couple of weeks?

They pulled up in front of the house with a jerk of brakes that brought them both back to the moment. "Wait until we get inside," he began, picking up the threads of their earlier conversation. "I only believed half of what I saw myself."

"Apparently everything I've ever read or heard about Daniel MacGregor's true." Gennie stepped out of the car with her eyes trained on the house again. "Forceful, eccentric, a man who makes his own deals his own way. But I'm vague on personal details. His wife's a doctor?"

"Surgeon. There're three children, and as you'll be hearing innumerable times over the weekend, one grandson. My sister married the eldest son, Alan."

"Alan MacGregor.... He's—"

"Senator MacGregor, and in a few years..." With a shrug, he trailed off.

"Ah, yes, you'd have a direct line into the White House if the murmurs about Alan MacGregor's aspirations become fact." She grinned at the man in khakis leaning against the hood of the rented car while the wind played games with his hair. "How would you feel about that?"

Grant gave her an odd smile, thinking of Macintosh. "Things are presently unsettled," he murmured. "But I've always had a rather—wry affection for politics in general." Grabbing her hand, he began to walk toward the rough stone steps. "Then there's Caine, son number two, a lawyer who recently married another lawyer who as it happens, is the sister of Daniel's youngest offspring's husband."

"I'm not sure I'm keeping up." Gennie studied the brass-crowned lion's head that served as a door knocker.

"You have to be a quick study." Grant lifted the knocker and let it fall resoundingly. "Rena married a gambler. She and her husband own a number of casinos and live in Atlantic City."

Gennie gave him a thoughtful glance. "For someone who keeps to himself so much, you're well informed."

"Yeah." He grinned at her as the door opened.

The redhead that Gennie recognized from the Mercedes leaned against the thick panel and looked Grant up and down. "Still lost?"

This time Grant tugged her against him and gave her a hard kiss. "Apparently you've survived a month of matrimony, but you're still skinny."

"And compliments still roll trippingly off your tongue," she retorted, drawing back. After a moment she laughed and hugged him fiercely. "Damn, I hate to say it out loud, but it's good to see you." Grinning over Grant's shoulder, she pinned Gennie with a curious, not unfriendly glance. "Hi, I'm Shelby."

Grant's sister, Gennie realized, thrown off by the total lack of any familial resemblance. She had the impression of hordes of energy inside a long lean body, unruly fiery curls, and smoky eyes. While Grant had a rugged, unkempt attractiveness, his sister was a combination of porcelain and flame.

"I'm Gennie." She responded instinctively to the smile Shelby shot her before she untangled herself from her brother. "I'm glad to meet you."

"Pushing seventy, hmmm?" Shelby said cryptically to Grant before she clasped Gennie's hand. "We'll have to get to know each other so you can tell me how you tolerate this jerk's company for more than five minutes at a time. Alan's in the throne room with the MacGregor," she continued before Grant could retort. "Has Grant given you a rundown on the inmates?"

"An abbreviated version," Gennie replied, instantly charmed.

"Typical." She hooked her arm through Gennie's. "Well, sometimes it's best to jump in feet first. The most important thing to remember is not to let Daniel intimidate you. What extraction are you?"

"French mostly. Why?"

"It'll come up."

"How was the honeymoon?" Grant demanded, wanting to veer away from the subject that would, indeed, come up.

Shelby beamed at him. "I'll let you know when it's over. How's your cliff?"

"Still standing." He glanced to his left as Justin started down the main stairs. Justin's expression of mild curiosity changed to surprise—something rarely seen on his face—then pleasure.

"Gennie!" He took the rest of the stairs in quick, long strides then whirled her into his arms.

"Justin." Laughing, she hooked her arms around his neck while Grant's eyes narrowed to slits.

"What're you doing here?" they asked together.

Chuckling, he took both of her hands, drawing back for a long, thorough study. "You're beautiful," he told her. "Always."

Grant watched her flush with pleasure and experienced the first genuine jealousy of his life. He found it a very unpleasant sensation. "It seems," he said in a dangerously mild voice that had Shelby's brows lifting, "you two have met."

"Yes, of course," Gennie began before realization dawned. "The gambler!" she exclaimed. "Oh, I never put it together. Rena—Serena. Hearing you were getting married was a shock in itself, I hated to miss the wedding…and a father!" She threw her arms around him again, laughing. "Good God, I'm surrounded by cousins."

"Cousins?" Grant echoed.

"On my French side," Justin said wryly. "A distant connection, carefully overlooked by all but a—" he tilted Gennie's face to his "—select few."

"Aunt Adelaide's a stuffy old bore," Gennie said precisely.

"Are you following this?" Shelby asked Grant.

"Barely," he muttered.

With another laugh, Gennie held out her hand to him. "To keep it simple, Justin and I are cousins, third, I think. We happened to meet about five years ago at one of my shows in New York."

"I wasn't—ah—close to that particular end of my family," Justin continued. "Some chance comment led to another until we ferreted out the connection."

When Justin smiled down at Gennie, Grant saw it. The eyes, the green eyes. Man, woman, they were almost identical to the shade. For some obscure reason that, more than the explanations, had him relaxing the muscles that had gone taut the moment Justin had scooped her up. The black sheep, he realized, who'd outdone them all.

"Fascinating," Shelby decided. "All those clichés about small worlds are amazingly apt. Gennie's here with Grant."

"Oh?" Justin glanced over, meeting Grant's dark, appraising eyes. As a gambler he habitually sized up the people he met and stored them into compartments. At Shelby's wedding the month before, Justin had found him a man with wit and secrets who refused to be stored anywhere. They'd gotten along easily, perhaps because the need for privacy was inherent in both of them. Now, remembering Daniel's blustering description of Grant's weekend companion, Justin controlled a grin. "Daniel mentioned you were bringing—an artist."

Grant recognized, as few would have, the gleam of humor in Justin's eyes. "I'm sure he did," he returned in the same conversational tone. "I haven't congratulated you yet on ensuring the continuity of the line."

"And saving the rest of us from the pressure to do so immediately," Shelby finished.

"Don't count on it," a smooth voice warned.

Gennie looked up to see a blond woman descending the steps, carrying a bundle in a blue blanket.

"Hello, Grant. It's nice to see you again." Serena cradled her son in one arm as she leaned over to kiss Grant's cheek. "It was sweet of you to answer the royal summons."

"My pleasure." Unable to resist, he nudged the blanket aside with a finger.

So little. Babies had always held a fascination for him—their perfection in miniature. This one was smooth-cheeked and wide awake, staring back at him with dark blue eyes he thought already hinted of the violet of his mother's. Perhaps Mac had Daniel's ears and Serena's eyes, but the rest of him was pure Blade. He had the bones of a warrior, Grant thought, and the striking black hair of his Comanche blood.

Looking beyond her son, Serena studied the woman who was watching Grant with a quiet thoughtfulness. It surprised her to see her husband's eyes in a feminine face. Waiting until those eyes shifted to hers, she smiled. "I'm Rena."

"Gennie's a friend of Grant's," Justin announced, easily slipping an arm around his wife's shoulders. "She also happens to be my cousin." Before Serena could react to the first surprise, he hit her with the second. "Genviève Grandeau."

"Oh, those marvelous paintings!" she exclaimed while Shelby's eyes widened.

"Damn it, Grant." After giving him a disgusted look, Shelby turned to Gennie. "Our mother had two of your landscapes. I badgered her into giving me one as a wedding present. *Evening*," she elaborated. "I want to build a house around it."

Pleased, Gennie smiled at her. "Then maybe you'll help me convince Mr. MacGregor that I should paint his house."

"Just watch how you have to twist his arm," Serena said dryly.

"What is this, a summit meeting?" Alan demanded as he strode down the hall. "It's one thing to be the advance man," he continued as he cupped a hand around the back of his wife's neck, "and another to be the sacrificial lamb. Dad's doing a lot of moaning and groaning about this family scattering off in all directions."

"With Caine getting the worst of it," Serena put in.

"Yeah." Alan grinned once, appealingly. "Too bad he's late." His gaze shifted to Gennie then—dark, intense eyes, a slow, serious smile. "We've met...." He hesitated briefly as he flipped through his mental file of names and faces. "Genviève Grandeau."

A little surprised, Gennie smiled back at him. "A very quick meeting at a very crowded charity function about two years ago, Senator."

"Alan," he corrected. "So you're Grant's artist." He sent Grant a look that had lights of humor softening his eyes. "I must say you outshine even Grant's description of you. Shall we all go in and join the MacGregor before he starts to bellow?"

"Here." Justin took the baby from Serena in an expert move. "Mac'll soften him up."

"What description?" Gennie murmured to Grant as they started down the wide hall.

She saw the grin tug at his mouth before he slipped an arm around her shoulders. "Later."

Gennie immediately saw why Shelby had referred to it as the throne room. The expansive floor space was covered with a scarlet rug. All the woodwork was lushly carved while magnificent paintings hung in ornate frames. There was the faint smell of candlewax, though no candles were lit. Lamps glowed to aid the soft light of dusk that trailed in the many mullioned windows.

She saw at a glance that the furniture was ancient and wonderful, all large-scaled and perfect in the enormous room. Logs were laid and ready in the huge fireplace in anticipation of the chill that could come during the evenings when summer warred with autumn.

But the room, superb in its unique fashion, was nothing compared to the man holding court from his high-backed Gothic chair. Massive, with red hair thick and flaming, he watched the procession file into the room with narrowed, sharp blue eyes in a wide, lined face.

To Gennie, he looked like a general or a king—both, perhaps, in the way of centuries past where the monarch led his people into battle. One huge hand tapped the wooden arm of his chair while the other held a glass half-filled with liquid. He looked fierce enough to order executions arbitrarily. Her fingers itched for a pad and a pencil.

"Well," he said in a deep, rumbling voice that made the syllable an accusation.

Shelby was the first to go to him, bravely, Gennie thought, to give him a smacking kiss on the mouth. "Hi, Grandpa."

He reddened at that and struggled with the pleasure the title gave him. "So you decided to give me a moment of your time."

"I felt duty bound to pay my respects to the newest MacGregor first."

As if on cue, Justin strode over to arrange Mac in the crook of Daniel's arm. Gennie watched the fierce giant turn into a marshmallow. "There's a laddie," he crooned, holding out his glass to Shelby, then chucking the baby under the chin. When the baby grabbed his thick finger, he preened like a rooster. "Strong as an ox." He grinned foolishly at the room in general, then zeroed in on Grant. "Well, Campbell, so you've come. You see here," he began, jiggling the baby, "why the MacGregors could never be conquered. Strong stock."

"Good blood," Serena murmured, taking the baby from the proud grandfather.

"Get a drink for the Campbell," he ordered. "Now, where's this artist?" His eyes darted around the room, landed on Gennie and clung. She thought she saw surprise, quickly veiled, then amusement as quickly suppressed, tug at the corners of his mouth.

"Daniel MacGregor," Grant said with wry formality, "Genviève Grandeau."

A flicker of recognition ran across Daniel's face before he rose to his rather amazing height and held out his hand. "Welcome."

Gennie's hand was clasped, then enveloped. She had simultaneous impressions of strength, compassion, and stubbornness.

"You have a magnificent home, Mr. MacGregor," she said, studying him candidly. "It suits you."

He gave a great bellow of a laugh that might have shook the windows. "Aye. And three of your paintings hang in the west wing." His eyes slid briefly to Grant's before they came back to hers. "You carry your age well, lass."

She gave him a puzzled look as Grant choked over his Scotch. "Thank you."

"Get the artist a drink," he ordered, then gestured for her to sit in the chair next to his. "Now, tell me why you're wasting your time with a Campbell."

"Gennie happens to be a cousin of mine," Justin said mildly as he sat on the sofa beside his son. "On the aristocratic French side."

"A cousin." Daniel's eyes sharpened, then an expression that could only be described as cunning pleasure spread over his face. "Aye, we like to keep things in the family. Grandeau—a good strong name. You've the look of a queen, with a bit of sorceress thrown in."

"That was meant as a compliment," Serena told her as she handed Gennie a vermouth in crystal.

"So I've been told." Gennie sent Grant an easy look over the rim of her glass. "One of my ancestors had an—encounter with a gypsy resulting in twins."

"Gennie has a pirate in her family tree as well," Justin put in.

Daniel nodded in approval. "Strong blood. The Campbells need all the help they can get."

"Watch it, MacGregor," Shelby warned as Grant gave him a brief, fulminating look.

There were undercurrents here to confuse a newcomer, but not so subtle Gennie didn't catch the drift. He's trying to arrange a betrothal, she thought, and struggled with a chuckle. Seeing Grant's dark, annoyed look only made it more difficult to maintain her composure. The game was irresistible. "The Grandeaus can trace their ancestry back to a favored courtesan of Philip IV le Bel." She caught Shelby's look of amused respect. In the time it took for eyes to meet, a bond was formed.

Though he was enjoying the signals being flashed around the room, Alan remembered all too well being in the position Grant was currently…enjoying. "I wonder what's keeping Caine," he said casually, aware how the comment would shift his father's focus.

"Hah!" Daniel downed half his drink in one swallow. "The boy's too bound up in his law to give his mother a moment's thought."

At Gennie's lifted brows, Serena curled her legs under her. "My mother's still at the hospital," she explained, a smile lurking around her mouth. "I'm sure she'll be devastated if she arrives before Caine does."

"She worries about her children," Daniel put in with a sniff. "I try to tell her that they have lives of their own to lead, but a mother's a mother."

Serena rolled her eyes and said something inarticulate into her glass. It was enough, however, to make Daniel's face flush. Before he could retort, the sound of the knocker thudding against wood vibrated against the walls.

"I'll get it," Alan said, feeling that would give him a moment to warn Caine of their father's barometer.

Because he felt a certain kinship with Caine at that moment, Grant turned to Daniel in an attempt to shift his mood. "Gennie was fascinated by the house," he began. "She's hoping to persuade you into letting her paint it."

Daniel's reaction was immediate. Not unlike his reaction to his grandson, he preened. "Well, now, we should be able to arrange something that suits us both."

A Grandeau of the MacGregor fortress. He knew the financial value of such a painting, not to mention the value to his pride. The legacy for his grandchildren.

"We'll talk," he said with a decisive nod just as the latest MacGregors came into the room. Daniel cast a look in their direction. "Hah!"

Gennie saw a tall, lean man with the air of an intelligent wolf stroll in. Were all the MacGregors such superb examples of the human species? she wondered. There was power there, the same as she had sensed in Alan and Serena. Because it wasn't wholly the same as Daniel's, Gennie speculated on their mother. Just what sort of woman was she?

Then her attention was caught by the woman who entered with Caine. Justin's sister. Gennie glanced at her cousin to see him eyeing his sister with a slight frown. And she understood why. The tension Caine and Diana had brought into the room was palpable.

"We got held up in Boston," Caine said easily, shrugging off his father's scowl before he walked over to look at his nephew. The rather hard lines of his face softened when he glanced up at his sister. "Good job, Rena."

"You might call when you're going to be late," Daniel stated. "So your mother wouldn't worry."

Caine took in the room with a sweeping glance, noticing his mother's absence, then lifted an ironic brow. "Of course."

"It's my fault," Diana said in a low voice. "An appointment ran over."

"You remember Grant," Serena began, hoping to smooth over what looked like very rough edges.

"Yes, of course." Diana managed a smile that didn't reach her large, dark eyes.

"And Grant's guest," Serena continued with the wish that she could have a few moments alone with Diana. "Who turns out to be a cousin of yours, Genvième Grandeau."

Diana stiffened instantly, her face cool and expressionless when she turned to Gennie.

"Cousin?" Caine said curiously as he moved to stand beside his wife.

"Yes." Gennie spoke up, wanting to ease something she didn't understand. "We met once," she went on, offering a smile, "when we were children, at a birthday party, I think. My family was in Boston, visiting."

"I remember," Diana murmured.

Though she tried, Gennie could remember nothing she had done at the silly little party to warrant the cool, remote look Diana gave her. Her reaction was instinctive. Her chin angled slightly, her brows arched. With the regal look settling over her, she sipped her vermouth. "As Shelby pointed out, it's a small world."

Caine recognized Diana's expression, and though it exasperated him, he laid a reassuring hand on her shoulder. "Welcome, cousin," he said to Gennie, giving her an unexpectedly charming smile. He turned to Grant then, and the smile tilted mischievously. "I'd really like to talk to you—about frogs."

Grant responded with a lightning fast grin. "Anytime."

Before Gennie could even begin to sort this out, or the laughter that followed it, a small, dark woman came into the room. Here was the other end of the power. Gennie sensed it immediately as the woman became the center of attention. There was a strength about her, and the serious, attractive looks that she had passed on to her eldest son. She carried a strange dignity, though her hair was slightly mussed and her suit just a bit wrinkled.

"I'm so glad you could come," she said to Gennie when they were introduced. Her hands were small and capable, and Gennie discovered, chilled. "I'm sorry I wasn't here when you arrived. I was—detained at the hospital."

She's lost a patient. Without knowing how she understood it,

Gennie was certain. Instinctively, she covered their joined hands with her free one. "You have a wonderful family, Mrs. MacGregor. A beautiful grandson."

Anna let out a tiny sigh that was hardly audible. "Thank you." She moved to brush a kiss over her husband's cheek."Let's go in to dinner," she said when he patted her hair. "You all must be starving by now."

The cast of characters was complete, Gennie mused as she rose to take Grant's hand. It was going to be a very interesting weekend.

## *Chapter 10*

It was late when Gennie lounged in an oversized tub filled with hot, fragrant water. The MacGregors, from Daniel down to Mac, were not an early-to-bed group. She liked them—their boisterousness, their contrasts, their obvious and unapologetic unity. And, with the exception of Diana, they had given her a sense of welcome into their family boundaries.

Thinking of Diana now, Gennie frowned and soaped her leg. Perhaps Diana Blade MacGregor was withdrawn by nature. It hadn't taken any insight to see that there was tension between Caine and his wife, and that Diana drew closer into herself because of it, but Gennie felt there had been something more personal in Diana's attitude toward her.

*Leave me alone.* The signal had been clear as crystal and Gennie had obliged. Not everyone was inherently friendly—not everyone *had* to like her on sight. Still, it disturbed her that Diana had been neither friendly nor particularly hostile, but simply remote.

Shaking off the mood, she pulled on the old-fashioned chain to let the water drain. Tomorrow, she'd spend some time with her new cousins by marriage, and do as many sketches as she could of the MacGregor home. Perhaps she and Grant would walk along the cliffs, or take a dip in the pool she'd heard was at one of the endless, echoing corridors.

She'd never seen Grant so relaxed for such a long period of time. Oddly, though he was still the remote, arrogant man she'd reluctantly fallen in love with, he'd been comfortable with the numerous, loud MacGregors. In one evening she'd discovered yet something more about him: He enjoyed people, being with them, talking with them—as long as it remained on his terms.

Gennie had caught the tail end of a conversation Grant had been having with Alan after dinner. It had been political, and obviously in depth, which had surprised her. That had surprised her no more, however, than watching him jiggle Serena's baby on his knee while he carried on a debate with Caine involving a controversial trial waging in the Boston courts. Then he had badgered Shelby into a heated argument over the social significance of the afternoon soap opera.

With a shake of her head, Gennie patted her skin dry. Why did a man with such eclectic tastes and opinions live like a recluse? Why did a man obviously at ease in a social situation scare off stray tourists? An enigma.

Gennie slipped into a short silk robe. Yes, he was that, but knowing it and accepting it were entirely different things. The more she learned about him, the more quick peeks she had into the inner man, the more she longed to know.

Patience, just a little more patience, Gennie warned herself as she walked into the adjoining bedroom. The room was huge, the wallpaper old and exquisite. There was an ornate daybed upholstered in rich rose satin and a vanity carved with cupids. It had all the ostentatious charm of the eighteenth century down to the fussy framed embroidery that must have been Anna's work.

Pleasantly tired, Gennie sat on the skirted stool in front of the triple-mirrored vanity and began to brush her hair.

When Grant opened the door, he thought she looked like some fairy princess—part ingenue, part seductress. Her eyes met his in the glass, and she smiled while following through with the last stroke of the brush.

"Take the wrong turn?"

"I took the right one." He closed the door behind him, then flicked the lock.

"Is that so?" Tapping the brush against her palm, Gennie arched a brow. "I thought you had the room down the hall."

"The MacGregors forgot to put something in there." He stood where he was for a moment, pleased just to look at her.

"Oh? What?"

"You." Crossing to her, Grant took the brush from her hand. The scent of her bath drifted through the room. With his eyes on hers in the glass, he began to draw the brush through her hair. "Soft," he murmured. "Everything about you is just too soft to resist."

He could always make her blood heat with his passion, with his demands, but when he was gentle, when his touch was tender, she was defenseless. Her eyes grew wide and cloudy, and remained fixed on his. "Do you want to?" she managed.

There was a slight smile on his face as he continued to sweep the brush through her hair in long, slow strokes. "It wouldn't make any difference, but no, I don't want to resist you, Genviève. What I want to do..." He followed the path of the brush with his fingers. "Is touch you, taste you, to the absence of everything else. You're not my first obsession," he murmured, with an odd expression in his eyes, "but you're the only one I've been able to touch with my hands, taste with my mouth. You're not the only woman I've loved." He let the brush fall so that his hands were free to dive into her hair. "But you're the only woman I've been in love with."

She knew he spoke no more, no less than the truth. The words filled her with a soaring power. She wanted to share it with him, give back some of the wonder he'd brought to her life. Rising, she turned to face him. "Let me make love to you," she whispered. "Let me try."

The sweetness of the request moved him more than he would have thought possible. But when he reached for her, she put her hands to his chest.

"No." She slid her hands up to his neck, fingers spread. "Let me."

Carefully, watching his face, she began to unbutton his shirt. Her eyes reflected confidence, her fingers were steady, yet she knew she would have to rely on instinct and what he had only begun to teach her. Did you make love to a man as you wanted him to make love to you? She would see.

His wants could be no less than hers, she thought as her fingers skimmed over his skin. Would they be so much different? With a sound that was both of pleasure and approval, she ran her hands down his rib cage, then back up again before she pushed the loosened shirt from his shoulders.

He was lean, almost too lean, but his skin was smooth and tight over his bones. Already it was warming under the passage of her hands. Leaning closer, Gennie pressed her mouth to his heart and felt the quick, unsteady beat. Experimentally, she used the tip of her tongue to moisten. She heard him suck in his breath before the arms around her tightened.

"Gennie..."

"No, I just want to touch you for a little while." She traced the breathless kisses over his chest and listened to the sound of his racing heartbeat.

Grant closed his eyes while the damp, light kisses heated his skin. He fought the urge to drag her to the bed, or to the floor, and tried to find the control she seemed to be asking him for. Her curious fingers roamed, with the uncanny ability to find and exploit weaknesses he'd been unaware he had. All the while she murmured, sighed, promised. Grant wondered if this was the way people quietly lost their sanity.

When she trailed her fingers down slowly to the snap of his jeans, the muscles in his stomach trembled, then contracted. She heard him groan as he lowered his face to the top of her head. Her throat was dry, her palms damp as she loosened the snap. It was as much from uncertainty as the wish to seduce that she loitered over the process.

His briefs ran low at his hips, snug, and to Gennie, fascinatingly soft. In her quest to learn, she touched him and felt the swift convulsive shudder that wracked his body. So much power, she thought, so much strength. Yet she could make him tremble.

"Lie down with me," she whispered, then tilted back her head to look into eyes dark and opaque with need for her. His mouth rushed down to hers, taking as though he were starving. Even as her senses began to swim, the knowledge of her hold over him expanded. She knew what he wanted from her, and she would give it willingly. But she wanted to give much, much more. And she would.

With her hands on either side of his face, she drew him away. His quick, labored breaths fluttered over her face. "Lie down with me," she repeated, and moved to the bed. She waited until he came to her, then urged him down. The old mattress sighed as she knelt beside him. "I love to look at you." Combing the hair back from his temples, she replaced it with her lips.

And so she began, roaming, wandering with a laziness that made him ache. He felt the satin smoothness of her lips, the rustling silkiness of her robe as she slowly seduced him into helplessness. His skin grew damp from the flick and circle of her tongue and his own need. Around him, seeping into the very air he breathed, was the scent she had bathed in. She sighed, then laid her lips on his, nipping and sucking until he heard nothing but the roaring in his own head.

Her body merged with his as she lay down on him and began to do torturous things to his neck with her teeth and tongue. He tried to say her name, but could manage only a groan as his hands—always so sure—fumbled for her.

Her skin was as damp as his and drove him mad as it slid over him, lower and lower so that her lips could taste and her hands enjoy. She'd never known anything so heady as the freedom power and passion gave when joined together. It had a scent—musky, secret—she drew it in. Its flavor was the same, and she devoured it. As her tongue dipped lower, she had the dizzying pleasure of knowing her man was absorbed in her.

He seemed no longer to be breathing, but moaning only. She was unaware that her own sighs of pleasure joined his. How beautifully formed he was, was all she could think. How incredible it was that he belonged to her. She was naked now without having felt him tug off her robe. Gennie knew only that his hands stroked over her shoulders, warm, rough, desperate, then dipped to her breasts in a kind of crazed worship.

How much time passed was unknown. Neither of them heard a clock chime the hour from somewhere deep in the house. Boards settled. Outside a bird—perhaps a nightingale—set up a long, pleading call for a lover. A few harmless clouds blew away from the moon. Neither of them was aware of any sound, any movement outside of that wide, soft bed.

Her mouth found his again, greedy and urgent. Warm breath merged, tongues tangled. Minds clouded. He murmured into her mouth; a husky plea. His hands gripped her hips as if he were falling.

Gennie slid down and took him inside her, then gasped at the rocketing, terrifying thrill. She shuddered, her body flinging back as she peaked instantly then clung, clung desperately to delirium.

He tried to hold on to that last light of reason as she melted against him, spent. But it was too late. She'd stolen his sanity. All that was animal in him clawed to get out. With more of a growl than a groan, he tossed her onto her back and took her like a madman. When she had thought herself drained, she revitalized, filled with him. Her body went wild, matching the power and speed of his. Higher and higher, faster and faster, hot and heady and dark. They rushed from one summit to a steeper one, until sated, they collapsed into each other.

Still joined, with the light still shining beside the bed, they fell asleep.

* * *

It was one of those rare, perfect days. The air was mild, just a bit breezy, while the sun was warm and bright. Gennie had nibbled over the casual, come-when-you-want breakfast while Grant had eaten enough for both of them. He'd wandered away, talking vaguely of a poker game, leaving Gennie free to take her sketch pad outdoors alone. Though, as it happened, she had little solitary time.

She wanted a straight-on view of the house first, the same view that could be seen first when traveling up the road. Whether Daniel had planned it that way or not—and she felt he had—it was awesome.

She moved past the thorny rose bushes to sit on the grass near a chestnut tree. For a time it was quiet, with only the sound of gulls, land birds, and waves against rock. The sketch began with rough lines boldly drawn, then, unable to resist, Gennie began to refine it—shading, perfecting. Nearly a half hour had passed before a movement caught her eye. Shelby had come out of a side door while Gennie was concentrating on the tower and was already halfway across the uneven yard.

"Hi. Am I going to bother you?"

"No." Gennie smiled as she let the sketchbook drop into her lap. "I'll spend days sketching here if someone doesn't stop me."

"Fabulous, isn't it?" With a limber kind of grace that made Gennie think of Grant, Shelby sat beside her. She studied the sketch in Gennie's lap. "So's that," she murmured, and she, too, thought of Grant. As a child it had infuriated her that she couldn't match his skill with a pencil or crayon. As they had grown older, envy had turned to pride—almost exclusively. "You and Grant have a lot in common."

Pleased at the idea, Gennie glanced down at her own work. "He has quite a bit of talent, doesn't he? Of course I've only seen one impromptu caricature, but it's so obvious. I wonder...why he's not doing anything with it."

It was a direct probe; they both knew it. The statement also told Shelby that Grant hadn't yet confided in the woman beside her. The woman, Shelby was certain, he was in love with. Impatience warred with loyalty. Why the hell was he being such a stubborn idiot? But the loyalty won. "Grant does pretty much as he pleases. Have you known him long?"

"No, not really. Just a couple of weeks." Idly, she plucked a blade of grass and twirled it between her fingers. "My car broke down during a storm on the road leading to the lighthouse." She chuckled as a perfectly clear image of his scowling face flashed through her mind. "Grant wasn't too pleased to find me on his doorstep."

"You mean he was rude, surly, and impossible," Shelby countered, answering Gennie's grin.

"At the very least."

"Thank God some things are consistent. He's crazy about you."

"I don't know who that shocked more, him or me. Shelby..." She shouldn't pry, Gennie thought, but found she had to know something, anything that might give her a key to the inner man. "What was he like, as a boy?"

Shelby stared up at the clouds that drifted harmlessly overhead. "Grant always liked to go off by himself. Occasionally, when I hounded him, he'd tolerate me. He always liked people, though he looks at them in a rather tilted way. His way," she said with a shrug.

Shelby thought of the security they'd lived with as children, the campaigns, the press. And she thought briefly that with Alan, she had stepped right back into the whirlpool. With a little sigh Gennie didn't understand, Shelby leaned back on her elbows.

"He had a monstrous temper, a firm opinion on what was right and what was wrong—for himself and society in general. They weren't always the same things. Still, for the most part he was easy-going and kind, I suppose, for an older brother."

She was frowning up at the sky still, and remaining silent, Gennie watched her. "Grant has a large capacity for love and kindness," Shelby continued, "but he doles it out sparingly and in his own way. He doesn't like to depend on anyone." She hesitated, then looking at Gennie's calm face and expressive eyes, felt she had to give her something. "We lost our father. Grant was seventeen, between being a boy and being a man. It devastated me, and it wasn't until a long time after that I realized it had done the same to him. We were both there when he was killed."

Gennie closed her eyes, thinking of Grant, remembering Angela. This was something she could understand all too well. The guilt, the grief, the shock that never quite went away. "How was he killed?"

"Grant should tell you about that," Shelby said quietly.

"Yes." Gennie opened her eyes. "He should."

Wanting to dispel the mood, and her own memories, Shelby touched her hand. "You're good for him. I could see that right away. Are you a patient person, Gennie?"

"I'm not sure anymore."

"Don't be too patient," she advised with a smile. "Grant needs someone to give him a good swift punch once in a while. You know, when I first met Alan, I was absolutely determined not to have anything to do with him."

"Sounds familiar."

She chuckled. "And he was absolutely determined I would. He was patient, but—" she grinned at the memory "—not too patient. And I'm not half as nasty as Grant."

Gennie laughed, then flipped over a page and began to sketch Shelby. "How did you meet Alan?"

"Oh, at a party in Washington."

"Is that where you're from?"

"I live in Georgetown—we live in Georgetown," she corrected. "My shop's there, too."

Gennie's brow lifted as she drew the subtle line of Shelby's nose. "What kind of a shop?"

"I'm a potter."

"Really?" Interested, Gennie stopped sketching. "You throw your own clay? Grant never mentioned it."

"He never does," Shelby said dryly.

"There's a bowl in his bedroom," Gennie remembered. "In a henna shade with etched wildflowers. Is that your work?"

"I gave it to him for Christmas a couple of years ago. I didn't know what he'd done with it."

"It catches the light beautifully," Gennie told her, noting that Shelby was both surprised and pleased. "There isn't much else in that lighthouse he even bothers to dust."

"He's a slob," Shelby said fondly. "Do you want to reform him?"

"Not particularly."

"I'm glad. Though I'd hate to have him hear me say it, I like him the way he is." She stretched her arms to the sky. "I'm going to go in and lose a few dollars to Justin. Ever played cards with him?"

"Only once." Gennie grinned. "It was enough."

"I know what you mean," she murmured as she rose. "But I can usually bluff Daniel out of enough to make it worthwhile."

With a last lightning smile, she was off. Thoughtfully, Gennie glanced down at the sketch and sorted through the snatches of information Shelby had given her.

"Frog-faced?" Caine asked when he met Grant in the hall.

"Beauty's in the eye of the beholder," Grant said easily.

With an appreciative grin, Caine leaned against one of the many archways. "You had Dad going. We all got one of his phone calls, telling us the Campbell was in a bad way and it was our duty—he being by way of family—to help him." The grin became wolfish. "You seem to be getting along all right on your own."

Grant acknowledged this with a nod. "The last time I was here, he was trying to match me up with some Judson girl. I didn't want to take any chances."

"Dad's a firm believer in marriage and procreation." Caine's grin faded a bit when he thought of his wife. "It's funny about your Gennie being Diana's cousin."

"A coincidence," Grant murmured, noting the troubled expression. "I haven't seen Diana this morning."

"Neither have I," Caine said wryly, then shrugged. "We disagree on a case she's decided to take." The cloud of trouble crossed his face again. "It's difficult being married and in the same profession, particularly when you look at that profession from different angles."

Grant thought of himself and Gennie. Could two people look at art from more opposing views? "I imagine it is. It seemed to me that Gennie made her uncomfortable."

"Diana had it rough as a kid." Dipping his hands in his pockets, Caine brooded into space. "She's still adjusting to it. I'm sorry."

"You don't have to apologize to me. And Gennie's well able to take care of herself."

"I think I'll take a look for Diana." He pulled himself back, then grinning, jerked his head toward the tower steps. "Justin's on a streak, as usual, if you want to risk it."

Outside, Diana moved around the side of the house and into the front garden before she spotted Gennie. Her first instinct was simply to turn away, but Gennie glanced up. Their eyes met. Stiffly, Diana moved across the grass, but unlike Shelby, she didn't sit. "Good morning."

Gennie gave her an equally cool look. "Good morning. The roses are lovely, aren't they?"

"Yes. They won't last much longer." Diana slipped her hands into the deep pockets of her jade-green slacks. "You're going to paint the house."

"I plan to." On impulse, she held the sketch pad up to her cousin. "What do you think?"

Diana studied it and saw all the things that had first impressed her about the structure—the strength, the fairy-tale aura, the superb charm. It moved her. It made her uncomfortable. Somehow the drawing made a bond between them she wanted to avoid. "You're very talented," she murmured. "Aunt Adelaide always sang your praises."

Gennie laughed despite herself. "Aunt Adelaide wouldn't know a Rubens from a Rembrandt, she only thinks she does." She could have bitten her tongue. This woman, she reminded herself, had been raised by Adelaide, and she had no right denigrating her to someone who might be fond of her. "Have you seen her recently?"

"No," Diana said flatly, and handed Gennie back the sketch.

Annoyed, Gennie shaded her eyes and gave Diana a long, thorough study. Casually, Gennie turned over a page, and as she had done with Shelby, began to sketch her. "You don't like me."

"I don't know you," Diana returned coolly.

"True, which makes your behavior all the more confusing. I thought you would be more like Justin."

Infuriated because the easily spoken words stung, Diana glared down at her. "Justin and I have different ways because we led different lives." Whirling, she took three quick strides away before she stopped herself. Why was she acting like a shrew? she demanded, then placed a hand to her stomach. Diana straightened her shoulders, and turned back.

"I'll apologize for being rude, because Justin's fond of you."

"Oh, thank you very much," Gennie said dryly, though she began to feel a slight stir of compassion at the struggle going on in Diana's eyes. "Why don't you tell me why you feel you have to be rude in the first place?"

"I'm simply not comfortable with the Grandeau end of the family."

"That's a narrow view for an attorney," Gennie mused. "And for a woman who only met me once before when we were what—eight, ten years old?"

"You fit in so perfectly," Diana said before she could think.

"Adelaide must have told me a dozen times that I was to watch you and behave as you behaved."

"Adelaide has always been a foolish, self-important woman," Gennie returned.

Diana stared at her. Yes, she knew that—now—she simply hadn't thought anyone else in that part of the family did. "You knew everyone there," she continued, though she was beginning to feel like a fool. "And had your hair tied back in a ribbon that matched your dress. It was mint-green organdy. I didn't even know what organdy was."

Because her sympathies were instantly and fully aroused, Gennie rose. She didn't reach out yet, it wouldn't be welcomed. "I'd heard you were Comanche. I waited through that whole silly party for you to do a war dance. I was terribly disappointed when you didn't."

Diana stared at her again for a full thirty seconds. She felt the desperate urge to weep that was coming over her too often lately. Instead, she found herself laughing. "I wish I'd known how—and had had the courage to do it. Aunt Adelaide would have swooned." She stopped, hesitated, then held out her hand. "I'm glad to meet you again—cousin."

Gennie accepted the hand, then took it one step further and pressed her lips to Diana's cheek. "Perhaps, if you give us a chance, you'll find there are some of the Grandeaus who are almost as human as the MacGregors."

Diana smiled. The feeling of family always overwhelmed her just a little. "Yes, perhaps."

When Diana's smile faded, Gennie followed the direction of her gaze and saw Caine standing among the roses. The tension returned swiftly, but had nothing to do with her. "I need to get a new angle for my sketches," she said easily.

Caine waited until Gennie was some distance away before he went to his wife. "You were up early," he said while his eyes roamed over her face. "You look tired, Diana."

"I'm fine," she said too quickly. "Stop worrying about me," she told him as she turned away.

Frustrated, Caine grabbed her arm. "Damn it, you're tying yourself in knots over that case, and—"

"Will you drop that!" she shouted at him. "I know what I'm doing."

"Maybe," Caine said evenly, too evenly. "The point is, you've never taken on murder one before, and the prosecution has a textbook case built up."

"It's a pity you don't have any more confidence in my capabilities."

"It's not that." Furious, he grabbed her arms and shook. "You know it's not. That's not what this is all about."

His voice grew more frustrated than angry now, while his eyes searched her face for the secrets she was keeping from him. "I thought we'd come farther than this, but you've shut me out. I want to know what it's all about, Diana. I want to know what the hell is wrong with you!"

"I'm pregnant!" she shouted at him, then pressed her hand to her mouth.

Stunned, he released her arms and stared at her. "Pregnant?" Over the wave of shock came a wave of pleasure, so steep, so dizzying, for a moment he couldn't move. "Diana." When he reached for her, she backed away so that pleasure was sliced away by pain. Very deliberately, he put his hands in his pockets. "How long have you known?"

She swallowed and struggled to keep her voice from shaking. "Two weeks."

This time he turned away to stare at the wild roses without seeing them. "Two weeks," he repeated. "You didn't think it necessary to tell me?"

"I didn't know what to do!" The words came out in a rush of nerves and feelings. "We hadn't planned—not yet—and I thought it must be a mistake, but..." She trailed off helplessly as he kept his back to her.

"You've seen a doctor?"

"Yes, of course."

"Of course," he repeated on a humorless laugh. "How far along are you?"

She moistened her lips. "Nearly two months."

Two months, Caine thought. Two months their child had been growing and he hadn't known. "Have you made any plans?"

Plans? she thought wildly. What plans could she make? "I don't know!" She threw her hands up to her face. This wasn't like her, where was her control, her logic? "What kind of a mother would I make?" she demanded as her thoughts poured out into words. "I don't know anything about children, I hardly had a chance to be one."

The pain shimmered through him, very sharp, and very real. He made himself turn to face her. "Diana, are you telling me you don't want the baby?"

Not want? she thought frantically. What did he mean *not want*? It was already real—she could almost feel it in her arms. It scared her to death. "It's part of us," she said jerkily. "How could I not want part of us? It's your baby. I'm carrying your baby and I love it so much already it terrifies me."

"Oh, Diana." He touched her then, gently, his hands on her face. "You've let two weeks go by when we could have been terrified together."

She let out a shuddering sigh. Caine afraid? He was never afraid. "Are you?"

"Yeah." He kissed a teardrop from her cheek. "Yeah, I am. A couple months before Mac was born, Justin told Alan and me how he felt about becoming a father." Smiling, he lifted both her hands and pressed his lips to the palms. "Now I know."

"I've felt so—tied up." Her fingers tightened on his. "I wanted to tell you, but I wasn't sure how you'd feel. It happened so fast—we haven't even finished the house yet, and I thought…I just wasn't sure how you'd feel."

With their hands still joined, he laid them on her stomach. "I love you," he murmured, "both."

"Caine." And his name was muffled against his mouth. "I have so much to learn in only seven months."

"*We* have a lot to learn in seven months," he corrected. "Why don't we go upstairs." He buried his face in her hair and drew in the scent. "Expectant mothers should lie down—" he lifted his head to grin at her "—often."

"With expectant fathers," Diana agreed, laughing when he swept her into his arms. It was going to be all right, she thought. Her family was going to be just perfect.

Gennie watched them disappear into the house. Whatever was between them, she thought with a smile, was apparently resolved.

"What a relief."

Surprised, Gennie turned to see Serena and Justin behind her. Serena carried the baby in a sling that strapped across her breasts. Intrigued by it, Gennie peeped down to see Mac cradled snugly against his mother, sleeping soundly.

"Serena hasn't been able to get close enough to Diana to pry out what was troubling her," Justin put in.

"I don't pry," Serena retorted, then grinned. "Very much. You're sketching the house. May I see?"

Obligingly, Gennie handed over the sketchbook. As Serena studied, Justin took Gennie's hand. "How are you?"

She knew his meaning. The last time she had seen him had been at Angela's funeral. The visit had been brief, unintrusive, and very important to her. In the relatively short time they'd known each other, Justin had become a vital part of her family. "Better," she told him. "Really. I had to get away from the family for a while—and their quiet, continuous concern. It's helped." She thought of Grant and smiled. "A lot of things have helped."

"You're in love with him," Justin stated.

"Now who's prying?" Serena demanded.

"I was making an observation," he countered. "That's entirely different. Does he make you happy?" he asked, then tugged on his wife's hair. "That was prying," he pointed out.

Gennie laughed and stuck her pencil behind her ear. "Yes, he makes me happy—and he makes me unhappy. That's all part of it, isn't it?"

"Oh, yes." Serena leaned her head against her husband's shoulder. She spotted Grant as he came out the front door. "Gennie," she said, laying a hand on her arm. "If he's too slow, as some men are," she added with a meaningful glance at Justin, "I have a coin I'll lend you." At Gennie's baffled look, she chuckled. "Ask me about it sometime."

She hooked her arm through Justin's and wandered away, making the suggestion that they see if anyone was using the pool. Gennie heard him murmur something that had Serena giving a low, delicious laugh.

Family, she thought. It was wonderful to have stumbled on family this way. Her family, and Grant's. There was a bond here that might inch him closer to her. Happy, she ran across the grass to meet him.

He caught her when she breathlessly launched herself into his arms. "What's all this?"

"I love you!" she said on a laugh. "Is there anything else?"

His arms tightened around her. "No."

# *Chapter 11*

Gennie's life had always been full of people, a variety of people from all walks of life. But she'd never met anyone quite like the Clan MacGregor. Before the end of the weekend drew near, she felt she'd known them forever. Daniel was loud and blustering and shrewd—and so soft when it came to his family that he threatened to melt. Quite clearly they adored him enough to let him think he tugged their strings.

Anna was as warm and calm as a summer shower. And, Gennie knew intuitively, strong enough to hold her family together in any crisis. She, with the gentlest of touches, led her husband by the nose. And he, with all his shouts and wheezes, knew it.

Of the second generation, she thought Caine and Serena the most alike. Volatile, outspoken, emotional; they had their sire's temperament. Yet when she speculated on Alan, she thought that the serious, calm exterior he'd inherited from Anna covered a tremendous power...and a temper that might be wicked when loosed. He'd found a good match in Shelby Campbell.

The MacGregors had chosen contrasting partners—Justin with his gambler's stillness and secrets, Diana, reserved and emotional, Shelby, free-wheeling and clever; they made a fascinating group with interesting eddies and currents.

It didn't take much effort for Gennie to persuade them to sit for a family sketch.

Though they agreed quickly and unanimously, it was another matter to settle them. Gennie wanted them in the throne room, some seated, some standing, and this entailed a great deal of discussion on who did what.

"I'll hold the baby," Daniel announced, then narrowed his eyes in case anyone wanted to argue the point. "You can do another next year, lass," he added to Gennie when there was no opposition, "and I'll be holding two." He beamed at Diana before he shifted his look to Shelby. "Or three."

"You should have Dad sitting in his throne—chair," Alan amended quickly, giving Gennie one of his rare grins. "That'd make the clearest statement."

"Exactly." Her eyes danced as she kept her features sober. "And Anna, you'll sit beside him. Perhaps you'd hold your embroidery because it looks so natural."

"The wives should sit at their husbands' feet," Caine said smoothly. "That's natural."

There was general agreement among the men and definite scorn among the women.

"I think we'll mix that up just a bit—for esthetic purposes,"

Gennie said dryly over the din that ensued. With the organization and brevity of a drill sergeant, she began arranging them to her liking.

"Alan here...." She took him by the arm and stood him between his parents' chairs. "And Shelby." She nudged Shelby beside him. "Caine, *you* sit on the floor." She tugged on his hand, until grinning, he obliged her. "And Diana—" Caine pulled his wife down on his lap before Gennie could finish. "Yes, that'll do. Justin over here with Rena. And Grant—"

"I'm not—" he began.

"Do as you're told, boy," Daniel bellowed at him, then spoke directly to his grandson. "Leave it to a Campbell to make trouble."

Grumbling, Grant strolled over behind Daniel's chair and scowled down at him. "A fine thing when a Campbell's in a MacGregor family portrait."

"Two Campbells," Shelby reminded her brother with alacrity. "And how is Gennie going to manage to sketch and sit at the same time?"

Even as Gennie glanced at her in surprise, Daniel's voice boomed out. "She'll draw herself in. She's a clever lass."

"All right," she agreed, pleased with the challenge and her inclusion into the family scene. "Now, relax, it won't take terribly long—and it's not like a photo where you have to sit perfectly still." She perched herself on the end of the sofa and began, using the small, portable easel she'd brought with her. "Quite a colorful group," she decided as she chose a pastel charcoal from her box. "We'll have to do this in oils sometime."

"Aye, we'll want one for the gallery, won't we, Anna? A big one."

Daniel grinned at the thought, then settled back with the baby in the crook of his arm. "Then Alan'll need his portrait done once he's settled in the White House," he added complacently.

As Gennie sketched, Alan sent his father a mild glance. "It's a little premature to commission that just yet." His arm went around Shelby, and stayed there.

"Hah!" Daniel tickled his grandson's chin.

"Did you always want to paint, Gennie?" Anna asked while she absently pushed the needle through her embroidery.

"Yes, I suppose I did. At least, I can never remember wanting to do anything else."

"Caine wanted to be a doctor," Serena recalled with an innocent smile. "At least, that's what he told all the little girls."

"It was a natural aspiration," Caine defended himself, lifting his hand to his mother's knee while his arm held Diana firmly against him.

"Grant used a different approach," Shelby recalled. "I think he was fourteen when he talked Dee-Dee O'Brian into modeling for him—in the nude."

"That was strictly for the purpose of art," he countered when Gennie lifted a brow at him. "And I was fifteen."

"Life studies are an essential part of any art course," Gennie said as she started to draw again. "I remember one male model in particular—" She broke off as Grant's eyes narrowed. "Ah, that scowl's very natural, Grant, try not to lose it."

"So you draw, do you, boy?" Daniel sent him a speculative look. It interested him particularly because he had yet to wheedle out of either Grant or Shelby how Grant made his living.

"I've been known to."

"An artist, eh?"

"I don't—paint," Grant said as he leaned against Daniel's chair.

"It's a fine thing for a man and a woman to have a common interest," Daniel began in a pontificating voice. "Makes a strong marriage."

"I can't tell you how many times Daniel's assisted me in surgery," Anna put in mildly.

He huffed. "I've washed a few bloody knees in my time with these three."

"And there was the time Rena broke Alan's nose," Caine put in.

"It was supposed to be yours," his sister reminded him.

"That didn't make it hurt any less." Alan shifted his eyes to his sister while his wife snorted unsympathetically.

"Why did Rena break Alan's nose instead of yours?" Diana wanted to know.

"I ducked," Caine told her.

Gennie let them talk around her while she sketched them. Quite a group, she thought again as they argued—and drew almost imperceptibly closer together. Grant said something to Shelby that had her fuming, then laughing. He evaded another probe of Daniel's with a non-answer, then made a particularly apt comment on the press secretary that had Alan roaring with laughter.

All in all, Gennie thought as she chose yet another pastel, he fit in with them as though he'd sprung from the same carton. Witty, social, amenable—yet she could still see him alone on his cliff, snarling at anyone who happened to make a wrong turn. He'd changed to suit the situation, but he hadn't lost any of himself in the process. He was amenable because he chose to be, and that was that.

With a last glance at what she had done, she looped her signature into the corner. "Done," she stated, and turned her work to face the group. "The MacGregors—and Company."

They surrounded her, laughing, each having a definite opinion on the others' likenesses. Gennie felt a hand on her shoulder and knew without looking that it was Grant's. "It's beautiful," he murmured, studying the way she had drawn herself at his side. He bent over and kissed her ear. "So are you."

Gennie laughed, and the precious feeling of belonging stayed with her for days.

September hung poised in Indian summer—a glorious, golden time, when wildflowers still bloomed and the blueberry bushes flamed red. Gennie painted hour after hour, discovering all the nooks and crannies of Windy Point. Grant's routine had altered so subtly he never noticed. He worked shorter hours, but more intensely. For the first time in years he was greedy for company. Gennie's company.

She painted, he drew. And then they would come together. Some nights they spent in the big feather bed in her cottage, sunk together in the center. Other mornings they would wake in his lighthouse to the call of gulls and the crash of waves. Occasionally he would surprise her by popping up unexpectedly where she was working, sometimes with a bottle of wine—sometimes with a bag of potato chips.

Once he'd brought her a handful of wildflowers. She'd been so touched, she'd wept on them until in frustration he had pulled her into the cottage and made love to her.

It was a peaceful time for both of them. Warm days, cool nights, cloudless skies added to the sense of serenity—or perhaps of waiting.

"This is perfect!" Gennie shouted over the motor as Grant's boat cut through the sea. "It feels like we could go all the way to Europe."

He laughed and ruffled her wind-tossed hair. "If you'd mentioned it before, I'd have put in a full tank of gas."

"Oh, don't be practical—imagine it," she insisted. "We could be at sea for days and days."

"And nights." He bent over to catch the lobe of her ear between his teeth. "Full-mooned, shark-infested nights."

She gave a low laugh and slid her hands up his chest. "Who'll protect whom?"

"We Scots are too tough. Sharks probably prefer more tender—" his tongue dipped into her ear "—French delicacies."

With a shiver of pleasure she rested against him and watched the boat plow through the waves.

The sun was sinking low; the wind whipped by, full of salt and sea. But the warmth remained. They skirted around one of the rocky, deserted little islands and watched the gulls flow into the sky. In the distance Gennie could see some of the lobster boats chug their way back to the harbor at Windy Point. The bell buoys clanged with sturdy precision.

Perhaps summer would never really end, she thought, though the days were getting shorter and that morning there'd been a hint of frost. Perhaps they could ride forever, without any responsibilities calling them back, with no vocation nagging. She thought of the showing she'd committed herself to in November. New York was too far away, the gray skies and naked trees of November too distant. For some reason Gennie felt it was of vital importance to think of now, that moment. So much could happen in two months. Hadn't she fallen in love in a fraction of that time?

She'd planned to be back in New Orleans by now. It would be hot and humid there. The streets would be crowded, the traffic thick. The sun would stream through the lacework of her balcony and shoot patterns onto the ground. There was a pang of homesickness. She loved the city—its rich smells, its old-world charm and new-world bustle. Yet she loved it here as well—the stark spaciousness, the jagged cliffs and endless sea.

Grant was here, and that made all the difference. She could give up New Orleans for him, if that was what he wanted. A life here, with him, would be so easy to build. And children…

She thought of the old farmhouse, empty yet waiting within sight of the lighthouse. There would be room for children in the big, airy rooms. She could have a studio on the top floor, and Grant would have his lighthouse when he needed his solitude. When it was time to give a showing, she'd have his hand to hold and maybe those nerves would finally ease. She'd plant flowers—high, bushy geraniums, soft-petaled pansies, and daffodils that would come back and multiply every spring. At night she could listen to the sea and Grant's steady breathing beside her.

"What're you doing, falling asleep?" He bent to kiss the top of her head.

"Just dreaming," she murmured. They were still just dreams. "I don't want the summer to end."

He felt a chill and drew her closer. "It has to sometime. I like the sea in winter."

Would she still be here with him then? he wondered. He wanted her, and yet—he didn't feel he could hold her. He didn't feel he could go with her. His life was so bound up in his need for solitude, he knew he'd lose part of himself if he opened too far. She lived her life in the spotlight. How much would she lose if he asked her to shut it off? How could he ask? And yet the thought of living without her was impossible to contemplate.

Grant told himself he should never have let it come so far. He told himself he wouldn't give back a minute of the time he'd had with her. The tug-of-war went on within him. He'd let her go, he'd lock her in. He'd settle back into his own life. He'd beg her to stay.

As he turned the boat back toward shore, he saw the sun spear into the water. No, summer should never end. But it would.

"You're quiet," Gennie murmured as he cut the engine and let the boat drift against the dock.

"I was thinking." He jumped out to secure the line, then reached for her. "That I can't imagine this place without you."

Gennie started, nearly losing her balance as she stepped onto the pier. "It's—it's nearly become home to me."

He looked down at the hand he held—that beautiful, capable artist's hand. "Tell me about your place in New Orleans," he asked abruptly as they began walking over the shaky wooden boards.

"It's in the French Quarter. I can see Jackson Square from the balcony with the artists' stalls all around and the tourists and students roaming. It's loud." She laughed, remembering. "I've had my studio soundproofed, but sometimes I'll go downstairs so I can just listen to all the people and the music."

They climbed up the rough rocks, and there was no sound but

the sea and the gulls. "Sometimes at night, I like to go out and walk, just listen to the music coming out of the doorways." She took a deep breath of the tangy, salty air. "It smells of whiskey and the Mississippi and spice."

"You miss it," he murmured.

"I've been away a long time." They walked toward the lighthouse together. "I went away—maybe ran away—nearly seven months ago. There was too much of Angela there, and I couldn't face it. Strange, I'd gotten through a year, though I'd made certain I was swamped with work. Then I woke up one morning and couldn't bear being there knowing she wasn't—would never be." She sighed. Perhaps it had taken that long for the shock to completely wear off. "When it got to the point where I had to force myself to drive around that city, I knew I needed some distance."

"You'll have to go back," Grant said flatly, "and face it."

"I already have." She waited while he pushed open the door. "Faced it—yes, though I still miss her dreadfully. New Orleans will only be that much more special because I had so much of her there. Places can hold us, I suppose." As they stepped inside she smiled at him. "This one holds you."

"Yes." He thought he could feel winter creeping closer, and drew her against him. "It gives me what I need."

Her lashes lowered so that her eyes were only slits with the green light and glowing. "Do I?"

He crushed his mouth to hers so desperately she was shaken—not by the force, but by the emotion that seemed to explode from him without warning. She yielded because it seemed to be the way for both of them. And when she did, he drew back, struggling for control. She was so small—it was difficult to remember that when she was in his arms. He was cold. And God, he needed her.

"Come upstairs," he murmured.

She went silently, aware that while his touch and his voice were gentle, his mood was volatile. It both intrigued and excited her. The tension in him seemed to grow by leaps and bounds as they climbed toward the bedroom. It's like the first time, she thought, trembling once in anticipation. Or the last.

"Grant…"

"Don't talk." He nudged her onto the bed, then slipped off her shoes. When his hands wanted to rush, to take, he forced them to be slow and easy. Sitting beside her, Grant put them on her shoulders, then ran them down her arms as he touched his mouth to hers.

The kiss was light, almost teasing, but Gennie could feel the rushing, pulsing passion beneath it. His body was tense even as he nibbled, drawing her bottom lip into his mouth, stroking his thumb over her wrists. He wasn't in a gentle mood, yet he strove to be gentle. She could smell the sea on him, and it brought back memories of that first, tumultuous lovemaking on the grass with lightning and thunder. That's what he needed now. And she discovered, as her pulse began to thud under his thumbs, it was what she needed.

Her body didn't melt, but coiled. The sound wasn't a sigh but a moan as she dragged him against her and pressed her open mouth aggressively against his.

Then he was like the lightning, white heat, cold fury as he crushed her beneath him on the bed. His hands went wild, seeking, finding, tugging at her clothes as though he couldn't touch her quickly enough.

His control snapped, and in a chain reaction hers followed, until they were tangled together in an embrace that spoke of love's violence.

Demand after unrelenting demand they placed on each other. Fingers pressed, mouths ravaged. Clothes were yanked away in a fury of impatience to possess hot, damp skin. It wasn't enough to touch, they hurried to taste what was smooth and moist and salty from the sea and their mutual passion.

Dark, driving needs, an inferno of wanting; they gave over to both and took from each other. And what was taken was replenished, over and over as they loved with the boundless energy that springs from desperation. Urgent fingers possessed her. An avid mouth conquered him. The command belonged to neither, but to the primitive urges that pounded through them.

Shallow, gasping breaths, skin that trembled to the touch, flavors dark and heated, the scent of the sea and desire—these clouded their minds to leave them victims as well as conquerers. Their eyes met once, and each saw themselves trapped in the other's mind. Then they were moving together, racing toward delirium.

It was barely dawn when she woke. The light was rosy and warm, but there was a faint skim of frost on the window. Gennie knew immediately she was alone; touching the sheets beside her, she found them cold. Her body was sated from a long night of loving but she sat up and called his name. The simple fact that he was up before her worried her—she always woke first.

Thinking of his mood the night before, she wasn't certain whether to frown or smile. His urgency had never depleted. Time and time again he had turned to her, and their loving had retained that wild, desperate flavor. Once, when his hands and mouth had raced over her—everywhere—she thought he seemed bent on implanting all that she was onto his mind, as if he were going away and taking only the memory of her with him.

Shaking her head, Gennie got out of bed. She was being foolish; Grant wasn't going anywhere. If he had gotten up early, it was because he couldn't sleep and hadn't wanted to disturb her. How she wished he had.

He's only downstairs, she told herself as she stepped into the hall. He's sitting at the kitchen table having coffee and waiting for me. But when she reached the stairwell, she heard the radio, low and indistinct. Puzzled, she glanced up. The sound was coming from above her, not below.

Odd, she thought, she hadn't imagined he used the third floor. He'd never mentioned it. Drawn by her curiosity, Gennie began the circular climb. The radio grew louder as she approached, though the news broadcast was muted and sounded eerily out of place in the silent lighthouse. Until that moment, she hadn't realized how completely she had forgotten the outside world. But for that one weekend at the MacGregors, her summer had been insular, and bound up in Grant alone.

She stopped in the doorway of a sun-washed room. It was a studio. He'd cultivated the north light and space. Fleetingly, her gaze skimmed over the racks of newspapers and magazines, the television, and the one sagging couch. No easels, no canvases, but it was the den of an artist.

Grant's back was to her as he sat at his drawing board. She smelled—ink, she realized, and perhaps a trace of glue. The glass-topped cabinet beside him held a variety of organized tools.

An architect? she wondered, confused. No, that didn't fit and surely no architect would resist using his skills on that farmhouse so close at hand. He muttered to himself, hunched over his work. She might have smiled at that if she hadn't been so puzzled. When he moved his hand she saw he held an artist's brush—sable and expensive. And he held it with the ease of long practice.

But he'd said he didn't paint, Gennie remembered, baffled. He didn't appear to be—and what would a painter need with a compass and a T square? One wouldn't paint facing a wall in any case, but…what *was* he doing?

Before she could speak, Grant lifted his head. In the mirror in front of him their eyes met.

He hadn't been able to sleep. He hadn't been able to lie beside her and not want her. Somehow during the night, he'd convinced himself that they had to go their separate ways. And that he could cope with it. She lived in another world, more than in another part of the country. Glamor was part of her life—glamor and crowds and recognition. Simplicity was part of his—simplicity and solitude and anonymity. There was no mixing them.

He'd gotten up in the dark, deluding himself that he could work. After nearly two hours of frustration, he was beginning to succeed. Now she was here, a part of that last portion of himself he'd been determined to keep separate. When she went away, he'd wanted to have at least one sanctuary.

Too intrigued to notice his annoyance, Gennie crossed the room. "What're you doing?" He didn't answer as she came beside him and frowned down at the paper attached to his board. It was crisscrossed with light-blue lines and sectioned. Even when she saw the pen and ink drawings taking shape in the first section, she wasn't certain what she was looking at.

Not a blueprint, surely, she mused. A mechanical…some kind of commercial art perhaps? Fascinated, she bent a bit closer to the first section. Then she recognised the figure.

"Oh! Cartoons." Pleased with the discovery, she inched closer. "Why, I've seen this strip hundreds of times. I love it!" She laughed and pushed the hair back over her shoulder. "You're a cartoonist."

"That's right." He didn't want her to be pleased or impressed. It was simply what he did, and no more. And he knew, if he didn't push her away then, today, he'd never be able to do it again. Deliberately, he set down his brush.

"So this is how you set one of these up," she continued, caught up in the idea, enchanted with it. "These blue lines you've struck on the paper, are they for perspective? How do you come up with something like this seven days a week?"

He didn't want her to understand. If she understood, it would be nearly impossible to push her away. "It's my job," he said flatly. "I'm busy, Gennie. I work on deadline."

"I'm sorry," she began automatically, then caught the cool, remote look in his eye. It struck her suddenly that he'd kept this from her, this essential part of his life. He hadn't told her—more, had made a point in not telling her. It hurt, she discovered as her initial pleasure faded. It hurt like hell. "Why didn't you tell me?"

He'd known she would ask, but was no longer certain he had the real answer. Instead, he shrugged. "It didn't come up."

"Didn't come up," she repeated quietly, staring at him. "No, I suppose you made certain it didn't. Why?"

Could he explain that it was ingrained habit? Could he tell her the essential truth was that he'd grown so used to keeping it, and nearly everything else, to himself, he had done it without thinking? Then he had continued to do so in automatic defense. If he kept this to himself, he wouldn't have given her everything—because to give her everything terrified him. No, it was too late for explanations. It was time he remembered his policy of not giving them to anyone.

"Why should I have told you?" he countered. "This is my job, it doesn't have anything to do with you."

The color drained dramatically from her face, but as he turned to get off the stool, Grant didn't see. "Nothing to do with me," Gennie echoed in a whisper. "Your work's important to you, isn't it?"

"Of course it is," Grant snapped. "It's what I do. What I am."

"Yes, it would be." She felt the cold flow over her until she was numb from it. "I shared your bed, but not this."

Stung, he whirled back to her. The wounded look in her eyes was the hardest thing he'd ever faced. "What the hell does one have to do with the other? What difference does it make what I do for a living?"

"I wouldn't have cared what you do. I wouldn't have cared if you did nothing at all. You lied to me."

"I never lied to you!" he shouted.

"Perhaps I don't understand the fine line between deception and dishonesty."

"Listen, my work is private. That's the way I want it." The explanation came tumbling out despite him, angry and hot. "I do this because I love to do it, not because I have to, not because I need recognition. Recognition's the last thing I want," he added while his eyes grew darker with temper. "I don't do lectures or workshops or press interviews because I don't want people breathing down my neck. I choose anonymity just as you choose exposure, because it's what works for me. This is my art, this is my life. And I intend to keep it just that way."

"I see." She was stiff from the pain, shattered by the cold. Gennie understood grief well enough to know what she was feeling. "And telling me, sharing this with me, would've equaled exposure. The truth is you didn't trust me. You didn't trust me to keep your precious secret or to respect your precious lifestyle."

"The truth is our lifestyles are completely opposite." The hurt tore at him. He was pushing her away, he could feel it. And even as he pushed he ached to pull her back. "There's no mixing what you need and what I need and coming out whole. It has nothing to do with trust."

"It always has to do with trust," she countered. He was looking at her now as he had that first time—the angry, remote stranger who wanted nothing more than to be left alone. She was the intruder here as she had been a lifetime ago in a storm. Then, at least, she hadn't loved him.

"You should have understood the word *love* before you used it, Grant. Or perhaps we should have understood each other's conception of the word." Her voice was steady again, rock steady as it only was when she held herself under rigid control. "To me it means trust and compromise and need. Those things don't apply for you."

"Damn it, don't tell me how I think. Compromise?" he tossed back, pacing the room. "What kind of compromise could we have made? Would you have married me and buried yourself here? Hell, we both know the press would have sniffed you out even if you could've stood it. Would you expect me to live in New Orleans until my work fell apart and I was half mad to get out?"

He whirled back to her, his back to the east window so that the rising sun shot in and shimmered all around him. "How long would it take before someone got curious enough to dig into my life? I have reasons for keeping to myself, damn it, and I don't have to justify them."

"No, you don't." She wouldn't cry, she told herself, because once she began she'd never stop. "But you'll never know the answer to any of those questions, will you? Because you never bothered to share them with me. You didn't share them, and you didn't share the reasons. I suppose that's answer enough."

She turned and walked from the room and down the long, winding stairs. She didn't start to run until she was outside in the chill of the morning.

## *Chapter 12*

Gennie looked at her cards and considered. A nine and an eight. She should play it safe with seventeen; another card would be a foolish risk. Life was full of them, she decided, and signaled the dealer. The four she drew made her smile ironically. Lucky at cards…

What was she doing sitting at a blackjack table at seven-fifteen on a Sunday morning? Well, she thought, it was certainly a convenient way to pass the time. More productive then pacing the floor or beating on a pillow. She'd already tried both of those. Yet somehow, the streak of luck she'd been enjoying for the past hour hadn't lightened her mood. Perversely, she would have preferred it if she'd lost resoundingly. That way, she would have had some new hook to hang her depression on.

Restless, she cashed in her chips and stuffed the winnings in her bag. Maybe she could lose them at the dice table later.

There was only a handful of people in the casino now. A very small elderly lady sat on a stool at a slot machine and systematically fed in quarters. Occasionally Gennie would hear the jingle of coins spill into the tray. Later, the huge, rather elegant room would fill, then Gennie could lose herself in the smoke and noise. But for now, she wandered out to the wide glass wall and looked out at the sea.

Was this why she had come here instead of going home as she had intended? When she had tossed her suitcase and painting gear into the car, her only thought had been to get back to New Orleans and pick up her life again. She'd made the detour almost before she'd been aware of it. Yet now that she was here, had been here for over two weeks, she couldn't bring herself to walk out on that beach. She could look at it, yes, and she could listen. But she couldn't go to it.

Why was she tormenting herself like this? she wondered miserably. Why was she keeping herself within reach of what would always remind her of Grant? Because, she admitted, no matter how many times she'd told herself she had, she had yet to accept the final break. It was just as impossible for her to go back to him as it was for her to walk down to that blue-green water. He'd rejected her, and the hurt of it left her hollow.

*I love you, but...*

No, she couldn't understand that. Love meant anything was possible. Love meant *making* anything possible. If his love had been real, he'd have understood that, too.

She'd have been better off resisting the urge to look up *Macintosh* in the paper. She wouldn't have seen that ridiculous and poignant strip where Veronica had walked into his life. It had made her laugh, then remembering had made her cry. What right did he have to use her in his work when he wouldn't share himself with her? And he'd used her again and again, in dozens of papers across the country where readers were following Macintosh's growing romance—his over-his-head, dazed-eyed involvement—with the sexy, alluring Veronica.

It was funny, and the touches of satire and cynicism made it funnier. It was human. He'd taken the foolishness and the pitfalls of falling in love and had given them the touch every man or woman who'd ever been there would understand. Each time she read the strip, Gennie could recognize something they'd done or something she'd said, though he had a way of tilting it to an odd angle. With his penchant for privacy, Grant still, vicariously, shared his own emotional roller coaster with the public.

It made her ache to read it day after day. Day after day, she read it.

"Up early, Gennie?"

As a hand touched her shoulder, she turned to Justin. "I've always been a morning person," she evaded, then smiled at him. "I cleaned up at your tables."

He returned the smile, while behind guarded eyes he assessed her. She was pale—still as pale as she had been when she'd so suddenly checked into the Comanche. The pallor only accented the smudges of sleeplessness under her eyes. She had a wounded look that he recognized because he, too, was deeply in love. Whatever had come between her and Grant had left its mark on her.

"How about some breakfast?" He slipped an arm over her shoulders before she could answer, and began leading her toward his office.

"I'm not really hungry, Justin," she began.

"You haven't really been hungry for two weeks." He guided her through the outer office into his private one, then pushed the button on his elevator. "You're the only cousin I have whom I care about, Genviève. I'm tired of watching you waste away in front of my eyes."

"I'm not!" she said indignantly, then leaned her head against his arm. "There's nothing worse than having someone moping around feeling sorry for themselves, is there?"

"A damned nuisance," he agreed lightly as he drew her into the private car. "How much did you take me for in there?"

It took her a minute to realize he'd changed the subject. "Oh, I don't know—five, six hundred."

"I'll put breakfast on your tab," he said as the doors opened to his and Serena's suite. Her laugh pleased him as much as the hug she gave him.

"Just like a man," Serena stated as she came into the room. "Waltzing in with a beautiful woman at the crack of dawn while the wife stays home and changes the baby." She held a gurgling Mac over her shoulder.

Justin grinned at her. "Nothing worse than a jealous woman."

Lifting her elegant brows, Serena walked over and shifted the baby into his arms. "Your turn," she said, smiling, then collapsed into an armchair. "Mac's teething," she told Gennie. "And not being a terribly good sport about it."

"You are," Justin told her as his son began to soothe sore gums on his shoulder.

Serena grinned, tucked up her feet, and yawned hugely. "I'm assured this, too, shall pass. Have you two eaten?"

"I've just invited Gennie to have some breakfast."

Serena caught her husband's dry look and understood it. Railroaded would have been a more apt word, she imagined. "Good," she said simply, and picked up the phone. "One of the nicest things about living in a hotel is room service."

While Serena ordered breakfast for three, Gennie wandered. She liked this suite of rooms—so full of warmth and color and personality. If it had ever held the aura of a hotel room, it had long since lost it. The baby cooed as Justin sat on the couch to play with him. Serena's low, melodious voice spoke to the kitchen far below.

If you love enough, Gennie thought as she roamed to the window overlooking the beach, if you want enough, you can make a home anywhere. Rena and Justin had. Wherever they decided to live, and in whatever fashion, they were family. It was just that basic.

She knew they worked together to care for their child, to run the casino and hotel. They were a unit. There were rough spots, she was sure. There had to be in any relationship—particularly between two strong-willed personalities. But they got through them because each was willing to bend when it was necessary to bend.

Hadn't she been? New Orleans would have become a place to visit—to see her family, to stir old memories if the need arose. She could have made her home on that rough coast of Maine—for him, with him. She'd have been willing to give so much if only he'd been willing to give in return. Perhaps it wasn't a matter of his being willing. Perhaps Grant had simply not been able to give. That's what she should accept. Once she did, she could finally close the door.

"The ocean's beautiful, isn't it?" Serena said from behind her.

"Yes." Gennie turned her head. "I've gotten used to seeing it. Of course, I've always lived with the river."

"Is that what you're going back to?"

Gennie turned back to the window. "In the end I suppose."

"It's the wrong choice, Gennie."

"Serena," Justin said warningly, but she turned on him with her eyes flashing and her voice low with exasperation.

"Damn it, Justin, she's miserable! There's nothing like a stubborn, pig-headed man to make a woman miserable, is there, Gennie?"

With a half laugh, she dragged a hand through her hair. "No, I don't guess there is."

"That works both ways," Justin reminded her.

"And if the man's pig-headed enough," Serena went on precisely, "it's up to the woman to give him a push."

"He didn't want me," Gennie said in a rush, then stopped. The words hurt, but she could say them. Maybe it was time she did. "Not really, or at any rate not enough. He simply wasn't willing to believe that there were ways we could have worked out whatever problems we had. He won't share—it's as though he's determined not to. It seemed we got close for that short amount of time in spite of him. He didn't want to be in love with me, he doesn't want to depend on anyone."

While she spoke, Justin rose and took Mac into another room. The tinkling music of his mobile drifted out. "Gennie," Justin began when he came back in, "do you know about Grant and Shelby's father?"

She let out a long sigh before she sank into a chair. "I know he died when Grant was about seventeen."

"Was assassinated," Justin corrected, and watched the horror cloud in her eyes. "Senator Robert Campbell. You'd have been a child, but you might remember."

She did, vaguely. The talk, the television coverage, the trial…and Grant had been there. Hadn't Shelby said both she and Grant had been there when their father was killed? Murdered right in front of their eyes. "Oh, God, Justin, it must've been horrible for them."

"Scars don't always heal cleanly," he murmured, touching an absent hand to his own side in a gesture his wife understood. "From what Alan's told me, Shelby carried around that fear and that pain for a long time. I can't imagine it would be any different for Grant. Sometimes…" His gaze drifted to Serena. "You're afraid to get too close, because then you can lose."

Serena went to him to slip her hand into his.

"Don't you see, he kept that from me, too." Gennie grabbed the back of the armchair and squeezed. She hurt for him—for the boy and the man. "He wouldn't confide in me, he wouldn't let me understand. As long as there're secrets, there's distance."

"Don't you believe he loves you?" Serena asked gently.

"Not enough," Gennie said with a violent shake of her head. "I'd starve needing more."

"Shelby called last night," Serena said as the knock on the door announced breakfast. As Justin went to answer she gestured Gennie toward the small dining area in front of the window. "Grant surprised her and Alan with a visit a few days ago."

"Is he—"

"No," Serena interrupted, sitting. "He's back in Maine now. She did say he badgered her with questions. Of course, she didn't have the answer until she spoke to me and found out you were here." Gennie frowned at the sea and said nothing. "She wondered if you were following *Macintosh* in the papers. It took me over two hours to figure why she would have asked that."

Gennie turned back with a speculative look which Serena met blandly. "Perhaps I'm not following you," she said, automatically guarding Grant's secret.

Serena took the pot the waiter placed on the table. "Coffee, Veronica?"

Gennie let out an admiring laugh and nodded her head. "You're very quick, Rena."

"I love puzzles," she corrected, "and the pieces were all there."

"That was the last thing we argued about." Gennie glanced at Justin as he took his seat. After adding cream to her coffee, she simply toyed with the handle of the cup. "All the time we were together, he never told me what he did. Then, when I stumbled across it, he was so angry—as if I had invaded his privacy. I was so pleased. When I thought he simply wasn't doing anything with his talent, I couldn't understand. Then to learn what he was doing—something so clever and demanding..." She trailed off, shaking her head. "He just never let me in."

"Maybe you didn't ask loud enough," Serena suggested.

"If he rejected me again, Rena, I'd fall apart. It's not a matter of pride, really. It's more a matter of strength."

"I've seen you making yourself sick with nerves before a showing," Justin reminded her. "But you always go through with it."

"It's one thing to expose yourself, your feelings to the public, and another to risk them with one person knowing there wouldn't be anything left if he didn't want them. I have a showing coming up in

November," she said as she toyed with the eggs on her plate. "That's what I have to concentrate on now."

"Maybe you'd like to glance at this while you eat." Justin slipped the comics section out of the paper the waiter had brought up.

Gennie stared at it, not wanting to see, unable to resist. After a moment she took it from his hand.

The Sunday edition was large and brightly colored. This *Macintosh* was rather drab, however, and lost-looking. In one glance she could see the hues were meant to indicate depression and loneliness. She mused that Grant knew how to immediately engage the readers' attention and guide their mood.

In the first section Macintosh himself was sitting alone, his elbows on his knees, his chin sunk in his hands. No words or captions were needed to project the misery. The readers' sympathies were instantly aroused. Who'd dumped on the poor guy this time?

At a knock on the door he mumbled—it had to be mumbled—"Come in." But he didn't alter his position as Ivan, the Russian emigré, strolled in wearing his usual fanatically American attire—Western, this time, cowboy hat and boots included.

"Hey, Macintosh, I got two tickets for the basketball game. Let's go check out the cheerleaders."

No response.

Ivan pulled up a chair and tipped back his hat. "You can buy the beer, it's an American way of life. We'll take your car."

No response.

"But I'll drive," Ivan said cheeringly, nudging Macintosh with the toe of his pointed boot.

"Oh, hello, Ivan." Macintosh settled back into his gloom again.

"Hey, man, got a problem?"

"Veronica left me."

Ivan crossed one leg over the other and was obviously jiggling his foot. "Oh, yeah? For some other guy, huh?"

"No."

"How come?"

Macintosh never altered positions, and the very absence of action made the point. "Because I was selfish, rude, arrogant, dishonest, stupid and generally nasty."

Ivan considered the toe of his boot. "Is that all?"

"Yeah."

"Women," Ivan said with a shrug. "Never satisfied."

Gennie read the strip twice, then looked up helplessly. Without a word, Serena took the paper from her hand and read it herself. She chuckled once, then set it back down.

"Want me to help you pack?"

Where the hell was she? Grant knew he'd go mad if he asked himself the question one more time.

*Where the hell was she?*

From the lookout deck of his lighthouse he could see for miles. But he couldn't see Gennie. The wind slapped at his face as he stared out to sea and wondered what in God's name he was going to do.

Forget her? He might occasionally forget to eat or to sleep, but he couldn't forget Gennie. Unfortunately, his memory was just as clear on the last ten minutes they had been together. How could he have been such a fool! Oh, it was easy, Grant thought in disgust. He'd had lots of practice.

If he hadn't spent those two days cursing her, and himself, stalking the beach one minute, shut up in his studio the next, he might not have been too late. By the time he'd realized he'd cut out his own heart, she'd been gone. The cottage had been closed up, and the Widow Lawrence knew nothing and was saying less.

He'd flown to New Orleans and searched for her like a madman. Her apartment had been empty—her neighbors hadn't heard a word. Even when he'd located her grandmother by calling every Grandeau in the phone book, he'd learned nothing more than that Gennie was traveling.

Traveling, he thought. Yes, she was traveling—away from him just as fast as she could. Oh, you deserve it, Campbell, he berated himself. You deserve to have her skip out of your life without a backward glance.

He'd called the MacGregors—thank God he'd gotten Anna on the phone instead of Daniel. They hadn't heard from her. Not a sound. She might have been anywhere. Nowhere. If it hadn't been for the painting she'd left behind, he might have believed she'd been a mirage after all.

She'd left the painting for him, he remembered, the one she'd finished the afternoon they'd become lovers. But there'd been no note. He'd wanted to fling it off the cliff. He'd hung it in his bedroom. Perhaps it was his sackcloth and ashes, for every time he looked at it, he suffered.

Sooner or later, he promised himself, he'd find her. Her name, her picture would be in the paper. He'd track her down and bring her back.

Bring her back, hell, Grant thought, dragging a hand through his hair. He'd beg, plead, grovel, whatever it took to make her give him another chance. It was her fault, he decided with a quick switch back to fury. *Her* fault, that he was acting like a maniac. He hadn't had a decent night's sleep in over two weeks. And the solitude he'd always prized was threatening to smother him. If he didn't find her soon, he'd lose what was left of his mind.

Infuriated, he swung away from the rail. If he couldn't work, he could go down to the beach. Maybe he'd find some peace there.

Everything looked the same, Gennie thought as she came to the end of the narrow, bumpy road. Though summer had finally surrendered to fall, nothing had really changed. The sea still crashed and roared, eating slowly at the rock. The lighthouse still stood, solitary and strong. It had been foolish for her to have worried that she would find that something important, perhaps essential, had altered since she'd left.

Grant wouldn't have changed, either. On a deep breath she stepped from the car. More than anything, she didn't want him to change what made him uniquely Grant Campbell. She'd fallen in love with the rough exterior, the reluctant sensitivity—yes, even the rudeness. Perhaps she was a fool. She didn't want to change him; all she wanted was his trust.

If she'd misinterpreted that strip—if he turned her away… No, she wasn't going to think about that. She was going to concentrate on putting one foot in front of the other until she faced him again. It was time she stopped being a coward about the things most vital to her life.

As soon as she touched the door handle, Gennie stopped. He wasn't in there. Without knowing how or why, she was absolutely certain of it. The lighthouse was empty. Glancing back, she saw his truck parked in its spot near the farmhouse. Was he out in his boat?

she wondered as she started around the side. It was at the dock, swaying gently at low tide.

Then she knew, and wondered she hadn't known from the first. Without hesitation, she started for the cliff.

With his hands in his pockets and the wind tugging at his jacket, Grant walked along the shoreline. So this was loneliness, he thought. He'd lived alone for years without feeling it. It was one more thing to lay at Gennie's feet. How was it possible that one lone female could have changed the essence of his life?

With a calculated effort, he worked himself into a temper. Anger didn't hurt. When he found her—and by God, he would—she'd have a lot to answer for. His life had been moving along exactly as he'd wanted it before she'd barged in on it. Love? Oh, she could talk about love, then disappear just because he'd been an idiot.

*He* hadn't asked to need her. *She'd* hammered at him until he'd weakened, then she'd taken off the minute he hurt her. Grant turned to the sea, but shut his eyes. God, he had hurt her. He'd seen it on her face, heard it in her voice. How could he ever make up for that? He'd rather have seen anger or tears than that stricken look he'd put in her eyes.

If he went back to New Orleans…she might be there now. He could go back, and if he couldn't find her, he could wait. She had to go back sooner or later; the city meant too much to her. Damn it, what was he doing standing there when he should be on a plane going south?

Grant turned, and stared. Now he was seeing things.

Gennie watched him with a calmness that didn't reveal the thudding of her heart. He'd looked so alone—not in that chosen solitary way he had, but simply lonely. Perhaps she'd imagined it because she wanted to believe he'd been thinking of her. Gathering all her courage, Gennie crossed to him.

"I want to know what you meant by this." She reached in her pocket and pulled out the clipping of his Sunday strip.

He stared at her. He might see things—he might even hear things, but…slowly, he reached out and touched her face. "Gennie?"

Her knees went weak. Resolutely, Gennie stiffened them. She wasn't going to fall into his arms. It would be so easy, and it would solve nothing. "I want to know what this means." She shoved the clipping into his hand.

Off balance, Grant looked down at his work. It hadn't been easy to get that into the papers so quickly. He'd had to pull all the strings at his disposal and work like a maniac himself. If that was what brought her, it had all been worth it.

"It means what it says," he managed, staring at her again. "There's not a lot of subtlety in this particular strip."

She took the paper back from him and stuck it in her pocket. It was something she intended to keep forever. "You've used me rather lavishly in your work recently." She had to tilt back her head in order to keep her eyes level with his. Grant thought she looked more regal than ever. If she turned her thumb down, she could throw him to the lions. "Didn't it occur to you to ask permission first?"

"Artist's privilege." He felt the light spray hit his back, saw it dampen her hair. "Where the hell did you go?" he heard himself demand. "Where the hell have you been?"

Her eyes narrowed. "That's my business, isn't it?"

"Oh, no." He grabbed her arms and shook. "Oh, no, it's not. You're not going to walk out on me."

Gennie set her teeth and waited until he'd stopped shaking her. "If memory serves, you did the walking figuratively before I did it literally."

"All right! I acted like an idiot. You want an apology?" he shouted at her. "I'll give you any kind you want. I'll—" He broke off, his breath heaving. "Oh God, first."

And his mouth crushed down on hers, his fingers digging into her shoulders. The groan that was wrenched from him was only one more sign of a desperate need. She was here, she was his. He'd never let her go again.

His mind started to clear so that his own thoughts jabbed at him. This wasn't how he wanted to do it. This wasn't the way to make up for what he'd done—or hadn't done. And it wasn't the way to show her how badly he wanted to make her happy.

With an effort, Grant drew her away and dropped his hands to his sides. "I'm sorry," he began stiffly. "I didn't intend to hurt you—not now, not before. If you'd come inside, we could talk."

What was this? she wondered. *Who* was this? She understood the man who had shaken her, shouted at her, the man who had dragged her into his arms full of need and fury. But she had no idea who this man was who was standing in front of her offering a stilted apology. Gennie's brows drew together. She hadn't come all this way to talk to a stranger.

"What the hell's the matter with you?" she demanded. "I'll let you know when you hurt me." She shoved a finger into his chest. "*And* when I want an apology. We'll talk, all right," she added, flinging back her head. "And we'll talk right here."

"What do you want!" In exasperation, Grant threw up his hands. How was a man supposed to crawl properly when someone was kicking at him?

"I'll tell you what I want!" Gennie shouted right back. "I want to know if you want to work this out or sneak back into your hole. You're good at hiding out; if that's what you want to keep doing, just say so."

"I am not hiding out," he said evenly and between his teeth. "I live here because I like it here, because I can work here without having someone knocking on the door or ringing the phone every five minutes."

She gave him a long, level look edged with fury. "That's not what I'm talking about, and you know it."

Yes, he knew it. Frustrated, he stuck his hands in his pockets to keep from shaking her again. "Okay, I kept things from you. I'm used to keeping things to myself, it's habit. And then…And then I kept things from you because the harder I fell in love with you, the more terrified I was. Look, damn it, I didn't want to depend on anyone for—" He broke off to drag a hand through his hair.

"For what?"

"For being there when I needed them," he said on a long breath. Where had that been hiding? he wondered, a great deal more surprised by his words than Gennie was. "I should tell you about my father."

She touched him then, her eyes softening for the first time. "Justin told me."

Grant stiffened instantly and turned away.

"Were you going to keep that from me, too, Grant?"

"I wanted to tell you myself," he managed after a moment. "Explain—make you understand."

"I do understand," she told him. "Enough, at least. We've both lost people we loved very much and depended on in our own ways. It seems to me we've compensated for the loss in our own ways as well. I do understand what it's like to have someone you love die, suddenly, right in front of your eyes."

Grant heard her voice thicken, and turned. He couldn't handle tears now, not when he was so tightly strung himself. "Don't. It's something you have to put aside, never away, but aside. I thought I had, but it crept back up on me when I got involved with you."

She nodded and swallowed. This wasn't the time for tears or a time to dwell on the past. "You wanted me to go that day."

"Maybe—yes." He looked past her to the top of the cliff. "I thought it was the only way for both of us. Maybe it still is; I just can't live with it."

Confused, she put a hand on his arm. "Why do you think being apart might be the best thing?"

"We've chosen to live in two totally different worlds, Gennie, and both of us were content before we met. Now—"

"Now," she said, firing up again. "Now what? Are you still so stubborn you won't consider compromise?"

He looked at her blankly. Why was she talking about compromises when he was about to fold up everything and go with her anywhere. "Compromise?"

"You don't even know the meaning of the word! For someone as clever and astute as you are, you're a closed-minded fool!" Furious, she turned to stalk away.

"Wait." Grant grabbed her arm so quickly, she stumbled back against him. "You're not listening to me. I'll sell the land, give it away if you want. We'll live in New Orleans. Damn it, I'll take out a front page ad declaring myself as *Macintosh*'s artist if it'll make you happy. We can have our picture plastered on every magazine in the country."

"Is that what you think I want?" She'd thought he'd already made her as angry as she was capable of getting a dozen times during their relationship. Nothing had ever compared to this. "You simple, egotistical ass! I don't care whether you write your strip in blood under the cover of darkness. I don't care if you pose for a hundred magazines or snarl at the paparazzi. Sell the land?" she continued while he tried to keep up. "Why in God's name would you do that? Everything's black and white to you. *Compromise!*" Gennie raged at him. "It means give and take. Do you think I care where I live?"

"I don't know!" What little patience he had snapped. "I only know you've lived a certain way—you were happy. You've got roots in New Orleans, family."

"I'll always have roots and family in New Orleans, it doesn't mean I have to be there twelve months out of the year." She dragged both hands through her hair, holding it back from her face a moment as she wondered how such an intelligent man could be so dense. "And yes, I've lived a certain way, and I can live a different way to a point. I couldn't stop being an artist for you because I'd stop being me. I have a show to deal with in November—I need the shows and I need you to be with me. But there are other things I can give back, if you'd only meet me halfway. If I made the ridiculous move of falling in love with you, why would I want you to give up everything you are now?"

He stared at her, willing himself to be calm. Why was she making so much sense and he so little? "What do you want?" he began, then held up a hand before she could shout at him. "Compromise," he finished.

"More." She lifted her chin, but her eyes were more uncertain than arrogant. "I need you to trust me."

"Gennie." He took her hand and linked fingers. "I do. That's what I've been trying to tell you."

"You haven't been doing a good job of it."

"No." He drew her closer. "Let me try again." He kissed her, telling himself to be gentle and easy with her. But his arms locked and tightened, his mouth hungered. The spray shimmered over both of them as they stood entangled. "You're the whole focus of my world," he murmured. "After you left, I went crazy. I flew down to New Orleans, and—"

"You did?" Stunned, she drew back to look at him. "You went after me?"

"With various purposes in mind," he muttered. "First, I was going to strangle you, then I was going to crawl, then I was going to just drag you back and lock you upstairs."

Smiling, she rested her head on his chest. "And now?"

"Now." He kissed her hair. "We compromise. I'll let you live."

"Good start." With a sigh, she closed her eyes. "I want to watch the sea in winter."

He tilted her face to his. "We will."

"There is something else…."

"Before or after I make love to you?"

Laughing, she pulled away from him. "It better be before. Since you haven't mentioned marriage yet, it falls to me."

"Gennie—"

"No, this is one time we'll do it all my way." She drew out the coin Serena had given her before she'd left the Comanche. "And, in a way, it's a kind of compromise. Heads, we get married. Tails we don't."

Grant grabbed her wrist before she could toss. "You're not going to play games with something like that, Genvième, unless that's a two-headed coin."

She smiled. "It certainly is."

Surprise came first, then his grin. "Toss it. I like the odds."

* * * * *